How Uncle Huey got Religion

Printed in the United States of America

Cover art design by Lynette Bonner

First edition published August 24, 2015

20 19 18 17 16 15

Squyres, David

How Uncle Huey Got Religion / David Squyres

p. cm.

ISBN-13: 978-1515043157
ISBN-10: 1515043150

This paper meets the requirements of ANSI/NISO Z39.48-1992 (Permanence of Paper)

Dedication

This book is dedicated to Rebecca Squyres, who makes life happy.

Acknowledgements

Great appreciation to Mr. Jim Wilson who edited this book. I am thankful for your attention to detail, love for the craft and our shared love of Christ. And — so long as I'm thanking you Gipper, I sure do appreciate all those checks you gave me that ended up in the hands of Cal Baptist. It was nice to walk away with a certificate in one hand and a "paid in full" note in the other. You're the best.

Thanks to Linda Wichman, who is not only an awesome writer but a great source of encouragement to me.

Summary of Contents

Introduction

The year 1938 was a long, long time ago. So long ago that sliced bread really was the greatest thing, since it was brand spankin' new! *Kraft Macaroni and Cheese* was also new, and *Google* was a solid fifty years away.

If 1938 seems like it was a long time ago, then Madison Creek is going to seem very far away. It was a place where the simplicity of enjoying an evening on the front porch would be lost on a generation glued to their *iPods, iPads* and *iPhones*. Back then, you really could eat your blackberry and if you were *bad* it meant you were rotten to the bone. Cool meant cold and radio was king. Marilyn Monroe was twelve years old, and the superstars were guys like Jack Benny, Edgar Bergen, and George Burns and Gracie Allen. Orson Wells made a habit of spooking people on *The Shadow*, but by far the scariest man alive was the ominous voice of Arch Oboler on *Lights Out Everybody*. Oboler was really a quirky little nerd, but no one needed to know that since it was radio.

What happened that fateful year is still talked about by locals. The names get confused sometimes, and little details have a way of stretching out into whale like fish tales, but the heart of the story remains the same. Come on back, you should know the whole story before it's lost all together.

The Idiot Storm

Jo House stretched out on the roof of the big red porch. She liked the way the morning sun felt—like it was breathing right down on her. As if heaven was saying, *Here ya go, Jo-girl, you just enjoy this fine summer day.* The porch roof stretched across Uncle Huey and Aunt Georgette's two story home. It was her favorite place in the world because it was so easy to get to; all she had to do was slip from her bedroom window onto the porch roof. Best of all, she was pretty sure no one knew it was her spot. After all, a spot wasn't any good if people knew about it.

She had lived with her aunt and uncle ever since she could remember. She didn't know what family discussions were held or how exactly she came into their custody after her parents died—just that she belonged to them the same way other kids belonged to their mom and dad. Once, in an attempt to show she cared, Minnie Belle Lawson had asked Jo if she was "happy."

"What?"

"Happy, child." Then she spelled it out, "H-A-P-P-Y! Are you happy living with your aunt and uncle?"

She wasn't sure how to answer that question and so she just shrugged. She didn't know if she was happy, because she never thought about it. Who goes through life asking themselves if they're happy or not—old people who mostly aren't, she decided.

Minnie Belle had asked her again, "Honey, I'm just wondering if you are happy?"

"Sure," Jo had finally said.

That was when she was a lowly nine, way back in 1936. Now that it was the summer of 1938 and she was a lofty eleven, Jo thought she might offer a bolder response if asked again. She would just say, *I reckon' I'm just as happy living with my aunt and uncle as you are living with Mr. Lawson.* She liked that answer, because the Lawson's couldn't stand one another. Minnie Belle treated her husband the way most people treat a dog.

Yes indeed, she liked her new answer! But, Jo knew that even some magic could transport Minnie Belle to the porch roof right that instant and if Minnie Belle asked her again if she was H-A-P-P-Y, Jo would still chicken out and just grunt an ole *uh-huh.*

The roof of the porch was more than just her spot; it was a safe place when things in the house got a little tense. Downstairs, Aunt Georgette was in the clutches of an idiot storm. That's what Jo called it when her aunt got all worked up and threw a big fit. Usually Jo was game to ease nearby and listen in so she could giggle at the made up curse words her aunt would spew. But today, Jo was pretty sure her aunt was mad at her. In fact, she had forecasted an idiot storm would be dropping by this morning.

The day before, Jo had gotten herself kicked out of the Christian Camp Aunt Georgette had shipped her off to for the summer. Jo reckoned any girl who got herself kicked out of Christian Camp in less than two weeks could expect some repercussions. Of course, you bet-cha Uncle Huey didn't care if she got kicked out of the stupid Mount Hallelujah Leper Colony. The church camp had been all Georgette's idea, and so she was likely to see Jo's early return as some kind of personal failure on her part.

Yep, Jo said to the sky. *This is going to be an all-out idiot storm.*

When Aunt Georgette got all worked up, Huey called it a tizzy. TIZZY! That just wasn't a strong enough word for Jo. A tizzy just sounded a little dizzy… or drunk… or tipsy. When Georgette was angry, she stirred up enough red hot electricity to power all of Madison Creek—if not the whole of North Carolina. Imagine wires and power lines sticking out of the middle aged woman's head, sucking up her rage and giving light to Minnie Belle Lawson's dress shop, Mr. Finch's Mercantile, the Sweet Tea Café, and even the Grimm brothers' peanut farm.

She could try and wait out the storm—but it wasn't like her aunt was just going to forget she got kicked out of Christian Camp.

Humiliation, Jo said out loud to the big oak tree that grew up beside the house. *She is going to say I humiliated her. You owe me a million dollars, Mr. Oak Tree, if she says it.*

■ ■ ■

As Jo came downstairs that warm August morning, she pretended to put on a raincoat, ready to weather the storm. She could hear her aunt in the kitchen, slamming pots, pans — oops, there went a plate! Holy smoke, another plate! *For crying in a bucket, at this rate we'll be eating out of our hands.*

She heard her aunt giving a pan a mouth full of Baptist curses. These were things like, *no good, down right, complacent, hopeless, ding-wit, nit-wit, shula-macher,* and *lizard breath.*

Jo headed into the storm.

"Well good morning Aunt Georgette."

Georgette had the frying pan up in the air and it appeared she was beating an invisible somebody with the pan. Jo was probably that imaginary person.

"Makes me so mad I could just bend this pan right in half," Georgette fumed. A smattering of broken plates and glass lay at her feet like wounded soldiers strewn across a battlefield. Georgette raised the pan, ready to give the imaginary person another beating.

"You need help, Aunt Georgette? I've got a pretty good left hook, and the best kick in Madison Creek."

Georgette's face did not brighten. "Don't sass me, Jo. Your uncle has gone too far, this time. Way over the edge!" She shook the pan at the invisible person — who Jo now understood was Uncle Huey. "Wants to humiliate me."

BAM! And there it was! Only, she didn't say Jo had humiliated her; now it was all on big fat Uncle Huey.

"Well, looks like you've about bashed his head open," Jo nodded toward the spot where Uncle Huey was taking his lickin'.

A hint of a smile edged Georgette's thin lips. Her eye — which had been pulsing like something out of a Boris Karloff horror film — began to slow.

"You'll need a mop to clean up all the blood."

"Jo, really!"

"I better call the mortician, Mr. Step, and have him pick up the body. Otherwise, people might puke when they see all the blood. Besides, his body will get rotten quick and fill the kitchen up with maggots."

"Jo!"

Jo snickered and her aunt snorted hard. It was loud, unwomanly and absolutely piggish. She probably got a mouth full of snot on that one.

"So what did Uncle Huey do? I'll bet it was bad. He and his buddy Boots sell moonshine to Government agents?"

"That buzzard done invited the preacher over to our house tonight. Asked me to fix up a big meal. We done good to keep out of the bread lines through the Depression, and he wants a big meal on a weeknight?"

"I'd sure like me some fried chicken," Jo said.

"It's not about the chicken, Jo."

"So what's the problem?" Jo kicked the invisible Uncle Huey who was bleeding the last of his invisible blood on the floor. "I'd a reckoned you'd be happy as a dog with two tails to have Uncle Huey ask to see the preacher."

"Last time that turkey saw the preacher was when his ma died. He asked Pastor Weatherwax if it would be any cheaper to hold the funeral right at the graveside instead of the church. When Pastor said there wasn't no charge for funerals, Huey told him he needed to work on his business skills. He even offered to write up a funeral and wedding price guide, if the preacher would give him a CUT!" She trembled and kicked the invisible Huey. "Whatever he has up his sleeve now is going to shame me."

"Well, maybe you've got this thing figured all wrong, Aunt Georgette. I'll betcha he's come to his senses and decided to talk religion with the preacher."

"I doubt it."

"He might have decided to repent. Men are like that ya know? They don't come out and say they done decided to do away with wickedness. Men don't say, "Why, I drink too much and doubt too much and cuss too much." Men don't say that, do they, Aunt Georgette?"

Georgette shook her head.

"They tell their wife that they want her to ask the preacher over for dinner that night. And then they horse around a bit at dinner, because they're fearful to get around to the business of repenting."

Georgette brightened. "You learned a lot at Christian Camp."

Mount Hallelujah Leper Camp.

"Sure! I'll bet ya Uncle Huey is going to give his heart to the Lord this very night!"

"Yes!" Georgette cried. "That's it! Heavens-to-Betsy, what am I waiting for? I got to get busy!"

Jo triumphantly slipped her rain jacket off—the storm had passed. She wondered just what Uncle Huey really was up to. Did he have any idea that Aunt Georgette had him laid out on the kitchen floor, half beaten to death with a frying pan?

■ ■ ■

Jo skipped through her uncle's backyard. Skipping was something adults forgot how to do. Huey's man village was tucked in the far back corner of the property, on the other side of Madison Creek which rambled right through Huey's land. The little foot bridge that the Baptist Men's Ministry had helped Uncle Huey build years ago was looking tired these days. It had become slippery with overgrowth and the wood darkened with rot.

She stopped on the bridge and looked down at the running water. Sometimes when things weren't going well, she would come out to the bridge and think about running away. She could build a raft, like that boy Huck Finn did, and sail all the way down Madison Creek. She wasn't sure where it led; but she liked to think the creek went right to the ocean where she could then sail her raft somewhere wonderful—like New York City and the Radio City Music Hall. She'd have to park her raft out back, but she always imagined everyone would be so impressed with her, they'd let her in for free and maybe put her on the radio.

Hey fish, Jo yelled at the water that spilled from under the bridge. *Did you miss me? I've been off learning to get saved and not go to Hell, where they cut your head off and skin you. Too bad for y'all, Jesus won't save ya from my fishin' pole.*

She paused to consider that her handling of Aunt Georgette's rage had been nothing short of masterful.

Georgette's idiot storms had put the House family in more than one unusual situation. When you live with an angry person, life gets even more difficult than it already is. Everyone else in Madison Creek got their mail delivered right to their house, but Uncle Huey and Aunt Georgette still had to go to the post office on Main Street. That was because Aunt Georgette rained an idiot storm all over the mail-boy, Clay Simons.

Clay was just fourteen back then, but was working hard to earn as much money as he could because his pop had left the family. Some folk said his pa was a bum or a hobo these days. Jo thought being a bum sounded almost as romantic as sailing a raft down Madison Creek; but Clay got all red and angry when she told him he should be proud his pa was a bum.

What brought on the idiot storm was when Clay lost Georgette's contributor's copy of the *Baptist Standard Quarterly*. It was that particular issue that included Georgette's article on the power of forgiveness.

When he found the quarterly smashed at the bottom of his mailbag, he spared no time trying to make amends. He showed up at the door while roosters were still cock-a-doodle-dooing and the milk truck finished its first delivery.

Georgette took the package and said through gritted teeth, "Clayton, this was a very important package to me." When she was angry, her blood pumped especially hard through her right eye, making it THUMP-THUMP-THUMP in the socket. "You should be glad to have a job with a father—well, like the one you have. Here you are making good money in hard times. Taking up a paycheck that could be going to a grown man with a family." THUMP! THUMP! THUMP! went her eye.

Stung and angry, Clay spit words that had been building up like a mouthful of tobacco. "I work to take care of my mother and my little brother."

"Clay, I'd be proud of you if you weren't so cotton pickin' careless. Mail delivery takes organization. Like most young men your age, you're just slothful."

"Slothful? I'm not half as slothful as your man Huey! Minnie Belle Lawson says you have to roll him out of bed for lunch. Everyone knows he only goes to your church on Christmas, Easter and potluck Sunday."

That vein that had been pumping through her eye now made her entire head begin to shake. And that's when she chased him off the property. But she didn't do it empty handed. Oh no siree, she went after him with a loose red board from the porch rail. Clay ran for his life. Georgette raced after him with surprising vigor. Every now and then she paused to take long swings with her club—missing him by miles. Georgette returned to the house dragging the rail behind her like a boy coming home from a badly lost baseball game.

That evening, as Georgette fawned over her publication and read her own article about the power of forgiveness, the Holy Ghost began to squeeze her—and then the Almighty rang her out just like a washrag. With big, heaving sobs, she picked up the phone.

"Rose," she said to the operator on Main Street. "Put the Simons household on the horn, would ya?"

Georgette shook with shame. "Oh Clayton, precious Clay, can you ever forgive me? I was *SO* wrong!"

For his sufferings, Clayton Simons became the recipient of a large apple pie, a peach cobbler, and a friendly invitation to church. He ate the cobbler and apple pie, but did not go to church. And Aunt Georgette and Uncle Huey now had to pick up their mail on Main Street.

■ ■ ■

Uncle Huey's *famous* Man Village was lined with a couple of dilapidated old shacks, a Model T and piles of glorious junk. There was also Huey's *secret* shack, which had a water mill attached. People sometimes came to get batteries charged, or just to see how the wheel made electricity. With each passing year, the Man Village crawled a few feet closer to the creek.

Most days there was a steady stream of people who came to do business. Huey's trading skills would have put any car salesman to shame. There was a plethora of spare car parts, hub caps and an array of odds and ends. Need a light switch? Huey had it. How about a half used can of *Johnson's Glow Coat*? Or a jar of gently used nails?

Huey had told Jo that the secret to a good Man Village was knowing where to look for treasures. Old houses were great because they were full of hardware — door knobs, fixtures and Huey was even known to go after pipes, window panes, and chimney bricks.

"Well lookie there!" Huey's voice boomed over the rubble. He was an enormous fellow — and almost all gut. Truly, his belly was unusually blessed for times as hard as these. He sat next to an old boiler that Sheriff Tuff had meant to throw away. Huey's old buddy Boots leaned against the Model T. Everyone called him that because it was pretty well known that in *the day* he was the best bootlegger in North Carolina.

"Josephine Jackson House! I thought for sure Georgette would have killed you already," Boots said.

A wry grin edged over Huey's face, "It's probably her ghost."

"It's Uncle Huey who ought to be scared," Jo announced. "Aunt Georgette has him dead and bleeding on the kitchen floor."

"Ah, I knew she was mad. She didn't say a word to me this mornin'."

Boots shrugged, "Maybe she just didn't have nothin' to say to you, ole boy."

"Nah," Huey was thoughtful. "I don't worry a bit when a man doesn't say much, because a quiet man is a thinking man. But a quiet woman is mad. Jo, I hope you put a good word in for me," Huey tugged at a bottle Jo hadn't seen at first. He took a long swig, followed by a hearty *ahhh*.

"What in tarnation are you up to, callin' for a preacher on a Monday night?" Jo demanded. "You better not try to sell him anything. I told Aunt Georgette you're probably aiming to repent and give your heart to Jesus Christ—and that got her happier than…" she searched for the right word.

"Happier than a coon dog on a bare leg," Boots offered and rubbed proudly at his bushy black beard. Dog gone it if he didn't look like a pirate right out of a Robert Louis Stevenson book.

"Uncle Huey," Jo put her hands on her hips. "You better repent! With big ole alligator tears and thick snot."

Boots was excited, "If you can't get no tears to spring from your old dried up eyes, stab yourself in the leg with a fork, that'll get 'em flowin'."

"I can't wait to see this," Jo said.

"Oh, you ain't gonna see none of it," Huey said. "I got an engagement for you. Consider it payment for your shenanigans."

"What shenanigans?"

"Getting kicked out of Christian Camp. And worse, who had to drive you home? Mr. Step himself!"

Mr. Step was the town mortician. He had been up at the camp to visit his sister, and when Jo got kicked out, Mr. Step drove her home in nothing less than his hearse. Jo reckoned that if a girl was to get herself expelled from Christian Camp, riding out of camp in a hearse wasn't a bad way to go.

Huey folded his hands over his enormous belly. "Mrs. Dotson from next door come by and asked if me or Boots could shoot her cat. Says the cat has a demon or somethin' like that. So I volunteered you. I taught you to shoot when you were just six years old, and I reckon you're a better shot these days than I am."

"Seriously?" Jo's voice teetered in disbelief. She got kicked out of Christian Camp, and so her punishment was shooting the neighbor's cat? "You know, don't you, that Mrs. Dotson is crazy—right?"

Boots looked surprised, "Why Jo! What would make you say Mrs. Dotson is crazy?"

For cryin' in a bucket! Everyone knew Mrs. Dotson was crazy.

- Just this summer, Minnie Belle Lawson had told all the women at the Baptist Church that Lutie Dotson had come in her dress shop looking for a job. But she wouldn't hire her because she was C-R-A-Z-Y. Minnie Belle couldn't say the word — that would have been gossip — so she spelled it out.

- The mortician, John Step, said she was absolutely out of her mind. He told a whole group of men playing horseshoes behind Finch's Mercantile that the old bat had come in to the funeral home looking to buy a coffin. She didn't say what she needed it for, but he had the distinct impression she meant to sleep in it.

Sheriff Tuff said she better be insane, or he would lock her up for the murder of her husband.

■ ■ ■

Boots had a mischievous gleam in his eye. "Time to fess up Jo, just what did you do to get your hind end thrown out of Christian Camp?"

What hadn't Jo done? Why, there was the underwear up the flag pole, sneaking out of her cabin, and a mouse in Tilly Vanmeter's bed as she slept. She accomplished most of her antics undetected — the Shadow would have been proud. It was her stories that got her in trouble. In her two weeks up there, she'd spent plenty of time building the legend of Uncle Huey.

When the lights were out and they were supposed to be asleep, the girls in her cabin would say, "Tell us about the time…

- "Uncle Huey fell asleep at the funeral and the preacher thought he had died.

- "Uncle Huey ate so many beans he blew the seat of his britches out.

- "Uncle Huey pretended to be sick so Georgette wouldn't bother him to go to church. And the church ladies felt so bad for him that they brought him pies and cobbler."

"Uncle Huey don't like church, none," Jo had told the girls. "His Bible still smells like new leather, and crackles like a fireplace when opened. He thinks David was thrown in the lions den, and that Moses built an ark."

Jo had enough of Mount Hallelujah Christian Camp when Miss Step took her aside and asked if she had any questions about the Blessed Lord Jesus Christ. No, she did not have any questions. "It's just that all the other girls have given their souls to the Blessed Savior, except you, honey."

"Am I throwin' off your averages?"

Jo tried to think of what her Uncle Huey would do if he was confronted with an appeal to make a decision for Jesus. She didn't have anything against Jesus but the Blessed Lord Jesus Christ of Hallelujah Christian Camp was not one she wanted to invite into her heart.

"Honey don't you someday want to see your mother and father again? You can if you go to heaven, ya know?"

"I think they went to Hell."

Miss Step demanded to know what exactly made Jo say that. Everyone knew her godly parents had died in a terrible car accident on the way to church.

"Miss Step, can you keep a secret? That's just what we tell everyone. They actually got all shot up in a bank robbery."

She always resorted to something she considered much more grandiose than a simple car accident: a terrible house fire — they sunk down in quicksand — they were still alive, living in the Caribbean, and when they had enough money they would send for her. They had indeed died in the service of the Lord. Only, they had gone as missionaries to Africa. But her father became a cannibal and ate her mother. She punctuated it with a hearty burp.

That night the girls asked Jo to tell them a Uncle Huey story. Instead she decided to tell about the strict camp director, Miss Step. Everyone knew her brother, John Step, was the undertaker back at Madison Creek. Well, the reason Miss Step was so full of Jesus was because she had actually died. Her brother was so grieved by her death that he called in a local evangelist to pray over her. He raised her from the dead like Frankenstein's monster.

One girl asked how Miss Step had died. That was the best part of the story. In a whisper so hushed the other girls had to lean in toward Jo's bed, she explained that Miss Step had died in the throes of love making to a wild stranger who had come into town. Little gasps went through the room. It had been adultery with a capital A, and not just once. It had been a full blown affair. And then, in the throes of passionate love, God in heaven had looked down in rage. He struck her dead right in the arms of her lover. The girls giggled.

The story quickly grew bigger than the gigantic lie it already was. When Miss Step went to investigate who was spreading lies, she was not surprised to discover it was the *depraved one.*

"I know you're lost, honey," Miss Step waved her finger in Jo's face, "But there is no excuse for that kind of blasphemy."

Could you really blaspheme the head honcho of a leper colony?

■ ■ ■

Jo looked at Boots, who was still waiting for her. "I got kicked out because of all that moonshine you put in my bag. Really, Boots, you shouldn't have!"

He shook his head and smiled.

Demon Cat

I need you to shoot Dixie," Mrs. Dotson said.

She was sitting on the front porch of her tiny house. The place wasn't much more than what Aunt Georgette would call a shanty—something one might expect to find across the railroad tracks in Jordan Town. Jo studied the woman with guarded reservation, and a little self pity. It was just like that rotten Uncle Huey and ole Boots to send her all alone to deal with the loony neighbor. Mrs. Dotson's graying hair was pinned up, but several strands of loose hair still waved and bounced as she talked. She was wearing a flowered house dress—something Aunt Georgette condescendingly called a *moo-moo*. She worked her rocking chair back and forth with an unnerving rhythm.

"Dixie?" Jo asked.

"My cat Dixie!"

Mrs. Dotson opened the table drawer beside her and drew out a handgun. "Do you know how my husband died?"

"No."

Mrs. Dotson popped the gun open and went back to the drawer for a box of bullets. Her hand was unsteady and the bullets scattered everywhere. "My husband died by accident."

"Accident?"

Mrs. Dotson had a fistful of bullets in one hand and the gun in the other. She held the gun with her finger on the trigger. She loaded the bullets one at a time as she talked. *Click... Click.* "He was killed by a widow-maker."

"Widow-maker? Is that a g-gun?"

"No, it's a tree." *Click... Click.* "It's a dead tree that every now and then drops a branch on someone. When trees die, they just start fallin' apart, and God help the poor soul that's under them when they decide to lose a branch. My sweetie was asleep under the big tree out yonder…" *Click*, "and the widow-maker decided to drop a big branch on him. Like a bomb." Snap, she closed the gun and examined it, her finger still on the trigger as she stared down the barrel looking for the bullets she'd just dropped in. "They said that it looked like he had been hit with a blunt object. Them people said that maybe I done it. But I didn't. Devil might have… but I didn't."

Mrs. Dotson pointed the gun at Jo. "Take it, girl. I bought this gun at the Mercantile after I won the annual fishing contest. I caught the biggest fish in all of Western North Carolina." She nodded toward the wall, which was tacked up with newspaper clippings. "And I got my name in the paper. But not my picture. You know, if you get your picture caught on film it might do funny things to you in the afterlife." She slapped her leg as if to put a big period on the end of that entire thought and said, "Dixie is out on the porch asleep."

Jo took the gun. "Why do you want me to shoot your cat? I'd take your cat, but my aunt won't let me have it. But I'll come over and feed it and love it."

Mrs. Dotson dismissed that line of thought right away. "Nah, you don't want that little devil. Dixie ain't Dixie anymore, Jo. She's got a demon in her."

Jo nodded like everyone knew Dixie had a demon.

Mrs. Dotson led Jo right through her cracker box of a house to the back porch.

■ ■ ■

The preacher showed up, and Huey got right down to the business of humiliating Georgette. He had positioned himself in the parlor with his nose in the big family Bible. Worse, as soon as the pastor stepped in, Huey had to announce that he was reading the Song of Solomon.

Georgette took Pastor Weatherwax's hat. He had a comb over that attempted to hide a bald spot big enough to land one of the flying saucers Lutie Dotson was always talking about.

The preacher was small and wiry. A widower, he always wore the same black clothes and red bowtie. His wife died the same year the stock market did the big nose dive and broke America. For a few years after his wife's funeral, the women in the church tried to find him a new honey. But in a small town, the pickings are a little sparse, and the preacher was a hard sell. He wasn't a spellbinder in the pulpit — the kind that kept girls on the edge of their seat and men hollering amen. He was more of a plodder, building his sermon toward a final big thought. Most Sundays the big thought never came.

There was an energetic knock at the door. Georgette cringed — it was Huey's nasty friend Boots Hickerson. At least he'd put on a clean shirt. But *that* smell — what was it? All the bathing in the world couldn't get it off him. Not alcohol exactly... or sweat... or tobacco — all of it seemed to mingle together and bleed from his pores.

If vile Boots Hickerson was at the table, the likelihood of Huey doing any serious repenting was about the same as Roosevelt deciding not to run for another term.

Georgette pulled the door in close and let it squeeze her neck as she leaned out. "Boots, what are you doing here?"

"The big fella himself invited me."

"Well, can't you come back tomorrow? I'll cook a real fine meal just for you then."

"Boots, ole buddy," Huey thundered as he swept the door open. "Come in! We were just headed for the table."

After taking a fresh whiff of Huey's friend, Georgette decided it was best to keep the front door open and let the air in. The dining room was spectacular. Georgette seated the pastor at the head of the table and Boots at the foot — as far away as possible. The room breathed feminine elegance. Not only was the good silver out, but the plates and glasses sat centered on placemats and doilies.

When the chicken was served, everyone waited for the pastor to bless the food. It was always the pastor's job to bless everything. Most recently, when Teddy Grimm bought a new tractor, his wife Greta had the preacher out to bless it.

Huey rolled his fingers through the air to signify it was time to get things moving. "Preacher, give us the grace."

"This is your table Mr. House. Only fittin' that you say grace."

Boots snorted and grinned. Too bad Jo wasn't here to see this, she would split her sides open trying not to laugh.

Huey took a moment to collect his thoughts, then another moment to clear his throat, then another moment to adjust his shirt — was it hot in here? Finally, he prayed "Lord, for what we are about to receiveth, make us truly… verily… thankful. And look after thy preacher; this here man of God who sittith at our table in the presence of the glorious hosts of heaven. And pour ye out thy great blessings on the church… the Baptist one, not the Methodist one. And we thank thee for thy Book, which commands us to spread thy Gospel like butter on bread. Amen."

Boots moved his eyes up toward Huey without moving his head. "Spread the gospel like butter, that's a good one, big fella!"

Pastor Weatherwax sank into the chicken, making the appropriate sounds of approval as it went down.

"I sure did think highly of your sermon Sunday," Georgette said.

The pastor grunted thanks and buttered his cornbread.

Huey and Boots exchanged several long looks. Huey jerked his head, indicating Boots should get on with it, and Boots responded with a shrug that said, *this ain't my gig*.

Huey picked at chicken lodged between his teeth. "Well, I reckon you get asked this a lot. But, now, supposin' a fella is a wicked, rotten type —"

"More rotten than you think," Boots interjected.

Huey nodded agreement, "But then he decides to spin around and take up with preachin' the Bible."

Georgette's eyes widened. What did Huey just say?

Pastor Weatherwax rubbed at his chin, "You mean serve the Lord? There are so many places to serve the Lord, Mr. House. God might call you to serve him on the grounds committee, or the choir, or the prayer team —"

"What about you?" Boots put his elbows on the table and cradled his chin. His black beard mushed up around him, "How did you become a preacher? I mean, do you write somewhere and get credentials?"

Pastor Weatherwax's face paled. "Well, I got a calling."

Boots was interested, "A calling, eh? And who makes this call?"

Georgette answered that one. "The Lord makes the call, Boots."

"Ever get a church that's not a *Pepsi*, or a *Cola*, or a *Jell-O*, or a *Lucky Strike*?" Huey asked. "One that's not a name brand, I mean? Does it have to be Baptist, Methodist, or Catholic? Can't a church just be a little of everything?"

"Heavens, Huey!" A warm tear stained Georgette's cheek—she was holding back a volcano of irritation—a tizzy. Had Huey really just compared the *House of the Living God* to gelatin, soda pop, and cigarettes?

"Uh, there's not exactly a rule book," Weatherwax said uncomfortably.

Huey poured a fresh ocean of gravy over everything on his plate. "Now, with the I-R-S, do you have to fill out a form and tell them you're a church or does God give them a call as well?"

"And the offering..." Boots leaned as far as he could over the table, his chicken almost touched his chest, "You just take that home, or do you have to split it with the ushers?"

"Really!" Georgette snapped, and reminded herself not to storm up in front of the preacher. "Whatever the preacher is paid, it isn't enough."

"But people give you stuff, don't they," Boots pressed.

Huey lit up, "That's right, they do! Chickens and free dinners and even firewood, I suspect."

■ ■ ■

Dixie, the demon cat—whose brains had been scrambled by aliens—was waiting for Mrs. Dotson on the back porch. The cat had two yellow eyes fixed on the door, like she knew death was on its way. Jo started to aim the gun, but Mrs. Dotson shouted, "Don't do nothin' while I'm right here!" She disappeared into the house.

"Okay," Jo said to the cat. "You be a good kitty and you'll be in heaven before you know it."

She pulled the trigger and felt that gun turn to fire in her hands. Jo hadn't expected it to kick back and it almost hit her in the nose.

Dixie meowed and took flight at the same time. She landed on the ground with her legs already in motion to scamper away. "Hold now. Stay!" Jo shouted after the cat.

The door behind Jo flew open, and she surprised herself by firing again at the spot where the cat had been.

"Beelzebub!" Mrs. Dotson screamed at the cat. "Get 'er Jo!"

Dixie shot up a leaning tree. Jo had a terrible premonition that this might be the very spot where Mr. Dotson had met the Grim Reaper.

"You got to get closer!" Mrs. Dotson yelled as she started across the grounds.

Dixie hissed from the safety of the tree and trained spooky yellow eyes on Jo. The gun kicked in Jo's hand. The bullet missed the cat and lodged in a branch.

"Watch out!" Mrs. Dotson shrieked as the branch cut loose and creaked toward Jo. The cat launched herself from the tree. For a moment both the branch and the cat were in the air. Jo dodged out of the way of the falling branch and rolled into Mrs. Dotson. The branch landed at their feet. The cat fled like Al Capone from the G-men.

"Get off me, girl! What's wrong with you? Haven't you fired a gun before? Get the cat!"

Jo stood up and honed in on the cat. She got another shot in as Dixie ran across the yard. Dixie easily leapt onto Uncle Huey's picket fence and then down into his front yard. The fence was still shaking when Jo got to it. She hopped the fence easily.

Dixie was fast and before Jo could get her in her sights again Dixie had made it to Uncle Huey's big porch.

"Oh no!" Jo breathed, inching forward.

Georgette had left the front door open to let the breeze in. The smell of fried chicken wafted from the house making Jo's mouth water.

Right when Jo's foot touched the first step of the porch, Dixie turned and scrambled into the house. Jo was right on that cat's tail, almost ready to run her over with the gun stretched out in front of her. The cat and the girl blasted through the entryway toward the steps. Jo was midway up the steps when the cat reconsidered and leapt to the tile floor below.

"Josephine!" Georgette screamed as the cat, followed by the girl, thundered into the dining room.

Everything froze for a moment. Pastor Weatherwax had a napkin tucked up around the collar of his shirt like a bib, with his bow-tie making a strange lump underneath. Uncle Huey had a leg of fried chicken in his mouth and Boots had his elbows on the table, cradling his chin as he talked.

Dixie jumped up onto the table as Jo tried to decide what she was supposed to do. In the absence of a clear thought, Jo kept running toward the cat.

Aunt Georgette yelled as Jo slammed into the table. "Put the gun down!"

Dixie scampered across the dining room table while everything parted like the Red Sea. Plates full of food crashed to the floor as the cat stepped in the cobbler. The sweet tea was so full of sugar it oozed toward everyone.

"Gracious!" Pastor Weatherwax managed to say as the cat came toward him. Dixie was now leaving a peach cobbler paw-print as she went.

Jo started around another way, "Get the cat!" she shouted to the pastor.

He did not get the cat. What he did was try to dodge the cat, which caused him to tip back in his chair. He was skinny and wiry, but he still didn't have any balance. His chair went backward just as Dixie scurried past.

Boots started to grab Jo by the suspenders of her overalls, but she jerked free and stayed locked on that cat's tail. The girl swept past the pastor, tracking after the cat into the washroom. Jo lowered her gun to shoot as the cat looked for safety. The washroom was tight quarters, and Georgette didn't allow laundry to pile up. There was nowhere for Dixie to hide. Jo fired at the cat, sure she'd get a hit this time. But Dixie disappeared behind the washing machine. The barrel of the washing machine began to spray a bullet sized stream of water.

Really? Jo mouthed to no one. She knew she had shot that cat dead on, and that the bullet had gone right through Dixie and into the washing machine.

Jo stayed real still, even trying to control her excited breathing as she waited for the cat to reappear.

"Josephine!" Georgette's voice was angry and demanding.

"Stay back, Aunt Georgette. Dixie has a bad demon!"

Her clothes were getting soaked as the last of the wash sprayed out on her.

■ ■ ■

"No, Jo, you stay still. Don't move."

Jo could smell her aunt's perfume, dripping like sweat. Georgette dropped down and wrapped her arms around Jo, like she was going to hug her. Georgette gently pulled Jo's arms back until she could open her fingers and lift the gun out of her hand.

"Kick the washing machine," she instructed.

"What?"

"Josephine, kick the washing machine."

Jo kicked the washing machine and Dixie came out with a fresh fire in her belly. She ran across the wet floor toward Georgette. Jo jumped as the gun exploded in Aunt Georgette's soft hands. The cat's sprint became a tumble as its head dropped to the floor, but its hind legs kept up the race.

"Holiness, Aunt Georgette, you shot Dixie right between the eyes! Done blew her cat brains out and probably slaughtered that there demon she had, too."

Huey, who was now standing at the doorway, said that the pastor and Boots had skedaddled. But the preacher had promised he would pray for them.

"Jo, go on up to your room honey," Aunt Georgette's voice shivered with anger. She didn't wait for Jo to leave before turning to Huey, "Look at this mess! Cat insides all over my washroom. And the man of God at my house had to leave in shame."

"I don't think there was any shame in it," Huey said.

Georgette forgot the gun was still in her grasp, and she pointed it carelessly at Huey. "Huey, I thought you called on the preacher to surrender your life to the Lord! I thought you were done with sin!" She waved the gun in his face, "I thought you wanted to *Repent!*" Her eye settled on the gun that was in her hand and realization spread over her. She took in a deep breath, then deliberately pointed the gun right at Huey. "Huey House, you are going to tell me exactly what's going on!"

His eyes moved between the gun and his wife.

■ ■ ■

"Alright, baby doll, this is what happened. When tax time came around I realized we was just plumb broke. And it's such a blame mess to figure out. 'Bout that time I got to rememberin' about how the preacher said churches don't pay no taxes. They're fixed up with some kind of exemption."

"That true," Georgette agreed suspiciously.

"Sure it is. The Government's real friendly about it, see. But doggone it, I got this idea in my head and wrote the I-R-S to explain that—"

Jo felt warm pleasure spread over her as she realized what he had done. "Hot dog, Uncle Huey! You wrote the United States Government and claimed you're a church!"

Georgette didn't even look back at the girl, but kept her eyes—and the gun—locked on Huey.

"Sure," Huey said. "If I'm a church they can't come after me for taxes."

"Tarnation, Huey, you are cheap!" Georgette growled. "You wouldn't pay a dime to see a Yankee pull a freight train. So you told them you were a church, did you!"

"Well… no… not technically." He gave her a dumb smile. "I didn't tell them I was a church. I told them *we* was a church. Me and you are in this together, sweetie pie." Everything stood still after he said that. Huey finally broke the icy silence with an attempt at rejoicing, "We're a church! Praise the Lord!"

Unmoved by the sudden praise to God, Georgette lifted one eyebrow. "Huey, I'm sure there's more."

"Well, there is just one more little thing." Huey rubbed his bullfrog wide neck. "I got a letter from the I-R-S the other day sayin' they wanted to come visit my church."

Georgette waited for more.

"They say they'll be out here September 4th. So I don't have long to get things rolling, baby doll."

"Strange they gave you a date," Jo mused. "They should have come as a surprise. Snuck in like The Shadow. They're probably just tryin' to frighten you. Like an I-R-S scarecrow."

Georgette's eyes widened. So that entire affair with the preacher, the whole mortifying event, had been nothing more than a fishing expedition to find out how to run a church? She started to say something through gritted teeth — something that seethed out from deep within — then stopped herself and stared at the gun she had trained on Huey. Georgette acted so impulsively that she surprised herself. With a single jerk of the hand, and perfect aim, she shot the cat a second time.

Huey moaned and fell backward as if he had been shot.

Huey's First Offering

Minnie Belle Lawson was once a very beautiful woman. Leonard assured her that she was still beautiful — for a woman her age.

She considered herself a problem solver extraordinaire. Folk would come into her dress shop and share all kinds of worries and concerns. Women flocked to the dress shop because Minnie Belle had magic secrets that could get the most out of shapeless figures into the most shapely dresses. Men would come looking for their wife a new outfit, usually after a fight. She was able to tell men what women were thinking in a way their wives couldn't.

One man came in looking for his wife a new bonnet. Some gentle prodding resulted in the man explaining that he had come home and asked his wife exactly what it was she did all day. This reduced the poor wife to tears behind a locked bedroom door. The fella spent the night eating cold beans and sleeping on the sofa.

"How many children do you have?" Minnie Belle had queried. *Four.* "And how many meals a day did the wife cook?" *Three.* "And who did the dishes?" He wasn't sure. "Really and truly," Minnie Belle finally put her hands on her hips. "You think you can just buy her a bonnet and make it all better? What's missing in your house is a holiday."

"A holiday, Mrs. Lawson?"

"Sure, a big holiday. And I don't mean Christmas. And heavens, I hope you don't celebrate Halloween. Mister, you're missing out on Thanksgiving. You think it comes once a year in November. But you need to celebrate some thanksgiving for that wife who feeds you and keeps you in clean clothes and runs that fine house of yours. She doesn't just want a bonnet after a fight, she wants you to show her some gratitude, some thanksgiving, all year long. Without her having to pay for it with tears. Every now and again you just need to have a heap of spontaneous thanksgiving at your place. It'll make a new woman of her, I promise."

"That's a real fine idea, Mrs. Lawson!"

She folded the bonnet and slipped it into a hat box. "How about I have a dress sent to your house. I have her size right here in my file. Assumin' she hasn't dug into the chocolates lately. I can write her a little note that says how much you appreciate all she does for you."

He brightened. Wasn't she the genius? Of course she was. And the problem, like so many in Madison Creek, was fixed.

■ ■ ■

Today she had a different kind of problem. One that couldn't be fixed with a bonnet or a dress or even a girdle.

It was Sheriff Tuff. That big hulk of a man was as stubborn as a Missouri mule, and in her opinion he looked like one as well. He had refused to come to the dress shop when she summoned — imagine the audacity of telling *her* that she would have to come to the Sheriff's office. HER! — who had babysat him when he was doing number two-dee-doo in his diapers.

It was humbling to have to go in the Sheriff's office, since Sticky Simpson was locked up in the cell, and he always made comments. Minnie Belle went into the office with her head held high. Her confidence wavered as soon as Sticky whistled. He pressed himself against his cell bars. "Oh, Minnie Belle, I's a hopin' you'd come to my rescue!"

It was hard to believe that Sticky had respectable kin in town. Earl and Dorothy ran the Sweet Tea Café just a few stores up from the dress shop. Their daughter Katie had given them their sole grandchild. The only problem was, Katie had gotten everything all mixed up. She had a baby before getting married. In fact — Katie never got married. She didn't even tell who the father was. Just went about the business of raising her boy, Dusty, like it was as normal as a hen laying an egg for a child to just have one parent.

Minnie Belle felt sorry for Dorothy. She'd been a baseball freak of some kind in years back. What had she said they called her? A *Bloomer Girl*? Whatever that was, no good could come of that, Minnie Belle thought. What kinda woman would want to play baseball?

"Shut up, Sticky!" Sheriff Tuff snapped from his desk. His beard, blonde and thick, looked like a lion's mane. Minnie Belle wished she could march him over to the barber for a shave—but best not to antagonize. *You catch more flies with honey than vinegar.*

"Have you seen this?" Minnie Belle slapped a handbill down on the Sheriff's desk. "That orphan girl—the one Georgette was Christian enough to bring in her home—she brought this flyer to my dress shop this morning."

Sheriff Tuff studied the flyer.

"So a new church is coming to town, huh?" He actually gave Minnie Belle a little wink, "You must be right excited."

"Not just any new church, Sheriff, look who the preacher is. That Huey House has no business tryin' to set up a church! He's got that orphan girl handing out flyers all over this town. You need to shut him down—and quickly!"

> LITTLE RICKETY CHURCH
> of MADISON CREEK
>
> Invites You to Be Our Guest
>
> Sunday, September 4, 11 a.m.
>
> Good Singing and Good Preaching
>
> Come on out to Our Special Service
>
> Meeting at the Old
>
> HILLTOP RESTAURANT
>
> Preacher HUEY HOUSE
> Song Leading KATIE SIMPSON

"Well, Minnie Belle, there ain't really no such thing as a law that says ya can't start a church if you wanna. Fact, I think it's probably protected by the Federal Constitution."

This surprised her. "Really? None at all? I mean, don't preachers have to have a license… or papers… or ordinations… or something like that?"

Tuff had never thought about this, but it gave him a small opening. "Well, I'll look right into that, Minnie Belle."

She pressed on, to no avail. What about that old restaurant he was setting up shop in, she demanded. Could you really, legally, start a church in an old restaurant? Everyone this side of the Mississippi knew that Huey's old restaurant building was rat infested and dilapidated and a hiding place for drunks and vagabonds and hobos.

"Well," Tuff rubbed at his beard. "I reckon if Huey fixes that old building up and starts a church in it, the hobos will move on or get saved."

Minnie Belle lowered her voice and sank toward the Sheriff's desk, "You really should lock that Huey House up, Sheriff."

"Why?"

"Why, everyone knows, he tried to kill the preacher the other night."

Tuff was taken by surprise. "He tried to kill the preacher? You mean Pastor Weatherwax?"

"Oh good grief." Minnie Belle felt annoyed that she had to fill him in on this.

"Why would Huey want to shoot Pastor Weatherwax?"

"Really and truly! It's as obvious as the nose on your face. To knock off the competition!"

She had more, but right then Sticky Simpson stuck his tongue out and dragged it along the jail bars, moaning as he went. "Ooh, Minnie Belle! Come to me!"

"You want to do me some good," the Sheriff said, rubbing his beard. "Why don't you get my boy Sticky over there to tell you where his moonshine still is hidden at."

"Heavens," Minnie Belle sulked, "Everyone knows that. It's up yonder on Blue Mountain somewhere."

"Somewhere be the problem," Tuff sighed. Speaking more to Sticky, but looking at Minnie Belle, Tuff said, "I sure hope it's not in a cave. That would be stupid, wouldn't it? Might blow the top right off the mountain. If you put a distillery in a cave, I mean."

"Jesus turned water to wine," Sticky said tugging at the bars. "Can you hold me with no proof of a crime?"

"More moonshine running through this town than water over Niagara," Tuff said. "They call it *Resurrection Juice* out here. Know why?"

Minnie Belle was a little interested. "Why?"

"I reckon it's because they're brewing it in a cave somewhere."

Sticky snickered, "So like Jesus come out the grave alive, this stuff comes right out alive. That's a good one, Sheriff."

Minnie Belle turned to Sticky, "I hope that's a big lie, Sticky. I hope with all my righteous heart that you're not brewing up the Devil's drink and calling it *Resurrection Juice*."

"I'll tell if you'll marry me," Sticky said, and once again dragged his tongue along the bars of his cell.

Minnie Belle huffed out. She tried to slam the door behind her, but it was heavy and just wheezed shut. She was unimpressed with her exit, so she opened the door again and slammed it shut.

■ ■ ■

Really and truly, this whole thing was Leonard's fault, Minnie Belle reckoned. If Leonard would be the cotton pickin' big boy in the family, he could have explained the whole thing to the Sheriff and gotten a totally different response. But it would take armies to get him away from that blasphemous radio.

And then—behold—there he was! Huey House himself came driving right up Main Street in his old 1928 green pick-up. She heard him coming before she saw him. That truck sounded like an old man with a chest full of rocks. That insatiable orphan was in the truck bed. She road with her head in that back window and her hind end sticking right out. Can you imagine? Georgette sure was doing a fine job making a Christian woman out of that child.

Huey slowed and the girl waved a handful of flyers. "Are ya comin' to our church, Mrs. Lawson?"

The truck backfired, burped, and almost died.

"Wait!" Minnie Belle yelled. "I want to talk to—"

The engine caught its breath and Huey rumbled away. *Godless*, Minnie Belle thought.

■ ■ ■

Huey, Boots and Jo stood outside the abandoned restaurant. The structure leaned, as if the shadow of Blue Mountain was pushing it down. The building sported several broken windows like black eyes;

it looked mortally wounded. The front door blew back and forth in the late summer breeze adding a ghostly sigh to the otherwise quiet street.

"Looks pretty pathetic," Boots said. "You gonna show me the guts?"

Huey motioned at the door, which was gaping wide open for the moment—then slammed shut with the wind.

"Wait, Uncle Huey." Jo pointed at the ground. "There's not even much of a porch here. Women aren't going to come in their heels and dresses if you don't even have a porch. Big Mule got a bunch of stepping stones free from the mercantile. Want me to ask him if we can have 'em?"

Huey shrugged. Stepping stones in front of the building was the least of his problems. He and Boots went inside, Jo trailed after.

Huey had done little more than clear the room. Even that was a work in progress. A pile of tables and chairs was shoved into the far corner.

"Ain't much of a church," Boots announced as if he was God come down for a visit.

"Uncle Huey!" Jo said, jumping away from the wall. "I think some dead people done already showed up for church. I heard somethin' move inside the wall."

"What the blazes is that girl talking about?" Boots demanded.

"Just listen!" Jo insisted. "You listen close, you can hear something… lots of somethings, I think… in the wall. Y'all think maybe it's a ghost?"

"Really?" Boots went to the wall and pressed his ear to it. "Oh boy. We got visitors, Huey. Lots of 'em. Would say it's squirrels or woodchucks. But there's too many."

"Rats," Jo breathed. "This place is rat infested!"

"Bingo! Give that girl a candy apple!" Boots nodded toward the wall, "this is gonna be a deal breaker. Can't have rats chewing on the hem of the ladies Sunday dresses, now can we?"

"Yeah, yeah, yeah." Huey groaned.

For a moment, the entire room swelled with the sound of them. Unseen little feet scampering about inside the walls. Daddy rats visiting mommy rats. Cousin rats going to one another's houses for sleep overs. Dog gone it, it sounded like they were having a square dance in there.

"Thankfully, I know how to get rid of rats," Boots announced.

■ ■ ■

Now that was a good idea!

The plan required nothing more than a single cut in the exterior of each of the buildings four walls. Just tiny cuts big enough for a hose to slip in. And then, Huey pulled his old green pickup next to the wall. The men attached a hose from the truck's exhaust into the wall, and then they left the engine running to do the work, chugging out carbon monoxide.

It was interesting, Jo reflected, that Huey's truck used to belong to the mortician, Mr. Step. He used it to haul caskets and dead bodies around. Now it was being used to move rats to the next world.

Jo was about to ask if any of them actually thought this was going to work, when she heard her first *THUD*. She was standing next to the exterior wall, staring out toward Main Street when it happened. She jerked around and stared at the wall, wishing she could peek inside. Then there was another — *THONK*.

"It's working!" Jo yelled. "They're falling like rain in there!" She pretended to pick up a telephone. "Hello, operator? Yes, connect me to Hell please... You heard me! Hell!"

Boots held a hand to his ear, "Hell here. How might we help you?"

"This the Hell with fire and brimstone?"

"Sure is. Got us some worms and even a bottomless garbage pit. You want to buy land?"

"No sir," Jo said. "I just wanted to call ahead and tell you to make room down there, because we're sending you twenty billion rats in one big package."

They all laughed, feeling very smart to have gotten rid of all the critters.

■ ■ ■

The problem was discovered at ten thirty the next morning. It was a sunny Thursday.

Huey, Boots and Jo arrived at the old building ready to get some serious work done. Huey was sharing with them his philosophy that Eve had not eaten an apple, but an orange in the Garden of Eden. He opened the door, explaining that the whole time Eve was talking to the snake, that ole serpent was peeling the orange for her right then and there.

They were all thinking so hard on the orange and the snake, that it took a moment to realize that they'd just been hit with a humongous wave of stink.

Huey paused in the middle of the room. "What is that smell?" he asked.

"The rancid smell of rotting rats!" Jo exclaimed.

One dead rat might make a distant stink. But there were more rats in those walls than Pharaoh had Egyptians in his army. There had never been such a rancorous — even palpable — odor in all of Madison Creek.

■ ■ ■

"Ah, it's a wasted day," Huey bemoaned. They were sitting on the steps of the old building. Jo was sure the step under Huey was starting to bow.

Boots had taken to smoking his pipe. "Well, we can work outside for today. Need to paint a sign for the church, and maybe put a cross on it, don't ya think?"

"Right!" Huey hadn't thought of that. All churches had a cross. "Better make it big, too."

"How many Sundays are your church going to be open, Uncle Huey?" Jo asked.

"Just one. Long enough to show the I-R-S that I really am a church. Then it's no taxes for life. It's like a get out of jail free card."

Boots nodded toward the road and pulled his pipe toward the corner of his mouth. "Look who decided to join the party."

Minnie Belle Lawson was actually stomping as she came toward the building. She looked a little childish to Jo. She was in early fifties with gray hair that she kept pulled back in a tight bun. Her blue dress was perfectly fitted, with ruffles at the hem.

"Minnie Belle, ain't it a fine day?" Huey grinned.

Minnie Belle stopped in front of them. She held up one of Huey's flyers. "Yesterday, that orphan girl brought this here handbill by my shop. Do you really mean to start a church?"

"That's what the flyer says. You want to come?"

"No. Really and truly, I want to know what's really going on here. You're up to somethin'. What is it?"

"Yep, you got us," Huey said cheerfully. "I's thinkin' I'd start a church and sell liquor under the pews. You want a cut?"

She shivered with frustration. "I tell you, I've been up all night trying to figure it out. You're not a religious soul; don't have a righteous bone in ya. Worse, you're proud of it. I'm not fallin' for your foolishness, Huey. I'm gonna give this here church of yours a wide birth."

Huey measured his words. "Gosh, that's too bad. I's hopin you'd come to church and catch a bit of kindness."

"More likely to catch a dose of drunkenness and debauchery at any church that would let you preach anything."

Boots coughed up a nasty cloud of smoke that was so thick, Jo reckoned it had been trapped in his chest since Lee whooped the Yankees at Chancellorsville. "Well good heavens woman, don't catch immorality or I'll have to run to the straight and narrow."

Minnie Belle reddened. "You are a sorry man! I want to see the inside of this here church. You have a pulpit in there? Really and truly, more likely you have card tables set up and ready to go."

Huey started to say it was none of her cotton-pickin' business what they had inside the building; but Boots said, "Go on in and have a peek-a-boo."

She stomped up the steps past them and marched in like a gunfighter entering a saloon. She got several feet into the room before stopping suddenly. She turned back. Huey and his gang clogged the doorway, watching her.

"Well, what do you think?" Huey asked.

It was nothing more than an empty room with a few piles of chairs and tables.

Her skin was ashen. "What is that smell?"

"I don't smell nothin'," Boots said. "Do you, Huey?"

"Not a thing."

"Really and truly!" Minnie Belle gasped. "Did you bury someone in here?"

Huey gave an innocent shrug.

She tried to look around, to take things in, but her eyes were starting to water. Sickness came over her in a wave. She couldn't take that smell anymore. She crumpled over and let out a surprised yelp as her knees hit the floor.

"You going to pray for us?" Huey asked.

Minnie Belle started to say something, but she was nauseous.

"Stop it, Uncle Huey. You better be kind to her, I don't think she's well. We better get her out of there! I think she's going to blow!"

It was too late. Minnie Belle Lawson threw up—hard. It came in long, gasping, heaving torrents. First, all over the floor. Then she looked up to tell Huey one more time that he was surely damned— when a fresh wave caught her and she spewed her mornings bacon, eggs, and waffles at him. All three stumbled out of the doorway and almost tumbled off the steps.

Minnie Belle took a moment to catch her breath.

"Help me," she shivered as gooey eggs slid down her dress.

Reluctantly, Boots and Huey slipped their hands under her arms to help her up.

Once outside, Minnie Belle fought for composure. "I have never smelled anything that bad. I think maybe some demons died in there."

When she was gone, Boots gave Huey a toothy grin. "Well, big fella, a church is not really been blessed until the righteous have left their breakfast at the altar. You done got your first offering."

Sunday Nights at the Radio Club

Sunday evening worship service was not a popular thing in Madison Creek—not among the men, anyway. The prospect of listening to Pastor Weatherwax stumble through a second sermon was about as appealing an idea as trading places with General Custer before the Indians came riding down on him. "Face it," John Step once told his wife Edith, "The fella couldn't preach his way out of a cardboard box."

"You must know what's going on, preacher," Minnie Belle Lawson once said at the end of another sparse evening service. The preacher said he had no idea what was going on, so Minnie Belle helped him. "Those men are spending all Sunday evening over at Step's."

"The morgue?" the preacher questioned.

"Yes the morgue. They have some kind of Radio Club they attend over there. But who knows what really goes on. More than once I smelled liquor on Leonard's breath when he came home."

"Ah, it's a dry county."

With growing pressure from the women, the pastor dared to bring the subject up at a deacons' meeting. He encouraged the men to be leaders of their households and attend all the Sunday worship services.

"Well now, I'd like to speak on that subject," Clyde Finch said. Finch was a deacon as well as the mayor. A widower, he'd found God when his wife died. "Why are we having church on Sunday night, preacher? I already heard one sermon, and am workin' hard to put it into practice."

Several other deacons agreed right away. No one had gotten saved at an evening service in… well… ever. And it was costing the church money to have the lamps burning. Clyde called for a vote. To the pastor's astonishment, four of his five deacons voted to close up evening service.

The Monday after the deacons' big vote, the preacher was sitting on a bench outside the church. Huey House rumbled by in his old truck, then circled back and stopped. This was a year before the incident with the cat.

Huey lumbered up to the preacher. "You okay, old man? You look about as low as a well digger's behind at the end of a long day."

"Well, the deacons chose to close up evening service Huey," the preacher confided. "Seein' as you never been much of one to frequent the service, I don't guess you'd understand how I feel about this."

Huey sank down next to the pastor. Dog gone it if that wasn't some bad news right there. Now Georgette would be home bothering him to fix this or do that. Church nights were his best alone time.

"Shucks, that's too bad," Huey bemoaned, much to the pastor's surprise. "But they're gonna pay you just the same as they always did, right?"

The pastor was a little befuddled at this. "Well, sure."

"Heavenly days! It looks to me like you've rigged yourself a bargain. If they ain't cuttin' your pay, and they're workin' you less, it reckons to me that you should be happier than a pig in poop."

The preacher just stared at Huey. Thinking he had left the man in speechless gratitude, Huey slapped him on the knee and bid him farewell.

■ ■ ■

Huey got kicked out of the Radio Club a couple years before the cat incident. His troubles started when he brought good hearted — but completely illiterate — Big X to a meeting. The problem had nothing to do with Big X's literacy and everything to do with the fact he was black — or, a *negro*, as Clyde Finch kindly put it when speaking to the man, and not so kindly when yakking behind his back.

Huey and Big X had been working that Sunday afternoon at the

Man Village, getting things ready for Monday. Big X had raked the yard, and Huey got him to help move his latest prize, a bathtub, to a more prominent spot in the yard.

"Anyone needs help installing that there tub, you tell 'em I'd be happy to do it for a dollar," Big X said.

"I'll tell 'em for sure," Huey agreed. "But make it three dollars. Don't sell yourself short."

"I'm happy with a dollar."

"Well, I'll take a dollar for recommending you," Huey said. "And you'll still get two. Which is twice what you asked for."

Big X shrugged, it didn't matter to him either way.

"Say, it's time for me to skedaddle," Huey announced. "I got my meetin' to go to."

"What kinda meeting?"

"A Radio Club. You listen to the radio?"

"Some of the ladies over in Jordan Town say radio is the Devil. But that don't scare me none. I listen to *Jack Benny, The Lone Ranger* and *Fibber McGee.*"

"Well, you just gotta come, then," Huey said. And after he said it, there was really no gracious way for Big X to back out.

■ ■ ■

In 1936 the Radio Club was still new. The men met in John Step's small apartment above the morgue. Edith, John's wife, was patient with the men filling her apartment, leaving her bathroom dirty and more than once emptying the icebox. When there was church, she would attend. When the church service died, she joined Minnie Belle and several other ladies in a weekly game of Bridge.

The men would huddle around a Zenith radio that crackled and popped with static as it magically grabbed voices from the air. What started as a time for the guys to sit and drink Boots' moonshine, and listen to Jack Benny be bested every Sunday night by his servant, Rochester — slowly grew into something more complicated.

Clyde Finch had come upon a new wire recorder, and began recording radio shows. Soon the guys weren't just stuck with the live broadcast of Jack Benny, but could drop in on *The Shadow,* and *Lights Out*—things their wives did not approve of.

Finch had brought the wire recorder to the club, hoping the men might get excited about the new product and order one for themselves. So far he'd only sold two. He encouraged the men to take it home and try it out. So, each week another member would take the recorder home and place it next to the radio during his favorite program, and return the next Sunday evening and play it back for the group.

One of Finch's sales was to Huey. But Georgette pitched a tizzy fit over the thing and declared it was a useless waste of money; she didn't want it in the house. Huey tried to return the item to Finch, who said that he did not take returns on special orders. Especially since Huey had already etched his name at the bottom of the machine. So, Huey donated his recorder to the club. And off it went each week with a different member to capture great radio moments.

The guys got the best kick out of the occasional background noise. There was the time Minnie Belle had no idea she was being recorded, and told Leonard that Greta Grimm had come into her shop to see if she would like to buy a sack of apples. Minnie Belle proudly told Leonard that she didn't buy a single apple, but sold the German immigrant two dresses.

Old man Lucius Jeremiah had a more embarrassing incident with the wire recorder. The ole fella had once been a sharecropper in Oklahoma until the bank took back his land. When everyone else headed toward California, he packed up and came to North Carolina to live with his daughter.

Jeremiah had left the thing recording his favorite radio show — *Ripley's Believe It Or Not*—while he went upstairs to take a nap. After all, why listen to a program he'd just be listening to again Sunday night? It wasn't until they listened to the recording at the Radio Club that they discovered Jeremiah's daughter and her husband had come into the kitchen where the radio was and had a little chat—about the old man.

They started out talking about how the old man shouldn't drive; after all, he couldn't see or hear. It was like Helen Keller on the road. But then things got more awkward.

"He about embarrassed the daylights out of me the other day," the old man's daughter said. The men at the Radio Club leaned in to catch every bit, even though her voice was louder than the radio. "I took him up to Finch's mercantile to pick up some flour. Know what I spied him doing when he thought I wasn't looking?"

At this point, the men were crowding each other to get closer to the radio.

"What's wrong with y'all?" Jeremiah asked.

The voice on the recording went on. "I saw him reach right out and grasp the mannequin Finch has in front of the women's dress section. Before I could stop him, he had run his hands all over her..." their voices dropped back as someone turned the volume up on *Ripley's Believe it or Not*.

Over time, the Radio Club would experience a slow creep, taking up more and more of Step's apartment. Soon they weren't just meeting upstairs, but gathering round in the basement to listen to the wire recordings and drink moonshine. In fact, things got cozy enough that they felt confident telling Boots he didn't need to slip in once a week before the meeting to bring them a delivery of moonshine; they could hide a month's worth right in the basement. After all, no one really wants to search through a morgue for contraband liquor. John Step hid the moonshine in a big wood coffin the guys named *The Beast*.

■ ■ ■

Huey arrived with Big X in tow on Red Heartland's night to share his radio program.

Instead of sharing a radio program, Red brought the men a pile of strange material that had fallen off a Government truck headed up Blue Mountain. The flashy fabric could have passed for a modern version of Joseph's coat of many colors. The men were unsure what to do with it, and in Red's opinion, not nearly as thankful as they ought to be for his unusual gift to the club. Finch said it was probably weather balloon material, but boy there was a lot of it.

The men had finished stacking the material and were listening to a recorded episode of *Light's Out* when Huey and Big X came down the steps. The entire staircase sounded like it might cave in under their weight. Huey came in with his usual energetic smile and handshakes all around.

"Huey, doggone it, it's good to see you." John Step pumped Huey's hand.

"I'm always afraid you'll be the last to see me before they drop me in a hole and bury me," Huey said.

Red turned up the volume on the radio. "You guys mind, we have a show here."

"Who ya got with ya, Huey?" Clyde Finch asked, nodding toward the doorway, which was filled by Big X.

"Ah, him. This is my buddy, Big X. We call 'em that on account of —"

"He can't read or write," Lucius Jeremiah jumped in. "Just writes a big X when told to sign his name."

"That's me," Big X said. "My real name's —"

"Boy, no one cares what your real name is." Red's face was tight with anger. "The only question is, what are you doing here?"

Big X looked trapped. "Why, Mr. House invited me. That's all. I just come for the radio."

"That's right," Huey said, still smiling. "He's my guest."

"No he's not," Clyde Finch said. "'Cause he ain't invited."

Huey tried a good-ole-boy grin. "Don't y'all be like that."

"I know all about radio," Big X offered. "My favorite is *Fibber McGee and Molly.* And it won't upset me none of you fellas listen to *Amos and Andy.*"

"Better not upset you," Red said through gritted teeth.

Huey's good nature had gone and now he sounded whiny. "No one said a fella can't bring a negro buddy to one of our meetings. Y'all have friends from Jordan Town, too."

Teddy Grimm spoke up. "But we don't bring them here. Cause this is the *White* Radio Club, see?"

Huey's eyes widened with surprise. "The *White* Radio Club?"

Red looked toward Big X, who still hadn't moved an inch. "You understand that, boy? It's the *White* Radio Club."

"Guess it depends on what Mr. House says," Big X said.

Cornered between his buddies in the club and his black friend, Huey didn't feel this was the hill to die on. "Well, my friend, I guess it was a mistake to bring you here. Seein' as how you might not be real comfortable since no one else here is quite like you, if you take my meanin'."

Big X shrugged, "I feel just fine."

"No you don't."

"Yes I do."

"W-w-well, just the same," Huey stammered. "I'm sure I'll sell that bathtub tomorrow, and whoever buys it will want it installed. You better go get rested up, my friend."

"So you're sayin' you want me to leave?" Big X dared.

Red answered that in a burst of anger. "Yes! Go!"

But Big X didn't move. "I want Huey to say it. He invited me."

The wire recording bubbled voices as Huey thought about what to do. Finally, he said, "Well, I reckon you best move along. And don't go tellin' no one 'bout this here Radio Club—"

"This here *White* Radio Club," Red cut in.

With that, Big X turned and lumbered back up the steps.

■ ■ ■

Things were strained between Big X and Huey for a spell after that. Big X didn't stop by the Man Village as often as he used to. His weekly visits became every other week, and he'd just ask if Huey had any work for him. Huey didn't; until that September, when the big storm hit and tore the property up. Several people offered to help Huey clean up, but he sensed they were just being nice. To make matters worse, if he let any of the church people help him then they'd make him feel obligated to attend worship service. When Big X came by and asked if Huey wanted any help, he jumped at the offer and put him right to work. Soon it seemed things were right back the way they always had been.

■ ■ ■

It was the winter of 1937 that Huey got himself kicked out of the Radio Club—the *White* Radio Club. Huey, who had been unwilling to let a small argument about race break his connection to the Radio Club would instead stomp off over twelve dollars and fifty cents.

It was the first meeting of the New Year, and the guys were all business. The club was behind six months rent to Step's, and while John Step was a happy member, he gently explained that as a local businessman, he couldn't just permanently house the club without the agreed upon compensation.

"Ah, come on," Huey spoke up. He was sitting in a big, oversized chair with his arm resting on The Beast. The room was unusually still; maybe because the radio wasn't playing and the only background noise was the *humm* of the oil lamp. "The club ain't costing you a cent."

Step stuck to his guns, "It's what we agreed on."

Red jumped right on that, "Yep, it's what we agreed on, Huey."

"Which brings me to a rather uncomfortable order of business," Clyde Finch said, opening a ledger. "Some of us haven't paid last year's dues." He waited, letting that sink in, and hoping the guilty party might step forward and clear his name on the spot. But no one moved.

"Huey," Finch tried to look the ole codger right in the eye, "You haven't paid a dime this year, or last year. That makes two years worth of dues. Plus, you're past due for December the year before that. At fifty cents a month, that's twelve dollars and fifty cents you owe."

"I never paid dues. No one ever asked."

"No one should have to tell you, Huey."

Huey ran his hand over The Beast. "The way I was figurin' it, I'm good friends with the mountain man that gets ya all that moonshine. I don't see any of you runnin' up and down Blue Mountain to get it."

"What's that have to do with dues?" Finch asked.

"Yeah!" Red was always glad to pile on.

With a wave of his hand, Huey said, "If twelve dollars is that important, I'll pay it right now."

"That might make things easier," John Step offered, glad the situation was calming.

"But now, what about my payment?" Huey asked.

They all looked at him with mouths ajar.

"Y'all owe me, by my calculations, three hundred dollars. Wanna just take my twelve dollars out of that and pony up?"

"Oh good grief!" Red exploded. "Where in the world do you get that?"

"Well, that is my recorder you men haul off with each week to record your radio shows."

Finch and Step exchanged knowing looks. Huey was just going to make trouble now.

"Way I figure it—"

"No need to figure anything," Finch cut in. "You never said anything about payment for that recorder. And at that price—"

"Seein' as how we moved from friends to business, I thought you'd be a little more friendly about it," Huey said, standing up. "All y'all have a strange way of doin' business. Want me to pay you for nothing more than sittin' in this room and keeping you company. All the while, you use my recorder and don't give me a dime. Bunch of rotten thieves."

Huey was enjoying himself.

"Why don't you just take your player and get out," Red seethed.

"Small town, you ought to be careful about makin' enemies," Huey said to Red. "I'll move along, because this just isn't much fun anymore. But y'all keep the machine, I would hate it if y'all couldn't listen to radio shows at a Radio Club."

With that, Huey stood up, patted The Beast one last time, the way a man might longingly pat his wife's behind before a long trip, and headed for the door.

■ ■ ■

Huey did not return to the *White* Radio Club until that summer of 1938. It was Teddy Grimm who suggested Huey should make amends.

Teddy came to the Man Village to see if Huey had any dining chairs. When pressed a bit, Teddy admitted that he and his wife Greta had gotten *into it* a couple nights ago and between the two of them, they'd busted all the chairs in the house. Huey had chairs.

"Say, you're pretty good with your hands, ain't ja?"

"Sure. I'm a peanut farmer. You can't—"

Huey cut him off. "I'll make ya a deal. I'll give you chairs, if you'll build me some benches. It'll give you the day away from Greta. Kind of a vacation."

Huey had a pile of wagon wheels Nettie Drake had sold him when her husband left her for a California floozy. Nettie's sweetie had thought he would make a fortune building covered wagons. When he deserted Nettie, he left behind an impressive pile of wooden wheels that landed themselves in Huey's Man Village.

"How about this," Huey proposed to Teddy, "We—and I mean you—just saw those wheels in half and use them for the ends of the benches."

It was a deal. And Teddy had a suggestion of his own. "Ways I see it, Huey, you don't want to go startin' a church and have ruffled feathers all over town. You best go fix it up with the Radio Club."

"Yeah, guess I ought to," Huey said.

Huey knew better than to show up empty handed. He went to his Man Village and began a search for something to bring as a peace offering. It was Jo who pointed to the big rocking chair sitting under the shade of an old shed. Huey had made her sand it down the week before.

"Yeah, I guess that'll do fine," Huey said with a bit of a sinking feeling. He'd been hoping to give that rocker to Georgette for Christmas. "Let's load it up."

"Ah, you can't just load it up and take it over there like this!" Jo objected. "You gotta put somethin' on it."

"What are you talking about girl?"

"Yeah, you gotta make it personal. Otherwise it just don't make no sense, Uncle Huey. Why you givin' them a chair?"

"'Cause it's what I've got."

"Right, but you can't let them know it's all ya could scrounge up. No one wants another person's trash, even if they play like it's a gift. You gots to personalize it. Let me paint their names on the head rest."

Huey eyed the chair. "Nah, not enough room."

"How about a Bible verse?"

"By Jav, I think I'll keep ya!"

"I think that's *By Jove*. Which Bible verse you gonna put on there?"

"I reckon we might as well use that one your aunt's all over like ole Boots on a plate of grits. Matthew 25:41. Paint that in red, right on the head rest of that there rocker, and we've got our peace offering."

■ ■ ■

On Sunday Huey did not attend church, because he had a bad case of a yeast infection. He'd heard about it on the radio. The truth was, Georgette was glad to be free of him. He was becoming more and more of an embarrassment. He had plastered Madison Creek with more flyers than a Yankee carpet bagger.

She was humiliated when Minnie Belle Lawson led a group of ladies to her pew as soon as Pastor Weatherwax gave the final amen. Georgette's pew rested under the big stained glass window. Of course, that meant there was only one exit, which was now blocked by Minnie Belle and crew.

"Really and truly, Georgette, can't you do anything about Huey?" Minnie Belle demanded. She was wearing her favorite yellow dress and enough perfume to wake the dead.

"What about Huey?" Georgette asked, drawing her Bible up to her chest.

"Why, this business of a new church," one of the other ladies offered. "We're concerned about it."

"Well maybe Huey has finally turned from slothfulness and decided to follow the Lord."

"Really?" Minnie Belle looked doubtful.

"And truly," Georgette said.

Jo suddenly appeared, standing on the pew next to Georgette. "My Uncle is gonna be the greatest preacher since Billy Sunday. But he might start havin' church on some other day, like Tuesday. And they'll call him Huey Tuesday."

"I doubt it," Edith Step said.

"Jo, get down," Georgette demanded. Jo obliged because she didn't want to bring on an idiot storm. Looking at the ladies, Georgette said, "I don't think it's for you to judge a man's heart, or what the Holy Ghost might do. Why, he might be at home right now fasting and praying, while you stand here in God's temple judging him. You should be ashamed."

Minnie Belle started to stammer, "W-w-we were just—"

"Ashamed!" Georgette put her hands on her hips and stepped forward. The women parted—just like Moses at the sea.

"Ashamed!" Jo mimicked.

■ ■ ■

That evening, as the Radio Club listened to Jack Benny descend into his vault, Huey House came knocking at the door.

"What in high heaven do you want?" Red Heartland asked.

"Now, H-Huey, we don't need no trouble," John Step stammered. Gosh-golly, he was a timid soul for a man who handled the dead for a living.

"Nah, he's not here for trouble," Clyde Finch said with a knowing wink. "He's come to right his wrongs."

"Well he better have two years' worth of dues ready," Red said.

Lucius Jeremiah waved his hand in exasperation. "Shut up! I love it when Jack-o goes down the vault after his money!" He put his pipe back in his mouth and leaned back in his chair to rest his head against the basement wall. He looked like the Devil, Huey thought, with smoke whisking all around him as he tipped back into the shadows.

Huey waited for the expected *Jell-O* commercial, then jumped in. "I come to tell you men that I sure do regret the little argument we had about..." he laughed jovially. "Why, I plumb forgot what we argued about!"

"Money," Alvin Grimm said.

"Hush up and let the man talk," Teddy urged.

"I brought you a peace pipe." Huey ducked into the stair well and said something.

"Is there someone with you?" Teddy asked.

Huey and Jo carried the newly painted rocking chair into the smoky basement.

"No girls!" Red declared. "No blacks, no Catholics, and no girls!"

Jo spoke up for herself. "I ain't here to spy on none of y'all. I just come to help Uncle Huey carry the peace offering down here. We thought you'd like it."

"Y'all could have brought a piece of the cloth from Jesus' robe and this crowd would have still wanted your head."

"Nonsense," Clyde Finch said. "I'm happy to make peace. All of us are, Huey. You wanna pay your dues?"

"Didn't come for that," Huey said, patting the chair. "I come to scrape up old wounds and make sure there's no hard feelings."

"You come to scrape up the wounds?" Alvin Grimm asked, looking cockeyed at his brother Teddy. "Wouldn't that make it bleed more?"

"What's the chair say?" Leonard Lawson asked.

"Matthew 25:41," Huey said.

"I can see that. But what's that verse?" Leonard seemed unusually bold. He was irritated, because just quoting the Scripture and acting like he was a pagan for not knowing the verse by heart was the kind of irritating thing Minnie Belle would have done to him.

"What's it say, Jo?" Huey asked.

Jo cleared her throat. "It says, 'And the King shall answer and say unto them, Verily I say unto you, Inasmuch as ye have done it unto one of the least of these my brethren, ye have done it unto me'." She smiled with self-satisfaction. Maybe they'd been a bit quick to kick her out of the leper colony after all.

The men shared impressed looks with one another. Not bad; and far better from the overused John 3:16.

■ ■ ■

That night, Leonard Lawson lay awake listening to the summer wind whip the gate next to the house back and forth. A thought had come to him, and he couldn't let it go. Finally he got up and turned on a lamp. That stirred Minnie Belle, who asked what in the blazes he was doing.

"Just looking for a Bible," Leonard said.

She sat up and rubbed sleep sand from her eyes. "You got an itching to repent in the middle of the night?"

He dug through his Bible. After a quick reading, he leapt up and declared that he had to go somewhere. Leonard threw on an overcoat and rushed across town to Step's morgue. The mortician was used to being roused at unusual hours, but not usually by friends toting Bibles.

"What in tarnation, Leonard?" Step demanded.

"Let me in, I wanna check something in the basement."

The two men descended into the basement.

"I knew it!" Leonard declared, holding his Bible up to the rocking chair.

"What?"

"That verse! It doesn't say nothin' about doing kindness to others."

Step sighed, "Don't keep me in suspense, morning's comin'."

Leonard read slowly, "Matthew 25:41, 'Then shall he say also unto them on the left hand, depart from me, ye cursed, into everlasting fire'."

He waited for that to sink in.

"What?" Step was suddenly fully awake. "Did it say cursed?"

"And everlasting fire," Leonard added.

"He painted that on a rocking chair? That man has some guts." Step sounded like an admirer.

Leonard felt his throat tighten. "That ole boy done told us to go to hell."

Courting the
Doctor's Tithe

Dark clouds crowded in on a warm Saturday. It was the last weekend in August, but it appeared the first really good summer storm was at hand. Jo pointed toward the sky, which thundered at her command and spit rain. Her head and shoulders were in the pickup cab, while the rest of her drooped out the back window. Her knees rested firmly in the truck bed. She wondered aloud what would happen if a storm wandered through next Sunday as the Little Rickety Church had its one and only service. People might not come if it rained; and what if the roof sprung a leak? She said all this as drops of rain stained her backside.

Boots, who was in the passenger seat, patted her head and told her not to get herself all wound up—this was just one of those rare summer storms.

"God just don't want ya to think he forgot how to spill water," Boots said.

That was stupid, Jo thought.

"Ah, it doesn't matter how many people turn out," Huey said. "Just so long as the I-R-S goes away content that I'm runnin' a church."

Boots shook his head. "He's probably goin' to jail."

"He is if no one comes to church. Do you really think they'll believe you're a church if no one is there except your drinking buddy?"

They had been headed up the steep hill on Main Street toward the restaurant when Huey made a U-turn and started back down the hill. He said he wanted to stop at the Mercantile to pick up a hat for Georgette.

"You ain't gonna settle her down with no hat," Jo warned.

Of course, no one listened to her, so they headed toward the Mercantile.

A huge new sign had been attached to the roof.

Finch's Mercantile
Everything You Really Need!

Finch had been in a two year price battle with Hub's Grocery. Of course, Hub's had a lot more food products than Finch's did; especially the cold variety. Huey had suggested Finch just give up on the groceries, which got him an aggravated snort in reply. Truth was, as less and less folk came in for farm equipment and seed, Finch had been relying on grocery sales. But those were slipping away — right into Hub's hands.

"Know what's I heard," Boots said, "I heard's me a story that ole Finch got his hands mighty dirty in his little fight with the Grocery."

"Ya don't say," Huey was as interested as Jo.

"Word was that Finch got his friend to pay the Grocery with some bad bills, and they handed those bills right on to the customers. People was talkin' for a week about the bad money comin' out of the Grocery. Ole Finch was the first one to warn folk not to trust Hub's."

Huey said, "Well, seein' how Hub always has a parking lot fulla cars, I'd say that didn't work any better than a woman squeezing a quarter between her legs will keep her a virgin."

Jo frowned and said, "Maybe it was Mr. Finch and some of his friends who cut the power to the Grocery's ice box."

"Hush up!" Boots snapped. "Now you just gossippin'."

■ ■ ■

Finch's Mercantile was the largest building in Madison Creek. Men played horseshoes in the back, gathered on the long porch to sit in rockers and talk, and found all kinds of everything inside. On the porch there were two drinking fountains, one for whites and another was designated for coloreds.

It was at the Mercantile that Jo found what Huey really wanted — Katie Simpson. He had been trying to find a way to drop in on her, or give her a call, without Georgette horning in. He needed Katie to lead music. Georgette had given Huey a flat *NO* when he asked her to lead music. He would later tell Boots, "She turned me down like a folding blanket."

Katie had the misfortune of being absolutely gorgeous. Blonde hair, deep blue eyes, and a figure she was not able to hide even under the most homely dresses. At twenty five, she was already known in town as the best voice around. It was too bad she was so pretty, it meant a charming fella like Huey couldn't just stroll up and talk to her without people thinking he wanted something more. Besides, Katie was not only pretty, she was a mother—and had been since she was seventeen.

A small scandal erupted in the church when Dorothy Simpson, Katie's mother, asked if the women intended to have a baby shower for her. They certainly did not, Edith Step had replied. Girls who have children out of wedlock could not expect the support of the church. What they could expect, Edith schooled Dorothy, was wrath on the big judgment day. A small group of concerned women, led by none other than Minnie Belle Lawson, had suggested to Katie that she might do well to *pray* about giving the child up for adoption.

The boy Katie gave birth to was an energetic bundle of happiness. She left school and started work at the Sweet Tea Café on Main Street.

■ ■ ■

While Huey and Boots perused the women's hats with all the skill of a monkey trying to paint a Van Gogh, Jo bopped from aisle to aisle. Hub's Grocery might have a better selection when it came to food, but Finch's had everything else. Shovels, bonnets, hats, rakes, seed, clothing, jars overflowing with candy, and even a few wood toys. Of course, the best dresses in town were over at Minnie Belle's. More important than Finch's huge inventory was the catalog. "If we don't have it," Finch would say, "We can get it."

"*BANG! BANG!*" An eight year old boy shot out from a rack. "Dusty, knock it off," Jo said, rolling her eyes.

"I'm the Lone Ranger, and you're Tonto. Come on, Jo, we have bad guys to fight!" He held his fingers out like a gun. "We can blow their brains out and feed them to Coyotes."

Dusty started to dodge back into the clothes expecting Jo to follow him.

"Hey, Dusty!" Jo called, "Is your mama here?"

"Yep. And if I'm good, she's gonna buy me a real toy gun."

"It can't be *real* if it's a *toy*."

Dusty aimed his finger at Jo, "It's better than my finger."

She moved quickly through the big store. Katie had to be there somewhere. She finally spied her at the front counter, thumbing through Finch's massive catalog.

"Say there," Jo said. Katie didn't realize she was talking to her, and continued turning through the slick pages.

"I said, SAY THERE!" Jo said, louder. Finch, who was working the register, gave her a disapproving eye.

"*BANG! BANG!*" Dusty shouted, popping up to Jo's side. He hoped she would pretend to be wounded and fall to the floor; maybe even making her feet jerk about as she died. But Jo ignored him.

"Well hi there, Jo!" Katie said. She smelled like sweet flowers. "Dusty, get over here!"

Dusty ran off, pretending he hadn't heard his mother.

"Hey, you gotta come with me right now! My uncle wants to talk to you about singing."

She heard Mr. Finch give a heavy, *oh good grief!* as she tugged on Katie's skirt. "Come on, now. This is important."

■ ■ ■

The dresses and hats were in the middle of the store; past the food but before the farming equipment. The dresses weren't as fancy as what Minnie Belle sold up at the dress shop; but they didn't cost as much, either. Jo couldn't believe what she saw. There was Boots sporting a large woman's hat. It was white, with a wide brim and pink ribbon. Katie laughed out loud before she could catch herself.

Huey, who had been trying various hats on his friend, put his arm around Boots. "Have you ever seen a finer fella? He's available, iffin' you wanna marry him."

"Marry him? I hate to see him in a weddin' dress," Katie giggled.

"You two better knock it off," Jo warned. "Ole Finch is already grouchy. He catches you two messin' with ladies clothes, he'll throw ya out. Last thing any lady wants is ah hat that's been on Boots' sweaty head."

"Ah, it's fine," Huey said. He took the hat off of Boots and returned it to the rack.

Katie caught a whiff of Boots and nodded agreement. "Jo said you wanted to see me, Mr. House."

Somewhere in the store Dusty was shouting "*BANG! BANG!*"

Huey could sense people edging toward their section of the store. Was that on purpose? He imagined the ears in Madison Creek tuning in. The sound of rain was beginning a steady patter against the big roof.

"Good gracious I'm glad to see you, Katie!" Then, he got right down to business. "I need a song leader, and I think you'd fit the bill better than Bette Davis fits her corset. You got a fine voice, and you'd make the place look a whole lot prettier just by bein' up there."

She blushed a bit, but didn't refute that. "You want me to lead worship?"

That gave Huey pause. He'd not quite considered it worship. "Well, just the singing part. People warm up a bit if I have a canary up there."

A canary was what the men liked to call a female singer.

"How long do we have?"

"A week and a day," Jo said.

"And I'll pay ya," Huey offered, but she quickly poo-pooed that, saying she'd do it for the Lord.

"But there is one thing I need," Katie said, putting a perfectly manicured hand on Huey's shoulder. "A piano would be helpful. It's just so hard to sing without any instruments. Your church isn't the no instrument kind, are you?"

"Oh heavens no!" Huey burst out. "We're the most instrument church there ever was!"

■ ■ ■

A new voice dropped in. "A church with lots'a instruments, eh?"

It was Doctor Banks. He was black, and as far as Jo knew, he only saw black patients. She wondered if blacks and whites were different on the inside.

Huey nodded emphatically. "Yep, instruments for sure. At least a piano."

"You here to buy a piano, Huey?" Doctor Banks asked.

"No. Are you here to buy a stethoscope, Doc?"

Doctor Banks smiled. When he spoke, his baritone voice was slow and precise. "No sir. I come after a Bible. I have to order it because no one in town sells good Bibles. I've been having my own devotions at home lately, since me and the preacher had a falling out."

"Pastor Weatherwax?" Huey asked.

Gosh he was dumb, Jo thought. Everyone knew the blacks didn't go to the Baptist Church; they went to the little Gospel Chapel over in Jordan Town.

"Nah, other preacher. He believes in handlin' snakes, and I don't."

"Ah, you oughta thank 'em," Boots said. "Ask me about it, he's just drumming up business for you."

"You know, Gideons give Bibles away for free," Huey suggested.

Huey sensed the doctor was about to leave, when he blurted, "Well, if you don't go to church, what do you do with all your tithe?"

Good heavens, Jo thought, could her Uncle be any more socially clumsy?

"I've saved the last few months' worth. Just waitin' for the preacher to realize he's killed the church and move on."

Inspired, Huey said, "You know, we have a brand new church openin' up right here in Madison Creek."

"Really? I didn't hear about this," Doctor Banks said. That was a little white lie. He'd heard about it, but no one had invited him.

Boots covered that, "Well, reason you haven't heard about it none is on account of the fact we didn't put word out through most of the..." he paused, trying to think of the right word for black. "Most of the—"

"People like you," Huey supplied. Taking the conversation back, Huey said, "Katie here is gonna sing the prettiest songs you ever did hear." Katie beamed at that. She looked like an angel. "So if you wanna come, you're just as welcome as the Devil."

Banks was openly amused. "As the Devil, eh? Just one question, do you handle snakes?"

"Not except to throw them out," Boots said.

"You believe in the Trinity?"

That didn't seem fair, he had proposed just one question. Jo gave an affirmative to the Trinity, before the doctor could spot Huey or Boots struggling for theological clarity.

"And Baptism by immersion?"

"And water, too," Boots said. At this Katie gave a little giggle.

"Well, I'll see what I can do. Might stop in one week."

"Oh no!" Huey blurted. "See, it's just a one week church."

"A one week church?" That caught the normally unflappable doctor off guard. "You serious, Huey?"

"Sure. Ole Jonah didn't have to set up church long in Nevada. Just called for folk to repent, and then moved on."

"Nineveh," Banks corrected.

Somewhere in the store, Dusty declared he was the Lone Ranger, followed by a series of *POW-POW-POW*'s.

"So it's just a one-time church service?" Katie asked.

Boots slapped Huey on the back, "Plan is: pray big, repent big, and tithe big. Right, ole boy?"

"Yep."

"Can I help y'all?" Clyde Finch approached the little cluster, arms folded over his chest.

"Just invitin' the doctor to church," Huey explained.

Finch looked surprised. "Really? Does your church allow blacks?"

Remembering the fiasco with the Radio Club, Huey sensed a possible trap. Boots jumped right in, "Well now, Clyde, I reckon when you're a doctor, you're not hardly black anymore, are you?"

Doctor Banks raised a single eyebrow, expressing both interest and amusement at the same time.

Outside, it had begun to storm.

Dusty stood at the huge window and mimicked one of his favorite radio shows. "Heavily days, McGee, I don't want to say it's wet, but the USS *Pennsylvania* just sailed under my left instep."

"Really, Kate, does that boy do anything but listen to the radio?"

"And how! He listens to so much radio, you ought to invite him into your Radio Club."

"No children allowed, I'd bet," Huey said.

Before he could say more, certainly in front of the black doctor — no point in chasing business off — Finch said, "Jo, darling, why do they call you Jo? Is that for Joanna?"

She was wearing blue overalls and old boots that could have belonged to any boy in town. A warm blush flowered across her cheeks. "No sir, not Joanna at all. My parents named me Josephine, after the great General Joseph Johnston." She seemed sad for a moment, then brightened. "But that's before they went overseas as missionaries to India and got attacked by rattlesnakes."

The Explosion

Some things came easily to Huey; like finding a song leader or thinking of a million uses for an old fan motor. "You know, you can use that to power a fishin' boat," Huey once told Teddy Grimm. It gave him a sale, but Teddy's wife Greta made him bring it back.

What did not come easily for Huey was finding a piano. It turned out the Baptist did not want to part with their piano; not even the one in the fellowship hall—or the one shoved into the storage room. Huey was sure he could convince crazy Lutie Dotson to let him use her piano; after all, it had been years since anyone had come to her house for a lesson, it was just collecting dust. What was more, Huey explained to Lutie, that big hulk of a thing was just sucking up space in her tiny shanty.

"Nope, not gonna part with it," Lutie said with decision.

"Well, that's too bad. I felt right Christian about the way I disposed of your cat for you."

"That was neighborly, Huey, not Christian."

Jo and Huey spent a good part of Tuesday discussing how they might steal one of the church's pianos. In the end, all those plans came to naught.

"I have it!" Jo declared. "Annie Evermund used to have an upright piano in the parlor. It was her husbands, and he's dead, dead, dead."

"With my luck, they buried him in that thing," Huey griped.

It was still there, in the parlor, waiting for someone with real skill to come and make music on it. Annie had gone away for the summer to New York.

Annie was a teacher during the school year, and a self-proclaimed world traveler during the summer months. A couple years ago she went to Peru, and before that she had visited Mexico. In Madison Creek, Annie was nothing short of controversial. Folks worried that she was teaching the girls feminism and had decorated her classroom like the jungle of Peru. Mostly, they complained that she left Mule alone while she adventured about.

In Annie's estimation, Mule was *right fine and dandy* by himself. She once pointed out to Edith Step that Mule was eleven years her senior, and didn't need a babysitter. Just the same, Edith had to squawk about it not seeming proper. Frankly, Annie didn't care what Edith thought. Had Edith seen the Amazon, or Mexico City, or even the Alamo? No, no, and nope.

Mule answered the door with the same slow pace he did everything with. As it eased open, Huey declared, "I've just got a hankering for a piano."

Jo thought that was a funny way to put it. He got hankerings all the time, which usually resulted in Aunt Georgette bringing him something—usually a grilled cheese sandwich.

Mule didn't give it any thought at all, Annie hated the monstrosity—that's what she called it. "In fact," Mule said, "I th-th-think it would be just fi-fine to get rid of it."

■ ■ ■

Mule stood six two, but hunched over when he walked. He had been born Murl Evermund, but the Murl turned onto Mule as he grew. Like a mule, he was mentally slower than molasses, but a tender soul who was well loved throughout Madison Creek. He had no problem getting manual labor jobs at Finch's, or doing odd jobs for Minnie Belle. He bopped between the Methodist and Baptist churches, enjoying the kindness he found in each house of worship. That February of 1938 he turned forty and the two churches had a huge surprise party for him. The surprise had worked, perhaps too well. When he came back from a fishing run with Big X and stepped into his house, everyone shouted the typical *surprise*. Only, Mule wasn't sure what the surprise was. Big X pulled the big guys ear down and explained in a hushed tone that this was his big birthday party. Mule couldn't comprehend that. For him? The whole town?

"Well, no," Mule finally said, examining the room. "Not the wh-wh-whole town. Just the white town and bi-bi-Big X."

Then, as it all settled over him; the cake, the little pile of presents, the warm faces; he sank down to the floor into what a teacher long ago had told him was the Indian style of sitting. Legs crossed, he began to sob. Big X tried to calm him, but he cried all the harder.

"You mean all this is fo-fo-for me? Well I'll be slapped silly!"

He declared it the greatest night ever; even better than the time Annie bought a radio.

Mule and Annie lived on what they called *The Farm*. They had a hundred ways of keeping food on the table, most of them having little to do with farming. The land was primarily taken up with a huge garden. Watermelon, grape vines, okra, and black eyed peas dotted the landscape behind the Evermund home.

Huey headed toward The Farm the Saturday before his church opened for business. Boots and Jo were with him, and Huey figured that was enough manpower to move the piano. Mule jumped up and down on the front porch when he saw the truck coming down the dirt road. A small cocker spaniel yapped at his feet.

"Are you sure it's okay with Annie for you to loan Uncle Huey that piano?" Jo asked as they stepped into the parlor.

"Oh sure! She's ha-ha-hated it ever since Roy died."

"We know, Mule," Boots said. "Everyone in town was at their wedding, then at his funeral."

"Well I'll be sl-slapped silly!" Mule laughed.

"So she won't mind," Jo confirmed.

Huey smacked Jo upside the head. "Girl, knock it off. You're gonna lose me this piano, and then I'll ground you for life."

"Well I don't want him gettin' in no trouble on account of us."

Huey pointed at Mule. "Fine, how about I buy this right off of you."

Mule shrugged. "Okay."

"How much?"

Mule thought for a moment. "Ten thousand do-do-dollars."

"Two," Boots said. "He'll give ya two."

"Yep!" Mule said happily.

Huey fumbled about for two dollars. He hated to part with money; especially money he suspected didn't really have to leave his wallet.

The cocker spaniel at Mule's feet began to bark and run a little circle around his big leg.

"What's yar dog's name?" Jo asked.

Huey rolled his eyes. There was work to do, and Jo wanted to chit chat with the village idiot.

"My dogs name is co-co-Cow," Mule said. Once this train left the station, Mule had to follow the tracks all the way home. "I have all kinds of things; like oakry, and pe-peas, and even melons. But I don't have a co-co-cow. Because I forget things sometimes. I might fo-fo-forget to m-milk my cow. She would get upset and leave me, all full of pain from not bein' milked. And then I wouldn't have a co-co-cow." He pointed, "So that's my co-cow!"

The dog chewed at his old brown shoe.

"Well what if you forget to feed your dang dog?" Boots asked.

Mule suddenly looked worried. "Oh no! I'd never forget to feed Cow!"

"But ya might," Boots pressed.

"Oh no, not me. I'd ne-ne-never forget to feed Cow. She's my ba-ba-baby."

"If you forget to feed her, she'll run away," Boots said. "She'll run away and break into the grocery store lookin' for food — ya see? She would break into the store, because dogs are sneaky, but she won't know what to eat. And she might eat chocolate."

"I like ch-chocolate!"

"But she won't," Boots said. "Because chocolate is poison to dogs. See?"

Mule swept the dog up into his arms. "No!"

Huey was getting impatient. "Hush up, Boots, you're meaner than the Devil on Halloween. Let's get this thing moved."

Huey and Boots knelt down at the piano, felt for the ridge to dig their fingers under, and on the count of three the two men heaved upward. The piano groaned, but it didn't budge.

"Hey, I said on three lift!" Huey griped.

"I did!"

They tried again: One, two, three—LIFT! And, again, the wood groaned, but the piano didn't move. They didn't slow down this time, but kept pulling upward until finally it lifted an inch. As the piano came up, Boots moaned. Huey's face was red as he tried to raise the instrument high enough to carry. After a moment the piano crashed down.

"Good grief, I've gotten old," Huey sighed.

"And fat," Jo offered with a little grin.

"Ya-ya know what it's like?" Mule asked with childish delight. "It's like the angel ga-ga-Gabriel came down to planet ea-Earth and done nailed the piano right to the ground!"

"Hush up, Mule," Boots snapped.

Cow—the dog—gave an irritated yap at Boots from the safety of big Mule's arms.

"Like ga-Gabriel do-done said, 'Now Piano, I like you right here, so don't you mo-mo-move'."

Huey suddenly looked back at Mule. How could he have been so foolish? Mule was stronger than a German tank.

"Mule, why don't you help me?"

"I'm too stupid," Mule said.

"We don't need your brains," Boots snapped.

Mule shrugged. "I got to hold on ta co-Cow so she don't run off and eat chocolate puddin' and die of the po-poison."

"Give the dog to Jo and come help us out," Huey suggested.

But Mule wouldn't help. As good natured as he was, there was no chance he was going to touch that piano until Boots apologized— and the two men did a good bit of begging. He liked to be needed.

With Huey and Boots on one end, and Big Mule Evermund on the other, they heaved and then lifted the piano up and out the door.

"I'm superman!" Mule declared as they slid the piano into Huey's green truck.

Red faced and out of breath, Huey wondered how they were going to unload it on the other side. For a simple upright piano, that thing was a beast. He tied a rope across the back, where once—long ago—a tailgate had been.

With the piano in the truck, Huey turned to Mule. "Okay, big guy, where's the stepping stones ya said we could use."

Mule grinned big, "I put them in the pa-pa-piano!"

■ ■ ■

Minnie Belle hid her exasperation. A dress shop was for buying dresses.

The two men, one in a wheelchair and his assistant, did not appear to be likely sales. The one in the wheelchair was dressed in a nice Windsor double breasted suit. His beard was poorly trimmed and graying—probably prematurely. His assistant, a nervous young man of maybe nineteen, had big brown eyes that scanned the room again and again.

They had come in that Saturday morning on the pretense of buying something nice for the one in the wheel chair's wife, *something that says I love you all over it*. He introduced himself as Buck Hardy, and the assistant was just plain ole Doug.

Minnie Belle doubted Mr. Buck Hardy really wanted a dress for his wife. For one thing, he didn't have a wedding ring. And he called his beloved by two different names. Was it Sadie or was it Tilly?

She pointed out several nice dresses and explained that if his wife came in, she could make any of the dresses a perfect fit. But he wanted it as a surprise.

"I'm a missionary," Buck said proudly.

A crippled missionary? Heavens-to-Betsy the mission board would send just about anyone overseas these days.

"Just back from the jungle, no doubt," Minnie Belle said.

"No, I was in Australia ministering to the pygmy Aborigines."

I, not *we*, Minnie Belle noted.

"I want to get my sweetie something now that we're home in the States. Something that pays her back for all those tribulations we went through. Right, Doug?"

Doug sputtered an uncomfortable, "Uh-huh."

"You'll be living in Madison Creek?"

He shook his head, "Nope. Just passing through. Hoping to maybe speak at a church and find some partners for my trip back."

"Gracious, I just can't imagine the honor of having a real, live missionary in my store," Minnie Belle feigned. "And all the way from Australia. And the people live in huts, no doubt."

"The ones that can afford a hut. If we in America took up an offerin', we could do right by these people. We could put roofs over heads and…" She saw him search for a name. "Help poor Sally-Anne. She's sick as can be, and needs a surgery. That's not her real name, of course, it's just what we white people call her."

Edith Step had come in and was obviously listening close as she pretended to shop.

"Australian rainforest. Let's see, you must have been in North Queensland," Minnie Belle said. "Did Doug here have to push you over all those bushes and vines and mud?"

"Oh no!" Doug said at once. "I didn't go to Africa."

"Australia is not in Africa," Minnie Belle explained. Edith snickered.

"My wife pushed me!" Buck declared. "She's strong as a horse."

"I can't imagine the tribulations you've been through. But I know this, and I know it with all my heart, hell's fire is fueled from the bodies of wicked men like you. Liars. Scoundrels. Trying to steal from the godly."

"Oh no, you have us all wrong!" Buck objected.

Doug's eyes were huge and fixed on Minnie Belle.

"There will come a day, not far my friends, when the Lord will come again. He'll bring goodness to his friends, and we'll meet him in the air. But when that music sounds and the righteous are called home, don't you think it will be a dark day for the wicked?"

"Really, Mrs. Lawson," Buck began, but he was cut off by Doug.

"What'll happen to the wicked?"

Edith, who was musing over a table piled up with the latest shipment of fabrics spoke up. "The wicked, young man, will be judged and thrown into a blazing fire, where they burn, but never burn up."

Minnie Belle picked up where Edith left off, "God has given man time to repent of the kind of nastiness you and Buck here are engaged in. But someday, Doug, time will be cut short. The trumpet of the Lord will blast across the earth and everything will stop."

Doug looked back at Buck. "You never told me that stuff!"

Edith shook her head, "The angels will gather up the false prophets with big chains around their necks. They'll throw them into the lake of fire, roaring with waves of flames and heaving volcanoes in the middle. The wicked'll try to crawl out of that fire, but that chain will pull them back."

Minnie Belle added, "Someday God will hit his timer and say, 'that's it. You've had enough time'."

■ ■ ■

When *it* happened—the big bang—the explosion—it just about wiped out John Step's beloved hearse.

Clyde Finch and his buddy John Step were coming back from the Wilson's place. Donner Wilson had died the night before of old age. The doctor would find some name for it; but the truth was, he was just old. It was Clyde's idea to stop by Huey's place and give him a good ole Howdy-Do. Step objected, he wanted to get on into town.

"No, not his house," Finch said, nudging his friend. "Let's go up the hill to that old restaurant he's converting into a church. I wanna check Big Boys cathedral out for myself."

"I wouldn't mind giving it a peek-a-boo," Step agreed. "I'm curious as a cat what he has in that place that caused Minnie Belle to throw up. She has it all over town that it smelled like General Pickett's entire dead army has been rotting up there. We can tell Huey we've been praying for him."

Truth be told, those two didn't pray for much of anything except in desperation, or for their favorite ball team, the Concord Weavers. The Weavers were part of the Carolina league, and they needed a healthy dose of prayer.

"Oughta drop Wilson's body off first."

Finch grinned. "Want to give Huey a scare? We could bring ole Wilson up there with us and ask Huey if he wants to host the viewing."

Step shook his head. "Not professional, you ole booger."

"Yeah, but just the same, let's do it."

They passed the dress shop and just then a green truck cut in front of them as it turned onto Main Street. Step stomped on his break and cursed under his breath.

The truck was loaded with—well, all kinds of strange things. There was a piano, and behind the piano a couple of chairs, blankets, an old lectern and—who knows what else. Worse, Big Mule Evermund was in the back of the truck holding on to the piano with the help of Huey's niece, Jo. A small cocker spaniel peeked from behind the piano, giving a frightened bark as the truck finally steadied itself from the sharp turn.

"Say, that's him!" Finch laughed, pointing. "You almost plowed right into Big Boy."

"He almost ran into me," Step countered, and blew his horn. "He still hasn't put a tailgate on that truck," Step observed. He pulled up closer to get a better look. The girl took a hand off the piano she was holding and waved. The dog gave another bark.

"You better back off," Finch warned. He didn't like telling the mortician how to drive his own hearse, but they were staring up at a piano that just looked like it wanted on them.

Step impatiently blew his horn again, and the truck slowed. Its engine sputtered, sounding like an old man with pneumonia.

■ ■ ■

The car behind them honked again.

Boots shook his fist out the window, "Ah, phooey on you!"

Just as he brought his fist back into the car, Boots pointed at the road. "Look out!"

Huey had been wanting to give his brakes a tap, just to get Step to back off. But he didn't tap his brakes — he pressed his foot all at once to the floor. The truck, which had been laboring under the weight, was all too willing to stop. In fact, it pitched back a bit, as if the hill was going to swallow it down.

Mule grabbed the piano to steady himself. He lost his balance and shoved the upright as hard as he could. The rope they'd tied at the tailgate didn't even slow the piano, which blasted out of the truck like a cannonball. For a moment it was in the air, seeming to fly with all the elegance of a trapeze artist. Then it hit the pavement with the sound of thunder. Several musical notes hollered toward heaven one last time when the instrument came to earth.

■ ■ ■

"Good gracious, that's it!" Minnie Belle shouted in the dress shop.

Edith saw an opportunity and looked right at Doug. "Repent, boy! The Judgment of the Almighty is upon you! Fire, brimstone, lava are at hand."

Doug turned on his heels and started to run.

■ ■ ■

The piano imploded on impact and sank into the street. A torrent of round, smooth stepping stones burst from the belly of the smashed piano and rolled down hill. A few of the stones thudded against car tires, while others simply tipped over. Jo watched the stones whirr down Main Street like hubcaps.

John Step swerved hard just in time to dodge both the piano and the stones that poured from the piano.

■ ■ ■

"Boy! Get back here!" Buck shouted.

Doug looked back for a split second, but he didn't stop.

Not only was there the crash of music, but the sound of thunder was coming down the street.

"Run!" Minnie Belle yelled. "Don't make God pull you up through the roof!"

Doug was quick on his feet, He didn't even pause on the covered sidewalk. He ran into the street, his big eyes on the sky, he searched for the angels and the Almighty coming in his wrath.

He did not spot the Lord. But what he did see was a stone — a river of stones that weaved among the cars. One stone in particular seemed it was coming right toward him, and picking up speed.

"Oh God, forgive me!" Doug cried.

A horn blew, and he turned to see a man in a black Ford. The driver braked hard and lifted his hands in exasperation. Doug threw his entire body onto the Ford's hood and began to sob.

■ ■ ■

"What are you doing?" John Step screamed at Huey.

"Movin' this here piano to the restaurant up yonder," Huey gestured. "Almost got there."

"Ne-ne-need a pian'er, Mr. Step?" Mule asked. He was just starting to get his breath back.

"Here comes trouble," Boots pointed down Main Street. Sheriff Tuff was on his way, the light on his car spinning as the siren pierced the air.

Huey looked sadly down at the demolished piano. It wasn't good for anything now but firewood. He wondered if the ivory keys were worth anything.

"Well look at what I just stubbed my eye on!" he blurted.

There was something in the wreckage. He blinked twice, thinking maybe it would disappear. It was a little box way down in the rubble. What was that? He bent down — causing his britches to give a sigh of warning — and picked the little box up. It was velvet, the kind of thing that might hold a real treasure. He slipped it into his pocket.

The siren died and Sheriff Tuff got out of his car and demanded to know what was going on. He looked and sounded like a lion, with a bushy yellow beard that matched his shaggy blonde hair.

"Lock them up!" Step demanded. "Put them in a cell next to Sticky Simpson!"

"What law did we break?" Boots asked. "We just dropped a piano."

John Step screwed up his face in frustration. "No, you didn't just drop a piano. You dropped a piano full of stepping stones. That's attempted murder."

"Attempted murder of who?" Boots asked.

"Of me!" Step shouted.

Mule's dog, Cow, barked from the safety of the truck bed. That jogged Huey's memory. "There was a cat! It went right out in the middle of the road."

"Sure was," Boots confirmed.

"The pi-pi-piano just sl-sl-slipped." Mule's voice was always something of a faltering roar. His dog finally leapt from the truck. Mule swept Cow up into his arms.

"But why is it loaded down with stepping stones?" Finch asked.

"Eh-eh-I did it," Mule said, straightening himself up. "I pu-put the stepping stones in the pi-pi—"

"No he didn't!" Jo said unexpectedly. "Don't let him fool you. I did it. I loaded that piano with every stepping stone I could find."

There was a pause, it seemed like the entire world stood still.

"But why?" Sheriff Tuff finally asked. "Why did you do it, girl?"

She shook her head in mock disbelief. "Goodness Sheriff, everyone knows that if you move a piano, it gets all out of whack. You gots to keep it solid on the inside." Jo stuck her hands in front of the Sheriff, "You gonna lock me up?"

The Sheriff was thoughtful. "No, I'm not gonna lock you up, girl. I'm gonna lock Huey here up, unless he can give me one good reason he doesn't have a tailgate on this here truck."

Huey moved fast and swept his arm around John Step. He pulled him in tight, "Bought it as is," he said.

"Let go of me!" Step squirmed free of Huey.

The Sheriff wrote Huey a citation and told them to pick up the stones. All of them.

"Oh boy, more trouble on the way," Boots announced.

Marching up the middle of the street—taking almost the same path the stone had taken—came Minnie Belle Lawson. She was followed by Edith Step, who dragged behind as if the trip up the hill was more like a climb up Mount Everest.

"Really and truly Huey House, what are you doing?" Minnie Belle huffed as she worked her way up the hill. Huey spotted a little gleam in her eye. What was that?

"Edith," John Step called to his wife. "Honey, watch out, these scoundrels have it in mind to kill us."

When Minnie Belle finally came to the broken piano—and the men milling about it like it was a campfire—she put her hands on her hips and looked up at Huey. "Alright, mister, I've just got to tell you, sometimes the Almighty works in mysterious ways! All my years running the dress shop, I've never had someone like I had today. But you..." she reached up and took Huey by the collar, "you did me the biggest favor in the world!"

"I did?"

"I want you to know that God himself used you to shame the wicked today."

Not only had the missionary-man left, he'd gone with his tail tucked between his legs. In fact, he'd walked out pushing his own wheelchair. Guess the lame will walk after all. "And I have you to thank for it, Huey."

And with that, she pulled him down toward her like she was going to whisper in his ear and kissed him on the cheek.

"Ohhh-eeee!" Boots whistled. He was leaning against Huey's truck.

"Now, tell me," Minnie Belle said as she let go of Huey. "What are you really doing?"

It was Boots who spoke up, since Huey was speechless. "Gosh, Minnie Belle, we were gonna have church right here in the street. You want to play the piano?"

■ ■ ■

That afternoon, Huey sat alone in the old building that was turning into a church. He was supposed to preach the next day. The thought hadn't settled fully upon him until just then. Sure, there would be music and an offering — but surely they would expect him to preach a sermon.

Huey did a short mental review of the Bible stories he knew. There was Noah and the Ark, Adam and Eve, and Jesus on the cross. But he didn't know how he might get a whole sermon out of any of those. It was a curious thing; Pastor Weatherwax always had too much to say on all those subjects, and Huey couldn't scrounge up enough words to fill a tea cup.

Oh! And there was Jonah. He was swallowed by a whale, even though Georgette told him it wasn't a whale but a great fish. Huey wasn't so sure about Jonah. Seemed like that boy would have had a heap of trouble setting up camp for three days inside the belly of a whale. Besides, Huey reckoned that in three days, that whale should have pooped Jonah out by then. He must have been a constipated whale.

If he was really at a loss for words, he could just say he felt lead by the Spirit to open it up for testimonies. It seemed like preachers always used the Spirit to get them out of a pickle; or to say what they really wanted to say but didn't have the guts to take the blame for it.

Nervously, he put his hand into his pocket, and immediately forgot about his sermon worries. There was that box he'd found in the midst of the piano wreckage! What was it? A treasure he hoped.

Huey popped the box open, and his mouth dropped. There was a diamond ring.

■ ■ ■

"Wh-why did you lie for me?" Mule asked Jo as they picked stones from the road.

"Ah, it was the Christian thing to do, Mule," Jo said. "Or, I think it was. I don't really know if it was Christian or not, seein' as how I flunked Christian Camp and all."

"I'm glad you di-di-did it. If they had locked me up, then no one would be around to feed Cow. And he might go cr-cr-crazy and eat chocolate and die." With sudden excitement, Mule looked at Jo. "You saved my do-dog!"

Jo nodded and picked up a stepping stone. Thinking about the next day, and Uncle Huey's new church, she said, "I wonder who's going to save Uncle Huey."

Wild Oats

John Step paced back and forth in the small apartment above the morgue. "Just tell him there's no place for him to sleep." The room was a living room, kitchen and dining room all in one.

Edith shook her head, "You can't do that, John."

She was sitting at the table watching him as he crossed the room again and again. A fan in the window chopped energetically at the thick, humid air. Each time he passed the fan, she would get a fresh whiff of his cologne, which she liked very much.

"It's a one bedroom apartment, Hon! He can't just bop in and out of our lives anytime he wants."

Edith nodded toward the sofa, "He can sleep right there."

"No," John said without much thought. "A sofa is no place for a grown man to sleep. Is he a bum? If he wants to be responsible, get a job… a real job… then maybe I could help him. But he's the one who had all the big dreams and went running off to New York. Now he comes back with his tail—"

"Oh, good grief! I'm right here, popsa-dillies! Don't talk about me like I'm not here."

The young man sitting at the table next to Edith had deep black hair. It reminded her of John's hair not so long ago; before it turned gray and then began to slide away. He was tall and wiry, like he hadn't eaten much in a long time. Edith nudged her son, "It's okay, Otis. Let me do this."

Otis' cheeks were hot with anger, but he still couldn't look his father in the eye. "I don't need you to fight my battles, Ma. He knows he's bein' a pig."

John bristled at the accusation. "As far as I know, you're the one who's been a pig. You don't write. You don't call. We never hear from you. Not even Christmas. Your ma hasn't heard anything for eight Mothers Day's."

"Ah, I sent her flowers," Otis protested.

"That's true, John, he did send flowers."

Ole John Step wasn't going to be derailed. "Nothing for eight years. And now you show up and think we can just take you in?"

"Otis, why don't you just give me a moment with your father?"

"My friends call me Oats. I wish you guys would."

"Oh my goodness!" John threw his hands in the air. "What a big baby! Oats? You still go by that? No wonder you didn't get anywhere in New York. Who hires someone named Oats? Sounds like a lazy farmer."

"You just gotta rub it in, don't ya big papa! You just gotta take my head like I's you're little doggie and rub my face in the poo—"

Edith pointed at the young man. "Out! I don't care if you go downstairs and polish the coffins, just give me a moment."

Otis stood up in a huff, about to storm out when he realized he'd have to pass his father. He delayed a moment, eyeing the old man.

John motioned toward the door, "Well, you got any respect left in you for at least your mama?"

Otis stormed past his father and out the door, slamming it behind him.

"Ridiculous," John declared. "He's never going to grow up."

"Sit down," Edith said. She pointed at her husband with the same finger she'd just directed the young man out of the room with.

■ ■ ■

That evening Edith and her boy sat at the table. The fan continued to chew at the air and the lamp on the table burned away a circle of darkness. She served him day-old cornbread and buttermilk. John had stepped out, saying he needed to attend to other business. That was fine with Edith, let him cool his heels for a while.

"So he said I could stay?" Otis asked.

"Well, I had to do some fast talkin'." She lowered her voice. "But you really should apologize to him, you understand?"

Otis stiffened. "He ought to apologize to me. Said I didn't have a chance in New York."

"That was eight years ago. Besides…" A smiled touched the side of her lip. "Well, you are back here, aren't you son?"

"Yep, and it's his fault. All his fault. If he had believed in me; if either of you had believed in me, I would have had the self-confidence I really needed to land some parts on the radio. Only part I got was washing dishes at Fran's Diner. And I did some sound effects."

"Did you meet anyone famous?"

"Sure. Fred Allen once, and a lot of other people, but I don't know who. But they sure sounded familiar. I came home because I almost died. Did you know that?"

She did not know that. He reached for the newspaper, which had been folded in front of his father's spot at the little table. The paper was fat from the morning's spilled orange juice that had dried into the pages. Otis held the paper in the lamp light and scanned the front page, then the second and third. "Ah, they don't report nothin' in a local paper."

"You were in the paper, son?" Edith sounded unconvinced.

"No. The accident was in the paper. Subway trains collided on a hundred and sixteenth street. Killed a couple of people."

"And you were on the train?"

"No, Ma, I wasn't on the train. But I almost took the subway that day, see? I almost got on. But I didn't because I had a feeling."

More likely he didn't have money to ride, Edith thought. "Well, thank the Lord he protected you. Your father was almost in an accident this morning. Strangest thing I've ever seen. They were hauling a piano when it fell out of the truck —"

"Pa had an auto accident with a piano?"

Under the paper, also stained by orange juice, was a handbill. Otis laid the paper aside and began to unconsciously fold and unfold the handbill. She nodded toward the paper in his hand.

"That reminds me. Listen, Otis, your father said you could stay here on the sofa. But I made one itsy bitsy promise, and you have to keep it."

"Sure, anything. Well, almost."

"I promised him you'd be in church. That's what you have to do, be in church tomorrow."

"Ah, Ma, not yet. I don't have any good clothes yet."

"But I said you would."

"And I will. Maybe next week. Every week after next, in fact. But not tomorrow. I'm tired from the long bus ride."

"Well, it's what I had to do to appease the old man."

The truth was, Edith hadn't said a word to John about church. What she had done was tell him directly that she had been without her boy for eight years, and she did not intend to put him back out onto the streets. She didn't know where all he'd been, but she suspected he was in trouble, and there was nothing—and she meant nothing—on God's big earth John could do that would stop her from letting her boy come back. And, what's more, she'd reminded him of all the years she put up with that terrible Radio Club meeting in the apartment. Thank God they'd finally taken their business down to the basement, but just the same, she'd suffered in silence with men tromping about in her home.

There was no reason for Otis to know what she'd told her husband.

He looked down suddenly at the paper he'd been toying with. Why did that remind her of church?

"Say, lookie there," Otis said with a wry grin. "I suppose you're all about this, eh?"

"Not a chance."

A moth had found its way through the open upstairs window and began to flutter about the lamp.

"Really? New church opens up, and you're not interested?" He held the paper closer to him, as if that would improve his reading. "Little Rocketty Church—"

"Rickety."

"Invites you to be our guest on Sunday, September fourth. Good singing—"

"Singing."

"And good…" he paused, stumped.

"Preaching. Good preaching."

"Come on out to our special service." He looked up from the paper. "What's wrong with this here church?"

```
LITTLE RICKETY CHURCH
    of MADISON CREEK

Invites You to Be Our Guest

Sunday, September 4, 11 a.m.

Good Singing and Good Preaching

Come on out to Our Special Service

     Meeting at the Old

   HILLTOP RESTAURANT

   Preacher HUEY HOUSE
Song Leading KATIE SIMPSON
```

"Trouble," Edith said succinctly. "It's got folks all stirred up. That rotten Huey House is doin' somethin' wicked."

"A church? Why's *he* opening a church?"

"He's not." She swatted feebly at the moth. "It's just a one-time service."

"Come again?"

She smiled, "Exactly."

"Is it a revival?"

"Nope. Just a one-time church service." She lowered her voice, even though they were the only ones in the apartment. "Some folks say Huey House is in some kind of trouble with the law, and if he tells them he has a church, they'll let him off the hook."

Otis' eyes didn't lift from the paper. "I don't see how starting a church would get a fella outta trouble."

"Just the same, you don't need none of it, you understand? That would set your father off something terrible."

She said it before she thought about it, and regretted it at once.

"Really? But it's just a one-day service. And, I'd keep that big promise you made on my behalf."

His eyes had settled on a name. So *she* was going to be there? He wasn't sure he could stay away. There wasn't much comfort in coming home, except the thought that maybe—just maybe—*she* hadn't found a man.

"Says Katie Simpson is leading the music," Otis said.

Edith had hoped he would give up reading the handbill before he got to that. "Sure, sure. One more reason you don't need to be there."

"Small town like this, not many options for a pretty girl like Katie." He rubbed at the prickly hairs that wanted to make a beard. "Not good options, anyway."

"A woman with a child will have trouble finding any good prospects," Edith agreed. "Sweet Katie should have given that boy up for adoption."

The front door eased open.

"Hey popsa-dillies," Otis waved at John as he stepped in. "Thanks for lettin' me stay." John hardly had the door closed before the young man offered his apology. "I sure have been a wreck lately. I'm sorry—I mean really sorry popsy. And I should have written and let you know what was going on while I was in the Big Apple. But see, I wanted to make it big in New York. I wanted you to turn on the radio one night and look at Ma and say, 'Honey-doodles, that sounds like our boy!'"

John didn't move. He hadn't expected all that—not all at once anyway. Was that an apology, or was it something else? It felt like it was something else, but he wasn't sure what. The fan whirred in the absence of voices, pulling in the sound of a car honking down below on Main Street.

"Well, John, say you forgive Otis," Edith prodded.

"You have to find a place of your own quick," John said.

Otis popped up out of his chair like a jack-in-the-box and gave his father a crisp, military salute. "Yes sir! Understood, sir!"

"And a job, Otis. I want you to find a job. Even if it's just over at the Drug Store as a soda jerk."

"Roger, roger," Otis held his salute.

"Alright, knock it off."

"Aren't you two gonna hug?" Edith asked.

"Better than a hug." Otis reached back and produced the hand-bill. "I have good news Mr. Pops. I'm goin' to church tomorrow."

It certainly wasn't the first time that day John had been caught off guard. Huey had almost killed him with his blasted piano. Now Otis wanted to go over there and see what the show was all about? It figured. He probably came into town just for this. Anger—the red lava kind that Georgette sometimes struggled with when an idiot storm would overcome her—now pulsed under John's skin. He actually wanted to punch the boy, and hard. But, that wouldn't do any good. He pushed back the rage. Saturday nights were the times he was most likely to get an offer from Edith. He didn't know about tonight, but there was one way to shut the door for sure, and that was to make a scene with the boy.

"I hope you enjoy that church," John finally said and started toward the bedroom.

"Oh no!" Edith sprung up with almost the same energy her boy had come up out of his chair. "He can't go to that church! It's not even a church, John. Tell him no."

"No," John said robotically.

"Good." Edith patted Otis on the back. "You hug your father and I'll find some bedding for you."

They did not hug.

■ ■ ■

For Jo, climbing out the window was the easy part. Landing on the porch roof without making a sound was more difficult. From her room she could hear her aunt and uncle talking, but their voices were muffled. Most nights when the weather was warm they would sit out on the porch in their rockers until late and have their talks. The porch light glowed a pale yellow, casting strange shadows on the ground below.

Georgette liked to fill Huey in on what she'd found interesting in that days newspaper. Huey didn't read the paper—why should he when he had Georgette to summarize the whole thing for him; with commentary no less. The news of late usually involved a German named Hitler. Aunt Georgette was against Hitler, but Huey wasn't too concerned.

Of course, Huey had his own supply of news and tidbits to offer up that were of a very different nature than Georgette's. Things he'd picked up on as people came and went from the Man Village.

Jo wondered if he would tell her about the busted piano and the flying rocks. She tiptoed across the porch roof and lay down with her ear right over the sitting couple. The canvass of night sky above was brilliant.

She picked up quickly on the gist of the conversation below. Georgette was giving Huey a list of reasons he should not try to hold a church service in the morning. Her voice was sweet as honey; but Jo sensed her aunt was using every bit of self-control. The idiot storm was brewing nearby, threatening not just rain, but maybe thunder and lightning.

"Seems it would be best to just fess up Huey," Georgette said. "Tell them Government boys you laid a whopper on 'em and ask forgiveness. Most they'll do is fine ya."

"Nah, that ain't what'll happen baby doll. They'll throw me in the big house. Probably haul me clear up to New York to do hard time."

The thought of going to New York excited Jo. She'd never been to a really big city, with traffic and all those shops and people stacked up on top of one another.

There was a change in Georgette's voice, as if all the muscles in her throat hardened. "I've not been a pest about this, Huey. Not a bit. I've held my tongue…"

Jo thought that was hilarious and swallowed down a snicker. She imagined the refined southern woman with an unbelievably long tongue clutched in her hands as saliva oozed through her dainty fingers.

"But you are just askin' for trouble. This is not the Radio Club that you can cajole with that big smile of yours. This is the I-R-S!" She was starting to lose control. "And what will happen to me and the girl? Will they take the property away?"

"Nah." Huey brushed her off. "Got too much junk on the property. Be a pain to clean it up and sell it."

Jo could almost feel the heat blaze up from Aunt Georgette. "Huey, that's not funny! Are you really going to have a church service, and you think those Government boys will just shake your hand and tell you never mind? Is that what you think will happen? And even if it could happen that way, and it cannot—LAWD IT CANNOT!—but even if it could, do you know what you are going to preach tomorrow morning? Maybe you should have stayed awake during some of preacher Weatherwax's sermons."

"They have sermons on the radio," Huey protested. "And I gotta tell you, baby, a lot of them preachers are an awful lot better than that fella up at the Baptist church."

Jo heard her aunt jump up out of her rocking chair, leaving the chair sighing back and forth against the porch boards. "Doesn't matter who can preach better than who, because you can't preach at all! You think Jonah was swallowed by an alligator, and Jesus was born in a junk yard, and who knows what else. But it's all apostasy. And you're about to rain it down all over our town. All your wicked doctrine and misconceptions and your…" she trailed off. After a moment Jo realized her aunt was weeping.

She heard Huey rise out of his rocker and she had the sense that he'd drawn Georgette into his arms. He was whispering something; probably that it was going to be okay, and she didn't need to cry.

When Georgette spoke again, her voice trembled. "Oh Huey, you're just lost. Lost as a goose. Lost in the night. Lost, lost, lost."

He was about to say something when headlights splashed across the property. The car drove slowly. Finding the road up to the house could be a challenge at night. It was rare for anyone to come up the overgrown road after dark. Jo wondered if maybe it was a contingency of Baptist deacons, coming to ask Huey not to hold his church service. Or maybe it was armed hit-men hired by—she searched her mind quick, who would hire hit-men? Her reasonable mind told her that no one she knew would pay to have someone knocked off. But that wasn't any fun at all. Minnie Belle Lawson! That's who she decided had paid the hit-men, and they were on their way right now, ready to blow Uncle Huey away with Tommy Guns spraying bullets everywhere. She was a little sad when she realized it was just Earl Simpson and his daughter Katie.

The car came to a stop at the porch, the headlamps shut off and snapped the world back into darkness. But Earl and Katie did not get out of the car, they just sat there.

Georgette spoke for everyone—even the unseen Jo, "Well I wonder what they want."

"Ah, she probably come to drop out on me."

The man and his beautiful daughter got out. Jo was a little disappointed Dusty wasn't with them. He was always a bunch of fun. But, undoubtedly, he was tucked into bed and dreaming about radio shows.

"Mr. and Mrs. House, I sure do need to speak with you," Katie said. Jo understood that at some point Mr. Simpson had told Katie she was a grown woman and would have to speak for herself.

"Well there!" Huey boomed. "You just come right on up here. Sit down. Right here."

They came up onto the porch.

"You come to say you can't sing, didn't you, honey?" Georgette prodded.

Katie confirmed that she did indeed come for that very reason. She felt horrible and sick and terrible and a lot of other words for leaving Huey high and dry and at the last minute, but she sure couldn't lead music the next day. See, she explained, it was all about the piano. She felt fine so long as there was a piano, but without a piano, it would just be her voice, and she didn't feel right about that.

Huey tried to squash that fear quick. "Ah, ways I see it, the voice is the first instrument God created. And when he made yours, he made the best."

She went on protesting. Her voice wasn't the best, and she got a bit nervous in front of people, and what's more—he had promised her a piano. That had been the deal all along.

"Well, we sure do understand," Aunt Georgette said. "No one can blame you, honey."

"No one gonna blame you," Huey agreed.

"Thank you for understanding," Earl said. "Katie just felt herself boxed in a little corner."

Huey invited the guest in, but they refused, explaining that it really was late.

Sounding almost inspired, Huey said, "Why, you can't leave just yet. Georgette has tea she just has to serve you. It's a new concoction."

There was a pause, and Jo imagined her aunt staring dumbfounded at Huey.

"Of course!" Georgette said. Earl tried to object, but neither he nor Katie could do so and still be gracious. After all, they had just let Huey down on a big promise, so the least they could do is stay for a bit of southern tea before heading on. They had to prove they weren't social baboons.

■ ■ ■

Almost as soon as Georgette went in the house, Huey got right down to business. "Alright, might as well tell me what happened."

"It's just the piano, Mr. House," Katie said.

Jo wished there was a window in the porch roof, it would make her spying so much easier. She had a little panic; what if Georgette came in to check on her?

"It's not just the piano." Huey's voice had a knowing, almost teasing, edge to it. "Come on now, might as well tell me the whole thing. Or should I tell you?"

"Now that would be interesting," Earl said.

"Okay, fine. Some ladies—maybe a few who call themselves the *Concerned Women of Madison Creek*—paid Katie a visit. They told the both of you they would stop frequenting Sweet Tea's if she had any part in tomorrow's little church service."

"Well, that is pretty close," Katie confirmed.

"Don't make me play detective."

It was Earl who did the talking. "Well, a little group from the church came to visit Katie, just like you said. And you hit the nail on the head, they sure did imply they didn't want anything to do with the Sweet Tea Café, or Katie, if she went ahead and directed worship tomorrow morning. And—"

Katie jumped in, "And they reminded me of how they always welcome Dusty and show him heaps of lovin', even though he doesn't have a pa. Reminded me of how good they've been to me."

The door creaked open and Georgette came out to the porch with her tea. Jo wished she was right down there with the rest of them, now sipping her aunt's secret tea recipe, which she called *Revolution*.

"Bananas," Huey said, quite unexpectedly.

"What did you say?" Katie asked. Georgette and Earl echoed her need for clarification. So, since they couldn't seem to hear what Jo on the roof heard so clearly, Huey said it again. "Bananas."

"You want bananas with your tea?" Georgette asked.

"I sure do!" Huey said. "Sliced up, but not too thin."

Georgette rushed off for bananas. She seemed quite accommodating now that Katie had come and given her resignation to the entire singing bit. Jo suspected Georgette thought that meant the whole thing was doomed. What would Huey do without a song leader?

"Bananas," Huey said again as soon as Georgette was gone.

"I just don't understand," Katie said.

"Those ladies are bananas. They don't treat you or Dusty good. And I'll bet they don't even go to Sweet Tea's. Ladies like that prefer to serve coffee and tea in their parlor. Have you made a dime off Minnie Belle in the last month?" He waited for them to answer, but they did not, so Huey pressed on. "Folk like Edith Step and Minnie Belle have a way of making you feel like you're just a few rungs lower than them because you had that boy Dusty out of wedlock. They might not say it to your face, but you can feel it. They pretend it's pity—that they pity you—but really it's big fat pride and a healthy dose of meanness."

"Ain't that the truth," Earl agreed.

"You can almost smell that little bit of condescension when they invite you to something. You know what I mean? They invite you, and then pride themselves for loving a sinner enough to show her some social grace. They make you feel that every kindness is their way to stooping down and loving the wicked."

"Oh my," Katie's voice was beginning to tremble.

"They don't just make you feel bad about a mistake you made some eight years ago, they make you resent the boy, as if he was God's mistake. He sure ain't the brightest kid in town, but he's a bundle of joy. I'm glad you have him."

Jo was startled to realize that Katie was stifling a sob.

Having hit a nerve, Huey struck again. "I'm glad you had him, Katie. Glad for it. Glad he was born. Glad he keeps you company. Glad for the fine young man he's gonna be. I think you giving this world Dusty is one of the happiest things you could have ever done."

Katie began to weep. Jo wondered if her face was buried in her hands, or if she was holding on to her daddy. Finally, she said, "No one has ever said that to me."

"Ah, now come on." Earl was defensive. "I've told you plenty that I love Dusty."

"But not that you're happy for him," Katie said. "No one ever says they're happy for him. All anyone can think about is that he was the result of S-I-N. Like they can't be happy for the boy because they're worried folk might think their happiness means they approve of my mistake. But know what, Pa, I'm happy." Her voice shivered a little as she spelled the word out, "H-A-P-P-Y. I'm happy to have Dusty. Mr. House is right, he's not a mistake, not at all. God meant it to be."

"Rotten bunch of hypocrites," Huey breathed. "Know what I think? I think you shouldn't let them win," There was gravity in his voice. "You come on to church tomorrow, and you stand in front of everyone and lead music. And put Dusty right on the front row. Let him sing loud if he wants. We'll love that boy."

"Now Mr. House." Earl cautioned.

"Nope, you shouldn't let them win. Don't let them bully you all over town, Earl. You should show them you choose to be happy."

"Happy about what?" Earl asked.

"Happy about that grandson of yours. Hung your head all over town the whole time Katie was pregnant. That was eight years ago, and your head still dips down when people talk about Dusty. Like he's a big oops. Well, don't you believe it, mister!"

There was a moment of stunned silence. Had all that just come from Huey?

"It's just one day, my friends," Huey said. "One chance to celebrate the Lord. One chance to be glad for all he's given us. And the best he's given us is peoples. I'm glad for Dusty. I'm glad for my kin, like Georgette, even though she is a big heap of trouble for me. And I'm glad for Jo. She makes me happy. And you should be happy for that boy, Dusty."

And now, it was Earl himself who let out a little sob. Jo couldn't believe it! Not that Earl was weeping, but that she was beginning to drip tears of her own. She'd never heard Uncle Huey actually say he was happy to have her. His way of being nice to her was to tease her; or take her fishing—but there was something so warm in actually hearing him say it. And *happy* really was such a wonderful word to use for a person.

"Bananas!" Georgette announced as she came onto the porch. She stopped cold, realizing the entire tone had changed since she left. Perceiving Huey's shenanigans, she asked at once, "What happened? Katie dear, are you okay?"

"I'm just so happy!" Katie sobbed.

The Pancake Church

It was going to be a bad day. The problem was Aunt Georgette. Oh boy, she was going to be a wreck. It was just as concrete a fact as Roosevelt was a Democrat and gas was ten cents a gallon—Georgette was not going to have a good day; and that meant trouble for Jo.

This was Uncle Huey's big day, and Georgette had not found a way to stop it. She had talked plenty, and in the end, she lost. Jo didn't know which upset Georgette more; that Huey was having a fake church service, or that she was unable to talk him out of it.

Huey was gone before the first sunbeams stained the big North Carolina sky. Jo was a little sad he hadn't kidnapped her, but he certainly did not want to upset Georgette even more.

BUT—when Jo tiptoed downstairs, she was surprised to hear her aunt humming *Tis So Sweet to Trust In Jesus*. She went to the kitchen, where her aunt sat at the table behind a massive pile of pancakes.

"Aunt Georgette, are you okay?" Jo asked.

"Sit down, girl," Georgette said through a mouthful of pancake.

"Well, aren't we goin' to church?"

Georgette shrugged, her mouth still full, "Not goin' to Huey's church."

Jo slid into a chair and snatched a pancake from the pile and dropped it onto her plate. She expected her aunt to chastise her for using her fingers, but Georgette just smiled. It was getting a little scary.

"Well, are we goin' to the Baptist church?" Jo finally asked.

"Nope," Georgette said decidedly, and doused already soggy pancakes with syrup. "We're gonna have our own church right here."

Jo wasn't the type to spit food out when she was surprised, and it was a good thing, because if she was she could have sprayed the entire kitchen in chewed up pancakes. WHAT DID SHE JUST SAY? But instead of making a scene, it seemed wise to just roll with the program. "I see. And who's gonna preach?"

"Me."

"What are you gonna preach on?"

Georgette thought for a moment. "Maybe I'll preach on Jesus' love."

"Oh my, that is so overdone," Jo said, emptying the glass bottle of syrup over her cakes. "If I was you, I'd preach on evil preachers. No one ever talks about wicked preachers, but the Bible says a lot about them."

Georgette was thoughtful. "Yeah, you're right. And heaven knows there are a lot of wicked, rotten, lazy, cowardly, preachers in this neck of the woods."

"But don't preach on Jonah, okay? If you wanna talk about rotten preachers, it seems Jonah is just too easy. You gotta dig down a little."

Georgette actually brightened. "Jo, did you know that there were two wicked preachers in the Bible God burned up with fire?"

"Really?"

"Yes! They were Moses' nephews, and they were supposed to offer a sacrifice on the altar. But the Book says they offered strange fire on the altar instead."

"Strange fire? What kind of nasty is that?" Jo asked.

Georgette shrugged, "Book doesn't say. But it does say that a big ole fire come out of heaven and—*WHOOSH!*"

"Burned 'em up?"

Georgette grinned a little and nodded. "You got it."

Jo could just picture that. "You should preach that sermon, Aunt Georgette! And tell how they probably went running all around the altar while they were on fire, crying and screaming."

"I hadn't seen it quite that way." Georgette shook her head as if to try and free her mind of the image Jo had just placed there. "Anyway, Jo, I figure we ought to just have our own church today. The church of pancakes."

"I like it!" Jo declared.

■ ■ ■

Georgette didn't get to preach her sermon, there was a knock at the door just as they began to do the dishes.

"Good grief, who could that be on a Sunday?" Georgette asked, glancing at the clock. She untied her apron and smoothed out her favorite church dress.

The man at the door was handsome and clean shaven. He smelled like — peppermint maybe. He wore an expensive three piece suit that was gray with dark pinstripes. He took off his hat and unconsciously ran his fingers through his short black hair. It was greased and probably wouldn't move in a tornado. But oh, he was beautiful. Even Jo knew that, and she was only eleven.

"Illegal to sell on Sunday," Georgette said.

"Unless you're sellin' Bibles," Jo piped in.

Georgette swatted at Jo, who ducked away with a little giggle.

"I hope you ain't with the bank," Jo blurted. "'Cause if ya are, we might have to shoot you. Bank sent all kinds of people with suits few years back to close up peoples land and send them—"

"Jo, stop it!"

"Well, if he's with the bank, I ain't gonna be nice."

The man's eye twinkled at that. He was not with the bank. "My name is Elias Moore. I'm looking for the…" he paused, knowing this might sound a little ridiculous. "The Little Rickety Church of Madison Creek."

Georgette stared numbly at him. "The what?" Then a red flush came over her. "Oh no!"

"So you know where it is? Because the only location I have is here. But I've had a time trying to find the address. You don't have a mailbox?"

"You don't work for the mail service, do you?" Jo asked. She wanted a bit of the handsome man's attention. "Is the post office going to start delivering on Sunday?"

"No. I work for the Internal Revenue Service." His voice was crisp without a hint of any country accent. He pulled a paper from his hat and unfolded it. "I am at the right place, aren't I?"

"No sir," Georgette said. "Place you're looking for is up on Main Street."

He looked a little surprised. "So there really is a church?"

When Georgette answered, she sounded like a defeated woman. "Yes, there really is a church."

"I don't guess you'd mind giving me some good directions, now would you? It's important."

"And how! We might as well take you ourselves. We're just running a tad late."

"And Huey House? Is he here?"

"Mister, just give us a ride and we'll get you there," Georgette directed. "They'll be startin' soon, so hurry up."

"Do you have a siren on your car, Mr. I-R-S?" Jo asked. He did not.

Jo felt excited to get to go to Uncle's church, but a little sad that it meant the pancake church had to end.

When the Saints Come

Otis had intended to show up at the new church a little early and survey the situation, but his old man refused to drive him—that cotton-pickin' weasel. If pops was anything, he was chicken. He'd rather sulk about the new church than find out what was really going on.

He had to walk from the morgue up the hill. He could hear Katie's soprano voice leading the congregation in *Onward Christian Soldiers*. Even after being away so long, he had a good idea who would be inside just by spying the cars squeezed around the church house. Was it a church house? There was no cross, and no steeple and only a makeshift sign.

He spotted Big Mule Evermund standing at the door. Mule was pretending to shake hands with people, even though it seemed everyone who was going to come was already there.

He'd spent a restless night, thinking about Katie and all that once had been. She'd been the first girl he kissed, and the first girl he'd squeezed and the first girl he'd run has hands all over. They'd just been kids, but she was the sweetest thing on earth. He'd thought about her on so many nights back in New York. Nights he'd be talking to other girls in a bar or on the trolley, he'd just trade their homely faces out for hers.

He had told his parents he wanted to go and investigate what was really going on. He would do it for them; do it for the town. But really, thoughts of Katie's sweet perfume and soft skin had him crazy inside. Last night, when he saw the paper advertising she'd be doing the music, he had known he wouldn't be able to stay away. They had enjoyed that one, wonderful, delightful summer together so many years ago. She had been his first love, and he compared every woman after to her.

■ ■ ■

When Jo would later try to recall the events of that warm Sunday, she would get flashes of things that had happened; or of people's faces, but much of it was jumbled in a glob of bitter sweet gumbo she would simply remember as *That Day*. Perhaps her mind had recorded things faster than her poor memory was able to replay. Sometimes, in the twilight between wake and sleep, it all came back at once. The music — Mr. Elias Moore and that rich smell that clouded after him — the way the church was set up, with all those benches facing the front of the room where a wooden cross filled the wall.

The tax-man drove a 1934 Ford Sedan, which was almost as pretty as he was handsome. The way some married people started to look like each other, some people looked a little like their car — or their dog. Jo was happy with the sedan, since it meant she didn't have to ride in a rumble seat. Mr. Moore drove like a fireman, apparently he didn't want to miss a thing.

"There's Otis Step," Georgette said, and pointed at the man hiking up the hill. "We should stop and —"

"He'll be just fine," Mr. Moore said.

Mule Evermund grinned big when they got out of the car. "Gosh, I di-di-didn't expect you today!" he said. Then, when he spotted Mr. Moore trailing after Jo and Georgette, he was flustered. Not sure what to do — run off or say something smart in the presence of someone who really did look very important — Mule surprised them and gave a sharp military salute. That made Mr. Moore laugh, and he returned the salute.

Jo felt kind of nice being near the tax-man. She tugged at his jacket, urging him through the door. Inside the church, the song moved from *Onward Christian Soldiers* to *Amazing Grace*. She was surprised at Uncle Huey's turn out. It wasn't a Billy Sunday crusade, but the little room was respectfully full.

Mrs. Dotson, believe it or not, was in the front row with a big hat on. Boots was there, of course, and the mail-boy, Clay Simons.

There were others, like Jonas Wilson who ran the filling station, and none other than Big Floyd Carson and his wife. Mr. Carson managed the coal mine that zig-zagged through Blue Mountain. He said he owned it, and people referred to it as the *Carson Mine*, but Uncle Huey said it really belonged to a big company. Most anyone who had a job in Jordan Town worked for Mr. Carson. Aunt Georgette said Jordan Town was really just the other side of Madison Creek—but it's where the blacks lived. Carson Mine preferred hiring from Jordan Town. He said it was because they worked harder. Uncle Huey said it was because he could give them low wages and make them work harder.

Jo had thought Mr. Carson was a Baptist man. He only attended church on his wife's birthday, where he would make a production of giving the church a big check.

Jo was also surprised to see Nettie Drake there. Everyone had just figured Nettie was lost. The rumble in town was that Nettie was secretly rich because her husband had run off with a wealthy woman from California, and she sued the lady. No one knew how much she got in the settlement, but some said it was enough to give Floyd Carson a run for his money. Of course, that was probably just Madison Creek hogwash. She avoided church because she said all they wanted was her money, which she had safely hidden in her house because—well, you couldn't trust the bank. There she was, all fixed up in a nice yellow dress and a white hat.

There was no pulpit or podium at the front of the room. Just a makeshift stage and that big cross that towered over everything. Katie held a song book in one hand, and waved her arm with the other, urging the makeshift congregation to lift up praises to the Almighty. They did not. They just stood and stared. Really, she did look like an angel up there. It seemed her white skin even glowed a little with a joyful radiance.

Katie's son Dusty was seated, while everyone else stood to sing. Mrs. Dotson and her big hat had caught his eye, and he was studying it—and her—with the open fascination that could only come from an eight year old boy.

Mr. Moore and Aunt Georgette slipped into a back row seat. After an awkward moment of shuffling about, Aunt Georgette took Jo by the shoulders and moved the girl between them.

The door flew open, and Otis Step came in. He stood still in front of the door. At first Jo thought he was leaning against it, but then realized he was just staring at Katie. The singing sagged, Katie seemed unsure of herself. Jo looked and saw that Katie's radiant glow had died away; her pretty round face had turned bright red.

Otis wandered down the middle of the aisle, his head cocked to one side as he gawked at Katie. Little whispers went around the room, and everyone's gaze shifted from beautiful Katie to her long forgotten love.

Katie stopped singing all together. She was, after all, the only one even trying to make this work.

"Amen!" Otis said enthusiastically.

That's when Uncle Huey turned around to see what was going on. A warm pride swelled through Jo when she saw him. He was wearing his dark jacket—the one Aunt Georgette had given him four Easter's ago. Of course, he hadn't just outgrown the jacket—his belly had exploded right past it, ballooning out like a pregnant woman. Running over that big belly was his bright red tie. The tie was the exact same color as Uncle Huey's porch.

"Why don't you find a seat," Katie said to Otis.

"Sure," Otis nodded. "Where are you sittin' pretty?"

That was awkward.

Huey suddenly held out his arms as if to hug the whole room. "Ah, Oats, my old friend! You come right up here and sit with me!"

"Well, I was hoping to sit—"

Huey's buddy Boots, who had been slouching in a corner, suddenly shot up and held out his own arms. "You can sit by me, baby boy! I'd love to cuddle up with you during the sermon."

Otis darted for the safety of Huey, and everyone snickered. And just under those little snickers—or maybe just over them—was the distant sound of music. Not from Katie. This was trumpet music—and what sounded like a big choir. Maybe, Jo thought, a window was open somewhere and it was the sound of a radio.

"I'm glad you come to church, Otis," Katie said. She was shaking, and Jo wasn't sure if that was good or bad. "What's the next song, preacher Huey?"

Jo didn't hear what Huey said, because Mr. Big Government-Man bent down a little and whispered in her ear. "Is that *her* man?" he asked, motioning between Katie and Otis.

"I don't think so," Jo said. "Not no more, anyhoo."

The door burst open with such sudden energy. Mule Evermund hulked in the doorway. "Ho-ho-holy gee mo-Moses!" Mule cried. "You ain't go-go-gonna believe this!"

"It's the Martians," Lutie Dotson immediately declared. "Using their music to hypnotize us."

That was funny, but the best part was the look on Mr. Moore's face. He wouldn't have looked any more surprised if the Martians actually did drop down from the sky and suck the entire church up with a light beam.

■ ■ ■

The little rag-tag — one-time only — congregation forgot all about Katie and her music and the promised sermon yet to come, and ran for the door. Mr. Big Government-Man asked Jo if this kind of thing was normal. She shrugged, "Ask her," nodding toward Katie who was about the last one to file past them and out the door.

Trailing right after Katie was Otis. He was stumbling over an apology that Katie was working hard to ignore.

"Well hi there!" Katie said as soon as she saw Mr. Moore. She said it with such affection, it seemed they were old pals.

"Do you know him?" Otis demanded.

"Buzz off," she said over her shoulder. Katie reached for Mr. Moore and took his arm. "I don't want to face whatever is out there alone," she whispered.

Unsure of himself, but perceptive enough to know Katie had found a way around dealing with her nuisance, Mr. Moore locked his arm into hers and lead her out the door. After them, Otis demanded to know who this new fella was. Was this her man? A boyfriend? What was his name, anyway?

"What's going on?" Otis shouted to the now empty room.

He was startled when Jo answered him, "I reckon you done been away in New York for just a little too long. Life moved on without you."

"Who is he?" Otis demanded.

"Ah, him," Jo smiled a little. "He's the best. Everyone likes him."

"Well I don't," Otis grunted as the music grew louder yet.

■ ■ ■

"It's a mi-mi-miracle!" Mule stuttered.

"It's a parade," Mrs. Dotson said.

At that, Dusty chimed in with his best radio announcer voice: "It's the *Jordan Wax Program*, starring Fibber McGee and Molly."

Jordan Wax, that was good, Jo thought. Everyone knew Fibber McGee was sponsored by *Johnson Wax*, but the folks in the parade were from Jordan Town. Maybe the gears up in Dusty's head weren't as gummed up as everyone thought.

- They were all dressed for church. The women not only had their best dresses on, but jewelry which sparkled in the September sunlight.

- They were all singing, or playing instruments.

- And... they were all black.

There were a few lighter skinned people, mostly older, with wisps of white hair, but no white skin.

Leading the parade was Doctor Banks, wearing a brown suit, a red bow tie and a brown hat.

There weren't just trumpets. There were banjos, guitars, a clarinet, and a saxophone.

"I wonder what them people want," Floyd Carson said in a voice that made it clear he thought this was trouble.

The voices got louder and the instruments gathered energy.

> *Oh, when the saints go marching in,*
> *Oh, when the saints go marching in.*
> *Lord, how I want to be in that number,*
> *When the saints go marching in!*

Blazing through the music was the familiar sound of old Mo's harmonica.

Mule, who had run into the middle of the street along with several others, jumped up and down and clapped his hands. He spun around in what could have been mistaken for a drunken circle and hollered, "I want to be in th-that numba!"

On the trumpets were Shorty Parker and Elijah Robinson. Shorty didn't like the name, but he was too small to escape it.

Doctor Banks baritone voice rang out, his cuff links glimmered as he waved his arms.

> *And when the sun begins to shine,*
> *And when the sun begins to shine.*

Everyone joined in.

> *Lord, how I want to be in that number,*
> *When the sun begins to shine!*
> *Oh, when the saints go marching in,*
> *Oh, when the saints go marching in!*

Dusty had joined Mule in the middle of the street. "Yee-haa!" he cried.

Mule echoed him, "Ye-ye-yee-haa!" He clapped his hands and smiled big toward heaven. God had dropped a miracle right on Madison Creek.

"Ride 'em cowboy!" Dusty shouted, "I'm the Lone Ranger!"

■ ■ ■

The blacks marched right into the church, passing all the whites who had run outside to see what was going on. Mule patted each musician on the back, and shook hands with those who weren't playing anything. Doctor Banks stood at the front left of the church as the musicians joined him.

Lutie Dotson shook her head in disbelief. It wasn't the Martians invading Madison Creek, it was the coloreds!

"What are we going to do?" Nettie Drake asked as she smoothed her yellow dress and then adjusted her hat.

Jonas Wilson scowled. "Seems to me someone left the door open and a swarm of horse flies flew in. Surely we're not going to have church with *them!*"

Otis had been studying Katie. Which way would she lean on this issue? He knew the Sweet Tea Café had a colored section, but he also knew they didn't enforce it too hard. It was just a couple tables with signs, and sometimes those signs got moved around. "I think the Lord Jesus would have us welcome them in the spirit of…" Otis paused as mental wheels whirred like a conveyor dropping deep into the mine of his memory. "In the spirit of Jesus welcoming the Samaritan woman."

Otis waited for a sign from Katie. Did she approve of his stand? She didn't give any hint that she even knew he'd said a word.

One who did not appreciate his point of view was Floyd Carson. "Jesus and the Samaritan woman has nothin' to do with this situation. Jim Crow laws don't stretch out to churches, but if you tell me, Huey, I'll go in there and let them know they're not welcome. They'll run fast if I tell them to. The company writes most of their paychecks."

The company might hand out a lot of paychecks, but Otis knew the company treated most of its equipment better than its black workers.

"Say, you're new around here," Boots said, pointing at Elias Moore. "Whatta you think?"

"I'm just a visitor today, passing through town," Mr. Moore said. "Never seen anything quite like this. I'm mostly just hankering to get an ear full of that sermon Mr. House is gonna deliver."

"You want me to tell them to go?" Floyd was getting aggravated. "They can't even take a sip out of the white drinking fountain, what makes them think they can invade a church?"

Huey shrugged. "Well, I did invite Doctor Banks. I didn't know all of Jordan Town would ride in the saddle with him. But I guess they feel they have an invitation."

"Don't be afraid of bein' rude," Jonas said. "Some of them people got to be kept in their place."

"Have it your way," Floyd said, and stepped away. He stopped, hands in pockets as he obviously thought over what to do, then with renewed decision, he headed for his car.

Floyd Carson might not approve, but Otis was sure he saw Katie give him a little smile. He'd taken the right stand.

"Is this kind of thing normal?" Mr. Moore asked Katie.

"Nothing is normal when Mr. House has his hands in the pudding," Katie said.

The music died away as the whites returned to the building. But the room was now packed, and the only places left were standing room only in the very back.

■ ■ ■

"This is a favorite of ours," Elijah Robinson said before lifting the trumpet to his lips.

Big X surprised everyone when his deep voice rang out.

Swing low, sweet chariot
Comin' for to carry me home.

The entire band kicked in and the congregation began to sway.

Swing low, sweet chariot
Comin' for to carry me home.

Elisha Robinson let his trombone drift to his side as he sang.

I looked over Jordan, and what did I see,
Comin' for to carry me home?
A band of angels comin after me,
Comin' for to carry me home.

As they broke into a fresh chorus of *Swing Low*, they were met on stage by Boots, who had an empty jug in one hand. He held it up, and after some applause and cheers, he began to play with the rest of the band.

With all the singing, Huey began to feel warm relief sweep over him. Maybe they wouldn't press him to preach a sermon. He was caught off guard when Elijah came to the end of *It's Me, O Lord, Standing In The Need Of Prayer.*

"Preacher, guess it's 'bout time," Elijah said.

Huey looked like a condemned prisoner.

The Princess
and the Pig

Reconstructing exactly what Huey said would be impossible. Everyone heard something a little different.

Rose Abernathy, who worked Sunday evenings at the switchboard, would later say that she was *right plumb stampeded*, as the phone lines hummed all over town. Rose knew what they were all talking about—Huey House and his sermon.

Everyone agreed on the first part. *Well, here we go*, Huey had said. And from there, the stories went in all different directions.

Otis Step told his mother, who promptly called Minnie Belle, that Huey immediately began berating Christians. He hated them, one and all. There had been some collective gasps, but no one else would remember that raw hate Otis would report.

Most remembered the sermon going something like this…

> *Beyond a sermon, I guess I just have a question for y'all this week. I's a wonderin', just in the depths of myself, what good is it to go all around with God in your heart but not on your lips.*

That had gotten some amens.

> *Isn't that what you folk say? That you got that there Jesus right in yar heart?*

Uneasiness wiggled in on the congregation.

> *Now that just don't make a lick of sense. You can't squeeze Jesus into yar heart any more than you could suck him into your lungs or drink him down into yar liver. And I haven't read a lot of the Bible, but I don't know of anywhere where it said you had to get Jesus into your heart.*

Meemaw Moses stood and pointed a crooked black finger. "Now you be careful Preacher House, because you don't want to lead no sinners the wrong way, sir."

It was bold. First her interrupting the sermon. But more than that, it took some courage because she was a black woman openly correcting a white man in public.

But Huey was drawn in.

Indeed sweet lady. You're makin' my point. Making it better than…

He searched for a metaphor but none came.

"Better than a well sharpened pencil," someone offered.

Huey jumped on that.

Yes indeedy! Now lady, I sure as blazes don't want to lead anyone the wrong way. And that's why I'm just up here askin' if anyone remembers the Big Book sayin' we's gots to ask Jesus down into our heart.

Pages of the Bible rustled as people searched the Scriptures. Some, who didn't even know how to read, like Big X, just flipped pages with the others and pretended to study hard. Big X had been given a Bible when he was eight for memorizing a handful of Bible verses. He still carried that Bible with him, and over the years it had grown tattered from being carried about.

With Meemaw Moses having led the way, Doctor Banks felt safe to stand, holding the Scriptures up for all to see, and read John 3. "It's right here," he said with great authority. "You must be born again."

Huey mused that one over a bit.

That sounds difficult, but as difficult as that is, it sure doesn't say you have to get Jesus into your blood pumpin' muscle.

"Good grief, Huey!" Georgette burst out. She was about to say something, but Dusty mimicked her perfectly, making it sound like there was an echo in the room.

"Good grief, Huey!"

Everyone laughed, and by then, someone had found another Scripture.

"It says you have to repent," Shorty Parker said, reading the text slowly. "That's what the ole Apostle Peter said. Gotta repent."

Huey took a moment to muse that one over also.

I's just a wonderin', Is repent the same thing as asking Jesus into your heart?

There was some whispering as people considered this.

Dusty jumped up and shouted, "I got Jesus in my heart. That's what the radio preacher done said. Deep, deep down in my heart. And if that don't work out, I got the Shadow watchin' over me."

Katie grabbed his arm and pulled him back into his seat.

Mr. Moore—the Big Government Tax-Man—who seemed quite infatuated with Katie, laughed first, opening the door for everyone to give a little snicker. Except Otis. His eyes were on Katie and Mr. Moore and his lips were pressed hard together. Beads of sweat had begun to pop up on his forehead.

■ ■ ■

Huey lumbered on.

Maybe instead of asking Jesus into your heart, you ought to repent like the Book says. I don't have a dictionary, but I'd bet dollars to doughnuts that repent means to stop actin' rotten.

"And how!" Meemaw Moses agreed.

I'd bet my whole Man Village on the idea that Jesus doesn't want in your heart so much as he wants you to stop saying bad things about each other when you've got your back turned.

What got people riled up is that some remembered him saying…

It just doesn't plumb matter if he's in your heart if you act like the Devil.

Huey got a little thunderous at that point.

Seems to me y'all put Jesus in your heart just so you feel right comfortable acting as sinful as ya want. Just mean and hateful and spiteful, that's how you treat each other. You're like pigs in mud pretending to be a princess going to a fine ball. You think God's nose don't smell all that stink you got comin' off ya? You have as much fun sinnin' as a drunk at an open bar. Then, after you gossip about and treat each other bad, you run home to Jesus and ask him to spill some holy red blood for yar sins. Then you think you're okay

> *with the Big Boy upstairs. But I'm bettin' God's no fool. Maybe the Big Boy's right tired of emptyin' your sin bucket when you're just gonna fill it up again with the same manure.*

What stuck with Otis was Huey calling God the *Big Boy* upstairs. That buzzed its way through the phone lines to Millie Belle Lawson.

Huey pressed on…

> *Don't you think God knows when you plan ahead of time to sin, but you think down in your heart that you'll just ask for forgiveness later on.*

■ ■ ■

In Jordan Town, where most folks did not have phones — the lines actually stopped at the train tracks — people sat on porches that Sunday afternoon and shared their thoughts; which, for the most part, were much more favorable than what was humming through the phone lines.

Big X told a group gathered around him that his favorite part was when Huey dug right into the town gossip. Huey had said…

> *Now y'all explain to me how you can hate your relatives, and then think you're friends with God in heaven? I brought little Jo right into my house when her parents died that awful death. And I treat her like my own daughter. I love her, and I clothe her, and I teach her the best I can. And Georgette does even better than I do. But I hear some of you behind my back say some things that aren't so kind about the way Jo's been brought up. My girl goes off and gets herself kicked out of Christian Camp for — gosh, I don't know what — and you all have to offer up all kinds of opinions. Everyone's got somethin' to say about little ole Jo. I don't care if she got kicked out of Christian Camp, I love her just the same.*

> *Huey gave Jo a little wink and Jo return the gesture with an enthusiastic thumbs up. "I love you, big ole Uncle Huey, yes-siree."*

> *You think it makes anyone want to come to your stupid church when you claim to burn for Jesus on Sunday, but burn up the phone lines on Monday talking hot fire trash about my girl?*

There were some appalled whispers.

No matter. You disrespect your parents, then think you're safe on Judgment Day because of Jesus in your heart. I don't know, I've never been to cemetery –

"Seminary," Georgette corrected. But he didn't hear her.

But I'm pretty sure on that big day when God gets out his movie projector and watches your life on the big screen, he won't be none too happy with all the bad you've done all the while thinking Jesus was in your heart. I hear everywhere that Jesus loves ya. Maybe. But I'm on the side that says that if you're runnin' around hurting people and using Jesus as your excuse, the truth is Jesus probably hates you.

They all remembered that line. *Jesus probably hates you.*

After that Huey bellowed even louder.

You wanna cuss? Be my guest! I don't give a rotten tomato if you cuss like a sailor. But don't do it and then think Jesus got-ja covered on the big court day.

"Oh damn it," Clay Simons sputtered. "We're all going right to Hell."

"You stop that!" Meemaw Moses shouted at Clay. "This is the house of God!" Only, she didn't say, *God,* she said, *Gawwwwwwd.*

Clay reddened. "I know. And I'm so sorry. Please go on, Preacher House. But I'll betcha most of us really are in some hot water with your Big Boy in the sky."

Huey ran his hands through his hair in frustration.

If getting a sermon started was a problem, he now realized finding a way to end a sermon was an even bigger problem. He began to mutter…

So, uh – ya gotta do somethin'.

"Well, preacher, what are we supposed to do?" Mr. Big Government-Man asked, his arm now protectively around Katie. He'd been to plenty of churches, but never had he heard a sermon like this.

Huey shrugged.

Ah, I don't know. I done run out of steam up here. I guess you ought to decide which way you really wanna go. If you wanna roll

*in the mud, then just come out and say yar a pig. And if you want
to be a princess at the ball, then act like a princess.*

For years to come, the sermon would be known as the *Princess
and the Pig*.

"Now what?" Huey asked.

"The offering," Boots prompted. "Take an offering and let's go
home."

"I think you're supposed to give an invitation," someone said.

Huey hadn't thought about that. "An invitation for what?"

"To ask Jesus into… ah, never mind."

So they took the offering.

Chicken Whoopin'

When the last amen was said, it was punctuated by a "yeee-haaa," from young Dusty. That wasn't a surprise, considering Dusty was an idiot — in Otis' opinion. What shocked him was when a few people began to applaud. APPLAUD! As if the whole thing had been a New York stage show. And the truth was, it had been a good show; even a little stirring. What — with the black band and the unusual preaching, it was the kind of thing a big time producer might say they could make a show out of.

Of course, good as they might have been, those rotten blacks had horned in on Katie's music.

The little crackle of applause picked up steam, and soon everyone was clapping.

"Hip, hip, hooray!" Dusty yelled.

"Hi-hi-hip hooray!" Mule bellowed after.

"And God bless America!" Lutie Dotson said.

Lawdy, Otis thought, *the Asylum must be letting the inmates out on day passes just to attend this freak show church.* To his own surprise, the voice that rattled that out in his head was his own mother's. He found it a little disturbing that sometimes his thoughts expressed themselves audibly in her voice.

As people filed out, Otis turned to find Katie. She was talking to Nettie Drake, who was telling both Katie and the entire room, what a great performance Katie had given before *them other people showed up.* Otis noticed that the fella Katie had been so attached to was off talking to a small group of blacks. Only, he wasn't talking to them; he was interviewing them. Yeah, that's it. It reminded him of the way a stage director in the Big Apple would linger around after the first few performances of a new show and talk to audience members. Only, they were never really talking to the audience, they were interviewing them, looking for little clues on how things might be better, or what they didn't like. Yeah, that's what this guy was doing. He might not be peppering them with questions, but he could tell just by watching that an interview of some kind was going down.

It was time to make his move.

Otis stepped beside Nettie and pulled her close to him. He gave her a little sideways squeeze. "Boy howdy, and you said it, Mrs. Drake! Katie here is an angel, isn't she?"

Nettie let out a sharp squeal of surprise, and then giggled like a school girl.

Katie's face froze in a tight smile; but her eyes didn't smile.

"She's an angel," Nettie drooled. "I was just telling her that. Telling her how she could lead heavens choir right here on earth. I hope like the dickens she doesn't feel bad no one was singing with her. But we were all just engrossed in her, that's all."

"Engrossed," Otis repeated with a raised eyebrow. "Katie dear, I think Mrs. Drake is a right smart woman, eh?"

"I love Mrs. Drake," Katie said with a guarded tone.

What Otis didn't see was that behind him, Katie's boy Dusty had mounted a wooden bench. He threw himself onto Otis, covering Otis' eyes with his hands and wrapping his skinny legs around the man's waist. Nettie Drake stumbled aside as Dusty yelled, "Guess who!"

Otis hadn't expected that, but he did expect any moment for Katie to chastise the boy and tell him to get off. But instead, darkness just hung over Otis.

"Gotta guess who!" Dusty giggled.

The eight year old was spoiled rotten; spent all his time in front of the radio, and then reliving the radio plays all day. In Dusty's world, the Lone Ranger really might come riding into town; or Flash Gordon could drop in from the sky.

"It's you, Dusty," Otis groaned.

The boys grip tightened. Of course, Otis could wiggle free, but if he was a bad sport it would just give Katie more reason to be annoyed with him. A good interaction with Dusty would mean extra points with mama.

"Not Dusty," the boy said. "You gotta guess. My dog's name is Yukon King."

"Ah, I know who you are."

"Say it, 'cause I ain't lettin' go until you say it."

Otis voice was warm. "You're Sergeant Frank Preston, of the Northwest Mounted Police."

Dusty was impressed. "And what's my radio show called?"

"The Challenge of the Yukon."

Dusty let go and dropped to the ground. "Look, a safe landing, just like Buck Rogers."

Katie had taken the opportunity to get away and was now back with her new man, trailing right behind him as the guy talked to Huey.

"Hey Dusty, you know that man over there?"

Dusty shrugged, "I can't say nothin'. Police work, ya know?"

"Pretend I'm your partner."

Dusty raised his eyebrows, "Those two," he pointed between his mother and the new guy, "That's my new dad."

Otis frowned. "Have you met him before?"

"Sure! And I'm his..." Dusty thought for a moment. "I'm his Green Hornet."

"That has nothing to do with anything," Otis said, suspicious that Dusty didn't have any more idea who the new guy was than he did.

"Okay, I gotta go, boy."

"You wanna play Green Hornet?"

"No."

"Lone Ranger? Shadow? How about—"

Otis had to push away from the boy and start toward Katie, where the new man was now having quite the conversation with the preacher man. Otis could tell that Katie had been watching him out of the corner of her eye, and now as he approached she put her hand on the man's shoulder to indicate they were together.

■ ■ ■

Otis wanted to ease up beside Katie and whisper, *Say there, toots, you look better than Claudette Colbert.*

But he could tell he needed to ease into things with Katie. Dog gone it, he had a suspicion starting to brew in him that he didn't like.

"Hey there Katie," Otis said.

She rubbed the shoulder of Mr. New What's-His-Face. "Hello Otis," she said. "That was certainly an awkward entrance you made to church today."

"I was just taken by how beautiful you were up there. Kinda brought back old memories from when you was sixteen."

"Lot of people thought you were dead, or in trouble with the law," Katie said.

The man she was with didn't even turn to look at him.

"I've been chasing dreams and living life in the Big Apple. Got on a lot of radio shows. Did you hear me?"

She shook her head, "Not a one."

"Well, I was there. With Jack Benny and — oh, so many!"

"This is my friend," Katie said, pulling a bit harder on Mr. Pretty's arm. He turned and smiled at Otis. "Elias, I want you to meet an old acquaintance of mine. This is Otis Step. Otis, this is Elias Moore."

Elias. What a stupid name, Otis thought. Sounded like a used car salesman — *A-LIE-US.*

"You familiar with this here church?" Elias asked.

Otis shrugged, "Sure. Good as anyone I guess."

Katie rolled her eyes in frustration. "Ah, he doesn't know a thing about this place."

"Sure's I do!" Otis exploded. "I'm a deacon."

Katie's mouth hung wide open, and Huey, who had started to use the opportunity to slip away, turned back. A quiet hung over them, even as other conversations carried on around them.

Big nasty Boots, who had been lingering nearby in a conversation with Doctor Banks, stepped toward them.

"I say!" Boots bellowed, towering over Katie and Elias. "Look what the cat drug in."

"Otis here was just telling us how he was a deacon," Katie said.

"Is that so?" Boots came around to Otis and put his arm around him. "I guess you missed the news Katie."

"So Otis is a deacon?" Katie inquired, looking to Huey.

"Sure he is," Huey agreed a little too easily.

"Just not ordained yet," Boots said. "That's what I was fixin' to do right now. Go ordain him."

"Wait a minute!" Otis felt a trap forming around him. "I don't want to get ordained by you. What do you mean by ordain me?"

"Just come on outside and I'll get it taken care of." Boots pulled Otis close to himself, and spoke to the new man. "I'm the chairman of deacons, you see? I'm just gonna take Oats here on outside and lay hands on him."

"Don't lay no hands on me!" Otis protested, wiggling free.

"Gotta do it," Boots turned to give chase. "That's how it works. You wanna be a deacon, you gotta have hands laid on ya." He looked over his shoulder, a twinkle in his eye. "Don't you worry Preacher House, I'll have him ordained by the end of the day."

"Yeah, well, ordain him good, would ya?" Katie asked.

■ ■ ■

That afternoon, while Rose Abernathy worked the switchboard and people filled Madison Creek with their chatter, Huey sat alone on his big red porch. His rocker worked back and forth, adding a rhythmic sigh to the crickets who had taken up chirping. Above him,

Jo lay on the porch roof and stared deep into the reddening afternoon sky.

"I don't guess we'll get no supper tonight," Huey said.

Jo wondered who he was talking to.

"Georgette's all worked up, and I can't blame her. Can you?"

Whoever was on the porch with Uncle Huey didn't answer.

"I guess it's more than a woman can take for her man to pretend to be a preacher and hold a church service in town. But the way I reckon it, she finally got me in church, don't you say?"

The rocker sawed against old porch boards, the crickets chirped, and no one answered Huey.

Jo had the distinct impression he was talking to her. She waited, and once again the rocker creaked as crickets flirted with one another. Jo wiggled to the edge of the roof and dropped her head over the side. There was Uncle Huey — only he was upside down — rocking away. The curtains in the big picture window behind him were pulled, and she could see clear through the parlor to the edge of the kitchen. Aunt Georgette was at work on something.

"You talkin' to me?"

Huey didn't seem surprised. "I was tryin' to, but you seem to be strugglin' to hold up your part."

"Well, I didn't know we was havin' any conversation, big uncle. Want me to come down there?"

"Nah. Just stay where you are every night, that's the way I like it."

"I kinda liked that tax-man. He smelled good, and looked real fine."

"Nosey nincompoop," Huey groused. "Fella just about put me through the Spanish Inquisition. Didn't matter how I answered that boy, he wasn't gonna get no satisfaction. Even if I's smart enough to buffoon Mr. Encyclopedia Britannica, he would have still had a mouthful of questions, and follow up questions, and follow up questions on the follow up questions."

Jo took the instant to bob up and let some blood ease away from her head.

"Try one of those questions by me, Uncle Huey."

"Well, let's see; 'Does the Little Rickety Church of Madison Creek belong to an established denomination?'"

"What-ja say to that one?"

"I said that Jesus didn't belong to a denomination, and neither did the prophet Paul."

"Apostle," Jo corrected. "Please tell me you didn't call him the prophet Paul."

"It's water under the bridge now. Wait, here's another," Huey shifted his voice to try and sound like the smooth, gentle tax-man, only what came out was a painful exaggeration. "Now sir, does this church of yours have a definite and distinct ecclesiastical government?"

"Gracious," Jo moaned.

"I says, 'Sir, I don't know what no ecclesiastical government is, but when it comes to Government, I'm a Democrat and so I'm generally for it. We have more government going on here than ole Roosevelt himself could cook up. Why, we thinkin' up committees on committees for the committee. Some of our committees are so complicated that the folk on them don't know their even on them.'"

"That's just stupid," Jo snickered and bobbed her head up and then back down.

"And then he goes and asks to see bylaws and all such as that, and I just told him I didn't have those documents handy. He wanted to know if the church had a distinct legal existence. When I explained that I am the church, that's when he got down to tellin' me how a person can't claim themselves or their personal belongings as a church. Seems that's a violation of some tax code. A person on their own can't be tax exempt."

"Gosh golly, are you gonna go to jail?"

"He didn't say. Just asked me a hill of questions, all the while our sweet Katie was standin' right behind him."

The red in the sky had finally given way to dark and Uncle Huey was just a shadow. Even in the darkness, Jo sensed him smile. He took from his pocket a long cigar and lit it. "I'd let you take a puff if you's down here with me, Jo."

■ ■ ■

They were interrupted by the steady whirr of a bicycle. Jo could see the shadow of the rider as he sped toward the house, then crashed into the dirt at the foot of the porch.

Uncle Huey let the silence settle with the dust.

The only person who would do something like that was sixteen year old Clay Simons. Jo held back a sarcastic greeting and decided not to let him know she was on the roof.

"Preacher House, can I talk to you?" Clay asked as he came up the porch steps.

"Sit down and make yourself at home."

After a moment Clay said, "Sir, I just gotta talk to someone. Pastor Weatherwax would hear me out, but he wouldn't understand. I don't think he's ever gotten in a fight or even said a bad word. But you've been in your share of fights, ain't ya?"

Huey didn't miss a beat. "Well, not when I could avoid them."

"Say, remember that time you ran against Mr. Finch for mayor? That was kinda like a fight, wasn't it?"

Jo's ears perked up.

"He licked me good," Huey agreed. "I sure shouldn't have gone off and said that Madison Creek should secede from North Carolina. Now what about you, boy? What fight did you get in?"

Clay's voice dipped toward guilt, "My pa."

The rocking chair slowed and the silence was metered out by crickets. The smell of cigar thickened.

"He lost his job long time ago. When the stock market derailed, we lost everything. Big fat man came and threw us out of our own house. I's just a kid back then, but I remember it. That man came in our house like he owned the place. My pa told him to get out and do you know what that fat bank hog did? He done hawked up a big ole wad of spit and spewed it on our rug. He said he could do that because it was his house now."

"Those were the beginnings of the bad times," Huey remarked.

"That's when my pa got serious about the bottle. He'd drink anything that would make him numb to the hurt. Pretty soon, Ma said he loved bein' drunk more than he loved us. My ma found some work, but Pa didn't like that none. He liked her money, but felt bad he couldn't support us. He got mean about it, preacher. He beat her and called her wicked things. Once, when she came home with some new shoes—they wasn't fancy or nothin'—he wrestled those shoes right off of her and beat her with them. He tackled her, and went after her like a man with a hammer. He about wore that shoe out on her face. He would have killed her if neighbors hadn't heard her screams."

"I remember," Huey said. "And you're mama, she's a wise woman. She kicked him out of that little shack y'all live in. Some women would've taken it."

"He comes back sometimes to ask for money. And Ma, she's soft about him and gives him what she can. But she won't let him back in the house. But know what I heard, preacher? I heard he was campin' up yonder toward Blue Mountain. I wanted to see him."

"Did you go huntin' for him today?"

"Yep. Right after church. I thought about what you'd said. About how we would live different if we really believed all that stuff in the Bible. Well, I can't just let my ole pa drink himself to death and die out there."

"It's a dry county," Huey objected.

"Well, up yonder on Blue Mountain, there's more bootleggers runnin' loose than chickens in our yard. Anyway, I think Pa and Sticky Simpson got themselves some secret stash up there. Your buddy ole pal Boots told me I'd find my pa if I just followed the stream on up Blue Mountain. It wasn't very far. He was all alone, sleepin' under an old green scout tent. He sure was in a sour mood when I found him. He wanted to know why I was snoopin' around his tent. He said that he didn't need nothin' from me, seein' as how I was a no account black boy."

"Black boy?"

"He said he'd spied people goin' in the church that mornin'. 'Don't that make ya uncomfortable?' So I says, 'That's what you're all poopy about? I went to church and a few blacks showed up?' And then he went and asked me if I planned to marry me a coon girl."

"Oh, I'll bet that lit your fire! Did you hit him?"

"I didn't lay a hand on my old man. I kicked him. He was all wobbly to begin with, so when I kicked him, he just fell backward. Know where he fell, Mr. House? He fell right into that green tent. But that lesson didn't help his mouth any. He started callin' me a darkie and sayin' my kids was gonna have the mark of Cain."

"So you left him there?"

"No, sir. I kicked him again, and he just rolled. He was all tangled up in that tent, and he just rolled right downhill. I went after him, shouting some bad stuff and kicking him as I went. It was like a good round of kick the can. He finally hit a tree and got real quiet. I started to ask if he was okay, but he beat me to it, and shouted a bunch of curses at me. Which is fine, I've got my own liking for salty language. But then he said as far as he was concerned, I wa-dn't his son no more."

"So what-ja do?"

Quiet sucked them in. Jo so wanted to peek down and see what was going on. She had the idea that Clay had come up and sat down in the rocker next to Huey and they were both smoking.

"Well, boy," Huey said, "out with it. What did you do to your pa? Did you kick him again?"

"I peed on him."

Even the crickets died down.

"Say what?"

"He said he'd rather live in a tent in a rainstorm than be with me. So I just gave him some rain. I was full, too."

Huey snorted. "That's wonderful!"

"No it ain't!" Clay shot back. "That's my pa! You're supposed to tell me that's sin, and that I am probably goin' to hell."

"Ah, you'd just pee the fire out."

Jo held back a snort.

Huey finally spoke with authority, "Well, it is sin. And ya know why you feel so low about it? Because God lives in ya belly and he won't let ya sin without givin' ya trouble over it." Huey cleared his throat, "Well boy, let's pray."

Jo couldn't believe her uncle was going to pray. Jo imagined angels in heaven gathering around to hear this. But only silence.

Finally Clay said, "Well, ain't ya gonna pray?"

"Me? Pray? I'm not the one who peed on my old man. You do the prayin', boy. Or go drench Weatherwax with your crocodile tears. You are in the drenchin' business today, aren't-ja?"

"Well, preacher, can I just do a prayer in my heart?"

"That prayin' in your heart business is just like the Jesus in your heart business," Huey said. "I think you better get the prayer onto your lips."

With frustration, Clay blurted, "Well, God, I'm sure sorry for what I done. Amen."

"That's it?" Huey asked.

"Yep."

"Well, that's fine if it's what's on your heart. But I reckon when you have time you ought to ask the Lord to kick your pa for ya. God kicks better than we do. Sometimes God can kick a man deep down and wake him up."

There was a quiet moment. Was he hugging Huey? Jo hoped not. She didn't like Clay. Clay picked on her, and she had the feeling that wasn't going to change.

Then Clay was back on his bike speeding away through the darkness.

■ ■ ■

"Wow," Jo said, looking down on Uncle Huey who was at the end of his big cigar. "I just can't believe he did that."

"Well, you didn't hear none of it, ya hear?" Huey warned.

Behind him, in the big picture window, Georgette was standing. The lights were off in the parlor, but Jo could see her silhouette. Georgette stepped outside and said loudly, "Might as well come on down here, Jo. I'm tired of you snoopin'."

"I prefer it up here," Jo said; but then, with sudden decision, she surprised herself and got up on her knees. She skedaddled to the edge of the porch, and wrapped her legs around one of the pillars. Her aunt let out an exasperated sigh as she came down.

Georgette had a huge chicken leg in her hand, and pointed it at Jo. "First of all, for you, I want to tell you that I am sorry."

"I forgive you," Jo said at once.

"No, child. I'm sorry for you."

Oh. That was different.

"I'm sorry your parents died that terrible death. I'm sorry you've been left to an uncle who's a no good and a rotten thief."

"Hey!" Huey objected.

She turned on him. "You are truly no good, Huey."

Huey gave an ah-shucks shrug, and Jo took the moment to slip toward the dark corner of the porch. She sat down, rested her elbows on her knees and cradled her head. She was ready for whatever show God had planned for tonight. *Hey, there, Mr. God,* she thought, *you might as well call up Gabe and Mike and them other angels, because this is probably gonna be a pretty good show.*

"Someone stopped by, who was it?" Georgette questioned Huey.

"That boy, Clay Simons. One that delivers the mail to every other house, but not this one because—"

"Don't make this about me, Huey." Georgette sat down in the chair next to Huey's. He reached for the chicken leg in her hand, but she waved it away. "Why did Clay come by here after dark?"

"Ah, he wanted to talk to me about his pa. Let me have a bite of that chicken."

She shook the chicken leg at him, "Nope. Tell me more."

"His pa is a skunk, and he went to try and make nice with the old man. But it didn't go well, so he peed on his pa." He grinned at Georgette with childlike delight. "Ain't that a great one?"

WHAP! She smacked him, hard, with the chicken leg.

Jo hadn't even realized her aunt had come out of the chair. But there she was, standing over ole Uncle Huey, her face bright like a blood moon glowing in the dark.

Then Georgette did it again; she smacked him with the chicken leg, her secret batter sprinkled all over him. Huey tried to fend her off as she knocked him in the head with the chicken. He pushed away from her, tilting the rocking chair. The entire chair careened toward the porch, landing Huey on his side. Georgette didn't miss a beat, she continued to whomp him with that chicken leg.

Huey laughed and wiggled free from the chair. It reminded him of Clay kicking his pa while he was down. "You gonna pee on me, Georgette?"

She dropped the chicken leg, which was nothing more than bone by now. Huey wiggled until he was sitting up, his back propped against the house. Georgette sat down beside him, pressing her back against the front door.

"What scares me, Huey, isn't the I-R-S. I'm sure they'll cause us some heartache. But it's Clay, and folk like him. Because he thinks you're real. He thinks you can help him. What did you do after he told you he peed on his pa? You probably laughed your silly head off."

Huey shrugged, "Well, somethin' like that."

Jo wondered why Huey didn't tell her he had made Clay pray.

"What hurts my heart, Huey, is that you really can preach. You dug down into my heart, and tore me up a little. But bein' a preacher is more than preaching. People are going to bring their problems to you, Huey. And know what? They want a word from the Lord. Do you have that, mister?"

Huey gave a defeated sigh, "Ah, shucks, I sure am hungry, and I know you're not gonna let me eat a thing until I say what you wanna hear. I sure as the Devil am sorry."

"Are you done with that church business?"

Huey shrugged, "Done as the snake was in the Garden of Eden."

"He means he's ready to repent," Jo interjected. Someone had to get this right or they might never eat.

He grunted agreement.

"And he's wicked," Jo added. "He meant to say that, too."

Not Stopping
the Tornado

Anyone could have seen it coming; except Uncle Huey. That ole buzzard couldn't just up and quit church. He'd gotten people stirred up. He'd said things they never heard. What's more, he had welcomed people into the church who usually felt shut out.

"You might as well have tried to stop a tornado," Boots would later reflect.

Hints that Huey's troubles had only begun were everywhere. There were the phone calls that Georgette fielded — folk calling to ask his advice on seeking a better prayer life, his council on marriage, and his views on tithing. Georgette listened to each caller, and then reminded people that the church had been a one-time thing, and that Huey had only been preacher for a day.

But most people did not call. They visited Huey at his office; his Man Village, where the steady flow of customers had increased exponentially.

If Huey had an office downtown, most folk would have kept their distance. But his Man Village made the perfect preachers study, since people didn't feel like they were going to visit a man of God; they were just stopping in to pick up old paint, bald tires, or charge their batteries. But, in the midst of their purchase, they found ways of asking their questions and dropping their prayer requests his way.

■ ■ ■

Otis waited until Tuesday morning to track Katie down. Of course, she was at the Sweet Tea Café. He asked if she would like to go on a date. She did not want to go on a date, or visit the Drug Store with him to sip at the soda fountain; and she certainly did not want to come over for dinner, even if his mama did make the best cobbler on the East Coast.

He quizzed her about Sunday's Mr. Handsome. "You were on him like a hungry bedbug. But it's okay. I don't hold it against ya none."

Katie showed Otis to a table. Old Lucius Jeremiah was sitting at the table next to him, staring out the café window at Main Street. "I've just about figured out what's goin' on," he said to Jeremiah.

"What's goin' on?" Jeremiah asked.

"Ah, she's found her a new prince, and they're lookin' to get hitched up," Otis said.

"What?" Katie had started toward the counter, but came back.

"'Course church won't have nothin' to do with Katie here, because she's had a boy out of wedlock. And I'll bet ya they won't marry her and her Mr. Super."

"Ya don't say?" Jeremiah said.

"That's quite a story," Katie said. "Are you going to order something?"

"How about some coffee and a tall order of you to sweet'n it up," he raised his eyebrows.

"How about a big tall order of no way. Besides, according to you I'm lookin' to get married."

Otis nodded. "Church won't have anything to do with it, right? So ole Huey House created a church for you, just so he could marry you. I saw you and that Mr. Handsome talking to the Preacher House afterward."

"Yeah, Otis, that's it. You're Sherlock Holmes."

Jeremiah chimed in, "Way I see it, if Huey House's church was just about getting Katie married, that boy she wants to hitch up with must have done somethin' bad. Maybe he's still married."

"Or a criminal."

After some more awkward banter, Katie sent Otis away, bluntly telling him to either order something or skedaddle. Otis tried to order some sweet tea, but she said they were fresh out of sweet tea.

■ ■ ■

Shorty Parker came to the Man Village on Tuesday morning on the hunt for a blacksmith's shaping knife, which he found wedged between two old gas cans near a pile of Model T parts. Two old crows, who had kept watch over the Man Village for the last few months, cawed at him from the roof of an old shed. Shorty cawed back, but the birds held their ground.

"Preacher House, I sure do need your prayers," Shorty said as he and Huey rambled toward the shed where Huey did his trading.

"Ah, never mind them crows," Huey groused, "They think the place belongs to them."

"No, I don't need no prayer over the crows!" Shorty laughed. "I was hopin' you might say a prayer for my mother. She got a bad case of the fever."

"Ya don't say," Huey sighed. "Ya call on Doc Banks?"

"Sure did. He fixed her up with some medicine. But she needs prayers, too."

Boots, who was leaning against the shed drinking something undoubtedly toxic, perked up. "I got medicine that would fix her right up."

"You hush up," Huey commanded. "I gots some prayin' to do." Then, with sudden thought, Huey asked Shorty, "I guess her bein' sick puts ya in quite a pickle. Seein' as how she's a teacher at the colored school, she needs to be well before school starts back."

"You got it, Preacher House."

"I sure do want to pray," Huey said with a sigh. "But I just don't know how."

Boots laughed, "Didn't see that one comin'!"

"Well maybe I can say the prayer," Shorty offered, putting his small black hand on Huey's big shoulder. "I mean, if you don't know how."

"I don't know how you'll do any better," Huey said. "Problem is, I can't think of what we're going to tell God that he doesn't already know. You think God's up there waitin' for us to ask him to heal your mama before school starts? I doubt he's going to say, 'Why! I'm sure glad you told me that! I sure wasn't gonna heal her until ya asked'."

Shorty was taken back. "Well, it does say we have not 'because we ask not'."

Huey was startled. "Really? It says that in the Book?"

"It does," Boots confirmed. "I remember that one, too."

A warm breeze sang through trees and whistled through piles of junk. The crows cawed as new visitors rambled toward the Man Village.

"Well, I have an idea how we might pray," Huey said, looking toward the sky. "Big God, we need ya down here. You already know that, so I reckon you have a mighty smart plan lined up. Now you let us know how we might help her. And I guess if it's your will she be sick, then help her suffer without bein' too terrible mean to her family. But we sure do hope you wanna get her well. So you just show my friend Shorty what you want him doin' while mama is sick."

"Wait," Shorty objected. "What's this got to do with me?"

"Ah, shucks, everyone knows you fight with her all the time. I don't even live in Jordan Town, and I know you two can't get along. She still treats you like a little boy, and you lose your cool and go around slammin' things. You think I don't know that? Hope you never lay a hand on her."

"No! No... never!"

"But you could treat her nicer, don't ya say?"

Shorty looked away and stared at the crows. "I guess I could."

"So that's my prayer!" Huey cried. "Hey God, while Mrs. Parker be sick as a dog with the fever, would you teach Shorty to treat her like a queen? And Shorty here sure is sorry it took his mama gettin' sick for him to learn to be nice to her." He nodded toward Shorty with satisfaction, "So there ya go. We're all prayed up."

"Gotta say amen," Boots grunted.

"Well, Shorty might have more to say to God on this subject on his way home, so no point in cuttin' the conversation off. Now, you gonna pay me for that blacksmith's shaping knife?"

■ ■ ■

When Sunday came, Huey kept a promise he'd made to Georgette and went with her to the Baptist church. He sat right beside her in the second row. Minnie Belle Lawson stood over the both of them and announced she was glad to see the prodigal home from feeding pigs.

"Ah, just movin' from one pigpen to another," Huey said.

The ruckus didn't come until announcement time. Pastor Weatherwax was explaining that the church picnic was a church event. Apparently tag-alongs were showing up just to bum a meal.

The church doors exploded open, and Mule filled the space in the door frame.

"Ya-ya-ya just gotta see it!" he cried.

The preacher was dumbfounded. "What?"

"Oh, he's simple!" Minnie Belle cried. She stood up and pointed at Mule, "Either sit down, or get out."

"Oh go-go-gosh golly! I am sorry!" Mule cried, and stepped back, slamming the door.

Several people jumped to their feet.

"You should all be ashamed of yourselves!" Minnie Belle chided, and received a hearty amen from Edith Step.

"Take heart sister," the local milkman wiggled in his pew to face Minnie Belle. "We ain't all heathens."

Huey used the seat in front of him to pull himself up. Georgette reddened. "Where are you going?"

Huey shrugged, "Sounds like somethin' is happin' out there, and I figure they might need a little help."

She let Huey squeeze past her, but held out her arm to block Jo. "Whatever is happening out there, it sure isn't going to be anything you can help with."

Glancing back, it seemed half the church had emptied out after Mule's interruption. Meanwhile, the preacher tried to find his place in the announcements.

When the preacher asked everyone to turn in their hymn book to page ten, Jo leaned in to her aunt and explained that she HAD to go to the bathroom, BAAAD! Georgette patted Jo on the arm and shook her head.

"I might pee right here in church," Jo warned. She was trying as hard as she could to squeeze some pee into her bladder so it wouldn't be a lie, but she was dry as the Sahara.

And then salvation came. Just as surely as salvation had found its way to Peter in that prison, or Shadrach, Meshach, and Abednego in the fiery furnace — God sent salvation to Jo House in Madison Creek.

The church door creaked open and sunlight licked fresh through the Baptist sanctuary. Dulling that sunlight was big Uncle Huey, who stood in the door way with his ah-shucks grin.

"Sorry preacher. But I need Jo, and quick!"

Jo leapt.

- She leapt to her feet like the lame man who had just found healing.
- She leapt past Aunt Georgette.
- She leapt down the aisle, and
- She leapt out of the Baptist church.

■ ■ ■

"God just d-d-done it again!" Mule cried.

"I'm really not surprised," Jo said.

And neither was most anyone, except Huey.

They were back. The blacks and their band; the whites, and even a few new people. Huey could see them at the top of the hill, gathering around the old makeshift church. Katie was there, he could spot her bright yellow hair from afar. Someone was tagging right beside

Katie. Huey groaned and wondered if it would fall to him to chase Otis off. That boy was like a mutt that wouldn't let go of your leg.

"I told them there was no more church," Huey grunted as he and Jo stepped down into the street.

Boots put his arm around Huey. "Boy, couldn't have stopped this any more than you could have stopped a tornado."

Huey ignored Boots and said, "Jo, I sure do need you."

"Well I'm right here."

"I don't have a sermon in me. So give me somethin' quick."

"You know Jesus was dead and come back to life?" Jo asked as they made their way to the car.

"I knew that," Huey agreed.

"Well, it seems you could get at least one sermon out of that. I mean, most people die and their bodies get sour and rotten and then they turn to bones. But Jesus kicked death in the face and climbed out of his grave."

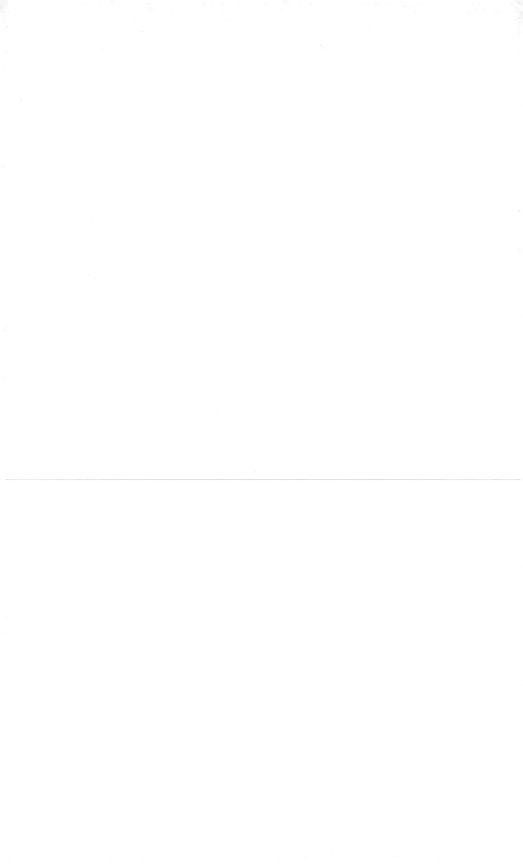

Martian Rock

When they arrived at the Little Rickety Church, Clay Simons was already there, standing on the roof shouting, "*DING, DONG! DING, DONG!*" Boots told him to get down or he'd tar and feather him. Jo was disappointed that Clay gave in.

Nettie Drake, whose husband had left her for the rich California hottie, stepped into Huey's path and held out her arms. The nice yellow dress she'd worn last week was gone, replaced with a house dress. At first Jo thought Nettie wanted to hug Huey, but then realized she intended to block his path.

"Move aside for the preacher," Doctor Banks said.

Nettie's hands went to her hips, her skinny elbows stuck out. "I have been robbed! Went out yesterday to take Lutie to the Grocery, and come home to a house that'd been tossed upside down. Made a terrible mess." She stepped closer to Huey. "You know what they took?" She whispered in his ear and Huey grinned. "Now that is a hoot, don't you say, preacher?"

"You don't seem so upset after all," Huey mused.

"Well, just the same, they violated me. And they took my bed coverings. What kind of sick pervert does that? Steals your bed coverings?"

"Did you call the Sheriff?" Jo asked.

Nettie looked at Jo like she was the smallest thing on earth. "Honey, it doesn't concern you who I called. But yes, as a matter of fact, I did call Sheriff Tuff. He just looked around, nosey little creep, and made a few notes. Said they was gonna investigate; but he ain't gonna." She brushed back mangled blonde hair with her fingers. "Preacher, I'll bet you'll say the reason I got robbed is because I don't tithe none, and so God brought down a curse on me."

"Nah, I think the reason you got robbed is because you let everyone know you hid money in yar house."

The sound of trumpets blasted from the door as the music grew even louder.

"Guess we oughta pray about it," Huey said.

"Guess so," Nettie agreed. "Pray they go to hell."

Huey started to lower his head to pray, and when Nettie closed her eyes, Huey stepped around her and into the church house.

■ ■ ■

Inside, the band seemed even more energized than the week before.

Huey surveyed the congregation. Of course, rich Floyd Carson wasn't back; but there were plenty of folk to take his spot. Every bench was claimed, and people, mostly black, pressed against the walls.

Huey was surprised to spot Earl and Dorothy Simpson up near the front with their grandson Dusty between them. Behind them was Katie and—AND!—that evil tax-man, Mr. Elias Moore.

He was back! Huey couldn't believe it. That rotten tax feller was like a boomerang that just kept coming round to hit him in the head.

Of course, hovering near by—one row over—was Otis Step.

"Sing it again!" Nettie Drake yelled when the band came to a stop. Her voice was angry. "This town needs some churchin'! And some hell fire."

"Hit it!" Dusty shouted, only to be elbowed by both grand-parents.

"Oh no," Shorty Parker objected. "It's sermon time. So come on up, Preacher House!"

"Come on, now!" Meemaw Moses called.

■ ■ ■

God was in the saving business that day. Sometimes he takes weeks or months or years to answer a prayer. But that morning, he not only plucked Jo out of the Baptist church, but he rescued Huey right at sermon time.

Huey started into his sermon about Jesus rising from the dead, when the windows shook and thunder crashed through the room. Only, it wasn't thunder.

"Good lawd! What was that?" Meemaw Moses gasped.

"Sounded like war cannons," Hammond Washington said. Hammond had served in the 369th *Infantry Regiment* during the Great War. It was a black unit that had gotten the nickname the *Harlem Hellfighters*. But ole Hammond was likely to declare any loud sound to be cannon fire, just to remind everyone that he was a real warrior. He also walked with a limp, a war injury, but sometimes he forgot which side his limp was on.

"That's not cannons," Meemaw shot back at Hammond. "Somethin' done blew up."

"Wrath of God," Nettie looked a little satisfied. "God got them people who ransacked my place."

"Nah, it's cannons," Boots chimed in. But he was already up and moving through the crowded room.

"Heavenly Days, McGee, we're all gonna die!" Dusty shouted. "Everyone out!"

Of course, he was slapped by both grandparents, but the stampede was almost immediate as people rushed for the door.

Outside, they found—

Nothing.

Maybe it was the wrath of God vindicating Nettie Drake.

Nothing except Lutie Dotson, staring numbly toward Blue Mountain and Boots standing right behind her, holding her extended hand.

Boots, who was the first one out, asked Lutie right away what had happened. She pointed at Blue Mountain and said, "I think something fell from the sky, and I seen a huge flame shoot up through the trees up yonder." She pointed to the mountain. "I don't see it now. But I saw it, I would swear to it."

Boots took the woman's extended hand in his own and moved it ever so slightly, so she was pointing at another ridge of Blue Mountain. "I seen it too, honey," Boots said. "But it come from over there."

She seemed a little confused. "Over there? Why, no! It came from…" she paused. "You saw it, too?"

"Yep."

"Fall from the sky and blow up?"

That was when everyone came out to see nothing but Lutie and Boots.

"I saw it first!" Lutie cried. "Right up there!" She pointed the direction Boots had given her. "Fell from the sky and done blew up. I saw fire come up in a big huff, and then just go away, like someone shut off the valve."

"You sure something fell from the sky?" Earl Simpson asked suspiciously.

"Sure it did!" Lutie said, adjusting her big hat with her free hand. "Martians probably! I think they have finally come."

"Martians!" Dusty echoed, perfectly mimicking the pitch of her voice.

"Ah, it ain't no Martians," Boots said. "Just an asteroid I think."

"Asteroid or meteor?" Shorty Parker asked.

"What's the difference?" Boots asked.

"I dunno," Shorty said. "Just so's we all talkin' 'bout the same thing. Giant rock comes from space and *WHAM*, gives planet earth a big kiss?"

"Sure," Boots agreed.

Shorty was excited, "There's a whole asteroid belt, and they bump one another, and go flying all over the solar system. Every day them rocks come our way to say howdy-do, but they get all burned up by our atmosphere. But every now and then the strong ones come on down to lay a big one on planet earth. Solar system's way of sayin' *I love you!*"

Elijah laughed, "More like a punch from the solar system. Like God's given the planet a black eye for bein' so wicked."

"Maybe we can find it," Dusty said excitedly.

"Nah, best leave it be," Boots said.

Elias Moore brushed at his suit and then pulled Katie back toward himself. "If it's a big one, the Government will be out this way to find it—if they can. I didn't hear an impact, but I sure did hear somethin' big."

"Not an asteroid!" Lutie was offended. "You and I both know the Martians landed right over there."

"This is ridiculous," Otis cried. "You people have got to have extra helpings of stupid! Whatever it was, I can guarantee you it wasn't Martians, and it sure wasn't an asteroid. If an asteroid hit the earth and made that big sound, Madison Creek would be leveled down to dust."

"Not necessarily," Mr. Moore corrected.

Otis rolled his eyes. This fella just wanted to say the opposite of whatever Otis point was.

"We need to hear the sermon," Meemaw Moses reminded them.

Huey was thoughtful. "I have a good sermon eatin' me up. It'd bring Billy Sunday back from the grave just to say amen and hallelujah. But, just the same, seems to me that if God is sending rocks our way, we should go find them. It might be a clue to some great plan he has for us."

"No!" Boot said at once. "Leave them be."

"No," Huey gave Boots a hard stare. "If things are coming from the heavens, it stands that the Little Rickety Church of Madison Creek wants to know what it is. We might drag that space rock—that Martian rock—into our church as a reminder of the God who made the heavens."

"Bad idea, Huey," Boots grunted.

"Not Martian rock," Lutie objected. "Martians. Their spaceship done crashed."

Shorty Parker said, "We would be famous if we found them. Get our names in the paper and probably a plaque from the Government." He looked toward Elias Moore. "You some kind of Government man, Mr. Moore?"

"Sure," Moore confirmed.

"What agency?"

"Federal Government. That's all I can say."

Katie smiled warmly.

"Let's go find it," Huey said excitedly. "And give praise to the creator."

Meemaw asked Huey to bless them before they left on their expedition.

"Lord," Huey called out. "If there be Martians, protect us from their death bombs. And if it be a rock from Mars or... or the asteroid belt—you help us find it right quick. Amen."

Dusty shouted, "Play ball!"

■ ■ ■

Huey had quite a group piled in his old pickup. For once, Jo didn't have to ride with her head in the window, she got to sit right between Boots and Uncle Huey. She could tell Boots was mad as a hornet.

Uncle Huey was leading a little parade of cars up the narrow mountain road. It was a makeshift road, and dangerous, since it sometimes gave way or washed out.

"You shoulda listened to me, Huey," Boots grunted.

"Well if stuff's fallin' out of the sky, don't you want to know what it was? Besides, I had just preached all the sermon I had."

Boots lowered his voice, "My friend, I don't think anything fell out of the sky."

"Well I heard it!" Huey's voice was loud. "I felt it! Somethin' came from the sky and kicked our planet in the behind."

"Nope," Boots whispered now. "That came from the ground. You get what I'm tellin' ya?"

Jo frowned thoughtfully, "What would come out of the ground? You talkin' monsters?"

Boots shook his head, and then stuck his thumb in his mouth and tipped his fast back as if he was taking a long drink.

"Whiskey?" Jo asked.

Boots motioned for her to quiet down.

"Ah, whiskey wouldn't crash into the earth," Huey said, his eye tight on the road.

There was a clearing ahead where the road came to an abrupt end. Towering over them was the mighty Blue Mountain. Jo wanted to climb Blue Mountain all the way to the top and then she might be able to pop her head into heaven and have a little talk with Jesus.

■ ■ ■

"I'm gonna be the first to find it!" Dusty exclaimed, breaking free of the hold Katie had on the boy's shoulder. Dusty ran hard toward the forest ahead. "Hi-ho Silver, away!"

"He's such an idiot," Clay said, loud enough for everyone to hear. "I can't catch him," Katie said, her eyes searching until she found Jo. "Would you just, maybe, follow him and make sure he's okay?"

Clay puckered his lips and made a kissing sound toward Jo.

"Knock it off." Otis gave Clay a light thump on the head. "You need to learn you some manners boy."

Clay reddened, "What you doin' hittin me, mister!" He spun around and slapped Otis in the face. Otis head turned toward the ground and he swung his arm around and caught Clay's neck. Otis locked the sixteen-year-olds' head between his armpit and his elbow and dropped to the ground.

"Let me up!" Clay shouted.

Otis laughed and rubbed Clay's head with his knuckles.

"You don't give Miss Simpson's boy no trouble," Otis demanded. "He's special and ought to be treated that way."

"I'll kill you," Clay growled. "Or my pa will. He'll find you and slit your throat."

"I ain't scareda your bum papa," Otis said, and gave Clay another rubbin' on the head with his knuckles.

"Let him up!" Katie pleaded. "Come on, Otis. I'm askin' ya real nice."

Otis looked thoughtful, but Jo could tell he was relishing the moment. "I'll do it if you're really askin' me to. But I think anyone who gives Dusty a hard time ought to be taught a lesson."

"Well, you taught it good," Katie said.

Otis let Clay go, and the boy squirmed away. "Bully," Clay grimaced.

"Jo, where's Dusty?" Katie asked.

Jo couldn't believe herself. She'd gotten so caught up in the fight, she'd forgotten all about Dusty. "Come on!" Jo said. "We gotta find him."

He wasn't far, she knew that as she took off toward the forest. She could hear him, talking to invisible Indians in his Lone Ranger voice.

■ ■ ■

Otis pressed his ear to the ground. He could feel the far away vibrations of — well, something. He stood up and dusted heavy dirt off his trousers. He glanced around, but Katie was gone, and so was Clay for that matter.

What was going on here? He still couldn't figure it out. Why had that man, Mr. Big Government, left all week, only to show up again on Sunday?

Otis thought he might be wrong about the reason for the church. Maybe it wasn't just a set up to allow Katie to get married and have a church wedding — or maybe it was. After all, this week her ma and pa had been the first to arrive at church. They beat all the blacks.

"Hey, you." A familiar voice startled Otis. He turned to see Katie standing there, beautiful as an angel.

"Hey back at-ja, doll."

She smiled a little. "Why'd you stick up for my boy like that?"

"'Cause I like your kid."

"You did it because you like my kid, or because you like me?"

"I done it 'cause I like Dusty. That's all. Whenever I'm around, he lights all up like a Christmas tree. And I like that, ya know?"

She stepped closer and put a hand on his arm. "Well, thank you. I do appreciate it. Sometimes you act like he's a big hassle."

He was overcome with the desire to beg her to take him back; to grovel. But after the last rejection at Sweet Tea's, he'd told himself he was done begging from her like a dog at the table. He was losing self -respect.

"Anyway, Dusty's my bud."

She leaned in suddenly and pecked him on the cheek. Her perfume wafted around him, mingling with the scent of trees for a moment.

"Thank you," she whispered in his ear.

He stood still, not sure what to do.

"Well, okay then," was all he could manage. Besides, coming behind Katie was Mr. Big Government-Man. He asked if everything was okay, and Katie said yes, except that she wasn't sure where Dusty had run off to.

■ ■ ■

Jo climbed up the steep grade. She dug her heel into bushes or tree trunks to give her leverage as she went. She called for Dusty, but he didn't answer. Besides, she could hear him, not too far away talking to Tonto. What was crazy was that she was pretty sure she heard Tonto speak back. *Was he with someone else?* The thought scared her a little. She wished Katie hadn't asked her to go find him. She felt responsible now, and that just sucked the fun right outta the day.

She pressed her foot against a tree trunk and launched herself forward. She ran up the mountainside until she could grab a tree trunk. Things leveled out a little, and she could see where the rain had carved a little landing. She hoped Dusty hadn't gone up any further.

Jo wondered what Boots was really upset about. Whatever had exploded, she was sure of two things: First, he knew what it was, and second, it involved—MOONSHINE! Doggone, either she was Sherlock Holmes, or Uncle Huey really didn't have any grain in his silo.

She followed the little path the rain had made, moving deeper into the trees and brush. Things felt darker, shadows moved with the wind. She spotted a blue-backed Barn Swallow with a bright red forehead up ahead. The swallow was sitting in the low branch of a spruce tree. The bird watched her as she maneuvered along the hillside.

Not far, she could still hear Dusty talking. She wished he would stand still. And she still wasn't sure who was playing his Indian friend. She slowed to catch her breath.

Dusty was a little below her, leaning against a tree and talking to—no one. He was the voice of the Indian she realized.

"Dang blasted Dusty," Jo griped. "I climbed way up here for nothin'!"

Dusty turned and waved. "Hi yo Jo-Jo. You want to be the Indian?"

"Don't call me Jo-Jo."

She worked her way to where he was. Still the forest was thick and she wondered if anyone else was worried about them, because she was starting to worry for the both of them.

"No, I don't want to be the Indian. I'm Ginger Rogers, the Lone Ranger's boss."

"Ginger Rogers is a movie star, she ain't the Lone Ranger's boss!" Dusty objected loudly.

"Where ya goin', Dusty?"

He pointed, "Right there."

She had to step down toward him to look.

"I don't see nothin'."

He shrugged. "I know. But that's where I'm goin'. That way."

"We might get lost."

"Lone Ranger never gets lost. Ginger Rogers would know that, orphan girl."

Rage suddenly burned up through her like hot lava. "Don't call me that!"

"Then don't be Ginger Rogers. Be that girl from the *Phantom of the Opera*, Christine, but I'll still be the Lone Ranger. And I'll ride in and shoot the Phantom and rip his mask—"

"Don't call me no orphan girl!" Spittle flashed from Jo's lips.

"Then pull your parents up out of the grave like Jesus and you won't be no orphan girl."

"Dusty, I'm gonna pop ya!"

He broke into a little run. He couldn't move to fast, because the slope was steep. She realized they had gone a good ways up and a fall would be painful.

"You're the Indian," Dusty cried as he ran, "Injun Jo!" He called for Silver to hi-ho once again.

"You know Injun Joe is from Tom Sawyer, right?" She put her hands on her hips. She was never going to catch him because he actually thought he was the Lone Ranger. "Listen Dusty, my tribe done kidnapped the banker, and I'm the only one who knows where's he's at."

"What's your tribe's name?"

"The Twain's."

"That's dumb. I never heard of no Twain tribe. But just the same, you better fess up and tell me where you done tied up the banker at, or I'll have to unload my bullets in ya."

Jo smiled, "Catch me." She took off in the direction they'd come from.

She ran as quick and hard as she could, but Dusty really was fast. It was as if Silver was right under him, galloping for all he was worth.

"Now you're mine!" Dusty cried.

He leapt through the air and landed on Jo. She hit the ground and started rolling down the slope. She tried to yell and tell Dusty to get off her, but it was hard to yell. She sensed the mountain side got steeper nearby and was about to use her elbows to stop them when she slammed into a rock.

"Ouch!" Dusty cried, falling aside.

■ ■ ■

The rock that had stopped their tumble jutted out from the green forested mountainside. It was dark brown, or maybe a little red. *Red*, Jo decided.

"Look at that stone!" Dusty said. His britches were torn and she could see blood on his elbow and forehead. But Dusty didn't seem to care about that. He was too interested in the rock. "Maybe this is the rock that fell out of the sky."

Jo sighed. "No. Look, it's coming out of the mountain, not going in."

Dusty shook his head, "Can't tell which side of a rock went in. I bet this is it, Jo. And the Lone Ranger found it."

More like Gracie Allen than the Lone Ranger, Jo thought.

The trees nearby had been burned recently, probably in a lightning storm.

"Come on."

He wouldn't come on. She tried another game, but he was too interested in the rock. It had to be *the* rock that had fallen out of the sky.

Finally, Jo made like she was going to leave, and started on without him. She was surprised he didn't chase after. She went a little ways and slid down behind a tree. She didn't want to get far. She only had a general idea of where they were.

He was fun to listen to. Dusty talked to the rock, asking it how far it had flown through space, and if it was from Mars. She thought at times he was waiting for the rock to answer him. It was from Mars, he decided out loud, and it was carrying Martian seeds. "Soon, the whole forest is going to be full of Martian plants."

Jo rolled her eyes. She was about to come get him and demand he come on—she'd have to use her firm Aunt Georgette voice—when the brush rustled nearby. Someone was coming. She slid back into her place beside the tree.

"Hey, Dusty, what-ja doin'?"

It was Clay. He sounded nice enough, but Jo had a suspicion that after a painful humiliation like Otis had dished on him, he wasn't going to be real friendly. She could hear them, but dared not look. She didn't want to have a scene with Clay.

DUSTY: Thinkin' that maybe this here rock is the biggie that fell out of the sky.

CLAY: You better believe it. Kinda red, ain't it? Like it fell from Mars. You know, the Martians are headed this way. For real, Dusty. They're comin' to land on earth. Some of 'em already landed. They send Martians ahead of the invasion force. They send them as babies, and the Martian spies don't even know they're Martians. They look just like us. But they don't quite… you know… fit in.

DUSTY: Really?! Like stupid Mule Evermund. I'll bet he's one, huh?

CLAY: Well, that's not quite where I was goin' with that.

DUSTY: I did! The Lone Ranger solved another puzzle. That's two for today. I found the rock and the Martian. I can't wait to tell Injun Jo.

CLAY: You ever hear of Hickory Joe, Dusty? He's a killer who roams Blue Mountain, slicing people up and eating their innards.

DUSTY: Yeah, I've heard of Hickory Joe. Everyone heard of him.

CLAY: Think about that name, Dusty. Hickory Joe. Jo House. I'll bet she's named after that ole bugger. You should tell her that, Dusty.

DUSTY: Ah, now you're just tryin' to get me in trouble. She'll sock me, and hard, too. But I'll bet you're right about those Martians. They're dropping stuff off on our world before their big invasion.

CLAY: Sure. But I just don't think poor Mule Evermund would be the only one to come on down here to our neck of the woods. Who else doesn't fit in? Who else might be a Martian, Dusty? I heard that radio waves go out into space. All over space. They got radio bouncing off the moon, and even the planet Mars. I think any Martian would have to the partial to radio. The Martian would feel like a real freak show, you know? Kind of like they don't fit in. The Martian might not even know they're a Martian.

DUSTY: Are you a Martian, Clay?

CLAY: You stupid! You're the Martian!

■ ■ ■

"Well now you're just askin' for it!" Jo said, coming from the tree she'd been hiding behind.

Clay's eyes were wide with surprise as Jo came toward them.

"Hey, Jo," Clay said with a polite nod. He combed his finger through his hair.

"You call me Hickory Joe, Clay? Is that what you called me?"

"I was just funnin' with him. Can't you take no joke?"

"You're a joke," Jo said. She stepped up onto the rock and traced her way along the top of it. It jutted out a good three feet from the mountain side, but it was narrow and bumpy. Jo eased her way across the rock until she stood at the edge. If there had been water below, it would have been a perfect diving board. "And I'm gonna tell you somethin', Clayton. Somethin' that might surprise you. This here rock, it's the real deal," she nodded with personal satisfaction. "Look at how the earth is scarred all around it. You think you're tricking Dusty, all the while you done found the real thing. Ain't you a fool?"

"Nah, it's just a rock," Clay said.

"A red rock, in the forest, with burn marks all around? Maybe I'd believe that, if lots of people hadn't seen fire blaze up from here."

Clay nodded agreement, "Well, yeah. That's true."

Jo scuffed her shoe across the surface of the rock, "Besides, I feel somethin' when I get near it. Don't you?"

Clay frowned, "Not really."

Dusty was enthusiastic. "Yep! Yes! I feel it!"

Jo shivered a bit, letting a wave of Martian energy pulse over her. "Don't tell no one, Clay, but I think this rock done give me powers."

"Shut up!"

"Really, Clay, powers!"

"What kind of powers?"

Jo opened her eyes wide, "Power to see into you. Through you. See the gunk all over ya heart."

Dusty clapped, "Clay got gunk on him!"

"Oh, he got it bad!" Jo declared, averting her eyes from Clay as if looking toward him was painful.

Clay laughed nervously. "Stop it. It's just a rock." Then, looking around at the burned trees, "And even if it is a Martian rock, it's not gonna give you no powers."

"I read *Action Comics* book number 1," Dusty offered. "A boy from another planet comes to earth, and he has powers."

"What planet he come from?" Clay queried.

"Didn't say. Mars, probably. Everything comes from Mars."

Jo looked right at Clay again, her eyes big. "You have evil down in ya."

"What evil?" Clay demanded.

"All I see is something green—a scout tent I think. And there you are, wicked as can be. I see you peeing all over that tent." She grasped at her eyes as if the vision was more than she could bear. "Oh no! Someone is rolled up in the tent! You aren't just peeing on a tent, you're peeing on a person!"

"Pa!" Clay cried, and realized at once he didn't want to reveal what he had done to his pa, he modified it to, "Po-possum!"

"No possum," Jo said, trance like. "Person." She held her hands to her head as if focusing. "Just trying to see who it is under there. The rock sees. It's comin' out of the rock. I think it wants you, Clay. Not Dusty, he's too simple."

"Hey!" Dusty shouted.

Clay punched Dusty in the arm. "Shut up, somethin' big is happening here!" Then, his eyes narrowed. "Did your Uncle Huey tell you what I told him?"

She shivered, "It's the rock, Clay." Then she decided to be a little more daring. She would have to rely on some good ole playground gossip, but she was willing to bet it was true. She'd heard that Clay had dropped a rat down Scabby Duncan's pants and Scabby had wet his pants. That was worth chasing. "I can't believe what I see."

Clay waved her off. "You're a fraud."

"A rat." Jo repeated.

"Yep. You're a fraud and a rat."

"RAT!" Jo screamed, horror brimming up. "It's sliding down..." She screamed in terror at what she saw. "A rat is sliding down Scabby Duncan's pants! Oh my. Is it alive, Clay?"

"No!" Clay shouted. His mouth hung wide in disbelief. He didn't know anyone knew about that except him and Scabby. "That happened a long time ago."

"I see it right now, like it's happening. It just happens over and over in the Martian time loop. He's so scared, Clay." She giggled, "But I do believe he sprung a leak in his pants..." She let out a loud moan and threw herself from the rock toward Clay. Clay backed away, stumbled over his own feet and bumped into a tree.

Jo sat shaking.

Dusty jumped on the rock, "Talk to me, rock!"

"Get ya self off of there, you moron!" Clay yelled. "We don't need anyone else seein' nothin'!"

Jo sounded tired when she finally spoke. "Everyone's gonna see it, Clay. They'll all see what I saw. I don't know what you told my uncle, because he doesn't say squat to me about church stuff. But I know you peed on that green tent, and someone was inside it. I don't know who yet, but I'll bet if I spent some more time on that rock, I'd figure it out. We gotta show everyone where the rock is."

Clay grimaced. "No, let's just leave it be. It's just a rock."

"I'll bet some people are sensitive, like me. Others will see what I saw, or more."

Dusty pointed at the rock, and spoke in broken English. Jo knew right away, he was doing the Mad Russian from the *Eddie Cantor Show*. "I claim this rock in the name of my native country, Russia, and my home city, Paris."

Clay looked confused, "Paris isn't in —"

Jo grinned, "Well hello, Mad Russian."

"How dooooo you do! And I now must warn you to keep the rock a secret. A big secret! It come from Mars but it belongs to Russia!"

"He's a moron," Clay grunted.

"You better stop messin' with him, or I might just bring the whole town up to this rock, and they can see for themselves what you done."

"You're full of horse poop," Clay said.

"You think I don't hear you?" Dusty was still in Mad Russian mode. "Horse poop man?"

"Let me ask you something, Russian," Jo said.

"Yes, speak, speak."

"What should be done with this simple American?"

"He should be peed on!" the Russian declared. "But he will probably run away, so instead he should..." he paused, thinking.

"He should say sorry for being a rascal to my friend Dusty," Jo suggested.

"Oh gosh, this is stupid," Clay moaned.

"Then just say sorry."

"Sorry."

"No," Jo said, indignantly. "Kneel down and apologize."

"No way!"

The Mad Russian liked that. "Yes, yes, yes! Kneel before the Russian!"

"No way!"

Jo stepped toward the rock. "I think maybe I didn't get all the information the rock wanted to give me."

"Your rock is just a rock."

She stepped out onto the rock. "It is warm."

"Fine!" Clay's eyes were narrow and angry. He knelt down in front of Dusty. "I'm sorry."

"Oh no, Russian not forgive you," Dusty said in his perfect Russian accent. "You must polish Russian's shoe."

"Polish your face."

"Dusty, accept the apology," Jo instructed.

"Fine, I accept your apology," the Russian said. "But when we invade America, you shall be peed upon!"

"Get lost," Clay said. He got up and headed back the way he came.

Glove Box

As soon as they were back from their trip up Blue Mountain, Boots told Huey they needed to return. Huey was ready, but Boots wanted to wait for the cover of darkness.

"Where you goin'?" Jo asked.

"Just to pray," Boots said at once. The old bugger was as nervous as a turkey before Thanksgiving.

Of course they weren't going to let her go with them. She waited in her room until the darkness came, and when Huey and Boots climbed into Huey's old truck, she slipped out her bedroom window and slid down the porch pillar. The old truck thundered to life and was moving before Jo expected.

I'm Flash Gordon, she told herself in Dusty's voice. She ran hard and was about to leap into the back of the truck when the heel of her foot struck a rock. She stumbled, but didn't lose her balance. She had to keep running, if she let herself fall—it was so dark—she might really hurt herself; and she'd never catch up with the truck.

Come on, Jo, you don't want to miss this, she said to herself, picking up the pace.

She leapt through the dark toward the bed of the truck. She landed just as Huey gave the engine some more gas, and the truck lurched with renewed energy. She fell backward, striking her tailbone on a rock. She rolled several times, feeling rocks bite at her as she went. She was surprised how hard she'd fallen, considering the truck couldn't have been going that fast. And, even as she tumbled, she was surprised that the old truck lumbered on. Hadn't Uncle Huey heard her? Surely he knew that big thump was her! Didn't he know she'd be coming along?

Pain screamed through her. Not just her tail bone, she'd struck her head on something, and something else snagged her leg. It had been a long scratching sensation that she'd hardly been able to take in when it happened; but now as she lay on the ground catching her breath, her leg became a giant exclamation point. Something was wrong. She wasn't sure if she was hurt bad, or if it was just a scrape. She reached to rub away the pain and realized her hands were full of dirt, and little rocks were pressed into her palms.

"You old skunk!" Jo yelled. The truck was long gone. But she knew where they were going — Blue Mountain; and in the dark. What could be more fun?

She started to stand, wobbled a bit, and fell back to the ground.

"Stupid old men," Jo yelled again. Warm tears, unbid and unwelcome, streamed down her cheeks. They must have known that was her trying to get in the truck. They couldn't even turn around and see if she was okay?

Jo dusted her hands hard, rubbing the rocks away. Then she pushed up her dress and reached for her leg. As she'd feared, it was wet; very wet.

She spoke to herself in the voice of the Mad Russian, *How dooo you do? I do think I peed myself.* She hoped that little bit of silliness might chase off the tears. She hated feeling sorry of herself, but how else was a girl to feel when those who are supposed to care for her drove off, leaving her bleeding in the dark?

She looked back toward the house with disappointment. Her heart had been so set on adventure. She really did hurt. She'd hate to have to admit —.

OH GOSH GOLLY! She hadn't thought of that. She was going to have to tell Aunt Georgette what she'd done. An idiot storm would ensue and she'd be grounded… or beat… or who knows what.

Well, they never actually beat her. "I'll tan your hide," Uncle Huey would say when he got riled up. But he never laid a hand on her. And for that matter, neither did Georgette. They might ground her to her room, or make her skip a meal, or chew her out — but she didn't get any of the lickins her friends got. Even when she got kicked out of Mount Hallelujah Leper Colony and driven home in Mr. Step's hearse, they didn't tar and feather her or even spank her with their bare hands.

She had always figured it was because she was good at getting out of trouble. Kids in her class were always talking about how they got taken to the woodshed and beat silly. *It's because they don't love me,* she thought as new tears salted her face. *If they loved me, they'd beat me hard and take me to the woodshed and do whatever angry parents do out at the woodshed.*

Then perhaps, she thought, because her Guardian angel had heard her little pity party — headlamps flashed up ahead.

She was on the side of the road, but she didn't want him to miss her. "You came back for me!" she cried with joy. Forgetting her pain for a moment, she stepped into the road and waved her arms. "You came back, you old nasty skunk of an uncle!"

But it wasn't Uncle Huey. This was a car. But not just a car, it was a sedan.

"Mr. Big Government-Man, you better not run me down!" Jo shouted. "I'm not a mobster!"

She imagined him slamming on the brakes, the car skidding sideways and dirt splattering the whitewall. He would come out of the car with his Tommy Gun and spray her with bullets.

Of course, he didn't, because the only adventure she might have had that night had driven on to Blue Mountain without her.

Mr. Moore stopped the car and came out, one leg still in the car, his elbows resting on the half open door.

"Josephine, right?" He sounded more proud of himself than the fact that he'd just discovered her alone on the long drive up to the house covered in dirt and blood. Gosh, even the big Government didn't care about her.

"Ain't ya gonna ask me what happened to me?"

It finally registered to him that something was unusual. "Well?"

"I got beat up by the mob and left for dead here on the side of the road. Same criminals that killed my parents. Come after me and pulled me out of my room. They were driving me off to shoot me, but I jumped out—"

"Really?"

She shrugged, "Ah, I's just out playin' and got hurt jumpin from a tree."

It was hard to see him because she was the one standing in the headlights, but she thought she saw his face tighten. "Are you running away?"

"Yeah, sure, that's what I'm doin'. Does the Government want to take me in? I'd like to live in the White House with Mrs. Roosevelt. She's the one that really runs this country, ya know?"

"Get in the car, I'll drive you on up to the house."

"Suppose I say no."

"You gonna tell a man who works for the United States Government no?"

She thought for a moment. What if he, with all his nice smell and pretty car, was really somethin' bad? What if he was one of those men who did unspeakable things to girls and then said they were full of lies? But he didn't give her that vibe.

■ ■ ■

Mr. Moore hesitated to let her get into the car. She was dirty, and he didn't even see how bloody her leg was. She pulled her dress tight around the leg and scooted down a bit so she wouldn't get blood on the car seat.

"You have children?" she asked as soon as they were moving. It wasn't far up to the house, and she wanted a chance to ask him some questions while it was just the two of them. But HOLINESS how her leg was starting to sting. She hoped this would not require a visit to the doctor. Aunt Georgette would tell her all about the Depression and being poor and not having money for a doctor. Guilt—that's how they punished her, Jo decided. They didn't take her to the woodshed; they guilted her, and that was worse.

"No, no children," Mr. Moore said.

"You married?"

"No," he said quickly. "Are you?"

"I'm eleven!"

Jo looked back to see a file on one seat, and a rag doll in the other.

"The doll is for my sister Norma. She loves dolls." He stopped in front of the house. "Well, I just have a little business to do with your uncle."

"You gonna take him to jail?"

"No. I do have to finish up some documents and get them sent on up to the office in New York. This story has been making the rounds, no one believes it, and —" he stopped himself.

"Remember the mobsters who came after me and I escaped?"

"Okay. Yes."

"Well, they stole Uncle Huey."

Mr. Moore opened his door. "Well, you coming?"

"I'd rather not."

"Might as well face the music, whatever you got comin' to ya."

"Why'd it take you all day to get out here?" Jo asked.

He was quiet for a moment. "You tell me somethin' Jo, and no fibbing, okay?"

"Sure. I hate fibbers."

"That girl, Katie, the one who lead the music last week — has she had many…" he wasn't sure how to finish his question.

"Many cats?"

He didn't answer. Of course Jo knew what he meant, but even with her leg and her head hurting, not to mention her behind, she couldn't resist playing this hand out.

"Many dogs? Many cars?"

"No, you know what I was going to ask."

"You gotta say it for me to answer it."

"Gentlemen callers," Mr. Moore finally said.

"Men! You want to know if she's had many men chasing after her? Boy, I don't know. I reckon plenty, 'cause she's pretty. And she works at a café, where lots of men come through. But I never seen her with any except her boy."

"And what about that troublemaker, Otis?"

Jo shrugged, "Never seen him before the other day. Why? Did he punch you?"

"Not exactly," Mr. Moore said.

"Reason you're late getting out here is because somethin' happened with Katie, huh?" Jo decided it couldn't hurt to press things a little. "You and her have a kiss and Otis beat you to the ground like he did Clay?"

The front door opened and Aunt Georgette stepped out. Light from inside the house cascaded around her. Jo thought she looked very pretty, and even a little angelic with the light making a halo all around her.

"What in the blazes do you want?" Aunt Georgette asked.

Mr. Moore swung his door shut and approached the porch.

Jo squeezed her leg, trying to force the pain to go somewhere else. She pulled down a little more of her dress and bunched the fresh fabric against her bleeding leg.

She was about to get out when she remembered the file laying in the backseat. That must be Uncle Huey's file. Suppose she swiped that file—would Mr. Moore still be able to mail off his report to New York?

She reached back, working hard not to let her leg touch the seat, and tried to grab the folder. It was just a little too far. She tried again, and again. Finally she wiggled around and got up on her knees. Just barely—she didn't want to get his seat messy, that would be impolite. She grabbed the folder and slid back into the seat. Sure enough, in neat handwriting across the top was:

House, Huey

There was a number with it, probably the number they were going to give Uncle Huey in jail.

She'd have to act quick, but if there was a way to cause that file to just disappear, she might make all Uncle Huey's troubles disappear with it. After all, they couldn't have a case without a case file, right?

She thought about getting out of the car and just stuffing it up her dress, but that was too dangerous.

Fire. If she could burn it. It was a crazy idea, but supposing he had a lighter in his glove box, then maybe she could find a way to slip out of the car with the file, run out into the woods — even with her bleeding leg — and give the file a little breath from hell with the lighter. She could run all the way out to where the family burned the trash, she knew the way by heart. Later, when she would tell Uncle Huey about it, he would be all the more thankful because she did it while in pain and…

No time to mess around. She snapped the glove box open, and the lighter rolled with a strange metal clinking sound. That wasn't a lighter, she realized. The glove box was empty, except she had heard something. She ran her hand through the glove box, and finally found what she was looking for in the dark. It wasn't a lighter at all.

On the porch, Mr. Moore was talking to Aunt Georgette, but looking back toward his sedan.

She pushed the glove box shut, which now sounded very empty, and held her new find tight in her fist.

"Jo!" Georgette stepped away from Mr. Moore and looked toward the sedan. Apparently he had just told her that Jo was in the car. Must be his way of getting her out without making a fuss himself.

"All right, all right," she said.

■ ■ ■

Her injuries and Uncle Huey's absence sent Mr. Moore on his way. He seemed suspicious that maybe Huey was hiding. He reminded Aunt Georgette that he could get the Sheriff and search the house. Georgette ignored him and told Jo to strip on down to her underwear. That got rid of the tax-man, who said he'd mail them a copy of his report.

Georgette laid out a towel on the floor for Jo to sit on.

"You are a barrel of trouble, child," Georgette said.

"Thank you." Jo was happy that her aunt launched right into guilt and shame. She didn't mind it so much, now that she realized guilt was Georgette's woodshed.

"Your calf is tore up somethin' fierce. I'm afraid we'll have to get a doctor to stitch it up. That'll mean money we don't have. Let me see your head."

Georgette wrapped Jo's leg tight with a strip she cut from one of Huey's old shirts. Of course this would happen when Huey wasn't home, she ranted. Of course he'd leave her with a mess.

"You know you are grounded forever," Georgette said.

"Maybe you could take me to the woodshed," Jo offered.

"What did you say, child?" Georgette felt Jo's head for fever.

"Listen to me, I want you to beat me," Jo said stubbornly. "Like real parents. I want you to take a switch and—"

"Stop your foolishness, Jo, someone's comin'."

Headlights beamed through the big parlor window as the car approached.

Georgette waited for the knock, but she didn't open the door. Instead she demanded the other person identify themselves. Jo realized her aunt must think that Mr. Tax-Man had actually decided to come back and make a search of the house. But it wasn't Mr. Moore, it was Katie Simpson. Jo was a little surprised she was alone; she didn't even know Katie knew how to drive a car. She was always with her father... or lately, Mr. Moore.

"Is Mr. House here?" Katie asked. "I need to talk to a preacher."

"He's out praying," Georgette said stiffly.

Peeking in, Katie asked, "Is she okay?"

"No, she's not okay. I'm going to have to call the doctor. More money we don't have down the drain."

"What's wrong with her?"

"She's a heathen," Georgette said at once, then realizing that was inappropriate, she said, "Sorry. I mean, she tore up her leg somethin' awful. Cut it up pretty deep. I got it to stop bleeding, but just the same, it won't heal right without some stitches. Probably let her rest tonight and take her on in to the doctor's office tomorrow."

"She bang her head?" Katie was quizzical. "Because it looks like she's pretty scuffed up."

"Deserves it, the rascal."

"I have an idea, if you want her seen tonight."

"That leg'll still be attached to her in the mornin'," Georgette said.

"True, but someone better clean it out, or it'll get infected somethin' fierce," Katie warned.

"I ought to make Huey take her in. Let him find the money to drop in the doctor's wallet."

"Really, my way won't cost ya much."

"Okay, where?" Georgette was suspicious.

■ ■ ■

Jo slipped on a nightgown that Georgette complained would be just ruined by the time this *episode* was over. Katie held off telling Georgette where they were going, the pretty blonde just insisted she knew someone who could help.

The Simpson's car was smaller than Mr. Big Government's, but Jo was happy it had a back seat, too. She was even happier when she found Katie's new beagle, Charlie Mac, was back there. Katie had named the dog after the radio program *Charlie McCarthy*.

As they drove off the property and toward town, it seemed the women forgot she was there.

"Mrs. House, I wanted to talk to the preacher, but maybe God wants me to talk to you. You *are* the preacher's wife."

"Honey, I'd be here for you even if I was a widow."

Jo reckoned her aunt enjoyed that thought way too much.

Katie talked in an ever lowering voice about being lonely. There were young men in town who gave her lots of attention, but they were either scared off by her pa or Dusty. It was one thing for a single woman to have a child, but Dusty was a special kind of child.

"Oh trust me, honey," Georgette said. "I understand special children."

Jo wondered what that was supposed to mean. She held Charlie Mac a little closer to her. She could feel his compassion right away as the dog snuggled, and then took to licking her face.

"Every time a man does take a liking to me, Rose Abernathy or Helen Card or one of those younger girls have to saunter by, and the gentleman just go chasing. I just hate those young girls."

"How old are you?" Georgette asked the same thing Jo was wondering.

"Twenty-five. Almost an old maid."

Georgette laughed, "Not hardly, honey. Besides, Rose Abernathy's nigh-about the same age."

"Sure, but she's not tied up with a kid." Katie turned onto Main Street. "It never works out for me. And then Elias came to town. He is a gentleman, isn't he?"

"Time will tell." Georgette was non-committal.

They passed Minnie Belle's shop, Sweet Tea's, the barber's and the corner of Main and Clark,

"Katie, honey, where are we going?" Georgette asked.

Katie paid her no mind and just rambled on with her earlier thought. "You know, a nice man—an employed man, no less, comes to town and pays me a little attention, and my heart goes all a flutter."

"You have feelings for him?"

"Well, he lives up state in Charlotte. But you don't think he came all the way back to Madison Creek today just to finish up business with the church, do you?"

The car tires did a familiar THUMP-THUMP over the railroad track.

"Katie, are we headed into Jordan Town?" Georgette demanded.

"We're in it now," Jo said and gave Charlie Mac an enthusiastic squeeze.

■ ■ ■

Jordan Town. It was mix of shanties and real houses popping up here and there. Most of the houses were down off the road, surrounded by other little dwellings and sheds. Jordan Town had a church, but no one went to it since the preacher took up snake handling. There were not even many lights. Barber shops and other little businesses were done out of people's homes. Most of the people worked down in the Carson Mine.

Katie slowed even more, it felt like they were crawling. "I don't want to miss my turn," she said.

"Okay, sweetie, time to tell me where we're going."

"Don't get mad."

Jo couldn't believe her aunt actually had to have it spelled out for her. *Good grief, we're either going to Doctor Banks' house or…* she couldn't think of an or. The only place they would be going would be to see Doctor Banks.

"Katie!" Georgette was distressed.

But, Katie had found her turn and didn't pay Georgette any attention.

Doctor Banks lived down off the road in a nice little cabin like house, with a big front porch that reminded Jo of Uncle Huey's big red porch. It was just a one story house, constructed of logs that Jo figured would have made Abe Lincoln proud. In the distance she could hear people talking and laughing. Someone was playing the harmonica. It was almost romantic, Jo thought — unless you had to live there.

The doctor had already gone to bed when the white women came knocking on his door. Georgette was mortified. Doctor Banks came out in his long night shirt, talked to the women for a moment. Jo couldn't hear what they were saying, but she could put it together just by watching them. Doctor Banks was much more happy to have them there than the ladies were happy to be there.

Finally, Jo was summoned. She had thought maybe some men might come out and carry her, but she had to walk on up to the porch. There was a wash tub leaning against the rail in the corner, and a considerable pile of newspapers beside the rocking chair. They were secured with a rock. Doctor Banks wanted them to come on into the house—he wasn't scared of a little blood—but Aunt Georgette insisted they could do their business out on the porch.

Charlie Mac followed after Jo, making joyful little circles around her. She almost tripped over the dog. Katie swooped the dog up and put him back in the car.

"I sure would like to hold Charlie Mac," Jo said.

"Don't you go getting attached to someone else's dog," Georgette warned.

She sat down in a big white rocker Doctor Banks had on his porch. With a kerosene lamp humming beside him, Doctor Banks knelt down and examined Jo's leg. It hurt to the touch, but he didn't back away when Jo squealed a little. "That's okay," he said, still examining the wound, "Gotta hurt for it to get better."

Doctor Banks wife, Bernice, stood in the doorway watching. She seemed as uneasy as Aunt Georgette.

"How'd ya do this?" Doctor Banks asked.

"Was runnin' in the dark and took a tumble. Scraped my leg on somethin'. A rock maybe."

"No, Miss Jo, not a rock. I'd take a guess it was somethin' metal."

Bernice excused herself, but didn't go inside; she stepped down off the porch, taking a lamp with her. The doctor asked where she was going, and she said she wanted to check on X.

"Well, you give me a minute; I think I can fix this up. Gonna hurt, because I gotta scrub it out first. Ya got all kinds of dirt and grime down under the skin. Wish ya hadn't taken so long to find me, 'cause it stands to get infected."

"Does that lead to rickets or scarlet fever?" Jo worried.

He said it did not lead to either of those, but he did seem concerned. The doctor went in the house to get supplies, and when he returned he warned this would sting just a little bit. It didn't sting a *little* bit—it stung a *lot*! That was just the disinfectant, he warned. He still had to get down and scrub the dirt out of there before stitching her up. The word stitches made Jo cringe.

Doctor Banks was well into his work when Bernice came back with Big X trailing after her.

"Howdy doctor," Big X said, and gave a nod to Jo and then the other two ladies on the porch. "Ladies, how you be?"

Georgette couldn't have looked any more humiliated. "We're just fine, Big X. How are you?"

"I fine and dandy. Just come over this way to, uh, watch the good doctor work. Thought I'd say howdy-do."

"Well howdy-do," Georgette said in a voice that wanted to dismiss him. Only, they weren't at Georgette's house, they were at the doctor's place.

Jo realized the harmonica music had disappeared and figured it must have been Big X sitting up late.

"You come on up here and hold the light for me," Doctor Banks instructed.

Jo wondered if Big X usually helped Doctor Banks.

When Jo looked down in a moment of pain, she saw children gathered at the porch and standing back in the shadows. "Hi y'all," Jo said with a little wave. Aunt Georgette shushed her, and the other kids did not respond.

The stitches hurt, and she worked hard not to cry. She might have cried if it was just her and the adults, but those kids gathered at the foot of the porch made her uneasy.

"You wanna scream ya ole head off, huh Jo?" A familiar voice asked. It was Virgil Parker, Shorty Parker's boy.

"Ah, it don't hurt me none," Jo boasted. "Feels a little good."

Doctor Banks had to pause to keep his hand steady. The mosquitoes had found them. They did a little fluttering dance around the kerosene lamp. Katie took her hat off and began to wave it up and down to keep the mosquitoes from her.

"Yep, I think I'll come get me some stitches every night," Jo said, and the children giggled.

Of course, it didn't feel good. A needle digging in and out of her skin felt like being stabbed over and over. What did feel good was when the doctor finally wrapped the wounded leg nice and tight and even gave it a little pat. "You can walk, but no more runnin' for a while, you understand?"

She said she did, and Aunt Georgette, who had been quiet as a mouse, asked what his fee was.

Banks looked from the girl to her aunt. "Well, if I don't charge you somethin' you'll object mighty fierce. So how about this, you keep those prayers comin' for me and Bernice. You pray that the Lord look over us here in Jordan Town."

"You want us to pray for Jordan Town?"

He shrugged, "Prayers be worth more than a truckload of money. As ole James said, it be far better to be lowly and right with God than rich and mighty in the world. God'll stomp out the rich."

Georgette nodded.

Doctor Banks added, "And while you're down on your knees talkin' to God, pray for the men who go down in the mines. We're right thankful for the mines, because they give us work. But they're dangerous, ya know?"

"Boy, are they!" Jo interjected. "Sammy Peak lost his eyesight —"

"Jo, hush up," Georgette warned.

Banks lowered his voice. "The Carson Mine is a small time operation, ya know? Not as big or safe as other operations. They might not have blown the mine up, but I see plenty of people who have had some kind of mishap down in the earth diggin' up that coal. But how about this, Mrs. House, I'll pray for your side of town if you pray for mine."

"Well, okay. I'll do that," Georgette agreed reluctantly. She swatted away a mosquito.

"Now what can I pray for?" Doctor Banks asked.

Jo jumped on that, "Pray they don't make me go to Christian Camp next summer."

■ ■ ■

It took a long time to get home. When they did, Huey was sour as a lemon. Where had they gone, he demanded, and what did they mean, leaving him to come home to an empty house with no note? Someone had cut up his favorite undershirt and there was blood all over.

Jo thought it strange that instead of being worried about them he was mad.

"I go out to see to a church emergency, and you go runnin' all over town?" Huey griped as soon as Katie had said her goodbyes and they came into the house.

"Emergency? You didn't run out to no church emergency. I've been the one seein' to the emergency, Huey! Oh, I could just wring your neck right now!" Georgette fumed.

Jo limped in and was actually glad to see Huey hadn't done any clean up. She had hidden her find from the glove box in her clothes, and they were piled up in the parlor. When she had secured it, she left Huey and Georgette to have their blow out while she worked her way upstairs. She could hear them from her room. The Huey side of the argument said that Georgette didn't have any business running around town, and certainly Jordan Town, after dark. And the Georgette side of the argument held that Huey had been doing too much sneaking around for her taste.

■ ■ ■

Too bad they had to have this fight, because Georgette really should tell Huey what Katie had told her on the drive home. They thought Jo was asleep, laid out in the backseat with Charlie Mac on her chest. But Jo hurt too bad to sleep. Katie drove them up the big hill to the church house. They sat, staring not at the church, but at the big grass field beside the church.

Katie had told Aunt Georgette what happened after everyone pooped out on searching for an asteroid. When everyone else went on down the mountain, she and Elias stayed to talk.

"Did he put his hands on you?" Aunt Georgette asked directly.

Katie looked out her window. "Well, not right directly. We did talk a while. Up there on that mountain, it felt like we was the only ones in the whole wide world. Elias told me he came back to see me. He said he was stretching things out as much as he could with the church situation just so he could keep visiting me. Ain't that kinda rotten?" She didn't give Georgette a chance to respond. "But sorta sweet. I said maybe I could come visit him some time, and he got funny about that. Said it wasn't safe for a girl to be traveling about."

"Try telling that to Annie Evermund. She rode her motorcycle to New York this summer."

"His father died in an auto accident, and he's the breadwinner for his mother and little sister."

"He lives with his mother?" Georgette queried. "Grown man with a good job, somethin's wrong, Katie, if he hasn't landed a woman yet. Don't you think?"

"Well, there's Norma to think of. That's his little sister. See, she got the polio real bad and can't walk. She's a sweetie, I can tell just by the way he lights up when he talks about her."

As she talked, her voice slowed and finally came to a stop. It was as if there was something ahead she didn't want to share. Georgette let the uneasy quiet settle around them. Finally, Katie took in a long breath and said, "Oh Mrs. House, I just gotta tell someone. You can hold onto a secret, right?"

Georgette put her arm around Katie. "You tell me what you like, so long as it makes your soul a little lighter."

Jo shut her eyes tight.

"He didn't kiss me, Mrs. House. He was as polite a gentleman as you might expect. Why, there we were, sitting on the hood of his car, talking like there was no tomorrow. And finally, I just couldn't help myself. I leaned in and gave him a little peck on the cheek."

"Nothin' sinful about that, you're a grown woman."

"Well, he kissed me back, but on the lips."

Georgette was getting aggravated with the play by play. "Honey, I'm not the judge of you."

But Katie needed to tell—and tell she did. How they kissed, and how it felt like heaven. How he smelled up close, and how she even put her hands through his hair. Jo had been unable to believe her aunt didn't cut this off. Maybe Georgette was enjoying the story as much as Jo was.

"And then, like a shotgun," Katie said, "Rotten Otis come and scared me half to death."

"He yell at you?"

Katie was suddenly sheepish, "No, not exactly. He just said he was surprised we were still there. And I got sore, Mrs., I got sore with him and I cursed at him. Can you believe that?"

Jo couldn't believe it, and she had to hold Charlie Mac a little tighter to keep from gasping out loud.

"I never cursed at nobody! But I did him. I told him he was making me so miserable. And Otis just said he was concerned about me, since no one ever saw this man before. He asked me if I was sure I knew who he was. Boy, I told him that I knew who Elias was; he's the tax-man. And Otis, he has to say, 'well what's a Tax-Man doin' in this neck of the woods?'"

"Well, did you tell him it's none of his business?" Georgette asked.

"Boy did I. And I told him more than that. I told him it didn't matter if Elias and I were having an all-out affair. Both men got all red when I said that. It was kinda funny, their faces were like matching red balloons. But Otis, he says to me, 'I just think you should find out more about a fella when he just rides into town out of nowhere. 'Cause I've seen him before up in New York. With his wife!'"

"Really? Do you think that's true?"

"Otis can spin a tale faster than a master weaver. But when he said Elias had a wife, my heart sunk like the Titanic. Elias, he got real mad at that. He told Otis he was a liar, and that he hadn't hardly been to New York except on a couple of business trips. Otis just shrugged and said he seen what he seen. Elias told Otis to stop stirrin' up trouble where there was none. Otis asked him if maybe his wife was a pretty brunette, and you know what Elias done?"

"I hope he told him to take a hike."

"Oh no, Elias come down off the hood of the car and he lifted his hand like he was gonna hit Otis. And Otis, he thought it was funny. He said, 'Wow, Mister Tax-Man has a temper when his secrets get exposed.' And then Elias punched him right in the face."

Jo gave Charlie Mac another squeeze. Good for Otis! But Aunt Georgette and Katie did not seem to see it that way.

Katie managed to calm Elias down, and then they drove on down the hill. Jo wondered how Otis got down, but no one else seemed worried about that. Maybe the legendary Hickory Joe would have to give Otis a piggy back ride.

Katie said she was able to cheer Elias a bit, and even convince him that she didn't believe Otis' lies. But the problem was, somewhere deep down—down there where the Titanic was resting at the bottom of her heart—she wondered if it might be true.

"Well, if you're askin' what I think," Georgette started.

"I'm ah askin', preacher lady, I am."

"Maybe you should be a little slower before you get too close to a man. I know he looks dignified, and he smells good, drives a nice car—but maybe under all that he just wants what all the other boys wants. You took to him right quick. I know he was a safe place for you to hide from Otis, but just the same, you locked on a little quick honey. If you act desperate, men are gonna take advantage of that."

Jo was surprised when her aunt offered to pray. "There are some prayers God says yes to right away," Georgette said. "If we ask for wisdom, God'll give it in a hurry. That's what I'm gonna pray for."

■ ■ ■

Jo was about to slip into real sleep when her door creaked open.

"Jo, you awake?"

It was Uncle Huey.

"Is Aunt Georgette asleep?"

"Sure. It's almost three in the morning. But I heard you tossin' about." Huey came and sat down in the chair by her bed. It felt eerie to be awake so late. Everyone said that three o' clock was the darkest time. "I hear you paid Doc Banks a visit."

"Don't worry yourself, none, Uncle Huey, he didn't charge us a red cent."

"Now say there, I wasn't worried one lick about the money. I've been thinkin' about opening up a printing press out in the old shed. We could print our own money."

"Well, if you do, put the Lindbergh baby on the money. He's more famous than those old dead presidents. But ya know what, Uncle Huey, somethin' confusing happened."

She told him how Bernice ran off and got Big X. And pretty soon, not only Big X, but kids from around Jordan Town had gathered at the porch. Why had Bernice wanted to get such an audience? It seemed to Jo like maybe the black doctor's wife just wanted to embarrass her.

"She's probably afraid of y'all," Huey said.

"We wasn't gonna hurt her none."

"Of course. But that's not what I mean, Jo. I mean that they might have been afraid because two white women show up at a black family's house in the dark of night. What if later on you accuse them of somethin' bad? They wouldn't have no defense, and everyone would believe you because you're white. Bernice was pretty clever, if ya ask me."

Jo felt strange about that. She didn't like people thinking she might be a threat.

■ ■ ■

"Uncle Huey, you come to tell me where you went tonight? Because I about lost my leg trying to catch up to you, you old rascal."

"Ah, shucks Jo, you probably know before I tell ya. Why don't you tell me, and I'll fill in the blanks?"

"Well, you went back up toward Blue Mountain."

"Yes sir, that's my girl. Smart as can be."

She was glad he was back to his jolly self. She didn't like the angry Huey.

Huey began to tell Jo how he and Boots had gone back up to Blue Mountain, but they took a very different road than the one they took the church folk up earlier that day. It was dark and Huey was worried the truck might not make it up the mountain. In fact, at one point Boots had to get out of the truck and clear away some bushes and branches to reveal a hidden road. Huey worried that the truck might slip off the road, or break down. He'd hate to be stuck up there. Not because of the legend of Hickory Joe, he didn't believe that nonsense.

What was up in that mountain, hidden away in deep pockets like a fine watch were the little makeshift distilleries.

"Moonshine!" Jo said with satisfaction.

Moonshine, Huey agreed. Also known as mountain dew or white lightening. What came down from Blue Mountain was called *Resurrection Juice*.

Boots and Huey didn't have to search long before they found what they were looking for. Boots had a lantern, Huey his favorite brass flashlight.

"I don't suppose you found Otis, wandering around up there, did-ja?" Jo asked with a little giggle.

"No. But we found what caused the big asteroid scare. Sticky Simpson left his distillery while the Resurrection Juice was cooking—probably to go have a smoke of his own—and he about blew it sky high. But it was hard to find by the time we got there, because the cave fell in on itself."

"Just askin' for trouble if ya cook moonshine in a cave."

Huey agreed. "Trouble found Sticky. In one big huff, it all went up in a giant flame. I guess that's the big flash and rumble everyone thought was an asteroid."

"I pretty much figured that out already. But what about Sticky? Is he dead as a doorpost?"

"Couldn't find him," Huey said. "Dug around a little in the mess, but it was dark up there."

■ ■ ■

She closed her eyes tight and tried to will herself to sleep. She sensed him rise up. She opened her eyes. A warm glow lit his face. "Well I'll be switched," he said in curiosity and amusement.

Jo was suddenly wide awake.

"Is somethin' on fire?" she asked.

Huey just loomed over her, staring out the window.

Jo kicked her blanket aside and sat up on her bed to stare out into the night. But indeed, the darkness was burning away — in the shape of the cross of Jesus Christ.

"Holy moly Uncle Huey! Someone is burnin' a cross on our yard!"

"Unless it came from the sky, like that asteroid did."

"This is serious stuff!" Jo said, her eyes widening like saucers.

Huey sighed. "Well, Jo, we best go get it outta the yard before your aunt sees it."

Fear radiated through Jo. It came from the center of her chest and pulsed out, making her legs and arms weary, then it all bunched up in her throat like a great ball. The sight of Jesus' cross burning, becoming a sign of hate, was something she'd heard of — but never seen. Not never.

"We have the K-K-K in Madison Creek?" Jo asked in a shiver.

"No. We have idiots in Madison Creek," Huey retorted. "Idiots who want us to be afraid." He then gave his own version of the president's quote, "We don't have nothin' to fear, but fear itself."

The yard glowed with the burning cross. Strange shadows danced back and forth. Jo imagined demons in those shadows and wondered if she could ever play in that yard again without feeling afraid.

"Well, whatever the president said, fear is pretty scary in itself. Do you reckon' this is on account of us going to Doctor Banks for help tonight?"

"Reckon that's part of it. Word travels fast in a little town like this. But I figure it's more about a church than the doctor."

"What's wrong with the church?"

"Little Rickety Church has got its arms open to whites and blacks. Sad thing, you know, because church used to be the one place everyone really was welcome."

"Maybe Ms. Drake's house got ransacked and robbed because she goes to the church," Jo said slowly. "Maybe they wasn't robbin' her, maybe they was tryin' to scare her."

Huey shook his head. "Nah. They was after her money. Money, she don't got none. Know what they stole, Jo?"

"Her bed coverings," Jo said. "And underwear, I'll bet." She tried a smile in the darkness, but it did not chase the fear away.

"They just stole a whole bunch of Confederate money. Probably thought it was the real thing. But it ain't worth the paper it's printed on, ya know?"

Jo wondered how Confederate money would make its way into a house in Madison Creek. And where had Ms. Drake hidden it? And what if—what if those men burning the cross down there were the same ones who broke into Nettie Drake's house? She imagined them tearing through her bedroom, turning things upside down. What if that evil that was outside found its way into her own house?

"Uncle Huey, I don't want to go down there. I don't want to go into the dark and take down that cross."

He thought for a moment. "Sweetie babe, you don't have to if you don't wanna."

He turned and headed for the door.

"You really goin' down there?" she asked, hoping he would change his mind and at least wait for daylight. He didn't answer her. She felt like a big coward as he left her room. But then she remembered with relief that her leg was hurt. She should have reminded him of that. But even she had forgotten about her leg. Strange how fear could erase pain quicker than stitches or medicine.

Jo slid her window open and took in the strange mixture of the night air and wisps of smoke.

Uncle Huey crossed the yard and stood in front of the burning cross. Jo sensed the shadow demons pulsing all around him, but for a moment, he was cascaded in light.

"You wanna come show yourselves?" he called out.

No one came. She thought about slipping down to the porch roof — Big Red — where she so often took refuge and then sliding down the pillar to help him. But the fear paralyzed her. A burning cross was not only threatening, it was spooky. As if God had gone bad and decided to burn the righteous instead of the wicked.

She watched as Huey stood, waiting for the flames to die out. The beams of the cross fell away first.

The sun was threatening to rise when he finally dragged the burned remains of the cross toward the Man Village.

Bones

Annie Evermund's long trip to New York came to an end the Sunday the rock from Mars struck Blue Mountain. Annie was Mule's younger sister. That summer of 1938, Annie completed what she called a *full circuit*—visiting family in New York. It might not have been like her trip to Peru or Mexico, but she'd had a blast.

To spice things up, Annie made the trip on her favorite horse, *Steel*. Steel wasn't really a horse, it was a 1917 Harley Davidson 11F. She loved it! It had a sidecar that she left sitting out in the barn because she really didn't need it. She traveled light. She had bought the sidecar thinking maybe Mule could ride with her, but he couldn't fit, even when he *he-he-held* his *br-breath*.

There was nothing like seeing the New York skyline appear as wind screamed in her face. She had actually slapped the motorcycle and yelled, *yee-haa!* Now that she was back in Madison Creek, she would have to return to her good ole automobile. She was going to miss Steel. She pushed it into the barn next to the sidecar. She swatted Steel on the backside and shut the door with a heavy heart. It felt like she was shutting the door on summer.

She had been thinking all summer of ways to turn her classroom into New York City. This year she would be teaching a combined 3rd, 4th, and 5th grades. Someone much higher than her had decided that making the first day of school a Wednesday might ease the children out of their summer habits a little more gently.

It was important to set the tone on the first day. She would be fun—but no pushover. She needed a fresh haircut—nice and short—one that said: *I'm not your mommy.* Of course, she did not intend to wear a dress, but her favorite wide leg trousers and her good-ole gray-fur Homburg hat. It had been her husband's hat, but she liked the way it looked atop her short blonde hair. She was a favorite with the students, and some of the parents. She'd gained a reputation for making learning an adventure.

Annie was pleased with Mule's upkeep of the family garden. Mule had dutifully picked black-eyed peas, but failed to shell any of them. There they were, waiting for her return, in buckets all over the front porch. She didn't really mind. Time spent shelling peas with Mule was also time she could listen to the radio.

She would bring some of the harvest with her to school and find ways of making sure the children who did not have a lunch got a bit of her bounty. The hardest part was giving the children something to eat without embarrassing them or making them think it was charity.

Mule might not have destroyed the house—and even if the garden was well kept—it still didn't forgive the sink full of dishes. Flies and gnats danced about the sink, which emitted a dreadful odor.

There was just one thing—where had her piano gone?

Mule explained with excitement that the piano had been given to the new church.

"New church? What new church?"

"The one that was searching for Martians and was full of black people."

She wondered about his mental health. He was slow as the dickens, but he had never been given to flights of fancy or any kind of self-deception. In fact, Mule was painfully honest. But this particular story just went on and on.

She sat at the table surrounded by a small mountain of notebooks. Cow, Mule's dog, had been hyper ever since she got home. The dog kept nipping at her toes. She thought about putting some shoes on, but there was no point in cramping feet up just to keep them away from dog slobber.

Even if his story of giving the piano to the church was true, she doubted that it had exploded and sent stones rolling down the hill. She liked that story—loved it!—but it seemed just too wonderful for Madison Creek.

"Where had the stones gone after the explosion?" He said they rolled down the street and cars had to swerve around them.

"And after that — where did those stones go after that?" Well they piled them up behind the church. It was a big ole pile.

"Well, it just sounds wonderful," she finally said from the table while he paced back and forth through the small kitchen. He seemed to take up all the space. "But, now, I've seen a lot in my young years — more than you have with an extra decade. I'm just having a little trouble believing you on this one, big brother."

"Tr-tr-truth is that the Martians took your piano," Mule said with joyful self-congratulation. He liked that one.

"That's the best story yet!" she laughed. "Martians took my piano and —"

"And they d-d-done dropped it off in p-p-Peru!"

"Great! I love it! But really now, Mule, it's time that you put on your big-boy pants and tell me the truth. There's somethin' you're hiding from me, so spill it."

Mule's face twisted with some guilt. "We-we-wellll —"

"Alright mister, you spill the beans or I'll whoop you good."

"You can't whoop me!" Mule was indignant and Cow agreed with a bark. "You ain't mama!"

She broke out her black gospel voice "Boy, I whoop you like there's no tomorrow! I whoop you with a fly swatter if I have to."

"Well then I whoop you li-li-like Jesus'll whoop the pa-pagans on big judgment day."

Still speaking like black mama, she said, "You sit your white behind down right here and you tell me what you've done."

"Alrighty," Mule said with decision.

He picked up Cow and sat down next to her.

Bathing. That was another thing he had not done since she left.

■ ■ ■

Mule told Annie how he didn't like what he called the little garden. It was a separate area next to the big garden, but walled off and set apart with a little gate. Mule had always complained about it because he didn't like fussing with the gate. He liked things big and open, where he could drag his wagons and hoses about.

The day before the Martian rock came and hit Blue Mountain, Mule was watering when he heard someone call to him. He thought at first it was Boots, because it was a gruff man's voice and it scared Mule. He looked all around, and couldn't find anyone. Then the voice came again. It scared him somethin' awful. Then, with growing dread, Mule looked to the little walled off garden. Was someone in there? Maybe someone wanting to hurt him, or someone playing a trick on him. Worse, Mule reasoned, what if it wasn't a living someone—what if a ghost lived in that secret garden? What if an evil spirit made its home in there?

"I don't see how that makes any sense, Mule. Why would a ghost live in my little garden?" Annie asked.

Mule shrugged, "Well, iffin' you're a gh-ghost, wouldn't you like a ro-room with no roof, so you could pop in and out without having to suck yourself through the walls."

It turned out to be Red Heartland—not a ghost. Red had come to explain to Mule, as simply as possible, that he was doing something bad by going to church with black people. He talked and talked, but Mule got tired of all those words.

Annie's stomach tightened at this. For the first time, she began to think that perhaps all these wild tales might have a ring of truth to them. Not only was there a church, but it seemed there were people against the church. And she wasn't a bit surprised Red Heartland would be leading the charge. It would be just like him to come badger her slow brother while she wasn't around.

The incident with Red had somehow left Mule spooked about that secret garden. Why, anyone could hide out and then come after him. Of course, Red hadn't even come near the walled garden, but that didn't stop Mule from worrying about it.

"So you tore down my wall? That wall was there when Roy's boss gave him this property."

Cow gave a short bark to make it clear he was on Mule's side of whatever this argument was about.

"But be-be-before you get all upset, let me te-tell ya what I fo-fo-found!"

He was stuttering hard, which meant it had to be pretty incredible. What on earth could he have found in an old garden wall?

■ ■ ■

It was the day before school, and there were plenty of other things Annie needed to do other than visit Huey House. In fact, she had never been out to Huey and Georgette's place.

Not knowing to take the side road up to Huey's Man Village, she parked in front of the house and went straight to the door.

"Ain't no one gonna come to the door," a voice from above said. "'Cause Georgette's gone to town to pay a bill at Finch's Mercantile. And Huey's down at the Man Village."

Annie recognized Jo's voice. So she was lying on the porch roof, huh? She decided to give the girl a surprise. She tiptoed across the porch, stepped up on the rail and then climbed the pillar. Someone had been making good use of that pillar, the red paint was chipping away faster than the other pillars. Annie kept her legs wrapped tight around the pillar and put her elbows on the porch roof. There was Jo, staring at the clouds in the sky.

"I think that cloud looks like the Hindenburg," Annie said.

Jo let out a scream and immediately laughed at herself. "Ouch! You made me wiggle my hurt leg." She rolled onto her stomach to look Mrs. Evermund in the face. "I like your hair."

"I just got it done. Have to get myself ready before the natives come to my village." She waited for Jo to get it. "My village is my classroom."

"I know," Jo said. "Ain't ya gonna ask how I hurt my leg?"

"I don't ask questions like that, because for all I know, the mafia did it to you and now they're layin' in wait to see if you'll squeal and rat them out."

"Ooh, that's a good one, Mrs. Evermund!" Then, with thought, Jo said, "Wait! Are you Mrs. Evermund, or Mrs. Roy… what was his name?"

"Parker," Annie said. "It used to be Annie Parker. But these days, I'm just going with the Evermund name for Mule's sake."

Gosh, it was getting hard for her to talk half on and half off the roof like she was.

"There's another village around here, and it's not my classroom. A Man Village?"

"Oh, that, Good Lady," Jo said casually. "You should have taken the other road. But you can get to it from here. You gotta follow that path over that there bridge. But you gotta pray on the bridge that it doesn't give way, because the Baptist men helped my uncle build it a long time ago and now it sighs every time someone walks over it. Like an old man getting ready to kick the bucket."

"I need to take my car. Think I can do that?"

"Sure. Just speed up when you go across the bridge, so it doesn't have time to get fussy."

Annie was about to slide down the pillar when Jo said, "Mrs. Evermund, can I tell you a secret?"

"Jo, I know more secrets than the F-B-I."

"Well, the other night, some rotten people come and burned a big ole cross on our yard. I think it's 'cause my uncle is friendly with black people. We took it down, but it sure did scare me."

Annie's face was indignant. "Oh you poor darling! I can't believe anyone would be that mean. Except, I sorta can imagine it. I'm so sorry that happened to you. I'm sorry you have to live in a world that's so mean."

"Me too. It scared me, and now it keeps me a little scared."

"Well don't you let it!" Annie said with determination. It was getting tiring to hold on with her legs to the pillar. "Don't you let them keep you scared. I don't know why anyone would burn a cross on your yard, but you gotta believe God don't like that, and he'll smack them hard for what they done."

"You believe in God?"

"Most of the time," Annie confessed. "Sometimes I find myself wondering. Mostly when bad things happen." She stopped herself. She didn't need to bare her soul to an eleven year old. "You better believe there's a God. Who else do you think made the Andes Mountains or the Amazon River?"

"Well, it's too bad you believe," Jo said with a sigh. "Because my uncle started a church while's you was gone. But it's more the sort of church for people who don't believe than do. Unless your black, and I think most of them believe."

Instead of trying to sort that out, Annie gave Jo a little wink and slid away.

She drove down the narrow path Jo had pointed her to, and gave a little speech to the oblong box next to her in the passenger seat. *Don't you cause me no trouble,* she said to the box. *I just have a little business to do here.*

Annie did drive a little faster over the bridge. Maybe it was just her imagination, but she thought she felt the bridge hiccup as her car rumbled over it.

■ ■ ■

"Now there's somethin' I never expected to see," Boots said.

Huey looked up to see a well-worn Buick coming through the trees. "Well, I wouldn't have expected that either. Not coming down the footpath, anyway. Guess she still thinks she's on her motorcycle."

"She calls that thing *Steel,*" Boots reminded Huey.

"I knowed she'd come on up our way sooner or later."

"She's probably gonna bawl you out for blowin' up her piano," Boots warned.

Annie parked awkwardly between a shed and an old bathtub. She really did drive the same way she rode Steel.

"You want me to wash and wax that car of yours?" Boots offered as Annie got out of the car and adjusted her hat. She brushed off the legs of her trousers, which appeared to have red paint chips on them. Either that, or it was her woman time, Boots thought. If she was cranky with them, he decided to chalk it up to woman time.

"You wash that car if you want," Annie said. "But it's not going to stop me from gettin' it dirty again."

Boots laughed, "My kind of girl! You lookin' to get married?"

She shrugged and gave him a naughty look with a raised eyebrow. "Maybe. But it would be nothing more than an affair, seeing as how you're already married."

"Oh no I'm not!" Boots declared. "And if I was, I'd divorce her for you. I'd leave her bawlin' in the mud if you'd take me."

"Oh, you ain't leaving your love, ole Boots," Annie said. "Because as far as I can tell, you've been married since you were neigh about fourteen."

"You don't say!"

"Yep. To Resurrection Juice, or whatever you whisky peddlers call it these days."

Boots put his hand on his heart, "If you married me, I'd never drink again."

"If I married you, I'd take up drinking more seriously," she said. Then, with a hand on her thin hip, Annie narrowed her gaze on Huey. "You have anything you want to tell me?"

"Well, I do believe Mule took good care of himself while you were gone. And we all thank the Good Lord you're back safe with us."

"Big coward," Annie shook her head. "What exactly did you do with my piano?"

"Mule said it was okay," Huey said.

"Mule is slower than a herd of snails digging through peanut butter."

"That's a good one!" Boots slapped his leg.

Huey's head dipped in shame. "I sure do apologize about your piano. You want me to pay you back?"

"I do!" She sounded quite serious.

Huey swallowed hard. "Okay, how much?"

"How about you just give me what ya found inside the piano."

Boots looked surprised, but Huey just smiled. "In the little box?"

"In the little box, you big moron. You have it. Now give it to me. It doesn't mean a thing to you."

"Suppose I sold it already."

"Then you're a dead man. I'll have to bury you in your church graveyard."

Boots cut in on that. "Our church doesn't have a graveyard."

"You don't say!" Annie frowned thoughtfully. "Here's the deal, Huey House. I'll forgive you destroying my piano. And I'll forgive whatever shenanigans you've got Mule wrapped up in. But I want that box back. But I know Mule gave you that piano, and I figure it was a legal transaction. Usually, whatever is inside what you purchase is yours as well. Did you pay him anything?"

Huey shrugged, "No. I think he said you wanted to get rid of it."

She held out her hand and gave her fingers a come-here motion. "Give me my box," she demanded forcefully.

Huey got up and headed for the shed she was parked beside.

"You keep it in a shed!" she shouted.

He ignored her and after a moment returned with her small box. "It's pretty, but probably not worth much," Huey said.

"Worth is in the eye of the beholder, Huey. I suppose I'd rather have that than a Picasso."

He gave her the small box and she immediately popped it open. There was her ring. Unexpected tears welled up and then spilled down her cheeks. It was a small ring—elegant was the way she would have said it—crowned with an *elegant* diamond.

"Roy couldn't afford much. He worked in the Carson Mine. He saved every penny he had for this, and still didn't have enough." She sat down on an old barrel. "Floyd Carson loaned him the rest and said he'd take payments out of his check. Only, Mr. Carson didn't do that. In fact, when Roy asked Carson about the loan, Mr. Carson said he couldn't remember ever loaning Roy any money. I don't know why he took such a liking to my husband."

She slid the ring on and off, happy with the way it still fit. Roy had been dead four years, and some people said she hadn't grieved properly. Well phooey on them. She didn't think Roy would have her lying around crying in a dark room while he enjoyed the big golden city. Besides, a lot of women lost their husbands and buried their pain in food. She was proud that ring still fit, and in her opinion she was still looking good. That opinion was apparently shared by the male species of New York, who had given her plenty of cat-calls and whistles.

"Well, what can I pay you for this? I'll give you everything I have."

"Marry me," Boots said at once. Huey swatted at him, hoping to shut him up.

"Great, we're engaged," Annie said with a little wink. "Really, Huey, I want this ring back."

"Ah, it's yours anyhow," Huey said. "Just take it. I was just keepin' it because…" He paused, why had he held on to it? "I guess I was looking forward to seein' your face when it turned up again. Kinda mean of me, now that I think on it."

"No, no," Annie waved that line of thinking off. "I can't just take it without paying you. The box in the car is for you. Simple as that, Huey House—I'll trade you boxes."

"The box in the car?" Boots stood up.

"Go get it, Boots," Annie instructed. She sounded like she was commanding a dog to fetch.

"I don't take no orders from you, my lady."

"You want to be my fiancé, you do as I say," Annie said. "And hurry, I don't have all day to waste out here."

■ ■ ■

The question was — what was in the box?

"Bones," Annie said. "That's what I figure. Gotta be bones."

Huey examined the wooden box, not sure he wanted to open it. "Well didn't you check?"

"Are you out of your mind, Huey House?" Annie shook her head. "You think I'm dumb enough to open that box with my brother Mule around? He's the one that found it, hidden in a garden wall he was tearing down."

The box appeared to be about 3' long, 2' wide, and 1' deep. After close inspection, Boots shook his head. "Not big enough for bones."

"Then open it and see," Annie said. "Maybe it's a jack-in-the-box."

"Why you givin' this to me?" Huey asked.

"Open the box," Annie pressed.

It took Boots a moment to figure out how to jimmy the lid. It seemed it had been shut for a long time. Finally, he slid it open and smiled big. "Bones!" he affirmed. "Long ones, skinny ones, hands, skull — the whole enchilada."

"Hush, the world'll hear ya," Huey said.

"Ah, they're old bones," Annie said. "I reckon at least seventy years."

The bones were stacked neatly in the box, nice and compact with the skull on top.

Boots and Huey nodded their heads in unison. "Seventy years is about right," they both agreed.

■ ■ ■

According to local legend, Joe and Bertha King had lived in the very house Roy and Annie would make their first home. Only, Joe and Bertha had not experienced the same marital bliss that Annie and Roy did. In fact, one night during a particularly heated argument, she hit him over the head with a pan. Enraged, he chased her all over the property while she laughed, "Ha-ha, you can't catch me, I'm the gingerbread girl."

He did catch her, only to discover she had slipped a Hickory hunting knife with a 7 inch blade in the big pocket of her dress. She drew it out and stabbed him hard in the leg. She didn't just do it once or twice, but over and over again. She ripped into his leg like a hungry hound dog into fresh meat. Now some folk say that she never intended to kill him, because she only went for that leg. Others say you can't stab a man that many times and not want him dead. Either way, it wasn't Joe who came to an end that day; it was Bertha. At some point, he kicked her away, got the knife from her and drove it right through her heart.

Now, the story really depends on who you ask. Some folk say it was an axe, not a knife. What's more, the legend eventually grew to say that she cut his leg clean off. In the end, however it played out between the two of them, she was the one who went missing. And he did lose a leg. He claimed he was robbed, and his wife kidnapped. Eventually he left town, and after a thorough search was made of the property, it was sold at auction.

But that wasn't the end of Joe King. Folk started seeing him outside their windows at night. Some saw him standing on street corners when it was raining. Most reports came from the hills, where a lone stranger was known to limp about and terrorize hikers and campers. He became known as Hickory Joe. Somewhere, hidden away on Blue Mountain, legend had it that he had built a cabin and lived off the wild. It was nothing for him to kill a raccoon, deer or even a bear with his Hickory knife. If anyone went missing for long, there were sure to be half-hearted jokes that maybe they'd been taken by Hickory Joe. Of course, by now Hickory Joe would have died of old age; but legends die slower than people.

Rumors or no rumors, what was fact was that Joe King's wife Bertha flat out disappeared, and soon after he did too.

■ ■ ■

Huey stared at the box. "You think we finally found ole Bertha? And to think she was hidden away in the garden wall all that time!"

"That's right, and now she's yours."

"Come again."

The look on Annie's face said it plain as day. "For your graveyard, Preacher House."

"I don't got no graveyard! Got somethin' like a junkyard maybe, but no graveyard."

"Well, iffin' you're a real church, you'd have to have a graveyard."

Boots nodded agreement. "It would help your credibility, Huey. Some crosses outside that church building might be the final touch you need."

A car was coming down the drive. Boots put the lid back on the box; it probably was not a good idea to let people come to the Man Village and find them inspecting old bones.

Huey was getting to where he knew the sound of that particular car engine. He closed his eyes and said, "I prophecy it is a 1934 Ford Sedan with whitewall tires."

He kept his eyes closed as the car approached.

"Bingo, you're a prophet!" Annie said.

"Ah, not really," Boots shook his head. "Ole Huey's been in the fight of his life with this fella."

"Who is he?"

"Government agent," Boots said.

Annie watched as the new man got out of the car. Now that is a handsome fella. He was well dressed, even a hat and pocket watch.

"Ooh wee!" Annie breathed softly.

"Ah, you leave him be," Boots warned. "He's been lip locked with Katie Simpson for the last couple weeks. And don't you forget, we're engaged."

"I break off the engagement," Annie said. "Skedaddle and don't cause me no trouble." She stood up and put her foot on an old engine, bending her knee as the new man approached. "Hi-Ho Cheerio!" Annie said with a warm smile.

He paused, staring at Annie. "You certainly are not anyone I expected to see out here."

Huey introduced them, and at once Annie stepped forward and held out her hand. For a moment he seemed unsure of what to do, then feeling the weight of expectation, Elias Moore took her fingers and lifted them to his lips and gave her hand a little kiss.

Mr. Moore turned his attention to Huey. "Mr. House, the other night, I gave your girl a lift. Just to be kind. But afterward, somethin' important of mine came up missing. I'm just wondering if maybe you have it."

"What did you lose?" Annie asked, and was greeted with an awkward silence. Mr. Moore did not even acknowledge her now, he just kept his eyes tight on Huey.

"If you have business with the girl, why don't you go ask her yourself," Huey finally said.

"What Government agency do you work for?" Annie questioned.

"Federal Government," Mr. Moore said in a tired voice. He was fed up with Madison Creek.

"Let me ask you somethin', Mister." Annie didn't give any of them time to cut in. "If you had a church, wouldn't you want that church to have a graveyard? Wouldn't you think it was all the more a church if it had a bunch of crosses outside? Used to be you could visit the Lord and pay respects to the dead all in one nice swoop."

Elias Moore sighed, "Gosh, why not. I think I've seen everything, so why the heavens not?"

Annie gave Elias a friendly wink, "Okay, now out with it, Mister, what are you missing? No one can help you if you don't help yourself."

"Did someone steal your report?" Huey asked.

"No sir. That's got to go off to New York."

Boots was thoughtful. "I wonder if you found what you're looking for if maybe you could be a little more generous toward the church."

"There is no church." Mr. Big Government-Man was holding back growing frustration. "A person cannot be a church. I already explained that to you."

"Makes sense to me," Annie said.

Huey shrugged, "Too bad I can't help ya."

Annie nodded toward the box, "Well, gang, it's been fun, but I think it's time I check out. I've got a classroom to decorate, and you have a body to bury."

Elias stepped back, startled. "You have a body out here?"

"Don't worry, it's goin' in the ground," Boots said. "Old bones. Hickory Joe's old wife, we think."

"You know this could just stir up even more trouble for you," Mr. Government-Man said. "Let me see those bones."

Boots smiled, "Well, their mostly just nothin' but powder now. So you gots to get close to see the bone specks." He motioned for Elias to come close. "No, come on now, get a little closer." Elias bent down some more.

That's when Annie gave him a firm swat on the behind. "Geronimo!" She laughed as Mr. Government-Man froze in astonishment. She marched off toward her ride, giggling as she went. "Thank you for my treasure," Annie shouted as she got in her car. "Make sure to bury them bones at least six feet deep."

"Come on now, you want to see these bones, you's got to get clooose as can be," Boots said.

Reluctantly, Elias bent down closer to the box. He was now almost face to face with Boots. The ole bootlegger reached for the box cover and then lurched at Elias. "NO!" he shouted. Elias stumbled backward and fell over the engine Annie had propped her foot on a moment ago. She waved as she drove by.

Now, with Mr. Tax-Man on the ground, Huey towered over him. "Wasn't nice of you to go chasing after Katie the way you have."

"What happened between me and Katie had nothing to do with my work," Elias stammered.

Huey nodded, "Sure. What about punching Oats, was that done as an official of the Government of the United States?" He didn't wait for Elias to answer. "And what about all that flirting you just did with Mrs. Annie Evermund?"

"I didn't flirt with her!" Elias was incredulous. "She was flirting with me! Come on, man, you were right here!"

"Why don't you just tell me what you're looking for? Maybe I can help you after all."

Once again that question was greeted by silence.

■ ■ ■

"I know why he doesn't want to answer you." Jo House stepped from behind an old water tank. How long had she been there?

"So what's he looking for?" Huey asked.

Jo smiled big at Mr. Moore, who was now propped up on his elbows. "You want to tell them, Mr. Moore?"

He sighed. "My wife died three years ago, gentlemen. It grieves me to talk about it. And I keep her ring in my car. Sometimes I wear it, just to feel a little closer to her."

"A day of boxes and rings," Boots marveled.

"Wait a minute!" Huey grinned. "Wait a minute! Did you say your wife is dead?"

"Yes sir. Grieves my heart. But I lost her ring—"

"Good heavens!" Huey cried. "Jo, give this man his ring back!"

"I would, Uncle Huey. But I can't. It's true, I did swipe it. But I don't have it no more. No sir, I don't."

"Where is it?" Huey asked.

"I done gave it to Katie Simpson. I figured she would be very interested in Mr. Moore having a wedding ring he don't keep on his finger."

Huey looked down at Elias. "Well, there you have it. I guess you'll have to go explain to Katie."

Elias struggled to get up. It seemed he thought maybe Boots or Huey might help, but they didn't. In fact, they enjoyed watching the man in a suit work his way upright. He dusted himself off, gave a little nod and then was back in his sedan — undoubtedly heading toward Sweet Tea's.

Huey patted Jo on the back. "That was brilliant! Giving his wedding ring to Katie like that."

"Gosh ain't you dumb as Mule Evermund!" Boots cut in. "Dog gone it, Huey, she hasn't seen Katie since the night Katie drove her out to Jordan Town."

Jo hung her head. "That's true. The ring is still up in my room. I just wanted to force him to go have a little talk with Katie. I sure would like to be a fly on Sweet Tea's wall."

"I ought to whoop you," Huey growled.

"Would you please? March me over to the shed and whoop me. It would prove you love me like a pa."

Huey shook his head. "Nah, wouldn't do you no good."

"Good grief, Uncle! Mrs. Evermund done spanked the tax-man because she liked his patoot, but you won't whoop me for being evil?"

"Holy Ghost'll get ya someday I reckon."

The Boys Radio Club

Stealing Popsie's booze should have been an easy thing, but it landed Otis in a Chicago overcoat. That was New York slang for a coffin.

Of course, booze was illegal in Buncombe County. Minnie Belle Lawson and the church ladies would fight tooth and nail to keep it that way. It didn't matter to those biddies that the Federal Government repealed prohibition with the Eighteenth Amendment. As far as they were concerned, Buncombe County was drier than the Sahara.

Well, no matter what the law said, Otis knew his father had it stashed somewhere. He searched the attic, closets, and even rifled through his pa's dresser drawers. Otis thought it was strange that his father never invited him to the Radio Club. Maybe he was ashamed of him. Or, maybe they were doing something they shouldn't be doin'. Could it be that the Radio Club was really Madison Creek's version of a speakeasy?

He hit pay dirt when he went down to the basement and peeked in the coffins. The liquor was stowed away deep in the belly of The Beast. Otis thought that was a ridiculous name for a coffin, but it undoubtedly made those turkeys at the Radio Club feel tough. Why his pa kept such a large coffin like that was really beyond Otis. Maybe pop was waiting for Mule Evermund to kick the bucket.

Once Otis found where the good stuff was, he made a habit of slipping away for just a sip. That's what he was doing when he heard someone — or several someone's — coming down the stairs. Otis eased The Beast shut and looked for the nearest, safest place to hide. He ended up in one of his father's handmade coffins.

He was tall and had to lift his knees a little in order to get his head and feet into the coffin.

It turned out that what he heard coming down to the basement wasn't just a couple people, but a sizable group of men — the Radio Club. Or, as he would learn listening to them, they were now the *White* Radio Club.

He learned a lot laying there like a corpse.

The men were greatly distressed, probably because their wives were — all about a church that included blacks and whites.

"They're just lowering the standards," Red Heartland griped. "And it's un-Christian. And they just keep on 'cause they ain't scared."

Teddy Grimm was angry. Usually Teddy was busy thinking of ways to work WC Fields lines into his conversation. Teddy was a serious WC Fields lover. He'd written the actor, asking if he might try out for one of his movies but got no reply. *Take me down to the bar, we'll drink breakfast together,* was a favorite that always got the Radio Club laughing. They also liked it when he broke into Field's voice and said, *Some weasel took the cork out of my lunch.*

But WC Fields was far from Teddy's mind. "See, y'all are just a lot of hot air," he raged. "Me and Alvin already done did somethin'. We done went to Huey's place the other night and lit up a cross."

John Step wasn't pleased. "You should have talked to us first! Suppose you had gotten caught?"

"Always scareda gettin' caught," Teddy snarled. "Y'all just a bunch of pussycats." Oats couldn't see out, but he imagined Teddy petting his dark goatee. "Huey might call himself a preacher, but what he's serving up is nothin' more than a good heap of mental cyanide. Arsenic for the soul."

"Yes, yes!" several agreed. Otis thought he heard his father in the chorus.

Sweat watered Otis' face, but he was unable to brush it away.

"He's giving our boys and girls a big dose of spiritual carbon monoxide. Cyanide, arsenic — know what those all have in common? You can't hardly detect that stuff until they're lopping dirt on top of your coffin. Things are changin' round here, fast. When that kid got herself hurt, know where Georgette took her? The black doctor. In the middle of the night! Aren't things just so cozy 'round here?"

"Well you didn't have to go burning the cross," Finch said.

"Now they'll think the Klan is in town," someone said. "That could be good."

Finch was nervous. "Y'all keep the Klan out of this. We don't need that kind of trouble. We can take care of this ourselves. Creek hasn't had serious Klan activity in years, and we don't need none of that. You get that kind of stuff stirred up, buildings get burned and —"

"Then do something!" Teddy shouted.

■ ■ ■

The Radio Club was nothing more than a bunch of hot heads letting off steam. Otis could decipher those tea leaves better than he could read the morning paper. The morons in the basement could do all the saber rattling they wanted, there wasn't a chance Clyde Finch would let it go anywhere. Clyde was interested in business, not who went to church where. But Red and some of those other guys could stir up a great big batch of trouble if they let their tempers get the better of them.

Later, after everyone had gone and he had escaped the confines of that horrific coffin — thank the Almighty he wasn't claustrophobic — he lay upstairs with his feet hanging off the end of the sofa while his brain raced. He was thinking mostly about Katie. All those girls in New York, every variety it had seemed, and still he could feel a lump somewhere deep down when he thought about her.

It was too bad, Otis thought, that the Radio Club wasn't more of a... well, Radio Club. In fact, he was pretty sure he'd heard the whoosh and pop of darts being played as the men talked. But no radio. Not until later, when they decided to really break out the booze and put on some music. The Radio Club had somehow become nothing more than a place for men to drink, smoke, spit tobacco and do some heavy duty squawking. What the town needed was a real Radio Club. What he needed was Katie.

Two ideas fused together. Katie~Radio Club — Radio Club~Katie.

He called Katie's house early the next morning. Of course, her mother answered and hesitated to give the phone to Katie. When she took the phone, Katie was obviously irritated. "Otis, what do you want?"

"I didn't call to bother you none. I'm starting my own Radio Club."

"Good for you."

He realized he sounded like he was announcing he'd just written Macbeth.

"An after school Radio Club for boys." He waited. She did not hang up. "I just wanted to invite Dusty. Starts today. He can come to my place right after school and I'll walk him up to the café when it's all done. You can't say no. It gets him out of your hair, and —"

"Fine," Katie sighed. "But when you drop him off, don't pester me, do you understand?"

Of course he understood.

"Otis, this better not be some low-life scheme to get me into your arms," Katie said into the emptiness after Otis had hung up.

"I bet it is."

"Dog gone it, Rose!" Katie snapped at the operator. "You don't have to listen in."

■ ■ ■

She really didn't know if it was a scheme or not, but that Thursday she prepped Dusty with the reminder that he was to behave and not show off. She worried constantly about the other boys mocking him.

It was hard for her not to hone in on the boy as soon as he was delivered to the café and ask every detail. They met upstairs, Dusty explained simply, around the radio at first. But then Mr. Oats, that's what he told the boys to call him, had brought out a box. Inside, the boys found a pile of papers that were labeled things like, *The Shadow*, episode 9 and *The March of Time*, episode 56. They were radio plays. Not ones Otis had written — but the real thing.

"I got to practice my reading," Dusty said energetically that Thursday night. "Because it's not like a movie, where you have to memorize the lines. No, no, that's not how it works." She could tell he was mimicking Otis. "In radio, we read the lines. So you gots to be familiar with them, and a good reader. Besides, we don't have copies of the script to pass around, you see?"

So with wonder, she sat up that night and worked with the boy on his reading. The next day when the club was over, Otis did little more than stick his head in Sweet Tea's, catch her eye, tip his hat to acknowledge that he had fulfilled his duty, and scamper off. In fact, he got away quicker than Katie anticipated. She had wanted to quiz him a bit about what was going on, but she didn't dare chase after him; and she wasn't about to call him — not unless she wanted Rose repeating everything she said to the rest of Madison Creek.

■ ■ ■

At the end of the song service that Sunday, Annie Evermund stood up and told the ragtag congregation that she was dedicating a dead body to the church. Huey announced that instead of having a sermon, they would have a funeral. They all marched outside and stood in the grassy field next to the church. Of course, Huey had never conducted a funeral either, so his comments still turned out quite hilarious.

Huey put his foot on the box of bones as he spoke. "I don't know nothin' much about this dear dead saint, except that she's been dead quite a while, and I reckon she's made the peace about which way she went. Guess she went on up to heaven if she was one of the gooduns, and on down to the sewer if she's one of the baduns."

"God help us," Meemaw Moses said. She held her hankie to her very dry cheeks and pretended to wipe away tears.

After the service, Hammond Washington, who had once dug trenches during the Great War, and Big X, carved out a grave in the big field next to the Little Rickety Church. The body was lowered into the grave, which looked to be more like nine feet deep than six. Everyone took turns throwing dirt into the grave. A solitary white cross marked the spot where — someone — was now buried.

Huey stepped onto the new mound of dirt and kicked it a little like he was going to pitch baseball. He prayed, "We thank you Lord for this dead body, and the gift it is to us. We look forward to the resurrection, and finding out who she is."

Huey had hardly said amen before that annoying Clay Simons jumped on top of the dirt and cried, "And dearest God, we pray you keep the dead in their graves. If you bring any ghosts out, send them on yonder to Asheville."

"Amen!" Dusty shouted joyfully. He darted for the mound of dirt to make his own speech, but Katie reeled him in.

"Well, we missed Memorial Day," Lutie Dotson said. "Ain't that a shame."

"Why?" Hammond Washington asked.

Lutie held her nose toward the sky. "Why, because we don't know but that maybe this dear one we just buried might be a war veteran. We could have decorated her grave with flags and sang."

"Yes!" Annie Evermund cried. "Yes, yes, and yes! I believe with all my heart she was a veteran. And probably not murdered at all, but killed in combat and shipped home. Maybe she was a war nurse, and was hacked up by the enemy. Her poor grieving husband buried her—"

"This is ridiculous!" Doctor Banks looked angry. "You teach children. You should know better."

Annie smirked, "Well, I do know this, women die in war and we never give them any credit. So I think the first grave out here should be to our woman war hero."

They agreed by a show of hands that on all national holidays, they would decorate the grave.

■ ■ ■

That Monday afternoon Katie realized how quiet things were now that Dusty was at his after school Radio Club. He usually came right to the café and found a booth to start his homework. Of course, the kid talked to everyone and that drove her crazy. But now, her heart ached without him. What's more, people asked about the boy. She explained where he was and that he must be having just the most wonderful time. She tried hard to sound positive. Everyone said how nice it was that he had something to be a part of; but a few seemed particularly sad the boy was gone.

Floyd Carson—who came in most afternoons to have a root beer float—nodded toward the radio, which was gurgling a mixture of static and the daily soap opera, *Painted Dreams*. "You can run the radio all day, but it's not half the show that boy gives us repeating the shows he hears."

The cafe's glass door burst open.

"Miss Simpson, I gotta talk to you!" Jo House shouted.

Jeremiah hollered at her to get in and shut the door. He had been gnawing at a sandwich for over two hours now, nodding off between bites. On the radio a news bulletin about Germany interrupted the music.

Jo, not worried about Germany, burst out, "They done set up a Radio Club and won't let no girls go. Do you think that's right?"

"Sounds right to me," Floyd Carson said from the counter where he was scraping up the last of his float. How did he stay so thin? "Boys need away from the girls."

Jo sidestepped Katie and stood in front of Floyd. "My teacher, Miss Evermund, told us that women have rights, too."

"You want to work in the coal mine, like men?" Floyd asked. He stood and slipped on his coat. "Men work hard. They need places to go where women aren't there to distract them."

"Hoggy-hog-wash and fiddle-de-foo," Jo sputtered. "These are just boys pretending to be men, Mr. Carson. They ain't worked in the mines or built on the railroad. In fact, I'll bet I work harder in school than they do. God bless the working woman."

Mr. Carson popped his hat on his head and touched the brim with two fingers. "I'll be seein' ya."

"You sure will. Down in the coal mine. I'll be the best coal miner you ever saw." Jo stuck out her leg to show the bandage. "I'm tough. See that? Sliced my leg up, and took stitches. But I didn't cry none like a big baby. My teacher let me show the whole class my bandage today."

"You tell them where you got that bandage?" Floyd asked, his head tilted a bit to the side in a knowing look. "Did you tell them the black doctor stitched that leg up? Or did you leave that part out?"

Jo's mouth went dry.

Floyd rubbed his boney chin. "Now tell me, child, why would you go running to Jordan Town for help? Because you're poor as dirt or because you prefer black folk?"

Jo didn't know what to say to that. It felt like there was more to the question than the words themselves. He didn't just want to know why she went to a black doctor, he wanted to know why her family was so friendly with black people. And, under that, it seemed maybe he was also giving her a little grief for being poor. She usually didn't worry about not having much, since neigh about everyone was poor. But it was like the time Minnie Belle asked her if she was happy and in the moment Jo had been unable to answer—now she had an answer for Minnie Belle, but nothing for Mr. Carson. Would it take another year for her to think of an answer for him? She wished she was a little smarter.

"Jo, let Mr. Carson get back to work," Katie urged. Then, almost apologetically, she said to him, "I am thankful for your business, sir."

When he was gone, Katie brightened a little. "He had me on edge. But Jo, dear, there's no way I can get you in a boys Radio Club. And I don't have time to start a girls club."

"I'll say you don't have no time," Jo giggled. "You got man trouble, don't ya?"

"Jo, I do not!" Katie laughed a little.

"Well, they line up to see you. What happened to that tax-man?"

Katie averted her eyes. "Him. Well, he headed on toward New York. Had to file his report."

"Will he be back?"

"Probably not. He made a fool of himself."

"You mean by socking Oats in the eye?"

"That's really none of your concern, child."

"Oh, I know. My aunt tells me that all the time. But then she goes and spills all the beans anyway. She doesn't really like keeping stuff to herself, she just likes pretending it's up to her to bear the weight of planet earth in the quiet of her big heart. But really, it helps to unload a little."

That was good, Katie thought. And she had to restrain herself all the more from telling the girl all about the last time she'd seen Elias. The memory itself made her both smile and miss that peppermint smell that followed him all around.

"Ah, what's it harm? Kid, you want a malt?"

"No, I want in the boys Radio Club. Besides, I don't have no money," Jo said. She stood up and pulled her pockets out to show that they were empty.

Katie looked around. Except for Jeremiah, who was dozing at his table by the window, Sweet Tea's was empty.

"We'll trade stories. I want to know about the other day, when we went up looking for that meteor that came from the sky. Dusty told me all about how Martians took over your body and you did somethin' to Clay to make him stop picking on Dusty. I want to know about that."

Jo grinned. "Fine. We'll trade."

■ ■ ■

They settled into a booth, and as customers came and went, Katie would see to them. But she always came back, to get more of Jo's story, and then to tell her own.

The last time she'd seen Elias Moore was a week ago Monday. That was after the Martian rock hit the earth and scared everyone. It was also the day after Jo had hurt her leg real bad.

Katie began to tell Jo what had happened.

Mr. Moore had come by Sweet Tea's that afternoon. He told Katie that he was on his way out of town. She sat with him as he ate a sandwich—in the same booth she and Jo now occupied. It was right next to the two tables with plastic signs indicating they were for the coloreds. It was her favorite booth because it was in the corner of the room and she could keep an eye on customers. She sat right beside the tax-man, running her hand affectionately over his shirt sleeve as he ate. But he seemed distracted.

Elias had asked if she had anything that was his.

"Oh my," Jo said softly.

Katie promised him that she didn't have anything of his. But Elias was distant and awkward. What's more, Sammy Peak had found his way into Sweet Tea's and was staring right at Elias. Sammy was a miner, and he hadn't washed up too good before coming to the café. His cheeks and hands were still black, and what's more, he was getting it on everything. He had eaten his sandwich with his bare hands. Katie wondered if he had more coal in his stomach than sandwich. Sammy was clear across the room, but his gaze seemed fixed on the tax-man.

"He makes me nervous," Elias told Katie.

"Well he shouldn't." Then, running her hand up and down his sleeve again, she asked, "So what is it you think I have that's yours?"

He asked if she was playing games with him. What in tarnation was he so worked up about? And then his big speech started; all the while, he wiggled under Sammy's seemingly tight gaze.

"Your voice, it reminds me of my wife," then, quickly, he added, "My dead wife. My very dead wife."

"Oh really?" Katie felt her heart fade a bit.

"Well, I just want to tell you up front what happened. Last night, I went by Huey's place to finish up some business. But I spotted that kid of his, and I gave her a ride on up to the house. I left her in the car for a few minutes. Didn't think nothin' of it at the time. If anything, I thought she might rifle through my folder. But that's not what she done."

He wiggled as Sammy's face tensed, and then Sammy's eyes went wide as if to swallow the room.

"What is his problem?" Elias asked. "Most people at least have the courtesy to look away when you look back at them."

"Maybe he just thinks you're handsome," Katie ruffled his hair like he was nine.

She asked again what Jo had taken, and Elias finally said that it was the wedding ring his wife — his dead wife — had given him. Elias has stared down at his fingers, which were locked tight together. "I buried her just six months ago. She died when a rabid dog bit her.

But I can't bear to let her go. So I kept her ring with me all this time."

"In your pocket?"

"No, sweetie. In the glove box."

"And that wife of yours is buried down deep? Like those bones Huey House buried up in the church yard? That's where she is? In a box?"

"Yes. You don't have to be so morbid about it." Elias fist had tightened and beads of sweat popped on his forehead.

"All that time we was together — with your lips on mine and it was gettin' hot and heavy — you sure as heavens didn't tell me about any wife. I just can't see keeping a wedding ring in a glove box if it means so much to you. Wouldn't you keep it in a dresser drawer or somewhere safe?"

"I like it close to me."

"But not on your finger," Katie had pressed. "Seems more likely you keep it in the glove box so you can put it back on when you get home." She nodded toward his hand. "You travel a lot. Pop that thing on and off is what I guess."

"What are you sayin', Katie?" For the first time that rich peppermint smell was beginning to stink to her.

"Maybe that wife of yours isn't buried so deep."

Elias looked up to see Sammy staring even harder at him. In fact, Sammy's face twisted in two directions at once. His eyes widened, and the left half of his face pulled into a frown while the other half reached upward.

Elias stormed up out of his chair and pointed at Sammy, "You have a problem with me, mister?"

Sammy just stared, his face working in new directions.

Teddy Grimm, who had been sitting at the window eating a bowl of grits laughed hard. "You talkin' to Sammy there?"

"Sammy's my angel," Katie had declared.

Surprised, Sammy's face had twisted again, his eyes bugged out at Elias. "You talkin' to me?"

"Yes I'm talkin' to you! Why do you have to stare at me like that?"

The restaurant was only half-full, but everyone began to laugh. Even Sammy's face reddened as he said, "I just can't get my eyes off you. You are the ugliest fella I ever seen."

Elias started toward Sammy, but at that moment every man in the restaurant stood up, ready to take on the newcomer.

"Are ya gonna hit me?" Sammy asked. "Go ahead! Do it! It don't make me no never mind."

"I oughta," Elias growled. *Boy, he did have a temper*, Katie thought.

"You can use his face as a punching bag if you like," Teddy said, "but you gotta come through all of us. I'd love it, I've been spoiling for a fight lately."

"Ah, this town isn't worth the dirt it sits on," Elias declared.

"Get outa here, ugly," Sammy laughed.

Elias put on his coat and hat.

Sammy was enjoying the spotlight. He reached down and took his cane—the long cane with a red tip. Everyone in Madison Creek knew that Sammy had lost his eyesight in a mine accident. He could still dig like a groundhog so they called him *The Blind Miner*.

"I'll beat you with my cane, ugly!" Sammy laughed.

Elias had bowed his head, "I pray your forgiveness." He leaned in to Katie and whispered to her before leaving the café.

Wait! Jo hated it when people did that. Left out some vital bit of something in a whisper. "Come on, Miss Simpson, you gotta tell me what he said."

Katie looked a little worried about that. But, she'd spilled this much all over the floor, she might as well empty the cup. "He leaned in close and he says, 'she's prettier than you.' And then he walked out."

"Who's prettier than you?"

Katie raised an eyebrow. "His wife, I reckon."

"Ah, don't that just get ya, Miss Simpson? Don't that just eat you up? That Teddy Grimm is mean as the Devil, but I wish he'd let loose on that tax-man."

"Well, everyone got a good laugh at him as he left. I figure he got his come-uppance. And from a blind man."

■ ■ ■

But Elias got the last laugh.

When Katie came home that evening, her mother had asked if Elias was with her. She hadn't told her mother her doubts about Elias because Dorothy liked him so much. He was so much better than that awful Otis character.

"No," she had said. "I don't know where Elias is."

Setting her purse on the kitchen counter, she called for her little dog, Charlie Mac.

But Charlie Mac didn't come.

Strange; he usually met her at the door, barking and nipping at her ankles.

"Honey, you sure everything is okay with Elias?" her mother asked.

"Just dandy." She called again for Charlie Mac.

"Sweetie, just a little over an hour ago Elias came by and said you wanted him to bring you Charlie. Said you needed him. I didn't question the man, but boy did I wonder what was going on."

Stunned, Katie reached for the counter for support.

A tear touched Dorothy's face. "He took the dog, hon."

"How could you?" Katie burst out. Tears and rage poured out at the same time.

"Honey, I didn't know better. Maybe you should have told me what's going on."

"Don't you turn it on me!" Katie hollered. "You did this! You just wanted to hurt me!" Then, in disbelief, she began to call for the dog. "Charlie Mac! Charlie! Here, boy!"

But Charlie didn't come.

She landed in her bedroom, curled up in a tight ball crying hard. Dusty came in, paced around their room in a small circle, and then stared at her with his hands on his hips. "Don't you worry, mama! I'm gonna go up to Martian Rock and call down the aliens on that evil man."

Katie didn't dare tell Jo any of that. She had already been too free with her heart.

■ ■ ■

The café door swooshed open. It was Otis dropping Dusty off.

"Hey you!" Jo motioned for him to come to the booth where she and Katie were sitting.

Otis sighed with exaggeration; apparently he wanted to look like he didn't have time to be bothered with Katie.

"Listen, buster," Jo said boldly, "I want in your Radio Club. I don't like this boys only stuff."

Otis was annoyed. "Don't call me buster. And, it's the Boys Radio Club. If you're a boy, you can come. If you're a girl, you can knit."

"That's just rotten," Jo sulked, looking to Katie. She had thought maybe if she confronted Otis in front of Katie, either Katie would take her side or Otis would soften up.

Dusty hovered behind Otis. "Mom! You won't believe what I just did! I rode home on a motorcycle."

Katie was not impressed. "You got a motorcycle, Otis? What do you mean riding my boy around on one of those? That's dangerous."

"Borrowed it from Annie Evermund," Otis said. "And don't get your panties in a wad, sweetie, it has a sidecar."

"Don't talk about my panties," Katie said in a hushed voice. "Why don't you skadat?"

He sulked off and after a moment, Jo decided to follow. Outside the sky had begun to fill with dark clouds. Jo wondered if a storm would pass through.

"Don't bug me no more about going to my club," Otis warned.

"I come to make a deal with you," Jo said, admiring the motorcycle. She made a circle around the bike and ran her finger over it as she went. Even the dust on Steel felt special. Maybe it was dust from somewhere magical, like New York City; or even better — the Radio City Music Hall. Jo reached into the sidecar and pulled some rumpled roses out. "These for Katie?"

"Skadat," Otis tried to wave her off.

"You were going to ask her out tonight, weren't you? Then you chickened out. Or you're just waiting for me to go away so you can go bug her some more." She looked hard at the bike. "You didn't need a motorcycle to take Dusty home. You been somewhere today. Where ya been?"

"Girl, you could write a book on being annoying."

"Thank you. Where ya been?"

"Winston-Salem," Otis confided.

"How about this, mister — just let me talk to the boys and they can take a vote. And I'll hook you up with Katie for tonight. Where you goin'?"

He looked doubtful. "I don't know."

"Well everything you've done lately has been a big boomtastic failure. Let me try." Jo cradled the flowers.

"Fine, give it a try, kid."

Jo marched the flowers in to Katie. Sweet Tea's was nearing closing time, and Katie was cleaning tables. She watched Jo enter, eyed the flowers and announced at once that she hoped the flowers were for Jo, because she didn't want them.

"You gotta take the flowers, and you gotta go out with him tonight," Jo said, holding the flowers out. "For two reasons: One, I really think he loves you. And two, it's the only way I can get in the Radio Club. And I prayed that God would let me in that club. Do you believe God answers prayer?"

"Yes, I do believe God answers prayer."

"Well, don't cause me to stumble in my faith." She held out the roses.

Defeated, Katie took the roses. "Where is he taking me?"

"I don't know," Jo said. "But good thing is, I don't think he knows, either."

Mashed Cotton Candy

Vrrrrm! Vrrrrm! The sound of the motorcycle engine sent squirrels and rats diving into their holes. Steel burped and coughed as it climbed the old road up Blue Mountain. This wasn't the same road everyone had taken on their Martian hunt. And it wasn't the bootleggers' secret road. This was a road that dipped and turned and finally climbed up to Lookout Rock. Katie tried to yell at Otis that she didn't want to go up to the rock — she knew what all the young people did up there. But he pretended not to hear her, and she wasn't about to jump out of the sidecar

The air was thick with the smell of pine, mingled with that distant scent of coming rain. This had been a bad idea, Katie told herself. Most men could at least haul a girl around in their car; but Otis had to borrow the school teacher's motorcycle. Humiliating!

When the motorcycle stopped, Katie wasn't impressed with the view. She should have been. The late afternoon sky — the town below — the trees — it was the kind of thing only God could paint. But her vision was fogged by anger.

"I told you not to take me up here," Katie fumed.

Otis ignored her. He took off his helmet, then the gloves, all the while pretending she wasn't there.

"This might be the worst date in history. You dragged me up a mountain hoping I'd..." she trailed off.

"I like to look at it all from the edge," Otis said. He took a thermos he'd strapped to the back of the motorcycle and walked to the mountain's edge. Below him, Madison Creek looked like a child's train set. That ledge would be hard to spot from the ground looking up. Otis sat down, then scooted a bit so that his feet were hanging down. He opened his thermos and took a long drink.

Moonshine, Katie thought. He was going to get drunk up here, and was hoping to get her drunk—and then he was hoping to get her legs pried apart while the alcohol made her silly. Well, that just wasn't going to happen she decided.

"Are you going to jump?" Katie asked from the sidecar. She didn't see any point in getting out.

"No. Are you going to push me?"

"More likely to take the motorcycle on down the mountain myself and let you hoof it down," she nodded toward the sky, "In the rain, maybe."

"The motorcycle is named *Steel*. You should call him that. And I'm willing to bet you can't ride it. Not without breaking your neck."

That was frustrating—probably because it was true. He'd maneuvered them through some tight spots on the road up.

Thunder echoed and emphasized the angry silence that hung between them.

When she looked out at those clouds and then down at the town, she wished things had unfolded a little different. Elias had left town in a terrible way. He had made sure that if she didn't cry over him, she'd at least cry over Charlie Mac. Somewhere deep down, Katie wished she had been with Elias as they raced to put Madison Creek—and maybe all of North Carolina—in the rearview mirror. He had said he had to go up to New York to file his report. She doubted that. He'd probably have some secretary type the entire file and mail it in.

She had been drawn to that mystery, imagining him whisking her away to some wonderful place where she could live free from the burdens of her past.

Her eyes moved along the side of the mountain until they rested on Otis, who sat still, feet hanging over the mountainside like a boy might sit on the edge of a bridge. What was wrong with him, she asked herself. Why was she so resistant to Otis?

Well, for one thing, everyone hated him. Her mother hated him; his own father hated him. He was full of himself, and annoying. But Dusty didn't hate him. In fact, Dusty was crazy about the guy.

Was he attractive? Maybe — probably — but not to her. And that's what mattered, right? Attraction wasn't like two plus two, always having the same answer.

"If you're going to just sit there, you might as well take the box out," Otis said, his gaze still fixed out at the town.

The box had been tucked down near her feet. It could have been a hat box, except it was square.

"What is it?"

"Why don't you open it and see. I drove — or rode — all morning to get that for you."

What kind of annoying gift could he have hidden in that box? He couldn't pop a ring on her, unless he had a box — inside a box — inside a box. But what if it was a dress or a skirt or something he wanted her to wear? Worse, what if he had paid a lot for some article of clothing; she would feel guilted into wearing it because she knew he would have paid for it with money he should have spent on some essential.

"Open the box," he said again. "It's not an engagement ring."

She smiled a little.

Inside the box was doughnuts.

But different than the doughnuts the Hub's Grocery store had. These were glazed with a fine, sticky sugar.

"What is it?" she asked.

"Bring me some and I'll tell you."

"I can't. Might be overcome by the urge to push you off the mountain."

She saw his shoulders bob up and down as he laughed at that. She got out of the sidecar. Her legs ached from being pinned up so long. They screamed with pleasure and pain as she finally stood up.

"I'm not sure I want to sit that close to the edge."

"Then don't."

She handed him the doughnuts and sat down beside him. Katie slid her legs down and let them hang off the mountain side. "If there's an earthquake we're dead."

He shrugged, "If a meteor hits Blue Mountain, we're dead."

"If lightning strikes—"

"We're dead," he finished.

"If there's an avalanche, we're dead."

He laughed hard at that and took a doughnut. "An avalanche is in snow, my dear." He held out the thermos to her. "They taste better with coffee."

She took a doughnut and inspected it. "I've never seen one quite like this."

"Taste and see that the Lord is good."

She bit into the doughnut and moaned with delight. "That is good." She took a long swig of the coffee and finished the doughnut.

"See, I think we could sell these in Madison Creek, don't you?"

She was on her second one and had to talk through a mouthful. "Sell them? Where did ya get 'em?"

"Up the road. Drove all morning. Guy opened a shop and is selling them. But he's looking for drivers and people to get them into local businesses."

"A salesman," she said with irritation. "He just wants you to be a salesman."

"Well, the truck is nice. Really nice. And if you have to sell something, might as well be something as good as this. Beats selling used cars."

She reached for the coffee and took a mouth full. "All right, I give. What are they?"

"Something called *Krispy Kreme*. You ever think of getting out of here, Katie?"

She let her eye run along the road that led from the high hill Huey's church sat on, down through Main Street and then stretched into the trees.

"Yes. But not on a Creepy Cream truck."

"*Krispy Kreme*. What about us, Katie? You ever think about us?"

"Sometimes. But I also think about what you've become—or what you haven't become. I have to work not to remember that wonderful summer we had. We were just teens."

"Summer and fall," he said. "Don't forget the fall."

"It tasted good. And I've tried to forget that taste, Oatsie." She stopped herself. Had she just called him Oatsie? It was like tripping on a jump rope. "I've tried to forget what being in love with you is like, because it was so terrible at the end. We did things we shouldn't have. But then you just had to show me, didn't you? Went off to New York and never came back. Just left me here in little ole' Madison Creek."

The sun had begun to set. Usually the sky would glow, but tonight it was just dark.

"I wanted to hit it big. But you know what I did? I worked where you'd never see me. Sound." He waited for a response, but she was watching the clouds. "You know, when there's a crash, I was one of the guys that made the sound of a crash. Or a boom. Or a doorbell. Or… whatever." He bit into another doughnut.

"You remember how sweet that summer was? Like these doughnuts."

"You drove all the way to Winston-Salem to buy doughnuts just to tell me that?"

"Maybe I did. Do you remember flying that kite off Blue Mountain? It was right over there." He pointed down the mountain. "And you remember going to the State Fair?"

"I do. You were so stupid."

■ ■ ■

The State Fair Otis was referring to was way back in 1929. They were sixteen and the two put their money together and decided to sneak away. They took a bus to Raleigh; but it was really two buses, because the first one broke down.

They got to the fair the day before it closed, October 18th. What a sight! Circus acts, animals, horse races, dog shows, food. That year there was the *Great Bonhair Acrobatic Troupe*, who claimed to be the 'Acrobatic Aces of the Ages.' Everyone *oohed* and *aahed* at them, except Otis, who said he could have done that if he had to.

There was also *The Great Wilno*, who was shot from a giant cannon a hundred feet through the air. As he whirred through the air, Katie had looked at her thin, gangly man and said sarcastically that he probably thought he could do that, too. After all, everything they saw at the fair, he said he could do it. He had gotten his feelings hurt and sulked off to buy food. She trailed after, dripping with apology for hurting his feelings. But he wouldn't listen to her. As he stood in line, ignoring her, she finally lost her cool. "You just think you're better than everyone and everything, Oatsie," she had blurted. "You probably think you could light up the sky better than the fireworks show. I know one prize you could take first in — the pig competition. That's what you are. You're just a big glory hog." And, to her shame, she snorted loud like a pig. He had turned red and stormed off without saying a word.

She wandered blindly into the crowd. Crying. And then, she got in line for the big Ferris wheel. Otis found her and told her she didn't want to go on that, she'd chicken out at the last minute. But she stayed in line, inching up one person at a time.

When they reached the front of the line, she starred up at the steel structure that would carry her to the top. Three hundred feet. It didn't look so tall until you stood right under it and looked up.

"Miss?" The ride operator motioned for her to come on.

It was Otis' turn to make a farm animal sound. It was just one little chicken BAWK. Katie's face went red and she jumped into the seat. Otis started to get in with her, but she shook her head hard. Speaking to the ride operator, "Sir, I'd rather go alone. Is that permitted?"

Of course it was. So up she went. Otis staggered away from the ride, not wanting to go up it himself.

She remembered riding up the Ferris wheel, trembling as the great machine lifted her ever higher. The sky was turning October red and as the sun went down and she could see the entire fairgrounds. This wasn't so bad, she had told herself. In fact, she might ride it again during the fireworks. That's what she would do. Teach Otis to cluck at her like she was a chicken. She was at the peak when the entire thing jolted and came to an abrupt stop. She let out a little gasp. Maybe they were just letting on passengers. But it seemed she could actually feel the power go out of the thing. Everything came to a stop; except her seat, which wagged back and forth like a puppy's tail.

Part of the fairground was plunged into darkness, and she let out a terrible scream. And she wasn't alone. Several other women cried out, both from the Ferris wheel and around the park. And then, she just sat there.

The sky getting darker; the wind became more than a whisper. She tried to pray, but that didn't seem right. God didn't want to hear from little Katie Simpson. She and Otis had burned their bridges with God a few weeks earlier. It had been both terrible and amazing. Terrible that every moment she allowed him to tear away her clothes and kiss her sixteen year old body, she had known the Almighty was taking notes for Judgment Day. When Oatsie entered her, she screamed in pain, pleasure and guilt. But at some point, the pleasure screamed louder than the other two.

So God wasn't going to listen.

In fact, maybe this was how God meant to end things with her. Maybe he had brought her to the top of this Ferris wheel the way he brought Moses way up to the top of Mount Nebo just to kill him.

The wind died for a moment and she felt a little hope, but it was just catching its breath before blowing even harder. She remembered the sound of the steel structure creaking as the wind hollered through it and the way her seat rocked.

God, I'm so sorry for the evil I've done, she started to pray, never actually got the prayer off her lips. Several loud *oohs!* and then some cheering broke her payer. What was this about?

"You go, boy!" someone yelled.

She glanced out, but didn't see anything. Some lights were back on, but the Ferris wheel wasn't moving.

Terrified, she inched to the edge of her seat to look down.

Even the memory of that October night, staring down into the shadows of that steel structure made her stomach queasy.

And then she saw it. Absolutely amazing! Maybe Otis *was* better than the *Great Bonhair Acrobatic Troupe*. They might flip and flop and do all those amazing things — but they didn't climb the Ferris wheel. And that's what the skinny, gangly Otis was doing! He pulled himself from bar to bar, level to level. He reached out at points to shake hands with riders, who were in awe. So *The Great Wilno* might get shot from a cannon, but her man was actually rising into the night by climbing up a Ferris wheel. Who did that? WHO?!

A sixteen year old knight in shining armor, that's who.

From the ground she could now hear people yelling for him to stop at once. Maybe she'd been hearing that all along and just blocked it out.

He had to work his way from one bar to another and then pull himself up. Then, horrified, she saw one of his hands slip. *Everyone* gave a collective gasp! But he kept his composure and in no time both hands were back on the steel and he was rising once again into the night sky.

Even at the memory her heart still skipped a beat. He had climbed all that way just for her.

When he got to her, she gave him her hand and pulled him into the seat.

"You're an idiot," she said, and kissed him on the lips.

He fumbled with his clothes and unbuttoned his shirt.

"Not here!" she chastised.

"You nut head," he laughed. Reaching through the open shirt buttons, he drew out cotton candy. It was the most beat up, sorry looking cotton candy she'd ever seen.

"You said you were hungry," he said.

"For ham!"

"Well, they're both pink."

She laughed and took the cotton candy.

■ ■ ■

Now, sitting there looking at the night, she wondered if they were really the same people. Was that boy who climbed the Ferris wheel for her still somewhere inside of him?

"That was a great time," she said softly, sipping his coffee. "You always bring me food. Cold doughnuts, mashed up cotton candy —"

"Or mashed up flowers," he said. "They locked me up after that. My parents had to come —"

"Yeah. And the judge chewed you out the next morning. But he and the whole courtroom laughed till their sides hurt when you said you did it because a girl was hungry."

"I'd do all that again for you."

"But I'm not the same girl who went up that Ferris wheel. You know, that summer, we had us a heap of fun. And I felt wrong about a lot of it. Every time you'd slip your hand on my chest or reach down to part my legs, I would tingle with desire and my heart would fill with guilt."

"That was a long time ago."

"But you'd do it again, if I let you," she said softly. "In fact, you'd do it right here."

"Maybe," he admitted. "You're all I've wanted."

"Except all them other girls you got your hands on back in New York. Did you pretend they was me while you… you know?"

"I did," he admitted.

"Know what changed in me, Oatsie? I didn't just become a good girl. Something in me changed over those years. When I told you we had to stop — and I broke things off all together, it's because I couldn't bear the guilt. I couldn't sleep at night. When I would take a shower, it was like immorality hung onto me and I couldn't wash it away. But that's not how it is now. I don't want to do right because of guilt; I want to do right because I love Him."

"Who? Elias? He's an idiot!"

"No, you clown!" She stuffed a doughnut into his mouth. "God. I love God. When you do right because you don't want to feel guilt, you always feel like you're missin' out on somethin'. But doin' right because I love God don't hurt so much."

"Fine by me. I like chasin' the church girls best," he said through a face full of doughnut. He lifted his thermos, but she snatched it from him and drank the last of his coffee.

"Now you need some help, don't-ja?" she giggled.

Half the doughnut was still sticking out of his mouth. Grabbing him by the hair, she pulled his head back until he could see the clouds above, and then she bent down into his face and bit off the doughnut.

"Mmmm," she moaned.

When he finally had the doughnut down, and he turned to kiss her, she was ready for him—with the last doughnut. She turned her face toward him, as if to kiss him. But as he moved toward her, she shoved that last doughnut into his expecting mouth.

"Do I taste sweet?" she giggled.

It felt so school-girlish. And good to tease.

■ ■ ■

As she pressed her lips toward him—toward the doughnut—she realized what a hypocrite she was. That's what Minnie Belle would say. Not just for kissing Otis after she told herself she wouldn't. But for telling him she wanted to please God, all the while she'd been running around with Elias. But this past week she really had tried to come back to God.

Once, long ago, when she was out later than she should have been with Otis, she returned home to find her father waiting on the porch. Earl didn't say anything to Otis; but he did increase Katie's chores that week. "Know why I punish you for bad relationship decisions, Katie? Because you'll always get punished for bad relationship decisions. Some day it won't be me who punishes you when you do something stupid with a boy; it'll be life itself. Life will tar and feather you if you make bad choices about a boy."

That had sounded high and mighty back then. But then she'd made a pile of poor decisions with men; and every one of them had brought their own punishment. Except for the one that brought her

Dusty. She used to think that Dusty was her punishment; until Preacher Huey had shown her that the truth was, Dusty was her blessing.

■ ■ ■

A tree branch snapped and both Otis and Katie cried out. Otis dropped a mouth full of wet *Krispy Kreme* onto his overalls.

Something was breathing heavy — and it wasn't Otis.

"What is that?" Katie whispered.

Otis scooted away from the edge of the mountain. "I don't know, but I almost slipped."

Katie also scooted.

The breathing had turned deeper. Whatever it was — it wasn't human, Katie decided.

Turning back she searched the darkness. Hunched over, near the motorcycle, was a shadowy figure.

"What is that?" Otis whispered. He started to get up, but the growling deepened.

The wind caught the empty doughnut box and it flew up. Katie grabbed it before it could go off like a kite into the wind.

"We're about to die, and you don't wanna litter?"

"At least I can die with one good deed on my record."

The figure by the motorcycle finally stood. "No! No! No!" he breathed ominously. He walked slowly toward them. His hair was ruffled, eyes wide and crazy and his face as dirty as a coal miner. His gaze was fixed on Otis. "You don't touch her!"

He jerked his hips back and forth in a motion another generation might identify with a singer from Memphis. "You caused her enough trouble. Now you keep your hands to yourself."

Otis started to rise up, but the man wiggled his index finger in a no-no gesture. His hand raised. Was he holding something? Moonlight flashed against his raised hand. It had to be a knife.

"Do I know you?" Katie called.

The figure giggled like a mad man. "Oh, you know me! I been watchin' over ya since you's just a little tyke. I be your guardian angel!"

"Do you know him?" Otis asked.

She didn't answer. Because maybe—just maybe—she really did. But knowing him wouldn't ease anyone's worries here.

"Now, you there boy," the man said, "You just step away from that pretty girl or I'll send you screaming down the mountain." He laughed like this was the funniest thing he'd ever heard. "I'll take this girl here on up into the mountains and train her right. They'll call me phantom of the mountain, you see?"

"Uncle Sticky," Katie finally hollered, "Is that you?"

"Twas me," the man giggled. "Till I blew myself sky high."

"Sticky Simpson?" Otis said slowly. "We did think you was dead."

"You're dead," Sticky said. "'Cause none of us like you, boy. I didn't like you when I was alive, and I don't like you now that I'm dead."

"You wanna come home with me and clean up?" Katie offered. "My pa sure would be happy to see you."

"Make me happy is to see him dead like me," Sticky said, nodding toward Otis. "Liked it better when this troublemaker was out of the picture." He had begun advancing toward them again. He was now just a few feet away. He might have blown his distillery up, but he still smelled like that special Resurrection Juice.

It was indeed a knife in his hand. As he approached Otis, the knife came up level with his ear. "Why don't you just leave Katie alone? I liked that other boy, the one in the suit, that she was chasing around with. You didn't need to horn in, boy."

Otis snatched the doughnut box from Katie.

"You stop that!" Katie yelled at Sticky. "Go on back where you came from if you don't want my help, but you—"

She was cut off by an old southern cry that had become almost forgotten. It was haunting and disarming all at once—the rebel yell.

"Wa-woo–woohoo!" As he screamed, Sticky sliced through the air with his knife toward Otis.

In an instant Katie pictured Otis laid out for burial. She wished she'd told him her secrets before he died. Wished she'd…

Otis held up the doughnut box, and Sticky plunged his knife in. Before he could pull the knife out, Otis kicked him in the groin. Sticky's eyes went wide and the battle cry fell away.

"You fake reb!" Otis yelled. He dropped the box and the knife and threw himself at Sticky. "You ain't old enough to…"

As they wrestled, Sticky began once again to give the Confederate Battle Cry. Sticky wasn't nearly as tall as Otis, but it was still difficult for Otis to pin him to the ground. Even with Otis holding his wrists down as he straddled his belly, Sticky hollered. It was as if he thought that at any moment reinforcements might rise up out of the forest and come to his defense.

"Shut him up!" Otis yelled at Katie.

Katie wondered if someone else was out there.

She knelt down next to Sticky, "Uncle, won't you please hush up now?"

He went quiet, his head turned to look her in the eye. Then, he screamed even louder. Startled, Katie let out a little cry and rocked backward. Dust and rocks went over the edge of Blue Mountain.

"You stop that!" Otis yelled at him. "You almost sent your angel to her death!"

Sticky became quiet at that. "I'm sorry," he said, sounding almost normal.

"Well, that's a bit better," Otis said.

Then, quick as a rattlesnake, Sticky thrust himself up and kissed Otis on the lips. With Otis caught off guard, he rolled him over and straddled him. Otis might be bigger, but Sticky was both strong and crazy. That wild look in his eye said he was willing to use every bit of energy he possessed to win this contest. He punched Otis in the face; once, twice, three times in a row. Otis tried to fend him off with his hands. Katie yelled and cried for him to stop, but Sticky went on as if he was Joe Lewis in the ring.

"You're gonna kill him!" Katie yelled.

"Feels good," Otis cried as he blocked another punch.

Katie grabbed the doughnut box and pulled out the knife. "You stop it, or I'll —"

Sticky laughed. "Ooh, do it, beauty! Stab me good, and I'll haunt you forever."

Katie tossed the knife aside and threw herself at Sticky. He gave a long, passionate moan as she knocked him to the ground. "Oh, baby, you go at it!" he sighed.

"Run, Otis!" Katie yelled.

He didn't protest, he didn't even hesitate in his heart. He jumped up like a jack-in-the-box finally sprung from his captivity and ran to the bike.

"Listen now," Katie whispered to Sticky. "Everyone wants to know what happened to you. What do you want me to tell them?"

"You tell them nothin'," Sticky said. "Ole Boots knows where to find me. But so long as I'm dead, I'm off ole Sheriff Tuff's radar."

"Now you get up and tell Otis you're sorry," Katie demanded.

"Ah, not a chance," Sticky said. He pushed Katie aside and stood up and dusted himself off. He reached up, tipped his imaginary hat, and wandered away into the forest. Otis looked at Katie and proclaimed, "He kissed me!"

■ ■ ■

Riding down the mountain in the dark was terrifying. Katie tucked herself deep into the sidecar and closed her eyes for as long as she could. But the curves made her sick, and she finally had to peek. She was glad when they whizzed into Madison Creek, blowing by the Little Rickety Church and the dress shop and the café.

"Stop!" she yelled at Otis. She had to tug on his arm.

"What?"

"Go back. Back to Sweet Tea's. I saw somethin'."

Dutifully, he turned back. Did she want to serve up a late night meal? Had she seen a burglar?

But as they approached, he spotted what she had seen.

Laying in front of the cafe's glass door was that little dog Katie loved.

"Charlie Mac!" Katie screamed as she got out of the sidecar. The dog jumped up and leapt into the woman's arms.

He was filthy and smelled like — a sink of dirty dishes. *No*, Otis thought, *that thing smelled worse than dirty dishes*. What's more, Katie seemed happier to see that dog than she'd ever seemed about him. She held Charlie Mac close and kissed him like he was a long lost love.

"You want me to take you home?" Otis asked.

She shook her head. "Nah. I'll just get questioned on where I've been. Best now to stay out the night. Besides, Dusty sleeps in my room and I'd wake him when I come in."

They went around behind the café. Otis watched the dog while Katie went in to get a bucket of soapy water from the kitchen. She fed Charlie Mac some leftover turkey she'd found in the fridge.

Later, with the dog clean and smelling like *Dreft Dish Soap*, they rode back up to the church house. Looking over the one-grave graveyard, they talked on until morning finally came. Katie ran her hands over and over the little dog, in total disbelief that she finally had him back. It almost made up for the misery Sticky had just put them through. Where had Charlie Mac been? It had been a good week now — had he just been running around? Had he escaped Elias' car and run home?

Maybe, Katie thought, *Elias had a change of heart and drove all the way back to Madison Creek to give the dog back to her*. That made her feel a little better about Elias.

"I do always bring you something mashed up," Otis said as the morning sun painted the sky orange.

"Mashed cotton candy was the best," Katie said, remembering the Ferris wheel.

"Tonight I just brought you a mashed up face."

Sheets

On Wednesday, September 21, Elias Moore stared out at the Atlantic from the window of a little clapboard cottage. The surf was rowdy this afternoon. He'd driven up Highway 1, chasing the deepest, bluest sky he'd ever seen. But now, the heavens were changing. The amazing calm that had rested over the highway was gone and heavy clouds raced overhead.

"I just don't know what to do with this, Papa," he said to the old man who sat across from him. Papa didn't respond. He just looked out at the surf and clouds.

"I can't file this report. Not after all I done. I'll lose my job for sure."

The little house on Long Island's West Hampton Beach had been his papa's place ever since he was just a boy. He'd known for a few weeks now that he had to get up here and talk to Papa. Papa would know what to do. About the girls. About the report he needed to file. Most of all, about his soul. That preacher—that fake—had made him uncomfortable with all that talk about God wanting more than a prayer.

The old man had raised him and schooled him in his own trade. As a boy, Elias had worked on the fishing boats with the ole men. But at night he taught himself to read. He was a natural at math and reading, a real book worm. Papa had always said that maybe, somehow, Elias would escape West Hampton Beach and go make something of himself. He thought Papa was just dreaming, until he asked a girl to accompany him to the church dance. She'd waved her hand in front of her nose and said absolutely not, she didn't want to be seen with a boy who always smelled like fish. He decided in his heart to work as hard as he could to never smell like fish again.

The wind was picking up outside, but Papa didn't seem worried.

A storm was coming, that was all.

"I got in some girl trouble," he finally said. The house sighed and moaned with the wind. "Government sends me all over the state, and Papa, I've sure piled up some serious sins."

Papa lit his pipe and tipped back a little in his chair. The surf was rising. The smell of the ocean was stronger than Papa's pipe.

Elias talked on. He told Papa about Katie. They hadn't done anything too bad, just kissed. But what if his sweetie back home, the one he'd put the wedding ring on and said he'd cherish forever — what if she found out? He told Papa how his ring got stolen. And there was more. Dare he tell papa? He was safe. He told the old man about the other women. The one in Charlotte and the one in Asheville. The prostitute right here on Long Island. He told the old man everything; and the old man listened without judging. In fact, it seemed he didn't even hear Elias. He just sat and smoked his pipe. Outside, the wind battered the house and rain began to sprinkle across the beach. No; it wasn't sprinkling. It was suddenly pouring down.

"Looks like this storm is gonna be a doozy," Elias said. He guessed he wouldn't be seeing Abby tonight, even though he'd spotted her on his drive into town.

The old man rubbed his chin and nodded.

And so long as he was coming clean, he might as well tell Papa how he'd taken Katie's dog. He had done it in a moment of spite. She'd taken his ring and then tricked him into a situation where the entire town laughed at him — so he took her dog. But he only got a few miles out of town before guilt slipped and began to strangle him. He let the dog lose on the side of the road, but it was such a small little rat, it probably got eaten.

The wind outside was violent.

"Papa, you there?" Elias said to the wind.

But Papa was not there. Papa had not been in this house for three weeks now. They buried the old man, and it was Elias' job to clean out Papa's belongings. His aunt had said she'd do it, seeing as how he was so busy with the IRS assignments. But he said he wanted to do it. He needed this one last talk with Papa — even if it was only with his ghost.

Incredibly, the wind outside grew stronger. The little wood house strained as if it might come apart. The ocean was growing, eating up the beach between him and the house. The only sound was the sound of the wind. It was eerie because the birds he was so used to hearing squawk on the beach had all vanished.

Papa, is that you? Elias asked again. He glanced toward the place where Papa had been sitting, smoking his pipe. No one was there. He began to weep.

Through his tears, he saw something unbelievable.

Outside, the ocean exploded onto the shore. The wind, which had been screaming, turned into a deep, low moan.

Is this about the file? he asked the empty house. He held up the Huey House file and waved it. This had to be a dream. Or maybe, he thought, Papa really was speaking to him. *I'm fed up with Madison Creek! Fed up with Huey House and his music lady and all those blacks! Never seen nothin' like it, and —*

A gust of wind blasted the beach, and the windows in the house crashed in. The file he'd been wagging in the air was snatched from his hand and blown across the room. The wind pinned it to the wall.

"I need that!" Elias yelled.

He glanced back at the beach. But there was no beach. Just ocean, and the biggest wave he'd ever seen was headed for the house. It was as if a great sheet of sea had decided to tuck the little town in for the night.

He looked from the door to the file. Should he run — dare he leave the house? — or should he secure his file?

It didn't matter. Because he realized in an instant that his time was up. The alarm clock was striking and it was time for him to exit the stage. As the water slammed into the little cottage, the walls folded in on themselves like a house of cards, and Elias Moore realized something terrible: He loved his wife. Really loved her. But she would never know it. Because he hadn't known it until this moment.

There wasn't time to reflect further than that. The hurricane smashed the house down as it surged forward, eating up West Hampton Beach.

The great hurricane of 1938 would take over seven hundred lives. It also swallowed up IRS file #3454598, with the name House printed neatly on it. The file was stuffed with over seventy pages of handwritten notes. They would never be filed, or typed, or even read.

"It's like Pharaoh's army," Elias said, holding on to a board as the tide carried him away. "I feel like Pharaoh's army, and ole Huey House has closed the sea in on me." He spit out salt water and laughed at that.

The water ripped at his legs and he tightened his grip on the board.

The house had just disintegrated all around him. And now the ocean wanted him. And he wanted his wife. Wanted to hold her hand one last time – or a thousand more. He wanted to feel her warm squeeze as she slipped her fingers into his.

Things rushed through his mind as the water carried him along. The way he'd punched Otis Step. The long, wonderful kisses from Katie Simpson. The way his wife had kissed him the day before he left for Madison Creek, even giving him a playful swat on the behind as he left. And he remembered the crazy lady at the junkyard; the one who slapped his behind. And there was Katie's dog. Why had he done that to her? Just to hurt her? She was right to be mad; he was married – to a truly beautiful woman.

There was more, so much more, to think over. But a floating telephone pole came between Elias Moore and his thoughts. Knocked unconscious, the water carried him along as it picked up trees, cars, and even houses.

■ ■ ■

Jo got the news about the hurricane before the paper landed on her front porch. She was up late supposedly doing homework, but it was hard to study without some background music. She was dial twisting the radio when she caught a distant report that came between local channels. Blasting through the static was a new bulletin warning citizens to evacuate. Through crackles and pops, she understood a massive hurricane had destroyed New York. She wondered if the Empire State Building was still standing. Good thing Miss Evermund had gotten away from New York before it fell off the map.

"Aunt Georgette, come here!" Jo called.

She got chewed out for messing around when she was supposed to do homework; but that was soon forgotten as her aunt listened to what news she could.

"A great flood — it's like the days of Noah, huh," Jo said to Georgette.

"Mayhap it is, Jo," Georgette said. "We have to get the church together to pray."

■ ■ ■

The next night after the big hurricane struck New York and ate up Long Island, the Little Rickety Church of Madison Creek opened its doors for prayer.

Inside the church, under the glow of oil lanterns, Georgette read from the newspaper about the big storm. The headline read:

MANY DEAD IN HURRICANE

The news article said that scores of bodies had been cast all over the Long Island shore, and that the subway had come to a stop. Hotels had gone dark and boardwalks were destroyed by the massive storm.

Many of the people couldn't read, so they had relied on what people told them had happened. Some had heard the Statue of Liberty washed away. Big X said that he'd heard the big storm had gone through Washington and that President Roosevelt had barely escaped.

Jo sat in the back of the room trying to read Macbeth. She rubbed her nose absently on the collar of her dress, then thought about how Georgette would give her a tongue lashing if she messed up one of her few school dresses. She rubbed at the collar, hoping to wipe the snot away. Miss Evermund said she knew Jo would like the book, but so far Jo was unconvinced. Shakespeare wrote plays, not books. She didn't understand reading something that was obviously meant to be watched and heard. It would make more sense on the radio.

Earlier that day Miss Evermund had called on Jo and asked her if she understood Shakespeare. Jo said she did, and Miss Evermund asked if she knew what a soliloquy was. "Sure," Jo had said, "That's when you get a far off look in your eye and you talk to yourself. You kind of mutter and say what you're thinkin'." Miss Evermund had been impressed, until Jo added, "Kinda makes ya look like an idiot, goin' around talkin' to your dumb ole self."

In the church house, Aunt Georgette divided the men and women into separate prayer circles. Jo got the feeling the women liked this a lot more than the men did. They'd hoped their wives would carry the prayer load. Jo certainly didn't want to get stuck in a prayer circle. She needed to get Macbeth read. She decided to go outside. Of course, it would be dark out there, but she might get some light by a window.

She eased the church door open, hoping no one would stop her.

There was light outside after all.

Fear that Jo had tried to tuck down inside of herself slipped loose and slithered up her spine. She stood in shock as the church door swung open. The darkness was alive again. Once more, Jo saw the dreaded symbol of Jesus Christ on fire. Two hooded men draped in sheets stood by the cross.

Spotting her in the doorway of the church, one of the men lifted his hand into the air. He was holding a large butcher knife. He made a slicing motion through the air.

"Y'all!" Jo yelled over her shoulder.

■ ■ ■

They clogged the doorway and finally spilled out of the church to see the burning cross in the vacant field across the street. Sometimes Jo played over there; but she thought she never could again.

"Nigga lovas!" one of the men yelled. His voice echoed, giving it a haunting sound.

The other one — the one with the knife — cackled like an old witch. It wasn't *spooky* scary; it was *crazy* scary. That made Jo even more frightened. If a person was really crazy, they might actually do crazy things — like hurt people.

The one without the knife stepped in front of the cross and yelled like a preacher. "God is bringing his judgment down on this nation! Liberal New York first, the whore of America."

"That's right," the one with the knife actually had a deep voice — despite his witch cackle.

"We'll rid the earth of the likes of you!" the preacher-one shouted. Behind him the cross blazed. "We'll find you at home and slice you up. We're not afraid of locked doors. You little kids hear that? We'll be comin' to get ya! You done stirred up the hornet's nest."

"Hey!" Nettie Drake yelled. They didn't hear her at first, and the preacher-one continued on trying to scare the kids. But Nettie was walking away from the cluster in front of the church and toward the men in sheets. "I said hey!" She sounded mad.

"You repent, woman!" the preacher-one commanded, his finger out as if to direct the judgment of God her way.

"Those be *my* sheets!" Nettie yelled.

The hand that had been pointed at her wavered. "What'd you say?"

The one with the knife lowered his hand. It seemed even the blazing cross dimmed a bit.

"I said those be *my* sheets! On your heads. Covering you up. Those are *my* sheets! They were stolen from *my* home!"

"Repent sinner!" the preacher-one commanded with new energy.

"Give the lady her sheets," Hammond Washington burst out, and several people actually laughed.

"Hush up!" someone from the church yelled. Jo felt sad when she realized it was Boots. She had hoped he would be the first to run out to protect Nettie.

Nettie slowed. She was halfway to them now.

Boots yelled across the yard, "Y'all made yar big point. We understand and don't want no trouble. Nettie, you come on back now."

"You stole my sheets!" Nettie cried again, enraged. She spun around to address the church people. "You folks remember when my house got broke into? They was lookin' for the money that rascal had to give me after he ran off with the California suntan girl!" She pointed at the men. "They ransacked my house looking for treasure. They found some money all right. A lot of it. And they hauled it out in my bed sheets. And there's my bed sheets!"

"We didn't do it!" the one with the knife protested.

"Maybe we did," the other contradicted. "We ain't afraid to go through your house. Slice you up if we find ya home."

"I know that voice!" Nettie exploded. "I'll have Sheriff Tuff on your doorstep first thing in the morning! Robbery. Breaking and entering. I hope you boys like jail."

The one with the knife lost his patience and broke out in a run toward Nettie. The other one, the speaker, yelled for him to get back where he belonged.

"Come on, sheet stealer!" Nettie screamed, opening her arms up in invitation. "They'll fry you in the electrical chair if you hurt me!"

The one with the knife was right on Nettie, ready to stab her, when dark hands came out of the night and grabbed him.

Hammond Washington pushed Nettie aside and grabbed the attacker's wrist. Then, sweeping in from the other side, Big X knocked him to the ground.

"My heroes," Nettie breathed.

Seeing his friend tackled, the preacher-one broke into a run of his own—toward the street and down the hill. He had to hold his sheet up—Nettie's sheet—as he ran. It reminded Jo of the way a girl with a long dress might run. "Bye-bye, you sissy!" Jo yelled.

At once, Georgette hit her upside the head. "What's wrong with you?"

"Let me go!" knife-boy demanded as he struggled between Big X and Hammond.

"That's my sheet," Nettie said again, folding her arms. "I can tell, it has faded yellow flowers all over it."

On the other side of the street, the beams of the wood cross broke away.

"Let go of me! I'll kill you!" His voice was full of desperation.

Hammond held up the knife the man had been wielding moments earlier. "Nah, you won't hurt no one tonight. I know who you are." He tugged at the sheet, but the man underneath struggled frantically to stay under it.

"You know," Big X said, "I think I do see yellow flowers."

"Stand him up on his feet," Uncle Huey said, stepping off the church porch and into the darkness.

Big X lifted the man onto his feet. The sheet was stretched tight now as he held on in desperation.

Uncle Huey stood in front of the man and held out his hand. He waited, but the man under the sheet wasn't going to let go.

"Sir, I have my hand out," he said. "Are you going to shake it and let me thank you?"

"Don't you thank him!" Nettie was indignant.

"He didn't mean nothin' by it," Huey said. "He was just bringing you your sheet back. Ain't that right?"

The man under the sheet didn't move.

"That's what he was doin', Nettie. He was just bringing your sheet back. Now, mister, you give Nettie her sheet back."

The man was pulling that sheet so tight over himself that Jo expected to see the thin material finally give up and his head come popping out.

He turned to the man and put his hand on his shoulder. The man tried to jerk away, but Big X and Hammond had him in their clutches. "If you won't give Nettie her sheet back, I reckon we oughta get the Sheriff out of bed right now and lock you up."

"Ah, we didn't even take nothin' worth anything," the man under the sheet said.

"Nettie, did they actually steal anything of value?" Huey asked.

"Messed up my house somethin' awful," Nettie said. "And stole lots of money."

The one under the sheet yelled, "You liar woman! Just some old Confederate money!"

"You ought to say sorry," Huey prompted. "Otherwise, we call the Sheriff."

Like a sulking child, the man finally said sorry. But he did not let go of the sheet.

"Gotta give Nettie her sheet back," Huey insisted.

"Okay. But let me do it myself."

Huey nodded for Big X and Hammond to let go of him. As soon as they did, the man broke into a hard run. Big X actually laughed.

"Run!" Hammond hollered as if a caged bird had just been set free. "You ain't gonna get nowhere, 'cause—"

The man tripped over a rock.

"'Cause it's dark out here. And you didn't cut your itty bitty eye holes big enough," Hammond finished.

Huey and Hammond started to run after the man, but the forest suddenly exploded with gunfire. It might have only been four guns, or perhaps as few as two—but it sounded like forty. The gunfire came from two directions. A loud scream pierced the air.

"We'll kill you all!" someone yelled from the forest.

"Nigga lovas!" a voice hollered from the other direction.

"That's Red Heartland," Jo said softly. "And I'll bet he means it, too. He really would kill us."

Nettie demanded they not let her sheet get away. But no one was interested in pursuing with real guns being fired.

"Ah, let's go pray," Huey said.

They gathered back in the church house to pray. This time, Jo joined the prayer session. Besides, talking to God was better than reading Shakespeare's characters that talk to themselves. She could tell, people were starting to get really scared.

"They won't kill you white people," Jo overheard Elisha Robinson tell Katie Simpson. "No they won't. But they'll drag us blacks right from our homes and terrorize us. Might kill us."

■ ■ ■

Several of those gathered offered up prayers to the Lord on high.

MEEMAW MOSES:	We beseech thee, Father, to help those poor people in New York. And give us a safe place to worship you right here in Madison Creek.
BIG X:	No foolin' Big God, we ah little scared. Threats and burnin' crosses got us thinkin' twice about church.
GEORGETTE:	Almighty God, you show us if it's time to maybe — maybe just call an end to this church thing and go back to our own churches.
SHORTY PARKER:	Oh God, don't you take our church away.
NETTIE DRAKE:	Now Lord, you know who took my sheets. Who broke in my house. Breathe down some fire on them.
DOCTOR BANKS:	Lord, you just calm things down around here. We're all a little timid to go home now. But forgive those who…
HAMMOND WASHINGTON:	Lord, this looks like it's gonna be trench warfare. Like it was back in the Great War. You gotta give us some deliverance.

■ ■ ■

Their prayers were cut short with a crash. One of the church windows burst, glass flew everywhere. Hammond, who had just prayed, didn't say amen, but let out a surprised cry and fell down hurt toward the center of the prayer circle. The rock that had come through the window had struck him in the head.

Red blood pooled around Hammond.

"I'll kill them!" Shorty yelled.

Jo's eyes moved between Hammond, who was grasping at his bleeding head and the rock that had struck him. There was a note attached.

"It's not bad," Hammond said. "I be okay."

Doctor Banks knelt down beside Hammond. "He'll be okay, but I need somethin' to sop up the blood."

Georgette told Huey to give her his undershirt. He was annoyed at that, since he was wearing overalls and didn't want to fuss with getting down to his shirt. But he did what he was told. Doctor Banks held the shirt to Hammond's wounded head.

When Jo looked back to the rock, she noticed the note that had been attached was gone.

"Where'd the note go?"

Meemaw Moses held her finger to her lips to shush the girl.

■ ■ ■

That night Jo lay awake thinking about the burning cross. First at her home, then at the church. But this time they hadn't just burned a cross, they'd fired shots and thrown rocks. They'd drawn blood. What was next? She'd heard someone say lynching. Wasn't that when they took you out into the woods and tied you to a tree and whipped you? Or worse, hung you?

Deep in the night, she sat up and looked down into the yard. She expected to see the cross on fire again, but it wasn't.

She looked from the window to her doorway. Maybe she should tell her uncle how scared—

Her heart skipped a beat.

Someone was in her room. Standing near the doorway, a solitary figure stood motionless.

She sat perfectly still, staring at the stranger. It was all shadows, and he was still as could be. As if maybe he was frozen in place like a great statue, waiting for just the right moment to lash out and do whatever he'd come for.

She waited. Stared harder into the darkness, and wondered if maybe it wasn't a person, maybe it was a — she didn't know what else it could be. It was a person… a man.

Outside rain had begun to tap the roof.

Maybe the person had come to lynch her. Maybe they would make a lesson of her. It would be the quickest way to get Uncle Huey to bring an end to this church business. They could cause him all kinds of trouble, but he would just find ways of turning the tables on them. She was surprised he hadn't somehow gotten Nettie's sheets back for her. But the way to really hurt Huey was to hurt her. She knew that. What if they ripped her from her warm bed and dragged her out into that rain? And what if those big men in sheets beat her?

She wanted to cry or scream, but fear paralyzed her.

Nothing to fear but fear itself, that's what the president said. But the president didn't have bad guys standing in his bedroom waiting for the right moment to kill him.

She looked away, then looked back thinking maybe the shadowy figure would be gone. But he was still there. Still hulking in that corner near the door.

She sat still and quiet, fear coursing over her as the night ticked away. She had to go to the bathroom, but didn't dare move. Uncle Huey was in the next room. She could hear him sawing logs and wondered if he'd lost a single night's sleep over this church business.

Finally, gathering all the strength she had, Jo whispered into the darkness, "Hey, you… what do you want?"

The person in her room didn't answer.

So she waited. Downstairs the big clock counted seconds and minutes and hours. It felt like years to Jo. Outside the rain continued to wet Madison Creek. Jo thought about all those people who lost their homes in New York. At this moment, she would trade places with any of them. Better to fight a storm than a man who wants to hurt you.

But then, as the sky breathed its first ray of morning light, the shadows began to change.

It wasn't a man in her room, waiting to kill her. It was her own clothes hanging on the closet door. Aunt Georgette had set out clean overalls and a shirt for her. But in the darkness, it sure had looked like someone was standing there.

She dropped back into the bed and gave a little laugh. How silly she'd been! Relief swept over her. She was surprised when tears even touched her face.

Doggone it, it was a school day; she'd be sleepy all day.

■ ■ ■

Three days after the big storm and two days after the prayer meeting, Nettie Drake woke up to the sound of something beating on her wall. When she got out of bed to investigate, she didn't find anyone there. Only, nailed to the wall next to her door were her sheets. They hung like twin ghosts, with tiny eye slits staring out at her.

It was such a haunting sight that she was unable to even touch them. It was scary to see something familiar, her own sheets, turned into something evil. She had once slept soundly on those very sheets, and now mean men had taken them right from her own home and worn them into the night.

She called Huey House, who came with his nasty friend Boots.

"Ah, they gave you your sheets back after all," Huey said, bemused.

"Why don't you go give it back to them," Nettie said. "You know it's got to be those Grimm brothers and Red Heartland. Maybe a few other rough characters around here."

Boots was thoughtful. "Might be somethin' more. What if folk from other towns have started comin' in to harass us? The gunshots in the forest, it sounded like a lot."

"Nah," Huey blew them off. "I'll just take the sheets and get rid of them. Don't worry none."

"I think it's time to worry," Nettie said.

When they were in Huey's truck, Boots said what he really thought. "It's the Radio Club."

Huey laughed. "The *White* Radio Club? Those bunch of cowards couldn't find their way out of a Cracker Jack box."

"The old ones want to keep the peace," Boots surmised. "But the younger crew is probably rocking the boat. And you're giving them boys' ammunition. Huey my friend, maybe it's time to call an end to this church thing."

Africa Calling

The man with the beard watched as the people filed into the church. He'd been promised that there would be music, singing, dancing and — well, who knows what else. But these people entered like it was a funeral.

He watched the last one go in, then counted to fifty.

"Ho-ho-how ya do-doin'?" a big oaf at the door asked. "If ya-yar new, be su-sure to say ho-howdy to my si-sister. She's a school te-teacher."

They shook hands, and the man with the beard went inside. It was indeed a strange mix of farmers, blacks, miners, women, and children. Up front was a fella wearing bib overalls that were stretched by his ballooning stomach.

The man settled down into a makeshift pew. It wasn't very comfortable.

"We had a good run," an older black woman said. "I made friends I would have never expected. Learned a little about the Lawd while I was at it."

"Just the same," a white man said, "it's time we called it quits. Give the Lord one last song and one last sermon and say amen to it all. We can't risk our houses... or our lives."

There was friendly banter in the congregation. Some agreed that it was indeed time to wrap things up. But there were others who insisted they hadn't done anything wrong. It was just church. It wasn't like they were asking for an end to segregated schools or restaurants or anything else that might seem controversial.

"Maybe we should vote," the old black woman suggested.

The man in front wiped sweat from his brow and shook his head. "No, that's not how we got in this mess. Reckon I got-ja in it. I started the church. You all showed up on accident."

"No sir!" a well-dressed black man said. "You invited us, and we took the invitation. Now unless you're sayin' you and you alone can decide if this is a church, I recommend we put it to the people of God."

There were scattered amens and more debate. It was obvious that those who were ready to call it quits outnumbered the ones who wanted to plow on.

The man with the beard waited until a vote was called for, and then stood up. "If you all don't mind, I have somethin' to say."

The preacher up front shrugged his big shoulders. What could it hurt?

The bearded man came to the front and introduced himself as Buck Hardy. "I'm home from Africa, where I've been workin' as a missionary. Came through town a few months ago, back when y'all was plannin' this here operation. Ran myself knee deep into some self-righteous, mean spirited church women. You know the types?"

There were a few knowing grunts.

"Judgmental… uppity. Lady folk like that are the very reason lots of people don't go to church."

"Ain't that the truth," the old black woman agreed.

"But I feel true religion in this room. I'm a missionary, home from the Belgian Congo. I've been ministering to the Mwamba." He turned to the preacher. "I have a word for this sweet church, if I can?"

The preacher slapped him on the back. "Ladies and gentleman, our last sermon will be given by the missionary-man, Buck Hardy, who took the Gospel to the Belgian Congo!"

There was cheering and applause. The heavy mood lifted as Buck adjusted his tie and smoothed his brown suit.

■ ■ ■

Mr. Missionary-man told about his adventures in Africa. About how he wanted the tribe to build a special hut for the study of God's Word. As the tribe was digging and packing mud, they came upon nothing less than a human skull. The tribe was convinced that this was an evil sign from the spirits. The tribe gave up on the hut that night, and the next day a terrible rain storm swept their work away. The natives were sure it was the work of the evil spirit that had been trapped in the mud, and they asked the missionary-man to leave.

Buck paused, until Hammond Washington asked, "Well, mister, did you leave?"

"Did David Livingstone leave when it got difficult? He did not! And what about ole Moses, stuck with those Hebrews. Did he give up on that tribe?"

"He did not!" the congregation said in unison.

There were more examples, followed by the line *he did not*.

   - Did David leave Goliath?

   - Did Nehemiah give up on the wall?

   - Did Job quit God when his life fell apart?

By the time he finished his examples, the congregation was rowdy with excitement.

"No, my friends, I stuck with them. They thought I had an evil spirit, but with time, my wife and I won them over. I was crippled back then, and she pushed me everywhere. Through the mud, the jungle. But if you love people, really love them — with a determined kind of love — you can show them the face of Jesus. God's color blind, ya know?"

"Amen!"

"My friends, I heard you talking about giving up on this here church of yours. I think if God is bigger than the spirits in Africa, he's bigger than any sprits here in Madison Creek. Don't any of you let that ole Devil scare ya! You just keep on doin' what you're doin'. Love the Lord and worship him."

"Sir," Nettie Drake stood to her feet. "I think the folks who hate this church are aiming to kill me."

Mr. Missionary-man held out his hand, "Lord Jesus, I bind our enemy in the holy name. I bind Satan from this woman. Free her house from any evil, and build a mighty hedge around her. Protect her in Jesus name!"

Tears streamed down Nettie's cheeks. Visible relief washed over her as she sank toward her seat.

He turned to Huey, "Sir, might I bless this church?"

"Sure, iffin' it's what God told ya to do."

"No!" Georgette said. "Because there's no church to bless. We're closing up shop."

"Not no more we're not," Huey said, straightening himself. With that, there was applause and shouts of hallelujah. "I'm not scared of no evil spirits. Not in Africa and not in Madison Creek."

"Thank the Good Lawd, we's be a church again!" Big X declared.

Mr. Missionary-man called for God to build spiritual walls around the church. The kind that could not be busted through by Satan or his minions. He prayed for peace and power and a great moving of the Holy Ghost. And what's more, he prayed for Africa and the Mwamba. He lifted up the people, who had been struck by the terrible plague. He poured out his heart to the Lord, wept with loud cries, as he recounted to God how the tribe was suffering under the plague because they did not have medicine. He put his hands to his face and sobbed as he recounted how he had to leave his beloved tribe. And oh how the children, the blessed little children, had suffered under the plague.

"Why did you leave?" Meemaw Moses asked.

"What kind of plague did they have?" Annie Evermund asked. She had planted herself as a spectator on the far side of the church.

Buck had to think for a moment. "Malaria."

Annie nodded, as if he had just passed a small test. "How did they get Malaria?"

"Mosquitos. Come down and ravaged the country. Same way grasshoppers tear up a farm, these little critters have destroyed the tribe."

Annie stood up now, very interested. "And sir, if I may just ask one thing; what is it that might heal the tribe?"

"Jesus!" Meemaw Moses cried. "Jesus will heal them!"

"No!" Annie's voice was strong. "Jesus gave us the answer. I just want to know if this man knows what it is."

Once again, feeling he was being given an examination, Buck said, "Quinine. It comes from a bug in Brazil. Ain't that just the way God works, ladies and gentlemen? Gives us the cure for Africa, but hides it in South America."

Annie stepped toward the center aisle. "Sir, Quinine comes from a tree in South America. Not a bug."

"And does it ever!" Then, backing off his enthusiasm a little — the way a man driving hard might ease off the gas pedal, he said, "But to tell you the truth, I'm not a scientist. A little medical training. A little preaching. A lot of Jesus. But I do have the connections to move the medicine on to the tribe. But our funds got cut short and I had to come home. But my supplier in Brazil is ready to move. If I move fast, raise the money I need, I can get them that medicine out of Brazil and the children won't die."

A gasp rippled through the congregation.

Then, as if a new idea had just come to him, hope filled the missionary-man's face. "But maybe — and I just say a little maybe."

Lutie Dotson was skeptical. "You're thinkin' *maybe* we might help."

"I didn't ask."

Nettie Drake was excited, "You didn't ask us to give?" It was a question. "Really? People are dying in your tribe, and you are their preacher, and you can't find it in yourself to ask others to help?"

"Well, times are hard in these parts."

"I want an offerin'!" Meemaw Moses said.

Others agreed. And soon, they weren't just asking for an offering to help the Mwamba, they were demanding one.

"You be out of town this week," Hammond Washington took to his feet and pointed. Buck looked worried. "You don't collect our money and then hang around here spending it. You get on out of here and raise the rest of what you need. Ya ole Jonah. God sent you to minister to your people, and you're back home moping around.

Get the money, get the medicine from Brazil, and get ya sorry self, back to the Congo."

Otis, who had almost squeezed Katie's hand in two, jumped up. "Ah, this is more than I can take! You all are being suckered in by the best of 'em! He might come up this way looking all spiffy and talking about some heathen tribe in Africa, but my mama didn't raise no fool."

Mr. Missionary-man didn't have time to defend himself. One of the miners came to his defense, "My mama didn't raise no fool, either. A fool chooses to disobey God. A fool don't help those in need."

Meemaw Moses gave a hearty amen. Even Huey nodded agreement.

Another miner, blind Sammy Peak, grasped the bench in front of him and spoke loud. "Ah, I smell a rat. Probably a whole nest of 'em. But just the same, it's the best story I've heard this week. Give 'em an offerin'!"

"Don't give him nothin'!" Otis was incredulous. "Shyster! Thief! Con-artist!"

"I understand your concern, sir," Buck said. "When I was prayin' up here, I had a short vision of you, Mr. Otis Step. Maybe I should share the vision."

"Maybe you ought to shut your pie hole! Come on, Katie, we don't need to listen to this clown."

Otis pulled Katie toward the door. "Wait!" she said. "I want to give an offering before we go."

■ ■ ■

Buck did not take immediate charge of the offering; Huey House did, as he did every offering. Hammond put it in the usual bag for offerings and gave it to the preacher. Everyone expected some kind of presentation, but Huey simply gave a prayer of thanksgiving and said that he would see that the missionary-man got the money.

"You come by my house around three this afternoon," Huey instructed Buck. "I'll have the money ready for you and say a prayer for ya."

An hour before Buck Hardy arrived, Georgette came out to the Man Village to tell Huey he had a telephone call. He asked her if she couldn't just take a message, but—of course—she didn't feel she could do that for him. It was Katie Simpson on the phone, and she sounded rushed.

"Preacher House, I just have a favor to ask of you. Maybe you could find out for me a little more from that missionary-man how he knows..." she paused, "you know."

"How he knows what?" Huey asked.

"I gotta go," she said, and hung up the phone.

Huey stared at Georgette, "That didn't make a lick of sense."

"She's worried the operator listens in on her calls," Georgette said.

"Ah, I would have done better with a smoke signal."

Buck Henry arrived five minutes early, and Huey invited him to the Man Village. Huey sat down at the splintered table where he did his business. Buck looked around at the old bath tubs, piles of wood, windows, car parts, engines and everything else imaginable.

"This is quite a place you have here. You could about build a city with all this stuff you have. God's sure blessed you, Reverend."

"Sit down and shut up," Huey instructed.

"Did I do somethin' to rile you up?"

"No. I want to get this over with. Ways I see it, the people gave for Africa. But they gave it in the church. So the church gets half, and Africa gets half. You're Africa, understand?"

Buck rubbed at his beard. "Way I see it, preacher, is all that money was given for Africa."

"It was. But, you owe me a scoundrel fee."

"Scoundrel fee?"

"Sure. I had that church business all wrapped up, until you came in there and got everyone all slap-happy about having church again. So in my eyes you're a scoundrel. I reckon you have been to Africa, and you have a heart for your people. But even the preacher has to pay the piper. You want to split it, or should I just keep the whole thing?"

"How do I know you didn't already swipe a little?"

Huey ignored that. "Here's how it goes. You reach in, take somethin' out, and it's yours. Then I reach in, do the same."

"We could just divide it fifty-fifty."

"Ah, you don't have any sense of adventure. We'll do it my way."

■ ■ ■

Buck reached in and drew out a dollar bill.

Huey withdrew a nickel.

BUCK: Dollar.

HUEY: Dime.

BUCK: Five dollars!

HUEY: Quarter.

BUCK: Dollar.

HUEY: Quarter.

They went on like this. Huey drawing change while Buck took the bills.

"You hoping for something special?" Buck asked.

"Just keep playin'," Huey urged.

This time when Buck's hand went into the bag, he rifled around more. He pressed past the tempting bills and dug down into the change. "I think I found it. Lucky draw." His hand came out of the bag in a fist.

"Now, show me what you have!"

Buck opened his fist. In the palm of his hand was a diamond ring.

"Good golly!" Huey cried. "That's a weddin' ring! Someone done gave you their wedding ring!"

"They must have told you they put it in the offering. You was digging around for it," Buck said. "Now it's mine—I mean Africa's." He admired how the diamond shined in the afternoon sunlight. "This beauty cost a pretty penny."

"Cost blood and sweat down in the coal mine," Huey said. He leaned on the table. "How about I trade you my take—all of it—for that there ring. See, I know who it belongs to, and it should go back to her."

"No, no," Buck smiled a little. "It belongs to Africa, fair and square. You made the rules."

"She's a widow, you see. And her husband sure did work to give her that ring. She dropped it in the plate so you could go to Africa. So, you better be sure you're goin' to Africa if you take it."

Buck was annoyed. "Don't doubt me now, preacher. She gave that ring to God's work. And if anything, you have to respect the work of God. Besides, she gave that ring away, probably to help her deal with her suffering. She probably teared up every time she saw that thing. I'm helping her by taking it off her hands."

"Taking it right off her hand," Huey said, remembering the way Annie Evermund had come looking for that very ring she'd hidden in the piano. Roy had given it to her, and had worked hard in the mines to pay for it.

Buck gripped the ring, "I think she gave it. So it's right for me to keep it—and give it to the Africa work."

"Then that's how it should be," Huey slapped Buck so hard on the back he almost dropped the ring. "But how about this, how about I buy that ring off of you?"

"You won't have enough in that bag to buy the ring. And there's nothin' I see around here I'd want to trade for it."

"No, no. I have a little stash hidden away. Moonshine treasure. I don't tell no one about it. How about this, you think about it tonight, and if you want, I'll buy that ring back from you. Pay you top dollar. Way I see it, it's gonna take you some time and effort to turn that ring into the cash you need."

"What do you think it's worth?"

Huey shook his head in disbelief, "Oh, a lot!"

"Well, I'm taking the ring with me," Buck said.

■ ■ ■

That night, Huey skipped his usual quiet time on the porch with Georgette. He was busy making plans.

The next morning, Jo set off for school and Georgette busied herself with a new Sunday School article. Huey waited on the big red porch and listened to Georgette's typewriter *clink* and *thunk* as she hammered out words.

"Well there's trouble!" Huey said as Buck drove up in his old Coupe. "You ready?"

"I just don't know if you'll really be able to pay top dollar for this here ring," Buck worried. "I mean, I would settle for far less, if it was just me here. But the children of the Congo are suffering and need the best relief I can give them."

Buck had started toward the porch, but Huey blew past him.

"Where you goin'?"

"Thought we'd take my truck. Get in, we can gab on the way."

"The way to what?"

"My moonshine loot. You come to cash out that ring, right?"

Reluctant at first, Buck got in the truck. Huey tossed a shovel in the truck bed and they were off. As they drove, Huey jabbered on about how much that ring was worth. Huey House was a bonehead, Buck decided. Buyers are supposed to try to talk you down, but this fool was so excited, he actually wanted to give top dollar for this prize. Yet the ring had been in Huey's own bag that whole time — what a twit.

As the road began to bend and wind, Buck finally asked exactly where they were going.

"Ah, my treasure is up yonder on Blue Mountain. Gotta keep it safe."

■ ■ ■

Buck complained that something seemed wrong when Huey parked the truck and said it was time to start climbing. Wasn't there a path?

But, the thought of all that promised money warmed his heart, and he followed Huey up into the trees. The climb was steep and Huey was slow. He had his shovel in one hand, resting against his shoulder, and he used the other hand to grasp trees to pull himself up the mountainside.

"God showed me this place," Huey huffed.

Up ahead a large rock jutted from the mountain side. It was the same rock Jo and Dusty had played on when everyone thought the asteroid had struck the mountain.

"See that burned tree right there? Finger of God swooshed down and struck that tree. Only an idiot would bury his treasure on the side of a path or in his own back yard. Huey House has brains, you see? That tree and that rock are my marker from God."

"Sure, sure," Buck agreed. "Just don't push me off that rock!"

"I didn't take you up here to kill you. I took you up here to do business. But I gotta dig up my treasure now, and I don't want you to see where it is. So I'm going to have to blindfold you."

"I'll look the other way. But I don't want to—"

"Then look the other way for a moment."

When Buck turned away, Huey swung his shovel and hit him hard in the head. Caught off guard, Buck fell back. He didn't have the ability to defend himself, since he was focused on not rolling down the hillside. Huey lifted his shovel again, this time Buck saw it and gave a pathetic cry of *Nooo!* He started to rise up, but the shovel smacked him in the face and the world went dark.

■ ■ ■

When Buck came to, he was tied up. His arms and legs were stretched out and tied to trees. His head throbbed. Sitting with his back against a tree, his feet angled up the hill, Huey gave Buck a childish wave.

"Well howdy there." His voice was friendly.

"What's wrong with you?" Buck raged. "You want to steal my ring? I didn't bring it with me. I'm no fool."

"Neither am I," Huey said. "Let's have a little church. You confess your sins, and I'll set you free. If not, I'll make a sacrifice of you."

"A sacrifice?"

"Sure. God told ole Abraham to take his son up into the mountains and sacrifice him. I think God wants me to sacrifice you."

"Jesus is the sacrifice, you fool," Buck said, and struggled at his ropes.

Where had he gotten ropes? He was sure Huey had not carried ropes up the mountain. This had been prearranged.

"I really am a missionary to Africa," Buck tried to sound calm.

"Maybe," Huey considered. "But the Quinine you talked about, it doesn't come from Brazil. It comes from Peru. My friend, the school teacher, she's been to Peru. She mentioned that to me on the way out of church yesterday. She suggested that if I tested you, and you turned out to be the real McCoy — to see to it that her ring went right to you. See, she really wants to help those people in the Congo. Especially the children. But she was suspicious, because you got the whole country wrong."

"I meant to say Peru." Buck fumed. "Don't judge me, you judgmental judger,"

"'Don't judge me,' that's what the fella says when he gets caught in bed with a woman he's not married to. And another slip she noticed was that they don't get the medicine from a bug — they get it from a tree called a Cinchona. Comes right from the bark of the tree."

"This is ridiculous. People are suffering, and you're picking —"

"People are suffering, and you're a thief," Huey declared. "And, we both know you haven't been to Africa any more than I'm the mayor of New York. So that makes you a double scoundrel in my book. Now, maybe I'll let you go if you're ready to spill some beans."

"What do you want to know?"

"Otis Step, that boy's a mess, isn't he?"

"Reckon. I just had a vision about him—"

"Ah, you stop that," Huey commanded. "No more of your visions and talk of tribes. I have a gun back in the truck, if I wasn't so lazy I'd go get it and sacrifice you right now. But I'd have to climb back up this hill, and my poor heart isn't going to let me do that. So I'll just have to leave you here for ole Hickory Joe."

"Hickory Joe?"

"Killed his wife a while back and went on the run. Strange thing, people been seein' him round these parts lately. Some people think the trouble we've had at the church is ole Hickory Joe."

"Probably the K-K-K."

"No, I think it's Hickory. Been seen standing outside windows and just lookin' for trouble. For the most part, things are quiet 'round here. Then, every few years, ole Hickory gets a hankering to cause trouble. Usually the killing kind of trouble. He starts with animals, but then moves on to people. Been about six years since he butchered anyone. I figure it's neigh about time he got it out of his system. This is his turf we're on. Seems reasonable to me that I just let you be the sacrifice and appease ole Hickory?"

"I don't believe you."

"Well, I'll just leave you here tonight. If you're still alive in the morning, I'll untie you and send you on your way."

"You can't do that!" Buck yelled. His voice repeated in an echo across the mountain.

"Well, I'm not the one tied up. You are. I'm not doin' nuttin' wrong. Just gonna give you the day to pray about it."

He slipped the blindfold over Buck's throbbing head. Best to pray in the dark, he explained. And then, with a final—playful—slap to the cheek, he said, "Aye be seein' ya, ole boy."

■ ■ ■

Buck yelled for Huey to come back. He listened as the ole codger began to work his way down the mountain side. The sound of branches snapping and leaves crunching had never seemed more crisp than they did with the blindfold on. Also, there was the sound of the big guys heavy breathing and grunting as he went.

Eventually the sounds died away, and he was left with only the birds chirping.

The terror didn't start for a few more hours. But blindfolded and tied up, it felt like much more than hours to Buck.

It was cold on the mountain and when night began to crawl in, the temperature dropped even more. When darkness came, a new sound greeted Buck. He'd listened to the forest for hours now — squirrels, birds, wind through the trees. But now he heard someone breathing.

Fear and hope gripped him at the same time. Maybe Huey was done with his games and had come to let him go.

"Help!" he cried. He knew he shouldn't. He should lay still and listen some more, but the urge to call out was insurmountable.

His plea was met by a deep laugh. He almost expected to hear *The Shadow Knows*.

"Who is that?" Buck demanded.

He was answered with the heavy sound of breathing. Whoever it was, Buck could tell two things: First he was huge, and second, it was not Huey House.

The someone was very close to him.

"I've had a dreadful time," Buck said. "I'm a servant of God —"

More laughter. Deep and hard. It sounded like an evil Santa. *Ho-ho-ho.* The sound rattled up from the man's chest. Spittle that punctuated the stranger's laughter sprinkled on Buck's face.

"Sacrifice," the stranger breathed.

"Now —"

He broke off and screamed as the stranger ran the edge of a knife against his cheek.

"Lay still," the stranger commanded.

There was movement. He felt the stranger's hands on the front of his shirt. He wanted to beg and plead, but he knew that wouldn't do a bit of good. He smelled terrible. A mix of cigar smoke, alcohol and body odor clouded around the monster.

"This is all because I didn't know Quinine comes from a tree in Peru," Buck whined.

The monster laughed and ripped Buck's shirt open from top to bottom. The same way Jesus rent the curtain of the temple in two, Buck thought.

Then the knife was back, sliding up and down his chest. It didn't hurt, because the monster wasn't pushing down yet.

His head already ached from the shovel attack. Still, through the fog and fear, a memory formed. The woman in the dress shop — Minnie Belle, he thought — had warned him of a judgment day. Had scared the life out of poor Doug. Even Buck had jumped out of his wheelchair in terror thinking judgment had come to Madison Creek that day back in August. Only, it wasn't the judgment of God, just some idiot moving stones. But now — now Minnie Belle's judgment was coming to pass. Not with the Second Coming, but with something that seemed worse. God had set a monster lose on him.

"I'm a man of God," Buck whispered, trying not to cry.

The monster actually growled like a dog and pressed the point of the knife at the center of Buck's chest. "David Livingston was a man of God," the stranger rumbled. "Went to Africa. You *like* him?"

"Yes!"

The knife did not ease up. In fact, it pressed a little harder. "You know, they cut David Livingston's heart out and buried it in Africa."

"NO!"

"I feel Africa calling," the monster hissed, and began to press down.

"No! I repent!" Buck screamed. "Don't sacrifice me! Don't send my heart to Africa!"

The pressure let up. What started as relief turned into fresh terror when Buck realized the monster was simply lifting the knife over his head. He'd been marking his spot, and now he was ready to strike.

"AFRICA CALLING!" the monster roared.

Buck sensed the movement as the strangers' arms came down and the knife plunged into him. He screamed, and his hollow echo screamed back at him a thousand times.

Only, when the strangers' hands came down, a knife did not plunge into Buck. Just the strangers' bare fists struck him.

Then he was struck in the chest again, this time harder. His scream hiccupped as the strangers' giant fist struck his chest.

■ ■ ■

Sometime during the night, after the monster — Hickory Joe? — had left him to whine and suffer and cry, Buck Hardy began to pray.

Salvation came as a motorcycle engine sawed away at the mountainside.

"Let this be you, Lord," Buck prayed. Would God ride a motorcycle? He hoped so, but thought not.

Eventually, the sound that had been coming ever closer, stopped.

Buck lay, hurting, crying and begging God as Annie Evermund climbed the mountain.

"You wretched sinner," Annie said. "I came to save you, unless you want another dose of Hickory Joe. And, iffin' you don't mind bein' saved by a girl."

"Save me," Buck pleaded.

"Well, I'm gonna untie you and you're gonna have to go down this mountain on your own in the dark. I ain't gonna carry you. And if you make any trouble for me, just know that ole Hickory is probably just traipsing along after us."

Annie didn't give Buck much allowance for his injuries. She rushed him along down the mountain, even as he groaned and cried about the pain he was in. He stumbled over rocks and growth several times, but she just gave him little kicks and told him to move his sorry self.

"I want my wedding ring back," she said when they came to where her motorcycle was. She had to help him get into the sidecar, where he folded up in pain.

"I'll give you your blasted ring," Buck cried.

His face was caked with dirt and bruises, his shirt was ripped and even in the moonlight, his beard looked red from all the blood.

"I saved you," Annie said. "I can drive you on down this mountain, or I can leave you here. But a ride from me is going to cost some information. And I'll warn you, I already know most of it, so if you lie to me, I'll hand you back over to the preacher."

"No!" Buck pleaded. 'I'll tell you everything."

And he did.

The ride down Blue Mountain in the dark was terrifying. She knew the old road so well, it was almost like she was part of the mountainside. They blasted right through the town; passing by the church and the dress shop, Hub's Grocery, Sweet Tea's and Finch's Mercantile like lightning.

At the edge of town she pulled over behind an old Coupe.

"The keys are in the car."

"Your ring? I got to get you your —"

"The church folk found the ring in your hotel room, in the Gideon Bible. Lying right under Matthew 25:41. You go look it up later, I think you'll find a word from the Lord." She patted him on his aching head. "Asheville is that way," she pointed, "and Woodfin is out yonder, but they're both a little close for us. You find yourself a good doughnut up there at Winston-Salem. But we don't want you near our doughnuts. So just keep movin'. Charlotte is on up that way, and if you gotta stay in North Carolina, I guess Charlotte or Raleigh is where you might land. Get any closer to Madison Creek, and I'm afraid I won't be able to save you again."

"Save me?"

"Sure. You come back, I'm sure ole Hickory and Preacher House will finish the sacrifice. See, preacher told me somethin' interesting today after school. Told me how he wasn't sure he believed any of this ruckus about the Almighty. But when you came and were ready to steal my wedding ring—"

"You gave it!"

"Shut up." She thumped him on the head. "When you stole my wedding ring, the one Roy gave me, some righteous anger burned in our friend Huey House. He got mad, and more than mad; he got religious. He found himself a hunk of the Holy Ghost he didn't know was in 'em." She pointed to the road ahead. "Now I've got class tomorrow, and I'm sick of you. So get out of town, or we'll kill you in Jesus' name."

■ ■ ■

That Monday night as the sun set, Huey and Georgette sat in their rockers on the porch and talked. They could hear Annie coming long before her motorcycle pulled up the drive. The surprise was that the giant of a man, Mule was squeezed into the sidecar.

"Well howdy-do!" Huey said as Annie and Mule came up onto the porch. She was holding a box.

"Ho-howdy d-d-do yarself! Sa-say ho-howdy, Annie."

"Howdy," Annie gave a tired grin.

"Did you get your ring back, honey?" Georgette asked Annie.

"I did," Annie said. Then, looking down at the box in her hands she giggled a little, "But goodness, this isn't it! Don't I wish I had a ring that needed a box this big."

"It's a pr-pr-present for you, bi-big preacher."

Annie held the gift out. "Mule and I just want to say thank you in a special way."

"Good grief," Georgette groaned as Huey took the gift.

"You didn't have to bring me no gift," Huey said.

"I wanted to — *we* wanted to. See, most preachers are shepherds. You're more like a guard dog. Nice to the family, but willing to rip up anyone who wants to come prowling around causin' the innocent trouble. So this is our thank you. Now you just hurry along and get into it."

He opened the box and smiled. It was a worn Bible. "Oh, I like this! Good and fat."

"Fat, but not too tall," Annie pointed out. "You could jam that in your pocket iffin' you wanted."

"It was our fa-fa-father's Bible," Mule explained.

Huey nodded with approval. "I like it that it's good and fat. Reckon every preacher needs a fat Bible. Makes it look like the pages got lumpy with tears."

"Well, there's be a little weeping over this Bible," Annie promised. "I carried it with me to Mexico, and used to hide it down in my sidecar. Sorry it's not new."

"No, new wouldn't be special," Huey said. He held the Bible to his nose, took a deep breath in as if to savor the smell. Then he kissed it.

"Have a seat, you two," Georgette said. "I'll get some tea. We want to hear about the missionary-man."

October Peanuts and Wedding Pumpkins

It was a cool October morning, and there was plenty of work to do at Finch's Mercantile.

Clyde and his new assistant, Clay Simons, spent the first part of the morning taking down the old sign. The sign had been part of his battle with Herbert Locks, who had opened up a grocery. Minnie Belle came in earlier in the week and told Clyde that his sign was starting to look ridiculous. It was time the sign come down. She was willing to poll the Concerned Women of Madison Creek, if he liked, but she was sure she spoke for all of them.

Finch's Mercantile
Everything You Really Need!

"Lookie there," Clay said, pointing as a big pickup loaded with peanuts turned the corner.

"Good grief," Clyde Finch shook his head. "Peanuts, peanuts, peanuts. No doubt they're headed back to the loading dock."

"You gonna dicker with them over price?" Clay asked. "'Cause I want in on that part of the business, too. Teach me everything, Mr. Finch. I don't want to go back to delivering—"

"Hush up, that's the first rule," Finch said and gave the boy a playful punch. "I'll deal with this one on my own. You dig the nails out of that old sign and toss it on the wood pile. After that, use the dust mop on the floor inside."

With that, Finch went on around the Mercantile to meet the Grimm brothers.

The Grimm brothers had been in the peanut business—forever. Their old man had run the peanut farm years ago, until his health broke and the boys took it over. What had been a thriving business under the old man dwindled before the boys' eyes. What's worse, the old man lived to see it and rub it in.

They had excuses, most of which involved the boll weevil and a lack of solid help.

These days there were tractors to make the work easier. Tractors were Alvin's favorite because they didn't talk all day. There was a big bank loan on the newest tractor—a Ford, Alvin named *Buffalo Bill*. When they bought the tractor, they had preacher Weatherwax over to bless the machine.

Teddy's wife, a fiery German immigrant named Greta, had saved their business. She lined up local stores as well as some larger companies who were interested in the peanuts. For the local stores, they were willing to salt and can the peanuts to make them ready for quick sales.

"Howdy," Clyde said as he strolled toward the truck. "Whatcha got?"

Teddy did all the talking. Greta often joked that the cat got Alvin's tongue and buried it in Peter Pan's Neverland.

"Gots us some peanuts. Canned and salted, ready for sale," Teddy said. "Raw ones, too. If you're interested in a barrel ah those. Seems like you sold raw peanuts last year, too."

Clyde nodded, "Yep. They sold pretty good last year."

"Well, harvest is done and here we are—"

"Glad you stopped by, boys. But I don't need no peanuts this year."

At once both men's faces dropped like boys who had been denied candy. "Whatcha say, Mr. Finch?"

"I said the Mercantile doesn't need your peanuts this year."

Teddy's face reddened, "Well that's interesting. See, I just come from Hub's Grocery, and he done told me the same thing. You men tryin' to drive our family outta business?"

"I just don't like buying from rascals," Clyde said casually.

"Come on, Teddy, let's go," Alvin said.

"No, WC Fields said that sometimes a man *must take the bull by the tail and face the situation*." But Teddy was thinking about Greta.

She'd wring him out if he somehow lost all the local sales she'd generated. "What's the problem, Clyde?"

Clyde mustered his courage. "I'm tired of the shenanigans. You cause trouble round these parts, and because you attend the Radio Club, people figure we're all in cahoots with you rascals. You run around burning crosses, breaking into folks homes — white folks — and cause all manner ah trouble. I'm done buyin' from you until you act like businessmen."

"You a nigga lova?" Teddy sneered, his voice lined with accusation. "I see them coons all over the Mercantile."

"Money's the same shade green no matter if it come from a black hand or a white hand," Finch said. "I'm fed up with Jordan Town, Teddy. Can't stand the likes of them. But know what makes money, Teddy? Peace. Peace makes money. Scared people don't spend money except on locks."

"I'll tell everyone you're a nigga lova," Teddy spit.

Finch shrugged, "You give Greta my regrets."

Only after they had driven away did Teddy realize Finch had said regrets, not regards.

■ ■ ■

By the time September had turned to October, the Little Rickety Church had established itself as something of a local staple. Huey preached strange sermons, the band brought energetic music, and outrageous things happened every week.

- Blind Sammy Peak gave his testimony, about how Jesus was his light. Someone, not to name names — but their initials are Lutie Dotson — said it was ridiculous for a blind man to say Jesus was his light. Sammy agreed, but said it made as much sense as Edgar Bergan putting his ventriloquist act on the radio.

- Nettie Drake asked to be baptized. Church was cancelled that week and they met at Huey's place where he baptized Nettie in the creek. Afterward, Huey opened up the Man Village, declaring that everything was half-price that day. Of course, nothing had a price to begin with, but he said he was giving everyone half-off.

One Sunday, when Boots and Mule were called forward to collect the offering, chaos ensued. As soon as Doctor Banks said "Amen" at the end of the offering prayer, Dusty shouted out a line from a commercial he'd heard a thousand times on the radio, "Time for Philip Morrrrrisssss!"

Cousin Pearly brought her twin nephews to church that Sunday. Everyone called her *cousin*, even though it was rather complicated trying to figure out exactly whose cousin she was. The twins had already gotten in trouble at Finch's for swapping the price tags while Pearly shopped. Clay almost sold a new blanket for ten cents.

As usual, when the jug came by, people dropped money in. Pennies and dimes and even a few quarters *thunk*ed about. Mule was helping Boots take the offering, using his customary skillet. As the offering went around the band up front played *Keep On The Sunny Side of Life*. It was an old song, and in no way religious — but they liked playing it, so they did.

Something chattered across the floor. No one saw it, but the twins had dropped a small mountain of marbles they'd been hoarding in their pockets. The marbles sprayed across the floor and Mule let out a sharp *oh*! He danced in the aisle as marbles chased him. His feet went two ways at once and he tried to use his hands to balance himself. Like a sailor in a storm getting rid of unneeded cargo, Mule threw the skillet into the air. The congregation responded with a long intake of breath, *huhhhhh* as the skillet and money went up toward heaven, and then a long *oohhhhh* as it all rained down.

The skillet whomped Lutie Dotson on the head. She had been bowing her head, pretending to pray so that the ushers would pass her by. She grabbed for the top of her head as the skillet landed on the floor behind her.

Mule finally lost his balance and found the wood floor about the same time the skillet did. People looked at one another nervously. Money was rolling across the floor, and some of it was leaking through the cracks in the boards.

"Uh, ain't I go-God's own fool?" Mule lamented.

Mrs. Dotson shot up, her hands grasped at her twisting head, "Who did that?" she demanded, looking toward the back of the room at Huey. She jerked the other way and narrowed her eyes at the band. The music had stopped all together. Shorty Parker met her gaze directly. Shorty's steady eyes gave her balance and the two stayed locked on one another. Then, just to confuse her a little more, Shorty puckered up and sent her a kiss through the air. Lutie dropped into her seat, red faced and a little smitten.

Cousin Pearly, who had been trying to sit as respectfully as she could and keep her boys from snickering, finally spotted the marbles. In one angry motion, she stood up and took the boys by the suspenders. She marched with a squirming boy in each hand, her pretty dark face chiseled with resolution.

"Don't beat us! Don't beat us!" one boy hollered.

"Don't beat us!" Dusty shouted, giving a perfect imitation.

"Whoop 'em good!" Boots cried out with glee.

"Whoop 'em good!" Dusty's voice changed and mirrored Boots.

The congregation roared with laughter. Meemaw Moses who had kept her composure through most of it, finally bent in half. When Meemaw Moses laughed, she sucked in hard and actually snorted. It was such a strange sound that it made everyone laugh even harder.

■ ■ ■

It was just over a week before Halloween when Katie made a big announcement. She had been meeting with the women, and they had decided the church would host its first ever Halloween Eve bash. What a great night to have a harvest celebration. Meemaw Moses asked everyone to bring pumpkins and to dress up anyway they liked—except no ghosts.

"I'm gonna dress like a pig!" Dusty declared. "I'm gonna eat and eat and eat. *Oink! Oink! Oink!*"

"I'll slaughter the pig," Boots grinned and made a slicing motion through the air.

Dusty squealed like a frightened hog.

"Slaughter pigs at the slaughter house, but I'll slaughter you on the Halloween Eve altar," Boots said and everyone laughed.

Katie told Dusty to stop it.

"I feel this is Devil work," Nettie objected.

Katie had an answer ready. "Ancient pagans celebrated their Sun god with every kind of wickedness. But do you know what ancient Christians did? They took over the holiday, which was held on December 25, and so they celebrated the birth of Christ. They recognized the light of the world while the evil Romans celebrated their wicked god of darkness. But soon, the good celebration overcame the bad one. I bet y'all celebrate Christmas without feeling any guilt."

Several people leaned forward with interest.

"The Christians didn't just take over December 25, they went further and even invented Christmas Eve. That's what we're doing; inventing out own holiday — Halloween Eve. We sure ain't askin' y'all to do nothin' bad. We're sayin' that maybe a church should do something good in a bad season."

Inspired, Georgette gave a hearty amen to this.

"Beautiful!" Otis declared from his seat.

Things had only gotten more intense between Otis and Katie since that night they sat on Blue Mountain and ate doughnuts. Still, each one harbored deep secrets they hadn't found the right moment to share.

Katie blew Otis a little kiss.

"Ah, knock it off," Boots gave a disgusted look. "Y'all are in church now. Behave."

There was new laughter. Katie finished up her announcement.

"We'll have the radio up here for music. And you all bring pumpkins carved and dress-up for fun. Bring candy, lots of candy for the kids. And if you have a crop that came in recently, bring a portion of that crop as a thanksgiving to the Lord. Finally, we'll have some games. Apple bobbing, maybe darts — "

"Oh no, not darts," Georgette vetoed that one right away.

"Well, anyhoo, we'll have us some games."

■ ■ ■

When the last amen was said in church, people got up ready to go, when the men began to hum the wedding march: "Da da ta da! Da da ta da!"

Katie was still up front after making her announcement.

Otis came down the aisle, fresh flowers in his arms, he knelt before her.

"Katie, dear, we've had some bad times. Some tough times. But I love you, lady. I'd climb to the top of the world for you; or at least the top of a Ferris wheel. I'd go to the ends of the earth to get you anything that would make you happy; even doughnuts." He spoke slowly, with metered precision he'd practiced for the past three weeks. "Baby doll, you would make me the richest man in the world if you would be my bride."

Katie's eyes filled with tears. But Otis felt conflicted by what that meant. Was she upset with him? He had sprung this too soon?

"But, baby," Otis stammered, unsure of himself and feeling embarrassed, "if you need more time, I can give you space to think it over."

"No!" Katie wept.

Now he was truly confused. "No?! You won't marry me?"

"No, I don't need more time, you oaf. Yes, Oatsie, I'll marry you."

Oats gripped the flowers tight to his own chest. "What a relief!"

That was too much for Dusty, who blurted lines from his favorite commercial, "What a relief indeed! Get rid of your gas and bloating with *Alka-Seltzer*." Then, coming up onto the little stage to stand beside his mother, Dusty pointed his index finger at Otis. "When do you plan to marry my mama?"

"Before the pumpkins go bad," Otis said, looking to Katie for approval.

She blushed, "I don't know, cowboy, you're in a mighty tall hurry."

He realized he'd been pressing the flowers against his chest. "Here, one more mashed up thing for you."

She took the flowers and laughed. "Mashed cotton candy, cold doughnuts—and now another batch of mashed roses."

"Well, let's stop mashing everything up and get somethin' done. I've waited long enough for you, my love. Let's do this before—"

"I heard you. Before the pumpkins go bad."

"Y'all ought to take an African honeymoon," Boots said. Then, breaking into his Hickory Joe voice, he declared, "I just feel AFRICA CALLING!"

"Stop it, you ole pirate," Katie chastised. "You're really scary when you make that voice."

Boots looked sheepish. "I know a missionary who might agree with you."

The Problem
with Halloween

Minnie Belle Lawson stomped into the Mercantile. Clay Simons asked if he might help her, but she said she wanted to talk to the mayor—right away. "I deserve it," she said.

Clyde stepped from the storeroom. "Minnie Belle, bless your heart, ain't I glad to see you. You wanna come back yonder and talk to me?"

There were several customers, and Minnie Belle's tantrums didn't usually make for easy shopping.

"I don't need to do this in secret, Clyde. I just need you to do something, understand me? I've been nice and civil for long enough. But this is over the top."

"Really, we can talk—"

She pointed at the floor. "Really and truly, we can talk right here, buster! Unless you want to throw me out of the Mercantile."

People peeked around the aisles and between clothes racks.

"Okay, sweetie, tell me what's got you stirred up."

"This!" She held up a flyer. "Got it this morning. Fresh off the press, no doubt." She held the top and bottom of the paper and shook it so hard that Clyde thought it might rip. "What are you going to do about this Devil worship?"

HALLOWEEN EVE

Bash for JESUS

Little Rickety
Church

5:30 p.m.

Dread and exasperation pulled at him. Huey House had finally gone too far. There wasn't going to be any way to appease Minnie Belle, or the other Concerned Women of Madison Creek.

He tried a few other avenues, before addressing the problem directly.

- Had she spoken to Georgette? Yes, and Georgette was concerned, but felt 'their hearts were in the right place.'

- And what about Sheriff Tuff? The Sheriff would just say there was nothing illegal about having a party.

- Finch reminded Minnie Belle that she was a married woman. Of course. And Leonard's terrible upset. But he's a follower, not a leader. Not that he's scared, he just needs some leadership.

When Finch finally spoke, he put his hand reassuringly on Minnie Belle's shoulder. "Well, rest your sweet soul, Minnie Belle. Leave it all to me. I'll go give Huey a talkin' to."

Minnie Belle shrugged his hand off of her. "You talk your face off and nothin'll come of it. No sir. I want you to stop this thing. Maybe it's time that Radio Club—what's it called?—the *White* Radio Club. Maybe it's time you all had a meeting and took some action."

"Yes!" someone in the store yelled.

"Do somethin' mayor!" someone else agreed.

Minnie Belle was delighted. "Or, maybe I should just go on up to the Grimm Peanut Farm."

Clyde shook his head. "I'll do something."

■ ■ ■

"Well now, look what the cat dragged in," Minnie Belle said as the dress shop door swooshed shut.

Katie Simpson was radiant. Her eyes shined with a new glow. She looked like she'd swallowed a lightning bolt. "Ain't it a fine day, Minnie Belle?"

Minnie Belle rolled her eyes. Even the promise of a new customer wasn't enough to make this day any better. "Ain't it sad some folk ain't educated themselves enough to stop sayin' ain't? What's got you all sparkled up?" Minnie Belle eyed her. "You're either pregnant or engaged. And I think you're a tad skinny right now to be pregnant."

"Why thank you, Minnie Belle!" Katie ran her palms over her smooth belly and narrow hips.

"You engaged to Otis? You know he doesn't really have a job, right? Just loafs around all day and makes a mockery of the working man. I hope he's not on Relief."

"He's holding out for something good," Katie said. "You have wedding dresses?"

"Honey, I make most of the dresses. If you want me to make you a wedding dress, I'll do it. But I won't make you a white one."

Katie reddened. "Why not?"

"Because white is for virgins. And you have that boy running around nipping at your ankles."

"Dusty? That's his name, you know?"

"I don't mean to offend, honey. I just can't see making a white dress if you ain't a virgin. I mean, somewhere out there that boy — I mean Dusty — has a father, and anyone can figure out how all that went. And it seems you have men lined up clear to New York interested in — "

"Good heavens you sure are interested in my woman parts, aren't you Minnie Belle? You've done more thinking today about what's between my legs than I have. As far as I'm concerned, God made me a virgin again — if you're interested in that — and it sure seems you are. I guess you don't believe in second chances."

Minnie Belle waved her off. "Don't make no difference to me. Just don't ask for a white wedding dress."

Katie's jaw dropped, "You just have that special gift, Minnie Belle. You can rip a person's happy heart right out of their chest and stomp all over it." She straightened up. "I'd rather wear the living room drapes down the aisle than something you made. And I'll tell ya somethin' else, Dusty makes me happy. That's what my preacher taught me. You don't need to worry yourself about *how* he got here, just be glad he *is* here."

"Ask those Devil worshipers you go to church with to make you a dress," Minnie Belle raged.

"The Devil party was my idea. And you know what we're going to do up there? Have an orgy. Sex and drinking and everything else.

Maybe we'll sacrifice a pig and have a hog roast." Katie smiled — it felt good to make Minnie Belle quiver with disgust.

"I'm prayin' for you," Minnie Belle said, which is what she always said when she didn't know what to say.

"Please don't talk to God on my behalf," Katie said before stomping out. "I'm not sure you're talkin' to the same Jesus I know."

■ ■ ■

Katie walked down the hill toward Sweet Tea's with a mix of delight and old hurt. It had felt good to fight with Minnie Belle, but she'd gotten wounded in the battle just the same. It took her heart a long time to heal up from insults about Dusty. Maybe, she considered, she could pay Preacher House another call and he could tell her again to be *happy* about Dusty.

As she passed the barber, the sound of a motorcycle caught her attention. It was Annie Evermund, fresh out of school and headed home. Mondays must be terrible for her, Katie considered. Annie didn't just blow by, though. She stopped, U-turned and then pulled up next to the sidewalk. She yelled something at Katie, but it was hard to hear her over the motorcycle's engine. With Annie pointing, Katie understood the schoolteacher wanted her to get in the sidecar.

"I gotta work!" Katie yelled.

Annie shook her head, "Get in," she commanded.

Katie looked down the street. Oh well, pops had said he would cover her work while she got fitted at the dress shop. Besides, Dusty was headed over to the Boys Radio Club, so he was out of her hair for a while. She slid into the sidecar and the motorcycle buzzed away.

■ ■ ■

At the Grimm Peanut Farm, it was Greta's job to answer the horn. She did the mail, advertising and lined up new business. Since she'd married Teddy, the farm's business had steadily improved. Too bad the old man wasn't alive to see it.

They were a match made in hell. The late night fights sometimes ended in broken lamps, smashed plates and once a busted door. But they were good business partners. Just as much as she could fight with Teddy — because he really was a knuckle head — she loved him even more. He'd fallen for her at the same time the women in town were trying to decide what to do with a German. Hitler made it difficult to be German in America, and so she tried even harder to be a Southern Belle.

She usually answered the phone on the first two rings. "Grimm's Peanut Farm, this is Greta."

"Greta, this is Rose Abernathy."

"The operator? Do I have a call?"

"Just listen, I've got to tell this to someone or I'll bust, okay?"

"Okay," Greta agreed, hating how even her *okay* sounded so German.

Rose was whispering and talking fast. Greta held the phone close to her ear, as if would magically make it easier to understand Rose. "I'm not supposed to do this, because I'm at work. Don't tell a soul."

GRETA: Uh-huh.

ROSE: You know how I am responsible over here for making the connections for the phones. And sometimes I hear things. I don't go stickin' my nose in other people's business, you understand? I mind my own yard, you understand that?

GRETA: I understand.

ROSE: I just think Teddy might want to know that the church is planning a big Halloween sacrifice — or Halloween Eve. But everyone's sayin' it's the same thing.

Her voice dropped. Maybe someone was passing by her that she didn't want hearing what she said.

GRETA: Rose, are you still there?

ROSE: Some folk are sayin' they're going to sacrifice a pig.

GRETA: Oh my.

ROSE: Like in the Old Testament, you know? Sacrificing — but not sheep, or goats — pigs! But I gotta go. See ya, love.

The phone clicked.

Greta took the phone from her ear and stared at it. What had that been about? It was probably just rubbish. Still, she liked it that Rose had thought of her as trustworthy.

The phone rang again. Greta thought it would be Rose with more information, but it was Minnie Belle, and she was wound up about the same thing. A Halloween Eve bonanza or something up at the church. Did Greta know anything about it? And who ever heard of Halloween Eve?

"Well, I'm not supposed to say," Greta spoke slowly, but that German accent wouldn't edge off. "But, you won't believe what I heard…"

■ ■ ■

The other boys were all gone, and Otis was about to take Dusty on back to Sweet Tea's, when someone pounded on the apartment door. Edith Step answered it, and then showed Katie into the main room.

"Mama!" Dusty leapt to his feet. He held up the Coke he'd been drinking and declared, "It's the best friend thirst ever had." He punctuated that with a hearty burp that would have made any grown man proud.

Edith Step was quick to reprimand Dusty. "We don't burp like that, boy!"

Katie said, "He has a name. I gave him that name. Everyone better stop calling him boy." She felt more feisty than ever since the fight with Minnie Belle and her conversation with Annie.

"Mama," Dusty held up some papers, "I'm gonna be Flash Gordon and Buck Rogers, all in one! That's the play we're making. It's called — wait, what's it called, Oats?"

"Space Crusaders," Otis said, looking a little proud of himself. "I made it up, Katie. I mean, we all did. We're making it up and writing it down as we go." He nodded to the typewriter set up in front of the window.

"Sweet." She wondered who was doing the typing, because he struggled to read the newspaper.

Otis stepped toward her for a kiss, but she wasn't in the mood.

"We need to talk, Otis. Right now."

"If this is about the church and that stupid Halloween—"

"It doesn't have one thing to do with the church," Katie promised.

From the kitchen, Edith offered to give them some space. Katie took her up on that, and asked if she might also take Dusty. The woman agreed, but Katie could tell she resented it. She didn't like Dusty, Katie realized; Dusty did not make her happy.

When they were gone, Otis reached a second time for Katie, hoping to embrace her. "Alright, sweetie, what has you all tore up?"

"Annie Evermund come by to see me. We had a little talk in her office—which is a motorcycle sidecar."

Otis tried a warm smile, "Last time you was in that sidecar, you was with me. Remember that?"

"Oh, I remember that. Let's see how good your memory is, hot stuff. Do you remember, oh, let's say, what happened those years you said you were in New York?"

Otis' face gave pause. "I told you. I was on the radio. I did sound effects, background noise, and washed dishes."

Now she took a step toward him and grasped the front of his shirt. "Otis, where did you wash dishes?"

"Restaurants. Just to pay the rent."

"Liar," Katie wanted to slap him, but she resisted the urge. In fact, she needed to let go right away or she might hurt him.

She went to the sofa, which was also where he slept, and sat down. He started to come around to sit beside her, but she shook her finger in a no-no gesture and pointed at the chair by the window— the one behind the typewriter. He obeyed her non-verbal commands. He pushed the typewriter aside and sat down.

"I wish you had the guts to tell me yourself. I know why you didn't want nothin' to do with that missionary. You said he was a fake. How did you know that? You knew right off the bat he was full of gas."

Otis tapped his nose, "I've got a good—"

"Can-it, Oatsie. Tell me how you know the missionary."

"I don't think I do."

"Well he knows you. Number 65876."

"What?"

"That's your number."

"What number?" Otis asked.

"Riker's Island!" She said it with conviction, but then unwanted tears sprung forth. She'd tried so hard to stay angry and hold off the hurt. "You big liar!" she sobbed. "You haven't been on the radio making sound effects or anything else. You might have been washing dishes to pay the rent, but—" she wept, and then blurted, "But rent was a prison cell. You've been locked up in the Big House. Of course, our missionary friend was right there with you, wasn't he? That's where you knew him from, but you couldn't say."

He was quiet as his face reddened with guilt.

She folded into tears.

"Honey, it's not quite like that," Otis said.

"I'm done bein' hurt," she said with decision. "I'm moving on without you. Or maybe you'd like to tell me what you were locked up for."

He looked away, "Petty theft. I stole some scripts."

"See, you can't tell the truth. You was locked up for statutory rape. How old was she? Have to be pretty young for those charges to have stuck."

His face, which couldn't have gotten any redder—did. "I didn't know—"

"You didn't know she was under age. You gonna tell me I ought to get over bein' mad at you, because the whole time you was with her you were pretending she was me."

He was quiet.

"I'm tired of secrets, Otis. I've got my own, and I'm gonna come clean with you. And then we're going to make a break of it. You aren't going to come near me at church or in the streets or at Sweet

Tea's. You're gonna go away. Maybe you'll just leave town, or I'll spread some terrible rumor about you."

"You have a secret?" Otis asked.

She shared her secret and then stormed off. Only, she forgot Edith had Dusty and had to come back for him. Then she stormed off again.

■ ■ ■

Otis wasn't able to eat any dinner. His mother hovered about, trying to get some information out of him, but he didn't share a thing. In fact, he made a silent vow to himself to speak to no one. Except, he did have to ask Edith to call off the Boys Radio Club, he didn't feel well. And by Wednesday, he had to endure a lecture from his father about how he couldn't just mope around all day because of a girl. He needed to pick himself up by the bootstraps and shake the dust off. He needed to find a job, even if it was something he didn't like at first.

"Tell ya what, Otis," John finally said. It was his lunch break, and he was standing at the window staring down at the street below. "How about I give you a job. You ever think of that? I've been waiting for you, boy. Been waiting for you to ask. I've been waiting for you to think, 'hey, maybe my pop has a job for me. Maybe he's built a life I can carry on and be proud of.' You ever think of that, Otis?"

Otis rolled his eyes, "No. I never thought of that."

"Well?" John was nervous. He'd just made a big offer to the boy, and now it seemed rejection was nearby.

"No thanks."

"No thanks? That's it? Not even going to give it the night to think on?"

Otis stood, "Maybe I ought to get out from your house. Go find me somewhere of my own, just a flop house if I gotta. But look, you won't even invite me to attend your Radio Club meetings. Why would you share your business with me if you can't even have me with your friends?"

"I didn't know you wanted to go."

"Yes you did."

John let out a breath of exasperation. Did everything have to be a fight with this guy?

"Well, you get all hot headed and embarrass me."

Otis sank down into the couch that was his home. "Might as well give me one of those coffins down stairs. I feel like life is over."

He began to weep. He sobbed and curled up on the sofa like a baby. John watched his son turn into a pile of mush and felt confusion tear at him. He hated seeing the boy act like that. This was his only child; and he'd dreamed big for the kid. Of course, the kid had gone and tried out his dreams in New York, only to come back defeated. He wanted to be proud of him. But if Otis wanted John to treat him like a man, he needed to rise up off this sofa and act like a man.

Finally, John said, "Well, I'll leave ya to it."

■ ■ ■

"I just can't see what the problem is," Huey House said the Friday before the Halloween Eve party.

Preacher Weatherwax had come all the way out to the Man Village, escorted by his chairman of deacons, Clyde Finch and his buddy John Step. All three were wearing dark suits and hats. They reminded Huey of the Three Stooges.

Huey stuck his thumbs in the straps of his overalls, "Let me guess, I'm cuttin' in on your profit margin, preacher."

Pastor Weatherwax gave an uncomfortable laugh and waved his hand in a gesture that said—*of course not... don't be ridiculous.*

"Preacher come tell you what the problem is," Clyde said. The mayor patted Pastor Weatherwax on the back to let him know it was his turn.

Pastor Weatherwax mustered his courage. "Well, it's like this, Huey... you see... Halloween is a bad, bad night. It's the night of the Devil. It sure isn't something the Christian Church celebrates."

John Step got in on it. "It would be wrong to have a celebration on Halloween."

Huey puffed up a bit. "Well, good news, we're not having a party on Halloween. We're having a party on Halloween Eve."

"Same thing," Step said.

The preacher was anxious to back down. "Might not be the same," Pastor Weatherwax said.

John shook his head, "Christmas Eve and Christmas are neigh about the same. Halloween and Halloween Eve are the same. Can't celebrate Halloween, or Halloween Eve, because it's sacrilegious."

"What's that mean?" Huey asked.

Finch tapped the preacher, "Sacrilegious, preacher, what's it mean?"

"Blasphemous."

"So you want me to call the whole thing off?" Huey asked.

"Yes!" Step was glad to be at the point. "And we mean the whole thing. Preacher here come to ask you to shut down the Halloween party, the pig sacrifice, the baptisms, the whole church gig."

"You want me to call it off because it's morally wrong, or because it has people upset? Because it just seems to me that maybe you aren't so worried about it really being right—as you're worried about other people who think it's wrong. You're not trusting your moral compass, you're just looking over someone else's shoulder."

"It's nothing like that," Step said. "We all, and I mean *all* of us, feel it is morally wrong for you to have this church. And a party on Halloween… Eve."

"All of us being… you? Or Minnie Belle? Or the Grimm brothers? Or Red Heartland? Because a cow breaking wind could stir some of them folk up. You gentleman just don't know when to pay knuckleheads no mind."

"Here's the problem with Halloween," Step offered, "It's the Devil's holiday. Maybe his birthday. It's a wicked day. And the day before is wicked, too. It just shows you're more wicked to jump the gun and have a celebration ahead of time. Like you can't wait. So we Christians should not have a party on Halloween or Halloween Eve." Then, thinking maybe he hadn't covered enough bases, Step added, "Or post-Halloween."

"Oh, I see. Because the Bible tells us to?"

"Yes!" the preacher was re-engaged.

"Great. You show me where it says in the Bible not to have a Halloween Eve party, and I'll shut it right down."

"Well it doesn't say it like that!" Finch tried to sound jovial.

"You heard we was gonna sacrifice a pig?" Huey asked.

"Well we didn't think it was true," Step assured him.

Huey nodded. "Get one story mixed up and say a dozen lies. Why don't you boys go to your Radio Club, have a good drink, and leave me be."

"Preacher, that's just not true," Finch said to his pastor. "We don't drink at the Radio Club. No drinking at all."

Huey looked to Weatherwax, "Pastor, I apologize I've been such trouble to you. In fact, as you men stand here, it occurs to me... I sure am a sinner."

"Now he sees the light," Step said hopefully.

"I am a big sinner. I am. And I know it. Preacher, I reckon I sinned terrible big when I sold the Radio Club all that moonshine. That big load of Resurrection Juice..."

Finch cut in, "Huey, don't go wasting your time on lies —"

"I'm talking to my pastor," Huey said. "But I really sinned, preacher, when I didn't go to Hub's Grocery and tell him the truth. I should have gone and done my Christian duty and told Hub about all the rotten things Clyde was doin' to run them out of business. Like passin' bad money and —"

"That's enough!" Finch said. "Preacher, let's go. There's nothin' but poison comin' up from this well."

Step agreed, "Ah, leave him be. Preacher, I apologize for taking up your time. Somethin's just catty-wampus about ole Huey."

Calm the Storm

As a mortician's wife, Edith Step was more than a little familiar with how people handled grief. At first they thought they were dreaming, and then they got mad, and someday they start to accept the truth. Watching Otis struggle with Katie's meanness made her think of that same path. He had buried his head in the sofa for most of the week in a state of miserable denial. He didn't want to talk or eat or do anything else. By Saturday, mad had taken over. But with mad, came something rather delightful; a need to burn off energy. He became a cleaning machine. By noon Saturday, the apartment above the morgue was sparkling. Not that she kept a dirty house, mind you, but he found places that hadn't been touched in years.

"Ma, would you look down on me any if I worked over at the fillin' station?" he asked.

"Not even a little," she said.

"But you wouldn't drive by and think, 'Boy, how I'd hoped that kid would have gotten a little further in life than he has now.' You wouldn't think that, now, would-ja mama?"

"No, no. I'd be right proud of you, Otis. You've picked yourself up from a lot. Went clear to New York, bustin' your tail after a dream. Not your fault dreams don't all come true."

"Did my time on radio. Got my fill of that life. I had my moment of fame. But now it's time to settle down for a real job."

She looked at him for a moment, wondering if she should call him on that or not. What moment of fame was he talking about? He washed dishes and did sound effects. To hear him talk, he'd been Jack Benny's sidekick. But if he needed to be big in someone's eyes, it might as well be hers.

"Oats... Otis darling have you thought any about your father's offer? He was serious, you know?"

"Sure, I thought about it. But I'm not sure I want to touch dead bodies for a living."

"It's a good living. Respectable."

"Oh, no doubt. Maybe someday later." He looked past her out the window. "Maybe if I had a job, not one my pop handed me — maybe Katie would see I've got more going than she gave me credit for."

Edith nodded distantly, "Maybe. An employed man is a good man. But if you were askin' me, and I know you're not, it won't hurt you any to say goodbye to your love feelings for her. She's trouble, always has been. Always seems to have a man chasing her caboose."

"Ah, it's not like that. And she's the one, mama. She's the one for me. It all blew up all over me, but my heart still says she's the one."

"You never did say why she left you. Was it for that other man, what's his name? Elias?"

"No, no. She's just jealous that I spent all that time in New York. And she doesn't believe I waited for her. But I did, mama. I waited for her, because she's the one."

A little pride sparkled in Edith's eyes. "You're a good boy, Otis."

Edith turned toward the stew she was cooking up. It was leftovers from their week's meals. After stirring the pot, she turned back and looked hard at her son.

"Otis, I don't like you being with that lady. She's not even much of a lady. You've never had another love. She's your first love and your only love. But maybe you've been more in love with love than you were with Katie Simpson. You were in love with the way love made you feel. She didn't have any business breaking your heart the first time. And here she does it again and again and again. And every time she whistles or shakes those hips of hers, you come panting after her. Well, I've said my peace, but you get the idea, son. You're just too good for her. You've already made a name for yourself on the radio, and worked some real jobs in the kitchens of New York. And here you are, with a good life ahead of you — iffin' you just tiptoe a little after your father."

"Katie's not that bad."

"Not that good, either. She might be pretty on the outside. But pretty on the outside and pretty on the inside are two different things. Runs around with that dog, Charlie Mac—"

"What's wrong with a dog?"

"Well, nothing's wrong with a dog, Otis, so long as you don't have other obligations. But she and her boy don't even have a place of their own, and she goes and takes in a dog."

"Wish I had a dog."

"I just don't like her, Otis. I don't. You can scold me for saying it, but she's immoral. A floozy." She lowered her voice, even though they were the only ones in the apartment. "I was talking to Minnie Belle, and you won't believe what Katie said to her. I wasn't going to tell you, because you don't need any more hurt in your life. But she let Minnie Belle have it the other day, when all Minnie Belle did was give her some righteous advice. But an immoral woman—and that's what she is—scorns the counsel of the godly."

"Broke my heart," Otis said softly. "That's the only immoral thing Katie done. Broke my heart."

"Well, I just don't like her," Edith repeated. "And there's that boy of hers, ain't he somethin' else? Always saying lines from the radio, and do you know why? Because his mama has to work and so he spends all his time in front of the radio. You'd think his grandparents would take some interest in him, but they're just as permissive as she is. I guess they figure if it's on the radio, it's free sitting."

"Ah, Dusty's okay, Ma. You'll warm up to him."

"Warm up to him nothin'," Edith reddened. "Don't you go back to that woman, Otis! Don't you do it! Don't chase her or that boy, you understand? That boy is not smart. In fact, he's just a tape recorder, going around saying what's already been said. I hate to say it, Otis, I just hate to say it, but that boy is as simple as a block of wood."

"No he's not."

"He is, Otis. Somethin' is wrong with that boy. He's got a little Mule Evermund rubbed off on him or somethin'!" That inspired a thought. *Maybe that's it. Maybe that boy is Mule's boy. That woman chases —*

"That boy is my son," Otis said finally. He didn't scream it or sulk, he said it with a firmness he'd long desired.

"What did you say?"

"I didn't know it all these years. But I felt somethin' for the kid. But when Katie told me goodbye, she told me her secret. And that boy is mine."

Edith shook her head. "No, you just gotta let them both go. Say goodbye to them in your heart."

"Mama, iffin' that boy is my son, that makes you—"

"That makes me nothing, Otis. Because that's a big iffin'. I have no relation to Katie Simpson or that boy. I'm sorry if she lied to you. I'm sorry if she laid a whopper on you."

"Well, my heart's still swollen up for her."

Tired of the banter, Edith said, "Otis, just ask your father for a job. That's what I want you to do. You get a job at the filling station, and I won't begrudge you none. But I wouldn't take pride in it the way I would if you follow after your daddy." With new energy, even a twinkle in her eye, she said, "Do it, Otis! Do it! Ask your daddy for that job he offered. Be done with Katie and all her lies."

■ ■ ■

That Saturday evening, Otis went downstairs and stood in front of the basement door; it was closed. That's how all the doors were for him now; closed.

Door with his father… CLOSED!

Door with Katie… CLOSED!

Door to his dreams… CLOSED!

One thing was for sure, no matter what happened with Katie, he was at least a little smitten with the Rickety Church. So far, no one had closed the church door to him. Besides, they might be the key to getting Katie's door open again. He wasn't sure about everything they did, but he didn't want those people hurt. He also knew the church people were in deeper trouble than they could really understand. Some of the local hotheads weren't just *willing* to hurt people, they would flat out *enjoy* it. They enjoyed drawing blood, enjoyed pulling the trigger, enjoyed smashing a face, enjoyed the sound of broken bones—the way Otis enjoyed a pretty girl.

If he was Jesus, he could just calm the storm. But he wasn't Jesus, he was Otis Step. But Peter had walked on water just the same as Jesus had. Maybe Otis could calm a storm. Dog gone it, he'd climbed a Farris wheel. This might be fun.

He could hear the men talking in excited voices and smell the cigar smoke. In the distance the radio was playing music. Just standing there, he got the gist of what was going down. Clyde Finch and Otis' own father were trying to convince the others to keep calm; but calm was a tall order to fill when most of their wives were stirred up.

Clyde Finch explained that they had already gone to visit Huey, and that it didn't do any good. "We ain't gonna talk Huey out of his church. And I don't think you can scare him. Grimm brothers tried that."

Someone said, "You can scare Huey House, if you want. Problem is, no one works together. That's what the women want, they want us to work together. Ought to burn down that church."

Micah Horn, a miner whose face was still dusty with coal spoke up. Otis could always spot Micah's voice because he talked loud, like he was still down under the earth. "Ain't no law that churches gots to be segregated. Maybe there ought to be. Huey probably don't like all them coons showin' up at his church, but he just don't have the backbone to tell them to get themselves back over the railroad tracks."

Otis was listening close to Micah when Jonas Wilson opened the basement door and just about scared Otis bad enough to put him in one of the coffins. "What are you doing?" Jonas asked. Otis couldn't believe he hadn't smelled Jonas coming. Jonas ran the filling station and always smelled like Ethyl gasoline.

"I just came down to say howdy," Otis said, giving a meek wave.

"Come to spy on us!" Jeremiah said. He was sitting in his favorite corner, a drink in one hand and a cigar in the other.

Clyde invited Otis to come on in to the meeting. There were more men there than Otis expected. A quick count came to fourteen. Hotheads like Red Heartland and the Grimm brothers weren't there. The room was stuffy with cigar smoke.

John Step put up his hand. "I'm sorry, son, but this is a private meeting of the club. The regular meeting is tomorrow night. This meeting isn't for everyone —"

"Ah, you fella's don't have to let me in. Can I just say one thing and I'll be on my way hummin' *Whistle While Ya Work*?"

They all agreed at once that he could speak his mind.

"Any of you boys ever thought that when it comes to ole Huey House and that church of his, that if you'd stop stirring the pot, it might just boil over on its own? But you keep it so stirred up, it ain't never gonna boil over."

"You sayin' we should do nothin'?" Jonas asked. He came around Otis and sat down next to The Beast.

"No. I'm not sayin' nothin' about what you should or shouldn't do. Burn down houses, blow up the church. I don't care. I've just noticed the more trouble Huey has, the bigger that church gets. A fella could shoot off cannons in the Baptist sanctuary and not hit anyone. Know why? 'Cause no one's payin' the Baptist any attention."

Clyde Finch was thoughtful. "Otis might be right. That church would've already caved in, if some folk around here didn't fuel the fire. No one likes what they're doin', but if ya go be mean about it, you just make 'em more determined."

Micah Horn nodded agreement. "When people get threatened, they huddle together. Let a mine shaft shake a little, and all the boys run for each other. But when there ain't no problems, people will pick each other right apart."

Otis said, "I been to that church; it's just waiting to fold in on itself, if y'all just stop propping it up. Let people really listen to what Huey is sayin' and they'll revolt. But y'all make so much noise, no one's really listening to Huey."

"They ain't gonna stop until their church and some homes get burned," Jonas said.

"Let someone find the end of a rope and they'll shut up," Leonard Lawson said. It was an unusually bold statement for Leonard, but they all knew he couldn't tie a hangman's noose any more than he could stand up to Minnie Belle.

Otis pushed on, "Why don't y'all just have your regular meetin' tomorrow night. Charlie McCarthy is on the radio. Bust out a little Resurrection Juice and enjoy the night. Tell the lady folk you'll get 'em another day, ya just got to pray about it. Put it in the Lord's hands. Ladies like that sorta talk."

"Huey put you up to this?" Jonas asked.

"No. I don't care what you guys do."

John saw a problem. "Son, you might get us to meet up around a radio and have a little drink tomorrow night, but those Grimm brothers are stirred up and they aren't going to be sweet talked."

Jonas was in agreement. "Someone's gonna get shot, or hung if it's just left to the Grimm's. We got to plan to do somethin', just so the hot-heads don't do somethin' worse."

Several members of the club stared openly at Jonas. So the reason they were talking about burning down a church was just to keep the real stinkers from shooting folks? When it was put together like that, they felt a little foolish.

Clyde was inspired, "We just got to keep them Grimm boys occupied." He rolled his eyes and smiled a little. "Leave it to me. Then when this Halloween — and Halloween Eve — business is all blown over, the town can talk about rules for churches. We'll shut them down."

■ ■ ■

Greta was glad when she saw Clyde Finch pull up in front of the house. Maybe he'd come to make amends. She kept an immaculate house, which was made easier because they didn't have kids. Teddy's brother Alvin lived in the bungalow on the far side of the property, and it was a mess. But she didn't have to go out there. Except that Teddy was spending more and more time out at the bungalow. Teddy said they were just playing cards — and they probably were. But as they played, they would talk — and the more they talked, the more they would get each other wound up with bad ideas.

She welcomed Clyde into the parlor, which was her office and after shaking his hand she invited him to sit down. He didn't sit, or accept her tea. She patted her short blonde hair involuntarily to make sure it was all in place. She was tall, with a strong German nose and fair skin. She felt out of place with Madison Creek's small women, but Teddy had a special gift for making her feel like the most beautiful woman on earth.

"Greta, where's the boys?"

"Out doing some work I hope. They've been falling behind lately." She stepped uncomfortably close to him. Did Germans not have personal space? He could smell her perfume, *Jean Naté*, a spicy citrus that he'd helped Teddy pick out for Greta's birthday.

"Listen," Greta said, "they have big plans for tomorrow night. I'm worried people are going to get hurt—buildings burned. And they even talked about tar and feather."

That gave Clyde pause. "Tar and feather? You mean the real kind? Or just that they're mad."

She started to explain the process to him, but he knew all about it.

"And I do mean the real kind. They get you all stirred up, and then mob that church. They'll tar and feather Huey House, drag him through the street on a cart. I hope that's all they do. But Georgette will be picking feathers out of Huey for a few weeks, and it'll lay him up in bed somethin' terrible."

"You have to talk them out of that, Greta."

"I was hoping that's what you came to do." She smiled warmly. "You can get people to do anything."

Her praise felt good. He didn't want to let her down. "Well, I did come to tell you that the Radio Club has invited them out this Sunday night."

"I'm not going to be able to get them to go to a club meeting when tarring and feathering Huey House is on their—"

"Wait. We want them to come because we want to present the White Radio Club *Business of the Year* award to the Peanut Farm."

She gave a respectful nod, then shook her head. "That's not going to do it. They're too set on their plan. Already got the tar and feathers. I hope that's all they do. Heard talk from Teddy about how people ought to hang — the black doctor in particular."

"Hold on, I got more." He felt good to have another splash magic to wow her with. "Part of the reward for being Business of the Year is that we want to give you a little somethin'. Somethin' small, don't have much to offer. But that tractor, what do you call it?"

"Alvin calls it *Buffalo Bill*." She sounded a bit annoyed.

"Have the boys bring Buffalo Bill to the club meetin'. We'll let everyone *ooh* and *aah* over it. Might even stir up some more good will for the Peanut Farm. I'll take them over to Jonas' Filling Station and fill the tank up all the way, till it spills over."

"Filling station's closed on Sunday."

"Not when you're the mayor." He gave her a sideways smile and raised one eyebrow. "We'll present them a certificate you can hang on the wall, and I'll see that their drinks don't cost 'em nothin'. But it's got to be tomorrow night, Greta. We'll deal with the church another day. There's more than one way to skin this cat."

"I don't care about the cat," Greta admitted. "I just don't want Teddy in trouble. I don't want anyone dead."

"Well, the ball's in your court," Clyde said.

She shrugged, not sure what that meant.

"I sympathize with the boys. I really do. That church and the whole of Jordan Town has been a real problem lately. I think Teddy and Alvin just need to know they're not alone."

She was excited and leaned toward him. For an awkward moment he thought she was going to kiss him, but instead she whispered in his ear. "Thank you."

■ ■ ■

Otis Step was glad when his father actually invited him to attend the Radio Club. It even came with a little apology that he hadn't done it sooner. John asked if Otis had given any further thought to joining him in the mortuary business. Otis said he was sixty-two percent sure that by Christmas he'd be working with his old man. It seemed strange to John to put a percentage on a decision like that.

"You be goin' to church with us tomorrow, right Otis?"

Otis shook his head. "No sir. Someone has to keep an eye on what's going on up yonder at that Devil church."

"You sure you're not just trying to keep up with Katie?"

"Oh, heavens no. I'm over her, really I am. She done broke my heart for the last time."

The truth was, Otis could never be over Katie. The way she smelled; the hue of her skin; the tiny mole she had on her back, right between her shoulder blades. He hadn't seen that mole in a long time, but he still thought about it—maybe because it was just about the only mark of imperfection she had on her entire body. It was the only thing that proved she was human, not an angel.

And there was Dusty.

Was he really Dusty's pop? Strange he hadn't put that together sooner. Or maybe he had and he didn't want to admit it, even to himself. He'd been sixteen and a kid would have messed up his life. He would have never made it to New York. Of course, he also would have never gotten locked up. He'd been glad to think the boy belonged to some stranger whose arms Katie had fallen into after him.

What had his father said? *Pull yourself up by the bootstraps.* He had to give Katie one more try. No, try wasn't the right word. He wasn't going to *try* to get her back; he was going to *get* her back. Tomorrow. It was a matter of willpower—and charm—but mostly willpower.

The Devil's Funeral

Sunday morning at the Little Rickety Church came even earlier because of *Fast Time*. (In years to come, Fast Time would become known as Daylight Saving Time. However, Huey himself would never make the adjustment and for the rest of his life would call Daylight Saving Time, Fast Time.)

Big X played his harmonica and Meemaw Moses sang along. The crowd was just a little thinner because some people wanted to sleep in; besides, they would be at church that night.

When Huey's turn came, he said, "I haven't read everything in the Big Book yet, but I just had to take a peek at the end."

"We win," Meemaw Moses announced.

"I reckon. But I read that an angel comes on out of heaven and wraps a big ole chain around this here dragon's neck. That dragon be the Devil, ya see? And then they throw the dragon-Devil in a bottomless pit. Kinda funny, iffin' ya ask me, to put a chain on him, then throw him in a pit with no bottom. So no matter how much he stretches out, he's still hangin' there choking on the end of that chain."

"Cool!" Jo House said, only to be mimicked by Dusty.

"Well," Huey said, "When they really get down to it, God'll put that rascal Satan into a burning pit. And that will be the end of him. His funeral's comin'. But I got to thinking, do any of y'all know the name of the angel who tied up Satan and threw him in that pit?"

There was some discussion. Gabriel? Michael?

"You don't know, 'cause that angel isn't named. It's just an ordinary angel. Think about that. God didn't call some big mighty angel to bind the Devil, he just chose a little ole ordinary angel. 'Cause it ain't so much how strong the angel be — as it is how strong the angel's God be. Ya se?" Huey grinned, proud of himself. "What I mean is, don't be afraid of trouble out there. God's got the Devil's funeral planned up already. In the end, the Devil goes up in flames like Fourth of July fireworks. We might as well have a party and celebrate the Devil's funeral ahead of time."

Before Huey let everyone go, Katie came to the platform, stood under the big makeshift that was attached to the wall. She gave last minute details about the Halloween Eve bash. She slowed in her announcement when she spotted Otis sitting in the back. Her eyes became hard. He better not get up and come down the aisle.

After church, he gave her the space she'd asked for. She was the one who edged near him as he talked to Doctor Banks. "I told you to let me be," she interrupted.

"I'm not here to see you. I'm here for church and to see the preacher. And maybe say howdy to my boy."

Her lips tightened. "You hush up about that. I told you the other night to go away."

He found Huey out in front of the church, smoking a cigar and talking to several men. He asked if he might have a word—just a short word—with the big fella. Huey wasn't quick to say yes. In fact, he stood for a long time without answering, and then finally said he'd chat when his cigar was gone.

■ ■ ■

Jo House thought that next to the first day of summer vacation, and Christmas morning… and Christmas Eve, Halloween Eve might turn out to be the best day ever.

Aunt Georgette tried to get her to come home for lunch and a nap, but Jo insisted she wanted to stay at church and help decorate.

It seemed everyone wanted a bit of Uncle Huey today. Otis was pestering him for a meeting, and there were people hunting him down with all kinds of questions about that evening's celebration. Poor guy, all he really wanted was to be with those men outside and have a smoke.

"Oh, you sure are pretty," Jo said when Katie Simpson breezed by. Jo was sitting on the floor watching men take up the benches to make the room bigger.

"Ain't you just the sweetest," Katie said.

"Miss Simpson, I sure am sorry for your loss."

Katie stopped in the doorway. "Why, Jo House, I'd have to say that's about the nicest thing anyone's said to me all day. I've had lots of folk tell me how lucky I am to be rid of him, or that I shouldn't cry. But 'sorry for your loss' is the best."

In the distance a motorcycle growled and burped.

"That's got to be my teacher," Jo said.

It was Annie Evermund, riding Steel, her old 1917 motorcycle.

"You know she's played with that engine," Katie said.

"Oh, you know it," Jo said. She loved it when adults forgot she was a kid and talked to her like she was one of them.

Annie pulled up into the church yard. Her sidecar was loaded with… something.

Jo watched as her teacher got off Steel, took off her leather helmet and goggles, then her gloves. She was beautiful, Jo thought. Not beautiful like Katie Simpson; beautiful because she didn't seem like she would break easily. Jo wanted to be like that.

"Whatcha got in the sidecar, Miss Evermund?" Jo asked.

"Come have a looksee."

The sidecar was jam packed with wooden crosses. Not big ones, like the bad guys had lit on fire; these were smaller and each one had been given a fresh coat of white paint. In fact, Jo could still smell the paint.

"These are grave markers," Annie said. "You need to go plant them over yonder in the graveyard. This is better than planting flowers, seein' as how they're already dead."

"Why?"

Annie blew Jo a kiss and wiggled her fingers. "Because it's Halloween Eve, silly. No Halloween party is going to be any fun with a graveyard that only has one dead body in it."

"I thought Katie said no spooks."

"Exactly! And a grave keeps the spooks down where they belong. Anyhoo, woman, go plant these in the graveyard over there."

Woman. Jo loved it that her teacher called her woman.

Jo loved her assignment. She got to work right away; first hauling all the crosses out to the field next to the church, then planting them down in the earth as if marking the location of a real grave. As she worked, she could hear singing in the church as people set up for their big night. There was laughter that echoed out of the building and the sound of things being hammered. Jo was pretty sure they were building booths for some of the games.

"Hey, Martian-head, what are you doing?"

Jo looked up to see Dusty crossing the yard toward her.

"Get out of here, Dusty. I'm planting a graveyard."

"I want to plant a graveyard."

"You can't. Besides, it's not easy. You have to dig up the crabgrass first, then dig the hole—"

"You're mean!" He stomped his foot in the grass. Then, with a spark in his eye, he grabbed one of the crosses and held it up. It was huge when he held it in front of him. "Get out of here, Jo House! Get out of here, or you'll die!"

"You scat, Dusty!"

"You are a vampire," Dusty declared. He shook the cross, but almost lost his balance. "Away from me, vampire!"

To humor him, she pretended to be afraid and even dipped her head a bit to show she was dead.

"That's no good," Dusty objected. "You can't just lower your head and be dead. You gotta twist and shake as evil quivers within you under the power of the cross. Now, do it again!" He steadied the cross in his hands and said, "Now die, you descendant of Count Dracula and—"

"Dracula!" Jo exclaimed. "That's a good idea! We should write names on the graves. Only we'll put monsters from the movies, you see? Like Dracula."

"And the *Phantom of the Opera*?" Dusty asked. Then in the voice of the Mad Russian, he declared: "It will be the swellest graveyard ever!"

"It'll be our revenge."

The Mad Russian disappeared as quickly as he'd come. "Revenge?"

"Sure! Revenge on those rotten adults for having a Halloween party, and then saying no ghost costumes."

"I'll go get a pen so we can write."

"No, you moron, not a pen. Get me some paint... black paint... and a brush. You got that?"

Dusty didn't come back with black paint, or anything very useful. Just a worn down crayon — and it was purple. She worked the crayon until it was nothing more than lumpy wax against her fingers. Dusty had to go find her another one — blue.

There was...

The Phantom
Frankenstein's Monster
Dracula

There was also...

The Invisible Man
King Kong

And *The Werewolf of London*, but she wrote it...

The Werewolf of Buncombe County

on that grave marker — and...

The Mummy

Dusty observed, "Two crosses left." Jo wrote...

Hickory Joe

"He's the best of the lot," Dusty said. "Only, he's not dead, dumb -dumb. He's still roaming these parts, terrorizing..."

Jo scratched out Hickory Joe and wrote a new name.

Satan

Dusty studied it.

"Sure, Uncle Huey just preached a whole sermon called *The Devil's Funeral*." She stood up and adjusted her dress the way a preacher might his suit. Then she began her own little sermon...

> *Ladies and gentlemen, I come here to preach the Devil's funeral. Lots of monsters in this here graveyard, but the wickedest of them all be dead and rotting right here in the ground of Madison Creek. Don't plant no trees near here, because they'll probably rot up and wilt, or give you poison fruit. Might not even want to step foot in this graveyard, or you'll get leprosy or polio.*

"Yeah!" Dusty shouted with excitement. "You come near Satan's grave, and your ears and nose might fall off. Maybe even your ding dong."

They were interrupted by Otis, who yelled at Dusty to stop doing—whatever it was he was doing—and go help move tables. Dusty hung his head and left Jo to finish the work.

In a final blaze of brilliance, Jo etched out her last cross...

Elias Moore

She didn't know what had happened to him, but he'd been a monster to her. He'd caused Katie all that heartache, and been a big pain in the rumpus to Uncle Huey. As she finished his cross, and came to the end of the blue crayon, she thought maybe she owed Mr. Moore and his peppermint cologne a debt of gratitude. If it hadn't been for him, she would have never had all the fun this church turned out to be.

She thought about what Uncle Huey had said about the Devil and his funeral. She wished it was true. But she knew the Devil wasn't dead. Jo sensed something bad was hovering over Madison Creek. Not the fun kind of bad; not just naughty bad. Something truly wicked was sinking its claws into the people she knew. She was beginning not to trust familiar faces. When she would see people in town, big men who would smile at her—she would smile back—but she also wondered if maybe they were the ones who burned that cross in her yard.

Setting Molasses on Fire

O tis' first two ideas to get Katie back fell flat. The easiest was to simply get Huey House to intervene in some way. Good pastoral council could go a long way. But Huey said he didn't think that was the place of a preacher to go courting girls for another fella. As if Huey knew anything about a preachers place. What's worse, Huey countered with a rebuke.

"Maybe it's time you put some prayers into where you might go beyond Madison Creek. You've burned some mighty big bridges in a short amount of time, young man."

Talk about burning bridges, Huey's bridges were worn down to tightropes. He wanted to tell Huey that he'd been his big defender last night when the Radio Club was ready to torch the church.

His second plan—a more unlikely one—was Annie... Annie Evermund.

"Can I have a short word with you?" Otis asked as Annie set up for apple bobbing.

"No."

"Just a short word. Please."

Annie sighed. "You're going to ask me to help you get back with Katie. And to do that, you probably have some idea that I should tell her I misunderstood what your jail bird friend told me. The one who pretended to be a missionary. Well I'm not going to do that, number 65876." She tapped her head proudly, "Photographic brain locked up in this skull."

He was a burning mass of rage by the time he started toward home. But then he spotted Katie sitting at a table under the shadow of the makeshift church house. Katie and several other church women—all black—were busy stuffing candy in bags.

"Katie, I've tried to keep to myself, but I'm just burning up. Please, can't we just have a little conversation?"

Meemaw Moses glared at him but didn't say anything. So did Cousin Pearly. Katie didn't answer. He tried again, but she ignored him. She tied an orange ribbon around a baggy of Jelly Beans and set it on the table.

"Hon, don't be like that."

Meemaw Moses finally said, "You's might as well go on yar way, Mr. Step. Seems yar good as dead to her. She thinks she's just-a hearin' your ole ghost."

"That's stupid! I'm right here!"

Katie looked up innocently and stared right through him. "Is someone talking, Meemaw Moses?"

"Nothin' but the wind, child."

Rage that Otis had been pushing down finally erupted. "I'm right here, you fool woman!" he shouted. "And don't you coon-women be telling me what's goin' on. I got eyes. I know what this lady's doin'. She's got her legs wrapped around every man in town. Well maybe I wanted to make a respectable woman of her — "

Meemaw Moses boldly held up her hand. "That be enough, Mr. Step. We all respect you. Don't you do nothin' to make us not respect you."

"You know what my mama told me? She told me that negroes don't got no soul. That y'all have them empty eyes because there's not nothin' behind them."

Meemaw Moses came right back, "Guessin' Jesus knows who has a soul and who doesn't. Soul be a little deeper than skin, and you ain't too good at seein' through skin, Mr. Step."

Otis let out an angry grunt, grabbed the edge of the table the women were working at and flipped it over. Candy that had been in little piles waiting to be bagged fell to the ground the way money did when Jesus cleared the temple. Katie tumbled backward, trying to avoid the table. Otis heard himself screaming as he did it. It felt good to finally let the anger out. It felt good for his muscles to stretch, even if it was just tossing a table over. The real satisfaction was the sound of all that candy falling into the grass.

"What's the problem?" Hammond Washington spun Otis around. "Don't give our women no trouble."

"These broads aren't women!" Then, looking to Katie, who was sprawled out on her back in the grass, he amended, "Well at least one of these ain't no woman. She's the kind of girl who's always running into the tall grass with some boy."

Hammond swallowed hard, and Otis thought he was going to tell him to leave. Instead, Hammond punched him in the nose. Otis went down in an explosion of pain. He bent over in the grass, holding his face. He'd been punched in the nose before, but never this hard. Blood stained the grass.

"I'd hit you again," Hammond towered over Otis, "but I want you to be able to walk on home. Get up and get out. You come back 'round here, Mr. Step, and I'll—" he stopped short, remembering he was speaking to a white man. "I'm sorry this happened," he amended. Then, he held out his hand, "We shake on it and it's all over, ya see?"

Otis rubbed his nose. Blood was pouring out like a river. He stated the obvious, "You busted my nose!"

Hammond kept his hand out, "We just shake on it, and it's all okay."

"It's not okay," Otis said and spit blood. "One more door shut in my face. And you had to be mean about it. If you'd told me to go, I would've. You're just spoiling for a fight, Mr. War Hero." His nose throbbed. "You'll be sorry you closed that door, you baboon. I'll make you sorry. I'll make all y'all sorry. All I asked for was a little talk, and I got my face punched in by this baboon"

"Don't you call me no baboon," Hammond warned. "I fought for this country, don't you call me a baboon."

Realizing the situation was about to be serious, Katie got up and came to Otis. "Listen, Otis, get out of here. We'll talk another time, I promise. You just go now. Go!"

"Don't order me around. I'm not your dog, Charlie Mac." He wiped blood across his shirt sleeve.

Katie cradled Otis in her arms for a moment, tipping back his head so that the blood might slow. "I'll drive you home."

"No you won't," Hammond said with authority. "Preacher will do it. That's preacher's job. Protect the flock."

Huey drove Otis home in his old Chevrolet pickup. Huey waited until they pulled up in front of the morgue, and said, "Some people gots to be smashed in the head before they really hear God clearly. You be glad you can go on upstairs to the apartment and clean up. If things been any worse, you would've landed yourself downstairs, in one of those coffins your father has."

Otis slammed the door and sulked upstairs.

■ ■ ■

When people began to arrive at five thirty, the sky was already turning orange. In the church house, oil lamps hummed and a woman on the radio sang like a canary. The benches had been pushed to one side, making a big open space in the middle.

Uncle Huey stood at the door to greet people. He was wearing his suit again with a brimmed white hat. The hat had a red ribbon around it that matched the handkerchief in his suit pocket. His gut still stuck out like he was watermelon pregnant; but to Jo, he looked like a fine southern gentleman. She was right proud of him. It was strange to her that he had preached in his overalls, and then dressed up for the Halloween Eve party.

As Huey shook hands, Georgette received the food. She was dressed in a beautiful white evening gown and had even put her grandma's pearls on. She said the same thing to each lady as she took their dish, "Best give it to me, honey, if you want anyone other than Huey to have a taste."

Papaw Mo brought corn bread that he swore he made himself, with no help from Meemaw Moses. Cousin Pearly showed up with pumpkin pie and a pot of spicy Gumbo. Katie Simpson showed up with cheesy beef stew her mother had made.

Dusty stood behind his ma as Huey tasted her bread. He recited one of his favorite commercials: *If you eat just one meal a day, make sure it's a bowl of tasty, zesty, out of this world Kellogg's Golden Crunch!*

"Dusty, knock it off," Katie said with irritation, and the boy shrunk away.

■ ■ ■

Edith Step stood at the big window of her apartment and stared out at Main Street. She didn't like Fast Time—it just got dark so early. If the farmers needed extra daylight, let them get up earlier. She had a party to be at and didn't like having to leave when it was already dark. Minnie Belle was hosting a special Tea at the dress shop instead of the usual Bridge Club. Edith was happy to have a reason to dress up. Besides, if they were lucky, Minnie Belle might let them try on a few of her dresses.

Otis had come in that afternoon with a busted nose. She fussed over him, but he was cranky and so she was glad to be leaving. He said he got punched at church. That was hard to believe. She wondered what he'd really been up to. She was growing tired of his shenanigans.

Along the sidewalk, she spied Mrs. Dotson carrying a box up Main Street. She looked tired. Edith had never seen Lutie out after dark. Undoubtedly she was headed up to that Devil party. Lutie looked tired, but just the same, offering a ride would be just like giving a hobo money when you know he's going to use it on booze.

But, as Lutie passed the morgue, Edith felt a little prick from the Holy Ghost. She tried to fight God for a moment, but she knew He would make her heart miserable if she didn't obey.

Edith took her hat and headed for the door. In a voice that didn't sound like him, Otis asked where she was going.

"Holy Ghost won't leave me alone," she lamented.

Edith went downstairs and called after Lutie.

"You can't have what's in my box," Lutie said at once.

"I was wondering if I could drive you on up the hill."

Lutie was about to say no, but then she looked up the steep climb and changed her mind.

Edith brought the car around and Lutie got in. Gosh she smelled strange. Most women smelled like flowers, but Mrs. Dotson smelled like—well, maybe wet newspapers.

As the engine idled, Lutie said, "Nettie usually drives me to church, but she told me the Halloween Eve party is Devil worship. She said some of you ladies invited her to your own shindig."

Edith did not want to invite Lutie to the ladies tea. She certainly did not want Lutie to be *her* guest.

"I got this box last Christmas," Lutie said. Inside Edith could see the tops of four large jars. "Church people, the Baptist ones, felt sorry for me bein' poor and a widow and brought me a box of food and Christmas Carols."

"What's in the box?"

"Pickled pigs feet!" Lutie said, and then blurted, "Does your husband smoke?"

"John smokes, Lutie. Does that bother you?"

"Cigarettes will kill everyone. People laugh at me. But know what I think—I think they were put here by..." she pointed up. "You know, by them-um's up there. Once we're dead, they'll take the planet."

"You don't actually believe that, Lutie," Edith said slowly. The engine was still idling.

Lutie shrugged, "I believe tobacco makes you sick. I also think that Martians are real. I just put the two together in my head and pretend it's true."

"It was not the Martians who gave us tobacco, Lutie, it was the Indians."

"Columbus saw a flying saucer!" Mrs. Dotson was hard to distract. Her box jiggled in her lap and the water in the jars sloshed. "Ole Chris was on the deck of the Santa Maria. Said he saw a light glimmering a great distance away. Then a thousand candles passed him at once."

Edith thought about Chris Columbus at the deck of his ship; the old boy was tired, hungry and close to a mutiny. By the time he was seeing flying saucers, he must have been as crazy as Loony Lutie.

"When I told Mule, of course he had to be an idiot about it and without missing a beat—without missing one single beat!—that big fool goes to stuttering. *I'm ch-ch-Christopher co-Columbus and I see aliens!*" Lutie rolled her eyes. "Can you imagine being mocked by a simpleton?"

Edith dropped the car into gear and pulled onto Main Street.

"See, I was excited because I heard about old Columbus seeing them aliens, so I told lots of people at church. My church — not that one you go to. And know what Big X did? He mocked me to! He says…" (Her rendition of Big X was spot on.) *Dat Christa Columbus couldn't tell a Injun from a real Indian. You'd a thunk a flying saucer might give him some learning.*

She was excited now, and the pickled pigs feet were sloshing even more as they went up the hill.

"And then ole Boots had to get in on mocking me, and he said, 'Mayhap them aliens led Chris to America.' And then Big X jumped up on a tree stump and says, 'All y'all can call me Professor Abercrombie, 'causin' I know it all. And I'll teach ya some history.' And then he goes right into mocking me. Even though he's black as can be, he didn't feel no reservation. He says, 'First, ya see, America was invaded by dim alien peoples. Dey gib dem Injuns de secrets of tobacco, knowin' it would kill us all.' And he just went on from there until I cried a little. I know what they call me, *Loony Lutie.* But I'm not loony. Wait until the spaceships come."

Edith stopped the car a little before the church house. It was already crowded with cars, and she didn't want to be seen. She needed to invite Lutie to the Tea. How could she not? The woman was right there, in her own car, telling her how the church people had laughed at her.

"Honey," Edith said suddenly, "I sure would love it if you gave up on this hootenanny and came to our Tea. I'll drive you right on over with me."

Lutie's rejection was quick and direct. "Nope, not gonna do it."

Lutie sat her pigs feet on the floor while she got out. When she went to pick them up, the box bottom gave up and the jars crashed to the floor. The glass broke and water and pigs feet went everywhere.

"Oh no!" Lutie cried.

ot happy about this. Edith started to comfort Lutie, but then she realized Lutie wasn't upset about the car, she was upset she wouldn't have anything to bring to the party. Lutie held the bottom of the box and began to scoop the pigs feet in.

■ ■ ■

At the dress shop, Minnie Belle was delighted as the women came to her Tea. They brought pies, cookies, and scones. Even Greta Grimm showed up with big sacks of apples for everyone. The Grimm's made their bread and butter on peanuts, but there was a little apple orchard that Greta had fallen in love with and made her own. Her harvest had been good this year and the apples were big and red.

Minnie Belle took her sack of apples and gave Greta a curious look. "Well, thank you, I think. Really and truly, apples aren't normal Tea Party fare, sweetie."

Red Heartland's wife Effie took a big bite of one of her apples. "Delicious!" she declared. Apple juice ran down her chin.

Minnie Belle showed the ladies upstairs to the little room Leonard usually held up in. He spent as much time as he could next to the radio, looking down on Main Street and doing—well, absolutely nothing. He called the room his vacation house; she called it a pigsty. She'd made him spend the day cleaning it, and then still had to take matters into her own hands. By the time the women arrived—all dressed like they were going to a grand ball—tables were set and the room was spotless. She had prepared much more than just tea. She had made little ham sandwiches and a large cobbler.

"If you listen close, you can hear the godless music commin' from that church!" Dorothy Simpson said.

For the past couple of weeks, Dorothy had been calling on Minnie Belle for prayer concerning her wayward daughter Katie. What Minnie Belle couldn't let go of was that Dorothy had roots in Minnesota, and she'd played baseball. Seemed a little liberal to her. It occurred to Minnie Belle that perhaps Dorothy was feigning contempt in order to please her new friend.

"I think they are playing live music," Effie Heartland said.

"Oh, they'll be at it all night," Greta said. "Let's enjoy the night and not pay them any mind."

A note of music caught on the tail end of a huff of breeze.

There was a knock at the door; it was Edith Step. She looked terrible, and smelled terrible. She had started out in her best dress — the blue one John had given her for their anniversary. But the dress was stained with — something — and even her hat looked like it had been sat on. "What happened to you?" Minnie Belle asked as she let her friend in.

"Loony Lutie happened to me," Edith griped. Then said, "Or the Holy Ghost just hates me. I can't decide which right now. I'm starved and I'm mad. Give me some of that cobbler you have and I'll tell you all about it."

■ ■ ■

As agreed, Jonas Wilson allowed Clyde and the other men to come by the filling station and put gas in the Grimm boys' tractor.

"It's like this," Clyde Finch told Teddy as Jonas pumped the gas, "We're not just a town, we're a community. I was wrong not to take your peanuts. We want to buy local and sell local. But I hope you remember what I said. Act like a businessman. So..." he held out his hand, "here's to a fresh start."

"You'd make a good preacher," Teddy said, pumping Clyde's hand.

When the tank was full, they parked the tractor outside the morgue and the men from the Radio Club gathered around to say how impressed they were with the machine.

"Well, let's go have us a good drink," John Step said. "We have the place to ourselves."

Music from the church chattered on the breeze.

"Negro music ain't so bad," Teddy said. "But that church still irritates me."

"That church irritates all of us," Leonard Lawson said. "I'd torch it myself, but I have an ailment."

Down in the basement, John gave out the rest of what the club had stored away in the belly of The Beast. He hadn't been able to restock it, because the Resurrection Juice everyone loved so much had gotten hard to come by since Sticky Simpson blew his still to pieces.

The men had settled into smoking and chatting when there was a knock at the door. John stood at the door and asked who it was. He always felt a little scared when the men were drinking. If Sheriff Tuff decided to clean up the town, he wouldn't bother climbing all over Blue Mountain, he'd most likely start at the *White* Radio Club.

"Who is it?" John asked.

"It's Otis, popsa-dillies. Open up."

John edged the door open, "You don't sound like…" then he pulled his son inside. "Otis! What happened to you?"

His nose was huge and red. It was too much for Jeremiah, who croaked, *Rudolph, won't you lead my sleigh tonight?*

"I'll flatten your nose, old man," Oats grimaced.

"Shut up, Oats, or I'll double break your nose," Red Heartland shot back. "We don't need you here. You just come for the free booze."

"Sit down, Otis," John said. Then to everyone he announced, "This is my boy Otis, and he come to join—"

"No!" Oats exclaimed. "I come to see what's wrong with y'all. You know what's going on up yonder. You know about the Devil worship. But y'all just gonna sit here and drink yourselves silly tonight?"

"It is Halloween Eve," Micah Horn said. He hadn't been in the mine for two days now, but he was still covered in sooty black dust. He was enjoying some strong moonshine. "Might as well enjoy yourself on Halloween Eve."

"Put a cork in it, Micah," Oats said. "There's no such thing as Halloween Eve."

"What happened to your nose?" Leonard Lawson asked.

"Went to church... house of God... thought it was a house of God, anyway... and got my nose busted by a colored."

Alvin Grimm narrowed his eyes. "Oats, maybe you ought to tell us what's really goin' on up there."

"Y'all don't care. Maybe you do, Alvin... and Teddy... and Red. I know you do, Red. But most of you are about as fired up as molasses."

Clyde Finch was already trying to think of a way to get rid of Oats before something bad got stirred up. But Oats launched into a tirade before Clyde could redirect him.

According to Oats, worshipping together had gotten people real friendly with one another. There was talk of serious change coming to Madison Creek. The churchers imagined a town where there wasn't a white and black water fountain; or separate bathrooms. In fact, they hoped that soon those two tables at Sweet Tea's marked *Colored* would come down and it just wouldn't matter where folks sat.

Of course, to really accomplish anything, they would need someone sympathetic to their viewpoint. There was talk, Oats reported, of running Huey House for mayor. Or, even whispers of putting Doctor Banks on the ballot. No one took that serious, but it had been said. Everyone knew blacks didn't vote because of the poll tax; but some had thought out loud that maybe the Rickety Church might use its funds to pay the poll tax for the congregation.

Oats said he tried to warn them. But no one would listen. In fact, when he told them, that what they were talking about was immoral and illegal, that's when the big colored man came and punched him in the face.

Tired of the ruckus, Lucius Jeremiah was the first to opt out. His knees popped when he stood up and he arched his back as arthritis screamed at him. "I come here to listen to the radio and have a good smoke. Leapin' lizards, all y'all are more wound up than a bunch of girls with their panties in a knot. Burn some more crosses... you think that'll scare anyone? You're going to have to burn more than a cross to scare those people. I'm too old to mess with y'all."

There were objections when he headed for the door, but he had made up his mind and went on out. On the old man's heels was Clyde Finch. He agreed, there was nothing but trouble ahead; and no real way to scare Huey House without crossing some lines that could get them locked up for a long time. They didn't have the connections others did. They were supposed to be a Radio Club. If folks wanted to vent, that was fine. But it was a Radio Club. But the men were riled up and they knew Oats had more to share. They wanted to hear the rest.

But, Oats found that outside of Finch and Jeremiah, provoking the Radio Club wasn't difficult. In the midst of his speech, Teddy Grimm declared that he was disappointed in himself. "I let my temper cool, and now I'm ashamed. All this goin' on right under my nose. I don't hate no one—not until they start ripping up the fabric of our town."

In Oats' opinion, he had helped the church. But the rejection he'd experienced today left him more than a little upset; he wanted revenge. On the old lady for laughing at him; on Huey for refusing to even help him when he just needed someone to talk to Katie for him; in fact, the school teacher was in that same boat. NO one would help a guy when he asked. And then they didn't just ask him to leave—they had to make a pancake out of his nose. Most of all, there was Katie. Who used the church, manipulated them, to keep him away from her. Well, he could do some manipulating of his own.

He had manufactured and saved his best tale for last. He told the Radio Club how even the most intimate barriers were breaking down. Not only did it not matter to the Rickety Church who sat where, or how people behaved—but relationships were forming. He didn't want to name names, but he told them how colored men were now inviting white women to dinner at their homes.

"Want their claws all over our women," Oats lamented.

"Is that why Katie left you?" Jonas asked. "For a black man?"

Gosh, some people just make you go and put two and two together for them. They're too dumb to connect the dots.

"You just have to know, don't you Jonas? Got a nose bigger than mine is right now. Well, that's between me and her. I'll preserve her dignity even if she's not worried about it."

Micah Horn took a long swig of moonshine after Finch left. "So you're telling us that after you practically begged us to leave the church alone yesterday, today they busted your nose and you decided to come tell us the truth?"

"I didn't want to say nothin'. I have friends at that church. I tried to protect them. Y'all know I tried."

"Old Lucius Jeremiah did have a point," Oats said. Actually, the old man had given him an opening to push things a little further; a little harder. "I respect you men going out there and taking your stand. But just burning crosses under Nettie Drakes sheets ain't gonna scare no one."

"I know what we can do," Alvin said thoughtfully. "John what happened to that weather balloon material that dropped off that Government truck while back? We had loads of it. I'm thinkin' on somethin' that'll really scare ole Huey more than me and Teddy in a sheet."

The Invaders

Jo slipped outside to get away from the noise of the music. A group of men were gathered around an old tree stump talking and smoking. As she approached, Jo realized that there was an arm wrestling competition going down, with the tree stump serving as a table top. Big X and Mule Evermund were about to go at it. They locked hands and Boots cupped his hand over theirs and counted. When he yelled, *GO!* the two men began to push.

Boots stepped back to watch the competition and let a long cigarette he'd been smoking slip from his mouth to the ground.

"Watch out, comin' through!" Dusty yelled as he bounded off the church steps toward Boots. In a single motion Dusty swept up the discarded *Lucky Strike* and stuck it in his mouth.

"Stop dat!" Big X grunted. He was in a dead heat with Mule.

"Luckies taste better," Dusty said as the tip of the cigarette caught new life. "Longer lasting!" he declared and sucked in on the cigarette. His eyes widened and he doubled over in a fit of coughing.

"Give me that!" Doctor Banks demanded.

"Cigarettes will kill us all." A woman's voice startled them. Jo glanced back to see Mrs. Dotson standing near the church house.

Mule finally groaned as his arm gave way to the steady force of Big X's hand. *Ahhh!* Mule put his hands to his face, a stubborn cowlick waved as his head bopped from side to side. "I-I almost h-had ya!"

■ ■ ■

When the sound of the band quieted down, Lutie Dotson decided it was safe to go inside. They had just been so extra loud tonight. She was anxious to find Huey. She had an offering of her own to give. Not the money kind of offering — she didn't have much of that. But she'd been thinking about how the school teacher had donated those bones to the church. Why, Lutie reckoned she might as well make a sacrifice of her own to the Lord. She was ready to have her husband's dead body dug up and moved to the new graveyard. Her heart skipped a beat at the thought. She didn't know why it made her so happy; except that she very much liked to be reminded as often as possible that he was indeed dead. Besides, it should make people very happy to have another grave in the graveyard. They might even give her a little more respect.

All of Lutie's thoughts about that very special donation disappeared as soon as she entered the church house. There was Nettie Drake, sitting by the radio fiddling with the dial. Nettie wasn't supposed to be here! She felt wounded.

"Where did you come from?" Lutie demanded.

"I decided to show up after all," Nettie said nonchalantly.

Lutie's face reddened and she stepped back into the night. Nettie had been giving her rides for weeks now; why would she have lied to her about coming to the party? Only one thing made sense: she was embarrassed by her friend. It hurt to realize her friend was ashamed of her. The teasing she'd taken a few days ago still stung; and now there was this insult from Nettie.

Lutie decided to walk alone down the hill.

■ ■ ■

Inside the church, Nettie Drake continued to toy with the radio. When she finally got a station to break through the static, Nettie patted the radio as if it was a good puppy.

"That's *Puttin' On the Ritz!*" Dusty shot both hands into the air. He gyrated his hips to the sound of the music in a motion that perfectly matched the beat of the song.

"Good grief!" Meemaw Moses shook her head with disapproval. "You stop that!"

Old Mo jumped toward the boy, but Dusty danced around in another direction.

"Can't catch 'em, might as well join 'em!" Mo shouted, and began to wiggle his body to the music.

There was laughter from the edges of the church. The lamps made the room flicker and the shadows wave as people began to dance.

The Ritz faded and the voice of Ella Fitzgerald breezed in with *A-Tisket, A-Tasket.*

■ ■ ■

"That church party sure is goin' late," Effie Heartland remarked.

Minnie Belle sat down by the radio, which was beside the window. "We can outlast them. *Chase and Sanborn Hour* is on the radio right now. That means Bergen and McCarthy."

The women joined Minnie Belle at Leonard's radio by the window. Minnie Belle toyed with the dial until she found Edgar and Charlie chatting about what a bad boy the puppet was. But they had hardly gotten into the show when Nelson Eddy began *Song of the Vagabonds.*

"Honestly, I have no idea what he's singing," Effie said.

Greta was pleased. "I thought it was just me. I can't make out a single word."

Minnie Belle sighed and spun the dial through a maze of static. Music filled the room for a moment, then they were dipped back into static.

"That music was good!" Dorothy Simpson said. She was across the room scrounging up a second helping of cobbler. Keep this up, and she'd need a girdle just to fit in her own clothes.

Minnie Belle worked back toward the station she'd passed up. The music faded to an announcer...

> Good evening, ladies and gentlemen. From the Meridian Room in the Park Plaza in New York City, we bring you the music of Ramón Raquello and his Orchestra.

As Ramón Raquello and his orchestra played, there was a pounding at the dress shop door below.

"Someone's at the door," Greta said and pointed at the floor to show she meant downstairs. But the gesture was exaggerated and she saw the little smirks on the ladies faces.

Minnie Belle commanded Greta to come with her. Greta was surprised, and a little honored. They hurried down the stairs and through the dark dress shop. Whoever was at the door was a persistent soul, knocking with what seemed to be steadfast assurance that surely someone would come.

"It might be trouble," Greta warned.

"Gosh, I didn't think of that," Minnie Belle snapped.

There was more pounding at the door. It was becoming rapid and desperate. A woman's voice called something. Minnie Belle threw the door open and Lutie Dotson almost fell in on her.

"Sanctuary!" Lutie cried. She didn't lower her voice now that the door was open.

"What?" Minnie Belle asked, confused.

"Sanctuary! Like a church! I want you to give me sanctuary."

"Welcome to our church," Greta said with a grin and waved Lutie in.

They brought Lutie upstairs. She was upset, or confused—more confused than usual.

"What are you doin' walking in the middle of the night?" Edith asked.

"What's going on out there?" Effie asked, her face pressed against the screen of the open window. She was sure she had caught a glimpse of a flash of some kind further down on Main Street.

They ushered Mrs. Dotson to a couch. Minnie Belle turned the radio up a notch. "Here, this is some solid listening. Found it while we was dial twisting. Some fella named Ramón Raquello and his orchestra."

The music on the radio was a swing band, but even with uplifting music, Lutie looked totally dejected. She told the ladies how Nettie said she wasn't going to the party, so she couldn't give Lutie a ride. But then she spotted her right at the radio having a good ole time. That's when Lutie realized none of these people were her friends—not really.

On the radio, the swing band died away and an announcer said…

We take you now to Grover's Mill, New Jersey.

"What's going on?" Minnie Belle asked. On the radio police sirens and the noise of a large crowd filled the airwaves. "Is there a war?"

A reporter named Carl Phillips was giving a live update from a farm in Grover's Mill. The ladies had grown used to interruptions on the radio with news about the war in Europe, but Grover's Mill wasn't Europe — it was New Jersey.

Dorothy Simpson was worried, "Oh no. Another hurricane, don't you think?"

Greta offered a silent prayer that the trouble not be Germany — not tonight.

On the radio, Carl Phillips was breathless. He was at the farm where something had struck the earth.

I guess that's the… thing, directly in front of me, half buried in a vast pit. Must have struck with terrific force.

The room tensed. "What hit with terrific force?" Greta asked.

"Shhhh!"

The women leaned toward the radio.

The ground is covered with splinters of a tree it must have struck on its way down. What I can see of the object itself doesn't look very much like a meteor. It looks more like a huge cylinder.

Mrs. Dotson sat up. She wiped tears from her cheeks. Something crashed in New Jersey?

On the radio, Phillips described the hundreds of parked cars as police tried to block off the road that lead to the farm where the object was half buried. People were actually venturing near the edge of the pit, and one man wanted to touch the object; of course, the police weren't going to let him do that.

"What do you think it is?" Minnie Belle asked.

Edith leaned forward, "Maybe a crashed German plane. I think the Germans are invading."

"No, no," Greta said, her German accent even thicker when she tried to force it from the edges of her words.

Carl Phillips told his radio audience the object that had landed at Grover's Mill was now making a strange sound. He held his microphone up to the cylinder and commanded the audience to, *Listen*. A hum pulsated through the radio.

"They're here!" Mrs. Dotson straightened up.

"Who's here?" Minnie Belle asked, giving Lutie a scornful look.

On the radio, Professor Pierson of Princeton, finally gave his opinion that the object was *definitely extraterrestrial*, and then clarified, *not found on this earth*.

A gasp went through the room.

"Oh!" Minnie Belle shivered. "You mean *them*!"

Mrs. Dotson nodded. "In September, a meteor crashed into Blue Mountain. We never found the crash site… maybe because it wasn't a meteor at all."

Greta was startled by this. "You mean… maybe one of those things that landed in New Jersey also landed here?"

On the radio, Carl Phillips was excited… something was happening.

> *Ladies and gentlemen, this is terrific! This end of the thing is beginning to flake off! The top is beginning to rotate like a screw! The thing must be hollow!*

There was a clanking sound on the radio as if a huge piece of metal had fallen to the earth. Voices screamed as Phillips came back to his radio audience to declare that what he was witnessing at that very moment was the most terrifying thing he'd ever seen. And then, with his own voice quaking, Phillips told the nation that something was crawling out of the hollow top. Its eyes were two black holes.

"We're not alone," Greta said.

"We are being invaded," Minnie Belle replied softly, trying to talk herself into the reality. Beings from another world — Martians — had indeed landed in New Jersey and were crawling out of their spacecraft. And she had indeed heard about the meteor that struck Blue Mountain.

Carl Phillips gasped…

> *Good heavens… something's wriggling out of the shadow like a gray snake. Now it's another one, and another. They look like tentacles to me.*

The women, who had been rendered speechless by the radio news, screamed in unison as people in New Jersey got the first contact with creatures from the planet Mars. Minnie Belle covered her eyes, as if she could see the entire thing.

The ladies listened as the creatures in the ship not only rose up out of their craft, but began to torch people with some kind of a heat-ray. The masses who had gathered at the farm in Grover's Mill were set ablaze by the Martian invaders. Unearthly shrieks pierced the airwaves.

> *Now the whole field's caught fire. The woods… the barns… the gas tanks of automobiles… it's spreading everywhere. It's coming this way. About twenty yards to my right.*

The microphone crashed to a dead silence.

And the silence lasted.

"Oh my!" Edith Step began to cry. In fact, all of the women were crying. That's what happens, Lutie considered, when one does not prepare oneself emotionally for the truth.

Finally the silence was broken when an announcer came on to say that circumstances beyond their control left them unable to continue the broadcast from Grover's Mill.

Minnie Belle stood up. "It won't take them long to get this direction if they landed a craft up yonder on Blue Mountain."

Effie Heartland looked out the window for a long time. When she looked back at the women in the room, there was terror in her eyes. "Lutie is right. The Martians are here," Effie reported solemnly.

"This is a big joke!" Minnie Belle snapped.

On the radio Brigadier General Montgomery Smith, commander of the state militia at Trenton, New Jersey announced that he was placing several of the counties in New Jersey under martial law.

"I'm telling you, come look!" Effie said sternly to Minnie Belle.

With exasperation, Minnie Belle stomped to her own window and stared out at Main Street.

And there they were!

Martians with strange flowing robes — space suits — and blazing torches marched confidently up the center of Main Street. They were almost to the Dress Shop.

They were led by a Martian on some kind of rolling machine. That was probably the heat-ray the man on the radio had been talking about. It was impossible to see exactly what the machine looked like because it was covered in that strange metallic space fabric. The Martians marched in silent procession, except for the steady grind of their death machine.

The Battle of Madison Creek

The women shut off the lamps and huddled at the window as the Martians passed. They were walking — almost floating — up Main Street.

"I count ten Martians," Lutie said.

"Eleven," Greta corrected. "One is on top of that riding heat-ray machine."

Over the radio, the Secretary of the Interior addressed the people of the United States. Only, someone at CBS had made a mistake. That wasn't the Secretary of the Interior; they all recognized the voice of President Roosevelt.

> *Citizens of the nation: I shall not try to conceal the gravity of the situation that confronts the country, nor the concern of your Government in protecting the lives and property of its people. However, I wish to impress upon you — private citizens and public officials, all of you — the urgent need of calm and resourceful action.*

"Ladies, it's up to us to defend our *heimat* — our homeland." Greta said boldly. It was the first time she had felt comfortable purposefully using a German word. "The president himself has called us to resourceful action."

"Really and truly, what do you think we're going to do against extraterrestrials with heat-rays?" Minnie Belle demanded.

Greta's dark eyes were steely with determination. "They prepared for the army. They came ready to be shot with bullets and cannons and bombs. They think we humans are afraid to get close. It's time for hand to hand combat. That's what the Martians aren't ready for. Minnie Belle, be a dear and turn up the warmer on that peach cobbler. "

"Are you hungry?" Minnie Belle asked.

"If we can't beat the Martians, we'll never beat the Nazis!" Greta said. "Okay, ladies, find your weapon and fix bayonets!"

■ ■ ■

"Preacher!" Shorty Parker rushed into the sanctuary. There was a hum of electricity as the radio spat mouthfuls of static. "There are fella's with torches comin' this way!"

"White Radio Club," Huey said. "Are they armed?"

"Just torches that I could see. But..." he paused with indecision. "Preacher, they don't look like anything I've ever seen before."

Georgette put her hands on Huey's thick shoulders. "Maybe it's time we pray, Huey."

The people of the Little Rickety Church made a big circle in the sanctuary. Black hands locked with white hands as Huey House sought the Creator's attention. "Well now, we might have a bit of trouble, big God. Maybe you might see fit to come on down and help us. Amen."

"We don't need to be afraid," Doctor Banks said, his voice reassuring.

"I best tell y'all somethin' dat I didn't tell ya sooner," Meemaw Moses said. "Remember a-ways-back when them boys burned the cross? They threw a rock in the window."

"Sure, I remember it," Hammond Washington said. "Had a lump for days after that. Hurt like the dickens."

"There was a note attached to the rock. I hid it because I didn't want to stir up any more fears. And, forgive me preacher, but I didn't want you to close up shop. This church has blessed me somethin' fierce."

"What did the note say?" Huey asked.

Meemaw looked down, as if staring at her old worn shoes would give her courage. "Note said: *Next time it won't be the cross that burns, it'll be the... negga church.*"

Hammond took charge. "Okay, this is going to be just like the Great War. Good thing is, we have the high ground. We should use that to our advantage." He began to give directions.

■ ■ ■

A familiar whirring sound caught Minnie Belle's attention. The last time she'd heard that was the day she and Edith had told that missionary — and his fool assistant — that the Judgment day was at hand. He had run outside as Huey House sent stepping stones right down Main Street. Now she heard the same sound and realized those church people were doing it again — they were sending a stream of stones down Main Street.

The Martians saw them coming, but it was hard for them to dodge the rocks in their space suits. Several of the stones hit the death machine with a very earthy bang. It was almost comical the way the Martians had to jump to avoid the oncoming stones. Several weren't fast enough and they stumbled when the stones rolled under their feet or struck their ankle.

At the top of the hill, Mule Evermund laughed with unbridled joy. He picked up another stepping stone, squatted down and launched the stepping stone into the street. Minnie Belle thought it must take something akin to perfect aim to get those stepping stones to roll on their sides like that.

Minnie Belle waited for the next stone, but it never came. They must be out, she realized with dread. Several of the Martians who had been hit now struggled to their feet.

■ ■ ■

With Hammond in command of the hill, and Greta leading the women from behind — the Martians were trapped. Above Blue Mountain, lightening lit the sky and was chased by the distant rumble of thunder.

Only, the Martians were trying to keep up with their death machine and didn't see the women trailing behind them. The death machine growled as it climbed the hill. The Martian in the machine was upright and stiff, his posture one of steely determination.

Stones had knocked more than one of the Martians down, but they had all gotten back up and kept moving. One of them had twisted an ankle and was limping, he frantically tried to keep up with the others who trailed behind the heat-ray. The Martian right beside the death machine waved his torch in a long arc that sprayed a trail of light.

The women silently shadowed the Martians. The invader's attention was on the church and the hill ahead.

The two women leading the charge, Greta and Minnie Belle, ran at one of the Martians. They were each armed with a broom. They pressed the bristle side of the broom under their arm and stuck the broom handle out like a great spear. When they were right on the invader, the ladies drove their sticks into the Martian's back.

"Our turn!" Greta yelled.

The Martian was taken completely by surprise, and not knowing what was being pressed into him, he fell face forward and almost torched his own space suit.

Minnie Belle followed Greta's lead. The two women pressed into the cluster of aliens, poking and stabbing and driving them down as fast as they could with their broom handles. Surprise was on their side.

When the Martians turned to see what was going on, Lutie Dotson dared to draw close to one of them and declared, "Take this, you Martian scum!" She flung a spoon full of hot peach cobbler. Most of it just splattered on the invaders uniform, but some found the eye slits. The Martian grasped at his uniform as the cobbler crusted around his eye. He brushed at his face, but with that head gear on, he couldn't wipe his eyes clean.

Minnie Belle reversed her broom and now held the bristles out toward the Martians. "You want our planet? You have to deal with the women of Madison Creek!" she exclaimed. She jammed the broom toward the Martian who had just gotten an eyeful of her cobbler. He knocked her broom out of the way with his torch. The broom caught fire, and Minnie Belle herself lit up with delight.

"You Martians like fire?" Minnie Belle asked as her broom began to blaze.

The Martian gave a GO AWAY motion.

Like baseball great Joe DiMaggio, Minnie Belle swung her flaming broom at the Martian's head. She stabbed him hard in the face with the smoldering broom. He fell back, arms flailing as he tried to defend himself.

From a little further away, Effie Heartland began to throw the apples that Greta had brought.

"Martian buggers wanna fight, I'll give 'em a fight," Effie huffed, and threw another apple. It nosedived in front of her.

"I like your spirit," Dorothy said. "Let me give it a try."

Effie handed Dorothy a fresh apple from the apple sack they'd brought down. Dorothy closed her eyes for a brief moment, then pitched the apple with surprising force. The apple buzzed through the air and struck a Martian in the head. She was dead on!

"Holy Moses!" Effie's eyes were huge. "Where did you learn to pitch like that? You just made apple sauce on that alien's head."

"Minnesota," Dorothy said. She felt like she was nineteen again. In a flash, she remembered her days as a Bloomer Girl. In fact, she didn't just remember it—she felt like she was there.

Ka-Wham! She sent an apple whirring through the air, where it struck yet another Martian dead on. This time, the impact wasn't as great as Dorothy might have hoped. But dog gone it, she was forty-seven and that had been one pretty good pitch.

"Quick, give me another," Dorothy instructed.

■ ■ ■

The stars and moon had disappeared. The clouds lit for a moment as lightening sparked behind them. The lightning was chased by a long rumble of thunder.

"Looks to me like the Martians are headed toward the Devil church," Minnie Belle said as she and Greta beat back another invader. The Martians waved their torches to drive away the women.

An apple struck the Martian Minnie Belle was contending with and he stumbled back, tripped on his own robe and went to the ground. Minnie Belle started to come after him, but Greta urged her to stay focused on the ones who were up and moving.

"Hand to hand combat," Greta reminded Minnie Belle as the German woman took on a Martian of her own. She had her own technique, which involved jabbing the handle of the broom at the alien's masked face. In particular, they seemed rather helpless when she aimed for the eyes.

"Poor creatures, they can't keep up with their death machine," Dorothy shouted, and pitched an apple.

The women circled the aliens they had cut off and began to close in. The Martians waved their torches to drive the women back. They were coming to an impasse.

"Stay there, you *dummes huhn*," Greta shouted.

"What did you say?" Minnie Belle asked as she pushed back on particularly angry Martian.

"Stupid chicken."

Lightening crackled and lit the sky. For a brief second Greta's face was lit and Minnie Belle saw her smiling. She thought at that moment, the German woman was absolutely beautiful.

■ ■ ■

Jo hovered near her Uncle Huey. They were standing in the middle of the road flanked by Hammond and Boots. Under Hammond's direction, the church people had armed up with clubs and rocks and gone into hiding. He said this was trench warfare. Jo didn't see any trenches, just people taking cover in the trees around the church and few going to her makeshift graveyard.

"Well would you look at that!" Uncle Huey said with satisfaction. "Those ladies done half our work for us. Split those men into two groups."

It was true. The truck or tractor they had draped with material continued to make its way up the hill. But now it only escorted three of their attackers.

Boots was impressed. "They're getting their tushies whomped by a bunch of ladies!"

"The ladies cut their numbers down," Hammond observed, "But I'm willing to bet the really dangerous ones are still headed our way."

"They're gonna use that tractor like a tank," Jo said. "Might not be many of them, but they could plow us right over."

"Jo, get outta here!" Huey said sharply.

"I'm your information getter," Jo said. She had slipped away and gone a little ways down the hill where she could hear some of the banter from the fight. Now she reported, "Those women down yonder think they are fighting a Martian invasion."

"Very good, now go away," Huey said.

Jo stepped back, but didn't leave.

Hammond was indifferent about her information. "It doesn't matter to me if this is an invasion from Mars, Germany or just plain ole rascals — they're the enemy. And Jo's right, so long as they have that tractor, they can make pancakes out of any of us."

The tractor was getting close. Hammond told them to follow him.

They ran toward the church, Huey following Jo and Hammond as he took gigantic breaths. The three of them stood in front of it as the tractor and the men following it turned onto the church property.

"You be-be-better watch out!" Mule Evermund yelled from the shadows.

The tractor came to a stop in front of the church. The three men who had kept up with the tractor now lined up in front of it.

One of the men shouted, "We tried to warn you people. Didn't want to take y'all to the woodshed. But some folk just need a whoopin'."

"Didn't you get my note?" another of the hooded men yelled.

The only answer he got was from the trees. A single stone flew through the darkness and struck the tractor.

"You better stop that!" The man speaking was angry. In fact, Jo didn't think she'd ever heard a man angrier. "I'll kill your preacher!"

"Y'all take your tank and your torches and go on home," Huey said calmly. He stood at the church door, his eyes narrow with determination.

Another rock struck the tractor — and another whizzed by the driver's head.

Jo looked toward the trees, and in a splash of lightening she spotted Big X... Mule... and Meemaw Moses.

Two gunshots came from the direction of the tractor and echoed all around Jo. *KABAM! KABAM!* Fire licked up from the finger of the driver. He was holding a gun that was now clouded with smoke. The rock throwing stopped and everyone became quiet. He stood up on his tractor and pointed his gun at Huey, then lifted it a little and settled it toward Boots, then lifted it again and pointed at Hammond. "I'm not afraid to lay you out in the cemetery," he warned, and pulled the trigger again. This time his shot didn't blaze up toward the clouds — this bullet whizzed by Hammond's head.

"Let us do our business!" the man on the tractor demanded. He pointed his Colt .45 at JO! She had been standing a little behind her uncle, just to his right. Now, the dark fear she'd first been introduced to the night she saw the cross on fire, crawled back over her with paralyzing intensity.

One of the men holding a torch in front of the tractor looked up at his buddy. In a loud whisper, he told his friend to leave the girl alone. The man with the gun lifted the Colt .45 and once again targeted Huey.

Jo wanted to fold up and cry. Just the thought that someone in *her* town would be willing to even point a gun at her crushed something inside. No matter what fight adults had with one another, they were supposed to love the kids.

■ ■ ■

When Dorothy was out of apples, Effie Heartland handed her the frying pan she'd been wielding.

"You're not a bad pitcher," Effie said. "Let's see how you are at bat."

Dorothy gave a little laugh and took the frying pan as one of the Martians pressed forward, torch extended. Dorothy swung and made contact, but she was a better pitcher than batter. He shook it off and tried to push past her.

"*KAR-AZ-ATTACK!*" the Martian shouted, and then began to growl under his uniform. As if on cue, the night growled with a belly full of thunder. A single raindrop struck Dorothy.

All at once the invaders began to swing their torches back and forth. The women backed up and the Martians made a break for it. They ran like terrified school children from a bully. One Martian limped behind the others.

"Oh no you don't!" Minnie Belle cried and chased after the limping Martian. Then, mimicking Greta's German accent she said, "*Dummes huhn!*"

Greta swelled with pride.

"*Dummes huhn!*" Greta yelled. "Get him!"

"Shouldn't we help her?" Effie asked.

Greta shrugged, "No. Let her have this one to herself. The others are all going back to their spaceship, no doubt. I want to see what's happening with that death machine."

■ ■ ■

Tractor-man held the gun on Huey. "Okay, boys, do what we came for."

One of the men pulled up his robe. Underneath, he had tied three towels drenched in gasoline around his waist. He wadded the towels up and told his two friends with torches to follow him.

Jo thought the one talking sounded just like Red Heartland. She wondered who the others were.

"You gonna torch da Lord's House?" Huey asked as the men passed by him to enter the church.

"This ain't no house of the Lord!" one of them said.

Huey looked from the gun that was aimed at him, to the man who was about to pass right by. "Running all around at night with torches, you men remind me of the mob in Frankenstein. There's no monsters here. Nothin' that y'all haven't cooked up in your own imagination."

"This church is the monster," tractor-man said. His arm was steady as he held the gun on Huey.

Overhead the sky flickered with lightning. There was a moment it felt like they were surrounded by blue and yellow light, and then it all went dark again. When the darkness came back, there were only two torches burning; tractor-man's and the other one of the man lying on the ground.

The one whose torch had become nothing more than a stick of smoke looked up at the tractor-man. "Give me your torch."

"You boys still got one torch. I'm not gonna be left in the dark out here. Go, before Sheriff Tuff gets a mind to come see what all this is about."

"Ah, don't act like this is a monster movie," Huey said.

This time the men ignored him and stomped past. The one with the dead torch struck Huey on the head as he went by. "Devil preacher," he snarled. Then he thumped Hammond on the head. Jo knew it took everything he had for Hammond not to smash into his attacker. But with tractor-man aiming that gun at Huey, Hammond couldn't do anything but accept the abuse.

■ ■ ■

It was dark inside the Little Rickety Church. The lamps had been put out and there was only the light of the torch.

They didn't see the woman sitting on the step of the little make-shift stage. She cringed as they broke windows to get a cross ventilation going. They didn't want to start a fire and not get the whole thing burned down.

"Right there, throw them rags on those benches against the wall," one directed.

"Otis Step," the woman said into the flickering light.

They all jumped.

"What?" Oats said, and then realized he'd just given himself away.

"Ah, why don't you guys just take your spook masks off," Katie said, still sitting motionless on the step. "I know who you are. Every one of you. You, right there, you're Teddy Grimm. Slim and tall. What happened to your torch? You just come to watch?"

Teddy looked from his torch, which was still smoking, to the woman. He wanted to hit her with it; just one good clunk would shut her up.

Katie pointed to the next man. "And you — the one who had the towels. Soaked them in gasoline, didn't-ja? I can smell it from here. You're Red Heartland. Anyone would know that voice. And this fine fella here with the torch, that would be none other than my old flame Otis Step. I know your shape, your walk and even your breathin'."

"Better get outta here," Red warned. "Oats here is about to put a torch to —"

"Wait," Katie demanded. "I just want to ask Otis one thing. You sure are willing to go to a lot of meanness and hurt a lot of people just because I hurt you. I don't know what you told these men to get them all wild eyed, but I'll bet it's the biggest barrel of half-truths since Roosevelt sold America the New Deal."

She motioned with her finger for Otis to come to her.

"Oats, leave her be," Red was feeling uneasy. They should have this done already.

"You gonna burn me in the church?" Katie asked Red. "At least at the Salem Witch Trials, they had a trial before the burning." She pointed at Otis. "Take off your mask and come to me. I want to have a chat with you."

Otis hated himself. She was a witch, he thought. She had cast a dark love spell over him years ago.

"I've been right here praying about us," Katie said. "Been right here at this altar, praying that maybe God might put us back together. I know you've been up to a lot of no good. Spreading lies and hurting people. But what if I told you that I realized Jesus forgives you? I mean, really forgives you. And I don't care about all that ruckus you did in the past. In fact, you coming in here by firelight, that was an answer to my prayers. Kind of a miracle, if you ask me. The kind of miracle only God could work out."

He was shaken by that. "Really? Did Huey House just put you in here? What kind of a preacher puts a woman in harm's way?"

"Huey doesn't know I'm here." Otis' eyes went wide as Katie stood up from the step and came toward him. "Give me the torch," she instructed. She reached for the torch, but he jerked it away. When his hand was up, she grabbed at his hood. "What do you have on under there? A party hat?" She pealed the hood off of him, the hat came off with it.

"What are you doing?" Red was angry. "Give me your torch, Oats."

"Kiss me, you sorry excuse of a man."

"Don't you kiss her," Red was getting more frantic. "I did my part. I got the rags up here. Now light them up! Or I'll have Teddy…"

Holding his torch up like the Statue of Liberty, Otis leaned in to kiss Katie. Just as his face came close to hers, she head butted him, smacking her forehead into his nose. He screamed in pain as his broken nose burst with new blood.

"That's what you get for stirring people up. And you deserve a lot more."

Blood covered his shirt and he started to lower his torch. She reached for the torch, but he waved it away from her.

She was angry, but he sensed she felt safe with him; safe enough to hurt his nose.

With his free hand he pulled Katie close and leaned in to kiss her, but he stopped himself.

"Go ahead, I won't head butt you again," she promised.

But she did.

This time, he pushed through the pain and pressed his face toward hers. His nose felt like it was on fire. Blood was dripping down over him. But he was hungry for her, and she for him. He kissed her as pain screamed over him and blood poured between the two of them. *But her kiss was worth a hundred broken noses*, he thought.

"You are an idiot, Oats," Red said decidedly. He reached for the torch, but Oats waved him away as he kissed Katie.

Blood was on her nose, her chin—he was even dripping it onto her dress.

"Shouldn't kiss in church," Teddy said simply, and joined Red in trying to get the torch away from him.

"What's going on in there?" the tractor-man yelled.

Otis broke away from Katie and flamed the torch toward the two men who were trying to take it from him. "Get out of here, you two."

Blood dotted the wood floor.

Angry, Red lunged forward and finally got the stem of the torch in his grasp. But Oats wasn't going to let go easy. Teddy leapt toward them both and tackled them. Katie stumbled aside and into the towels. She felt gasoline soak through her dress.

"Stop it!" Katie cried, untangling herself from the rags, she threw herself at the men who were fighting. Finally, Teddy snatched the torch, and pushed the others away as he stood up.

"YES!" Red gasped. He felt sticky with Oat's blood all over him. And then, with real delight, he said, "Light 'er up, Teddy!"

Teddy went to the towels, stood over them for a moment with the torch blazing in his hand.

"Teddy, what's the problem?" Red asked. "Don't study the rags, do it!"

With sudden decision, Teddy threw the torch out of the window they'd broken earlier to allow for airflow.

"What are you doing?" Red screamed.

Outside, the tractor-man demanded again to know what was going on.

Lying on the floor, Oats pulled his shirt up to his face and held his nose.

Teddy pulled off his hood. "I can't burn down a church. We can say it ain't no church, but Greta isn't going to buy that. I'd never taste her lips again if I harmed the house of God." He slapped his own head. "What was I thinkin'? If our ladies find out the trouble we've made, we might never get invited to bed again."

Katie tugged at Otis' shirt, which he was holding up to his nose. He shook his head hard. He wanted to kiss her, but his nose hurt too bad. And, there was always the risk she might sock him a third time, and he wouldn't be able to bear it.

"Trust me," Katie urged, and eased his shirt away from his face. He was smeared with blood. She kissed him — and then again.

They kissed until Red kicked Oats in the face. He planted his foot on Oats cheek. "I've had enough of you, New York boy. I've got half a mind to kick your teeth out and lodge my shoe in your throat."

Out of the darkness, Teddy swung at Red, hitting him in the jaw. Then a punch to the gut. Red stumbled backward. He tried to defend himself, but he was still draped in that ridiculous material and he was getting tangled. Teddy hit Red again, and this time Red bumped the window sill.

"Say goodbye, my friend," Teddy laughed, and shoved Red through the window onto the smoldering torch.

Katie sat up and blew Teddy a kiss through darkness.

■ ■ ■

Outside, the tractor-man was getting more and more nervous. They should have done this already. He heard them fighting inside, and then the torch came out the window.

"A miracle," Huey declared when the torch huffed out and lay smoking on the ground.

"You shut up!"

There was talking and fighting inside. Tractor-man was angry. He shook his gun at Huey. "You hid people inside your church? You knew we was gonna burn it, and you coward, you hid people in there to fight us. We shoulda come with shot guns and…"

The fighting inside got louder, and then a hooded figure fell out of the window of the church and landed on the torch.

"Now that's a sh-sh-show I'd pay a whole qu-qu-quarter for!" Mule Evermund shouted from the trees. There was applause and cheering.

"Admit it, you've lost," Huey said to the man holding the gun on him. He tugged at his suit jacket, smoothed his tie, and even ran his fingers through his hair. "Lost my hat in all this commotion," he observed. Then, to tractor-man, he said, "Call it quits, and we'll see if we might repair your tractor. You ever read about Elisha? Not Elijah—"

"Shut up!" Tractor-man was nervous.

"Elisha was surrounded by the enemy. But God didn't let the ole Devil have Elisha. He surrounded dim bad boys with chariots of fire. That's what I've got, mister. Chariots of fire all around me. They're in this forest, and out yonder in the graveyard. One of them might just take a mind to pop your head off iffin' you don't repent."

"That's the thing," tractor-man said, his grip on the gun tightened. "You think you're Elisha, surrounded by the enemy. But in my book, I'm Elisha. I ain't here to do no Devil work. I come because—"

Thunder boomed. Startled, his nerves on edge and thinking it was gun fire, tractor-man pulled the trigger. Echoing the thunder that had just popped, the Colt .45 banged and light flashed at the edge of the muzzle.

Huey let out a surprised cry as the bullet ripped through his suit jacket. He fell to the ground.

■ ■ ■

"You shot my baby doll!" Georgette House screamed from the makeshift graveyard. Forgetting the danger, she ran to him and knelt down. Trailing right behind Georgette was Doctor Banks.

"They sh-sh-shot our preacher!" Mule lamented.

Stunned, tractor-man stared at the smoking gun in his hand.

"What have I d-d-done?" tractor-man stuttered. He dropped the gun, which rattled on the ground and stumbled off his tractor. "What have I done, what have I done?" he wailed. Looking to Boots he said, "Tell me he's not dead!"

"You stay away," Boots instructed.

"Eye for eye!" Meemaw Moses cried from the bushes.

"They shot Huey!" Georgette sat beside her husband and cradled his head.

Hammond looked up from Huey, "Stone the murderer!"

Tractor-man pulled off his hood. Underneath was a terrified Alvin Grimm. "No, no! I didn't mean to shoot him! I got startled by the thunder and—"

A small stone struck Alvin.

"No!" Alvin was desperate. He shouldn't have dropped his gun. Gosh, he shouldn't have fired his gun.

"Teddy!" A woman with a German accent called as she came up from the road.

"Greta, stay away!" Alvin yelled. "I shot the preacher and now they're going to kill me!" His voice was a mixture of regret and fear.

Another stone, this one a little larger, struck the tractor.

"Look, it's me!" Alvin panted in desperation. He pulled on the coverings that had been draped over his tractor. They fell away. "Look! It's just me and Buffalo Bill!" He hugged his tractor. "Don't hurt us!"

Another stone came out of the dark and almost hit Alvin, but instead it thudded against Buffalo Bill.

Then something strange happened. Alvin heard his own voice come back at him. "Don't hurt us!"

"Who said that?" Alvin yelled at the darkness.

"It's me, Dusty! You sure do love your tractor, mister." The boy was excited. Then he repeated in Alvin's voice, "Don't hurt us!"

"Alvin, move to the other side of Buffalo Bill," Greta directed.

Glad to have some guidance, Alvin pushed away from his tractor and started to run around it. A rock hit Alvin on the shoulder, and then another struck his head.

"Stop it!" Greta yelled through her German accent. She ran to him and pulled him away from the tractor. His head was bleeding just above his eyebrow. As soon as they were away from Buffalo Bill, a storm of rocks flew at the tractor. It sounded like hail on a metal roof.

"Ah, that's too bad," Greta said. "I liked Buffalo Bill. And we still owe money on that big boy."

"No more rocks!" Doctor Banks yelled. The rocks stopped. "Preacher House is suffering something terrible. But he wants to speak to his killer before he dies."

Greta gasped. She stood up, "He can't come to you. He's hurt. But I will if you'd like."

There was some whispering between Hammond, Huey and Georgette.

"Alvin, get yourself over here!" Georgette stood up and pointed at the ground, indicating the exact location where she wanted Alvin to stand.

Greta let out and exasperated grunt. Mustering all her courage, she stood up and began to walk from the side of Buffalo Bill toward the slain preacher.

"We said Alvin!" Hammond shouted.

Greta kept walking. "Stone me if you want, but Alvin's head is bleeding."

She came to where Huey lay.

Georgette pointed her long finger at Greta. "This isn't about you. You go on back and get Alvin."

Greta looked down at Huey. He was breathing. His suit jacket was open, and there was a pin-size drop of blood soaking through his white shirt. Greta knelt down. "You didn't even take his shirt off?"

"You have guts, Greta," Hammond said, and patted the German woman on the shoulder. Then, looking back at the church he yelled, "Teddy, get out here with your wife!"

"Wait!" Greta wasn't content with a compliment. Pointing at Huey she demanded, "Why isn't he dead?"

Doctor Banks took a tattered Bible that was resting beside Huey. It's small but thick—and there was a bullet lodged in it.

"A Bible saved him?" Greta said slowly. "Really? No kidding? This is no joke?"

Doctor Banks shook his head. "Lady, I don't joke. I pray and I practice medicine and I go fishin' on Saturday and church on Sunday—but I don't joke."

Greta took the Bible in her hands and marveled at the bullet ridden pages. Then, with refreshed firmness, she said to Doctor Banks, "Well, if he's not dead—or even wounded—what are you doing here? Get to Alvin. He's hurt."

As the doctor and Greta got up, Hammond wasn't feeling so charitable. "Ahhh, did little Alvin get a rock thrown at his head? Seems he did that to me—"

"You stop that," Georgette said. She had been listening so intently to Greta for the past few minutes that her voice sounded German.

■ ■ ■

Leonard was running from Minnie Belle. She didn't know it was him, limping and hurting and even shedding a few pain filled tears under his hood and cape. He tried to lose her by running toward Sweet Tea's, but she stayed right on him.

At the front door of Sweet Tea's, Leonard Lawson fell down in total defeat.

But Minnie Belle wasn't hoping to just knock her Martian down—she wanted him dead. Dead! Dead! Dead! She drove the handle of the broom into his stomach. Leonard let out a loud cry and grabbed for the broom. Minnie Belle pulled the broom away and backed up. She held it like it was a rifle.

"Shucks, woman!" Leonard cried. "Knock it off! You want to kill me!"

"Leonard?" Minnie Belle looked questioningly at the fallen thing in front of her.

"Yes! It's me, Leonard. Your sweetie."

"How do I know you're Leonard? Martian could have stolen your body." She stabbed hard at his belly and enjoyed the sound of a long moan that escaped him.

Thunder and lightning did another dance in the sky as they chased one another.

"Minnie Belle, it's me!" Leonard pleaded. "I'm speakin' plain English, not Martian!"

"Well, maybe," Minnie Belle edged toward him. She flipped her broom around, so that the burned bristles were in his face. "If you're not a Martian, you'll know what my Leonard knows."

"Fine. Ask me anything."

"What is our wedding anniversary?"

He was quiet and then said, "August twenty-third!"

Mercifully she lifted the broom bristles from his face, but just as he started to lift his head she brought the handle down hard across his back. A surprised *OH!* was forced out of him. She did it again, and then again.

"It's the twenty-fourth you extraterrestrial maggot!"

"Oh, Minnie Belle, spare me!"

THUNK! She hit him again, this time across the back of his legs.

"Alright, you Martian hammerhead, how old was I when you met me?"

He was quick on that one, "Eighteen!"

THUNK! Her broom smacked the small of his back.

"I was eighteen when you married me. Sixteen when we met!"

She sat down beside him, using the broom like a staff to guide her. "Really and truly, you are an imbecile."

"Why did you do that? You hurt me!"

She shrugged un-apologetically, "I thought you were a Martian. I still don't believe you're Leonard."

He worked to sit up then pulled the hood off. His face swollen face was wet with tears and sweat. "See, it's me."

"Nah," she shook her head. "A bad replica. Look too good to be Leonard." She grabbed his hair. "Leonard is an ugly brute. Sorry man who wastes his time in front of the blasted radio. You look too good for him."

She kissed him hard on the mouth. He had forgotten what that felt like.

Huey's Funeral

Sheriff Tuff was surprised it took Minnie Belle until four thirty Monday afternoon to show up his office. He had expected her first thing. When she did arrive, she came in carrying a box of invitations.

"Really and truly, where were you last night?" She sat her box right on top of his desk.

"Trouble up on Blue Mountain. Boys went hiking and came back sayin' they saw Hickory Joe. But I went up there and it was just ole Sticky—"

"I don't care. You know, the town about fell apart. Thankfully you had the Concerned Women of Madison Creek watchin' the streets for you. We were almost invaded."

"By Martians?" The Sheriff pushed Minnie Belle's box to the side and pointed to the newspaper on his desk. The headline read:

Radio Listeners in Panic, Taking War Drama as Fact

"You know, poor Huey House almost died." Then, with rehearsed exaggeration, she declared: "Dereliction of duty!" She smiled, proud that she'd remembered the word. "You failed to protect this town. The Grimm brothers' tractor got all smashed up by people throwing rocks. And that's not all, my poor honey-pie Leonard got whooped somethin' fierce."

"Who beat Leonard?" the Sheriff asked.

"Not for me to say. You should have been here doing your cotton pickin' job and we wouldn't have had this hullabaloo."

"What's in your box?"

"Invitations. And you're going to deliver them."

Sheriff Tuff tipped back in his chair. "Minnie Belle, I am not the post office."

"No one would show up if the post office delivered them. And we wouldn't need them if you had done your job. So, you'll deliver the invitations and tell each person you expect them to show up, or you'll draw up charges."

"I can't do that," the Sheriff said patiently. "I can't threaten people."

She shrugged. "I don't care how you do it. You just see to it that these folks get my invitations."

"What's it an invitation to?"

"Huey House's funeral."

■ ■ ■

Curious, Sheriff Tuff opened the white envelope with his name on it. It was indeed an invitation to Huey House's funeral. It was set for the next Saturday afternoon over at the Grimm Peanut Farm.

Tuff fanned through the envelopes — who all had Minnie Belle invited? The question was more *who had Minnie Belle not invited*? He didn't see any notes for residents in Jordan Town, which was fine by him; he didn't like having to go out that way. So that's what Minnie Belle had spent her day doing — planning Huey's funeral and preparing invitations.

He wondered what they were up to. Huey was alive and well. He had seen the ole boy earlier that morning cleaning up at the church house with several members of his congregation. Sheriff Tuff had gone up to the church to see if Huey wanted to press any charges against Alvin Grimm for shooting him, or — shooting *at* him. He could certainly lock Alvin up for attempted murder, and disorderly conduct, not to mention destruction of property — the Bible. But Huey insisted that he didn't think Alvin meant to shoot him. There had been a thunder clap and it had startled Alvin. When asked why Alvin was pointing a gun at him in the first place, Huey simply asked the Sheriff if he hadn't heard that Martians had come down last night and invaded Madison Creek.

■ ■ ■

In Europe, a German was busy making plans to tear the world apart. In Madison Creek, a German busied herself on rebuilding a town.

Greta spent her week getting ready. She didn't have any patience with the brothers when they would whine about not wanting to hold the event on the farm or help her get ready. When they complained, she reminded them they were getting away with attempted murder.

Almost everyone in town was skeptical except Greta. Even Minnie Belle, who had gotten the Sheriff to do her bidding, told Greta that she still didn't believe in that church. But, Minnie Belle did believe in Greta. They had fought together against those Martian invaders, so how could she tell a good war buddy no?

By Saturday, Greta had the backyard ready for her big event. Well, she didn't have it ready — Teddy and Alvin did. The yard had been cleared of its weeds and overgrown grass. Edith Step, who was also doubtful — but pushed aside her reservations because Minnie Belle said it was going to be okay — loaned Greta her red, white and blue tablecloths.

At the last minute, after a visit from Annie Evermund, Greta made a new decision. She didn't want to use the patriotic tablecloths after all. Where had all that strange fabric the boys had worn on Halloween Eve gone? Dusty had gathered up a lot of it from behind the church where Teddy and crew had discarded it. There was more, Annie discovered, all over Main Street. Mostly behind buildings, like the Sweet Tea Café and the dress shop. She guessed the men had run behind the buildings to tear off their costumes before the lady folk killed them. Greta delivered the costumes to the dress shop, where Minnie Belle spent considerable time cutting and sewing until she had her own pile of tablecloths.

■ ■ ■

Jo objected to riding with her aunt to the funeral. She wanted to go with Uncle Huey. After all, she'd been right there when Alvin shot him. She had reflected more than once this past week that if that gun had been aimed at her when the thunder clapped, then she would have been the one to take a bullet — and she didn't have a fat Bible to protect her. Uncle Huey might be getting ready to forgive all these folks — if that's what this was about — but that didn't mean Jo had to.

"Why didn't we just have this thing at church?" Jo asked.

"Because then no one would have come for sure," Georgette said. "Besides, by going to the Grimm's Peanut Farm, it shows some good will on our part."

Jo figured they'd shown enough good will. In fact, for all she'd been through, she hoped Jesus was right proud of her. She hoped they let her go back to Mount Hallelujah Leper Colony next summer. She couldn't wait to tell a cabin full of girls all her most recent adventures.

They were greeted at the porch by Greta, who warmly hugged Georgette. She pointed to the side of the house, where Sheriff Tuff was waiting. "He'll show you to the backyard," she said.

Sheriff Tuff ushered them around the side of the house where they passed by Greta's apple orchard then through the side gate to the backyard.

"Look at that!" Jo pointed at the tablecloths as Sheriff Tuff directed them to their seat.

People sat with their friends, but no one said a word. They weren't even whispering. The Little Rickety Church crew was on one side of the yard, and the Radio Club crew on the other. Jo guessed Greta had told the Sheriff to seat people that way. And boy, were they ever the somber group! Everyone just sat, staring forward with angry expressions. Even the church people looked like they'd been drinking vinegar.

It was too much for Jo, who did not sit down right away when she found her assigned spot. Instead she waved her hand and broke into her best impression of the Mad Russian. "How dooo you do!" she said to everyone.

Aunt Georgette smacked her hard upside the head. But Dusty, who was sitting with Katie at the next table, laughed and slapped the table with both hands. Dusty responded in an even better impersonation of the Mad Russian. "You better watch out, the Russians are coming! We got you scared with the Germans and the

Martians, but—" Katie grabbed his ear and told him to stop it now. "Gosh, this is going to be boring," Dusty sulked.

Now that's where he was wrong, Jo thought. No matter what else this might be, she doubted it would be boring.

Jo watched as people came. The men all had the same reaction when they stepped into the backyard; a deep intake of breath. It was almost painful for them to come face to face once again with that unearthly metallic material that now graced each table.

"You all planning to kill us," Red Heartland asked when Sheriff Tuff ushered him in. He pointed to a pile of white crosses against the fence. Jo recognized those as the same ones she and Dusty had written monster names on. But doggone it, someone had painted out all her great monster names.

Sheriff Tuff patted Red on the shoulder, "I don't know, buddy. They might kill ya. It is a funeral, after all."

■ ■ ■

"Well, here we go," Greta said, and stood in front of her little crowd. "I want to thank you all for coming."

"Wasn't exactly our choice," John Step grumbled. It had been a bad week for John. He was angry, really angry, at Otis, who had stirred everyone up and then fallen once again into the arms of that tramp. He hadn't seen the boy since that terrible night.

"We're here to say goodbye to Huey House," Greta said. "And to try and bring a little peace to this town before we get ripped apart and divided up the way my homeland is right now." She put her hand on her heart. "I love America. And I love Madison Creek. And I love Teddy, even though he's a big idiot. And—"

She was interrupted by the sound of a motorcycle.

Jo sat on edge; she knew that could only be her hero, Miss Evermund.

"H-h-here she comes!" Mule cried.

She'll be comin' round the mountain when she comes, Dusty sang.

Sheriff Tuff opened the gate wide and Annie road in on her motorcycle. Crammed in the sidecar was big Uncle Huey. Jo thought the motorcycle looked tired.

"Well, here I am," Huey said, and struggled to get out of the sidecar. But he couldn't. He pushed and sucked in his gut, but he was jammed in there. Jo imagined him having to live in the sidecar until he lost some weight.

"Use *Johnson's Glow Coat* to get him out!" Dusty suggested.

Big X and Mule ran forward and with some pushing and pulling and shoving, Huey finally got out of the sidecar.

■ ■ ■

"Well howdy, all y'all," Huey said. He was wearing his favorite overalls and his big white hat.

"Howdy," a few of the church people responded. Everyone else just gave him hard stares.

"Thanks for comin' to my funeral. I know, lots of you are thinkin' to yourselves, *that big mess ain't dead yet*. You might wish I was. You might wish it way down deep in your heart, the way you also wish Santa was real and you wish winter wasn't on its way. But wishin' won't do ya no good. I got myself shot, but it didn't kill me. Jesus killed me."

There were some gasps. Here he was, once again spewing heresy.

"Alvin, bring me one of those crosses piled up back yonder," Huey pointed.

Obediently, Alvin brought Huey a white cross.

"My favorite niece, Jo there, she wrote monster names on these for Halloween Eve. I liked that. But what I learned on Halloween is that the monsters are in us. And I wish that was just true of y'all. But when I dropped the bucket deep in the well, I drew up some water in my own heart that wasn't so good. Some stuff in me that Jesus probably wants to kill. So, I'm gonna let him do it. I'm gonna let Jesus kill me."

"We don't need a sermon, Huey," Clyde Finch said. He hadn't been part of the Sunday night fight, but Sheriff Tuff had insisted he needed to be at the funeral just the same.

"I'm not here to preach to you. I'm here to tell you that I was wrong to feel as angry as I did at some of you. Alvin, I was right plumb mad at you the other night. I hated you." He held out his hand and Greta gave him a marker. Huey wrote on the cross...

Hatred

"That's what was in my heart. And it's what Jesus wants to kill. My hatred."

"You mean you hated him when he shot you?" Nettie Drake asked.

"No. I didn't think nothin' when I got shot except that I couldn't believe it didn't hurt a little more. I hated him when he held that gun on my girl Jo. I don't think I mind it so bad if you do rotten things to me. But anyone picks on Jo, and my heart doesn't feel so kind toward them." And then, he wrote something else on his white cross...

Pride

"I thought I could just make up my own church and it would just roll along. But I learned the big King makes war on the arrogant. In fact, he will reach down from the sky and cause trouble for the prideful. Might even send Martians."

"Amen!" Lutie and Nettie both said. The women were sitting beside one another, though they hadn't spoken all week.

"Well, I just learned there's a lot of me that needs to be dead so that I can be a little more like heaven wants me. So I'm declaring this my funeral. Ole Huey be dead. I'll still do some rottenness and cause you all some heartburn, but I want you to know, I'm tryin' to get some of the poison out of me." He pointed to the crosses. "Anyone else need to take a cross?"

He waited for them to the point that it was uncomfortable. Most preachers, if they call for input and no one answers, finds a way pretty quick to cover up the silence. But Huey just stood there, letting the quiet go on and on. Finally, Jo got up. "I guess I need to forgive some of you," Jo said. "You adults, I mean. Kids like Dusty and Clay and me, we all might have fights, but we're just kids. But you grownups made the world pretty scary for us kids. I'm working on forgiving you." She took a cross and wrote with the marker…

Forgiveness

That's what she needed to bury.

That opened things up a little bit.

- Nettie Drake confessed her own pride and that it had been wrong for her to be ashamed of her friend Lutie just because Mrs. Dotson wouldn't stop talking about Christopher Columbus and the spaceships.

- Katie Simpson said it was wrong for her to let herself be ashamed of her past. In fact, feeling so bad about her own past had made her hard on others with a bad past. People she loved. She told them all that she hadn't seen Otis in a few days, and looking toward his father, she said, "I miss him." Most of all, Katie said she was wrong to let people make her feel bad about Dusty. She looked right at him and said, "Dusty Simpson, I'm the most proud mama in the world." He gave her an energetic thumbs up, and thankfully said nothing.

Finally, John Step came forward.

"This has been a terrible week. Just terrible. I'm not sure where my son is, and I admit that part of me struggles to love that boy. But I do." He thought for a while, the pen in one hand, the cross in the other, and finally said, "I sure do wish I was a more kind and loving sorta fella. But I'm not. And I can try to bury this meanness — gosh, I passed it right down to Otis, so you be careful Miss Katie — I'm not sure the meanness won't just follow right after me."

"You gots to keep burying it," Huey suggested.

■ ■ ■

In the distance, there was the sound of music. As if heaven was coming their way. Or, more specifically, the saints were marching in.

As there had been that first Sunday, the trumpets blared, there was the tambourine and harmonica — and their voices lifted high.

Oh, when the saints go marching in,
Oh, when the saints go marching in,
Lord how I want to be in that number
When the saints go marching in!

The gate opened, and Doctor Banks stood beside the Sheriff, his parade waited behind him.

"What in the name of all that is holy are *they* doing here?" Teddy Grimm stood up, his face so red it looked sunburned.

"You could tell them to leave," Huey said. "Because this is your property. That's how it works in America. You don't have to like a fella—"

"Stop preachin' at us!" Teddy raged. "I don't want them on this property!" He looked to the Sheriff. "You tell them to go away."

"Over my dead body!" Greta stood up and shook an angry index finger at Teddy. "You tell them to come on in."

The blacks filed in. There were no more seats, so they gathered up near the front with Huey.

"I got somethin' else to bury," Huey said, looking at Teddy. "I just don't know the word for it. But sometimes, I feel good when somethin' bad happens to someone I don't like. Teddy and Alvin, I felt pretty proud when the church stoned your tractor. In fact, it might be one of the only times I was really self-righteous. But, then the Holy Ghost bothered me about it. And so, I guess, I ought to say sorry to you for feelin' so good about your little heartache."

Neither Alvin nor Teddy answered.

Doctor Banks handed Huey a shoe box.

"Gentlemen, if you'll take it, I want to give this to you as a sign of our goodwill."

Huey held out the shoe box. The men didn't move. There was nothing Huey could give them that they wanted. Worse, they were afraid it would be nothing more than a Bible with a bullet in it.

"What is it?" Alvin asked.

"Gotta take it to find out. Might be a dead rat," Huey said.

With a nudge from Greta, Teddy got up and sulked over to Huey. He took the box, which wasn't heavy the way he had expected, and started back toward his chair.

"What is it?" Red Heartland asked. "If it's money, I want a box."

"Probably more confederate money," Nettie said, and a few people laughed.

Teddy delivered the box to Greta at the table. She told him to open it up, but he said she should. They squabbled for a bit, and finally Greta stood up and opened the box. As she took the lid off, she gasped with surprise. "Oh my! It *is* money! A lot of money! Ones and fives and tens all crumpled up."

"Just under seven hundred dollars," Huey said with satisfaction. "Finding I'm a little proud at the moment. And I'm too lazy to write that on my cross. Jo, go write —"

"Pride is already on your cross, Uncle Huey."

"Well, anyway, this is all those offerings we collected. Some weeks would be ten or twenty dollars. But then we collected for that missionary, and y'all give like there was no tomorrow. Well, we had a church meetin' and all agreed that since the missionary turned out to be a big phony, we ought to do somethin' good with the money we collected for him. So we want to give it to the peanut farm for a new tractor."

Alvin stood with his mouth agape. "Are you serious?" Then, tearing up, he started to say something but he was unable to speak.

Huey wrote something new on his own cross…

Greed

"I've been thinkin' on a verse that goes somethin' like this: I am crucified with Jesus, therefore I no longer live, Jesus now lives in me." He looked around at white face and black. "That's what I want. I don't just want to ask him in my heart and feel better about myself. I want Jesus to kill me and bury me, and then I want him to pull a brand new me up out of the ground."

"Me too," Teddy Grimm said softly.

Tears finally broke over Alvin's hard face. He moved toward Huey to hug him, but Huey wasn't ready for that. He shooed Alvin away, indicating that if he wanted to hug up on someone to go hug Georgette or maybe Big X.

"I'll hug-ya," Big X said, with outstretched arms.

"Buffalo Bill rides again!" Dusty declared.

■ ■ ■

That Saturday evening as Huey sat on the big red porch thinking over what he might say the next morning, Jo came down and sat in the rocker beside him.

"Well, I guess you got outta this mess," Jo said.

Huey looked at Jo for a long time, studying her face. "I think we'll be in a mess for a long time. Not me, and not some old rickety church, but all of us. We'll be here hating until we learn to talk and worship God together."

"That wasn't a bad sermon right there."

"Problem is people want sermons and talk more than they want to change. They want a talk that makes them feel better about the way they already are instead of a slap in the face. More I read the Bible Jo, the more slapped in the face I get."

"But what about the Government? Are they gonna lock you up?"

Huey shook his head. "Nah. I heard our tax boy got eaten up by the hurricane. All the tax papers went with him. I think the I-R-S is going to call this one a wash. But I have to get my tax papers in order next year or there will be trouble all over again."

"Well don't mess around with the Government, Uncle Huey. You hear me?"

He lit a cigarette and rocked back.

"Big Uncle, how much did you give those Grimm brothers?"

"Six-hundred and sixty-six dollars. But I held out fifty dollars."

"Why fifty dollars?" Jo asked.

"Well, for one thing, I like the idea of giving the Grimm's six-six-six. But I admit, I'm not sure what it means."

"Ah, that's kinda mean, Uncle Huey. You were supposed to bury that today, remember? Now it's already crawled up out of the grave and that ole rascal is grasping at your heel."

He nodded, "Yeah, you're right. I'll toss them another dollar when I see 'em to straighten that out. Then it won't be six-six-six no more. But also, I had to charge them a fifty dollar fee."

"A fee?"

Huey nodded seriously, "Like I told that missionary, I got myself a scoundrel fee." He reached into his pocket and pulled out several crumpled dollar bills. "You take this and hide it, Jo. Hide it in a can, I reckon. But not with the banks, they'll steal it all. You take it and start savin' it up so you have some college money."

Warm tears rolled down the girl's cheeks. "Ah, Uncle Huey, that's the sweetest thing you done for me. Not as sweet as beating me might be, but almost just as sweet." She stopped and looked at him in the eye. "You know, if you really loved me, deep down, you'd beat me."

"Ah, no point in beatin' you. You're too rotten. Just gonna let Georgette save it all up and then one day she'll kill you. Probably call on me to hide your cotton pickin' body."

Epilogue

(Space Crusaders Take the Doughnut Truck)

Katie Simpson sat on the porch steps and watched Dusty play with Charlie Mac. She liked the way he talked constantly while he played, even if it might drive other people bananas. She pulled on her jacket as if that would make her warmer. It had rained on and off all week, and more was expected Sunday. They needed to let the dog—and the boy—get some fresh air. On the radio the Seven Dwarfs wrapped up their hit song, *Whistle While You Work*, and were followed by Artie Shaw's *Begin the Beguine*.

It had been two weeks since she'd seen Otis. He had hit the road after the fiasco, probably worried Sheriff Tuff was about to arrest them all. Or maybe he was sick of sleeping on his father's sofa. Just the same, he was out of her life once again and she was trying to find some peace with that.

Dusty was playing his favorite game, Space Crusaders. It's was just about all he really wanted to play ever since Otis had started the boys on writing their own radio script. Dusty had said it was a mix between Flash Gordon and Buck Rogers? Katie didn't understand either of those things.

"Mama, Charlie Mac just wanders around. We need a dog that'll chase me. Or a brother. Can you make me a brother?"

"No."

He nodded toward the late morning sky. "What we eatin' for lunch? I want *Kellogg's Rice Krispies*—crisp to the last spoonful."

"I don't have *Rice Krispies*, honey."

He stared off into the distance. "What about *Campbell's Soup*? It's mmm mmm good."

No. There was some up at Sweet Tea's, but she didn't want to go there because her mother had just hired a new girl and she would hound Katie with all kinds of questions.

"I want *Krispy Kreme* doughnuts," he said with decision. "That's what I want. Give me some good ole *Krispy Kreme* doughnuts, mama. Give me a whole truck full."

"What?"

He pointed. "That truck right there is full of doughnuts. I want some."

She stood up on the porch and realized just how wet her backside was from sitting on the steps after the rain. The truck coming up the drive was white with a green swoosh along the bottom. Even the long, round cutout where a window had been, was now painted white and said…

Eat Krispy Kreme Doughnuts

"Look who got himself a job," she said, more to herself than to Dusty.

Otis stopped and rolled down the window. The engine gave a steady purr—it wanted to keep moving. "Hey, toots, you want a ride?"

"Look who got himself a job," Dusty repeated what his mother had just said, then added, "Boy howdy, it's about time buster."

"A good job, boy," Otis said. "Come on, I'll drive you out of here. I got me an apartment in Winston-Salem. A new start. But it would be a great start with you and Dusty."

"You think I'm just going to walk off this porch and…" she stopped as Dusty went around the truck and climbed in. "Dusty, get out of there!"

"Come on, mama. The Space Crusaders, they like this doughnut truck. In fact, it's not even really a doughnut truck. It's a spaceship that looks like a truck."

"You want a wedding? I'll give you a wedding. I promised to marry you before the pumpkins go bad. But, I think the ground is getting cold and I'm late for the harvest."

"I don't ride with morons," Katie said.

Dusty climbed over Otis to stick his head out the window. "We're not morons, mama, we're Space Crusaders in the doughnut spaceship truck. Come join our team."

"Good grief."

Katie turned to see her mother standing at the screen door.

"I'll be switched, you aren't going to go with him, are you?" Dorothy asked. "Otis, I wish it had been me who caught up with you the other night. I would have loved to have pummeled you with some apples or hit some home runs off your head with a frying pan. Katie, get away from him."

Katie hung her head, not ashamed, but thinking hard. "It's time to start over, mama. Otis and I are gonna drive on over to Preacher Huey's and tie this knot. You can come or you can stay. And then we're gonna go start a family."

"The family is already started," Dusty declared. "What we're going to do next is launch this puppy into space."

■ ■ ■

As they drove out of Madison Creek, crammed in the cab of that truck, Dusty petted Charlie Mac.

Otis talked on and on as if that would eat up the miles. He had dreams, big dreams. Doughnuts were just the beginning. Soon they'd find their way to New York, and he'd strike it big. And if he didn't, then Katie would hit the jackpot with that voice of hers. Folk in New York were gonna say she was a canary. That was the word, he reminded her, don't forget it—it meant she had a good singing voice. And if she didn't swing in a home run on radio, Dusty would for sure. He was a natural.

"I am!" Dusty said. "I can make any voice. I belong on radio."

"You do, boy!" Otis went to slap the kid's knee, but ended up giving Charlie Mac a pat on the head.

Otis told her how the apartment was small, and not in the best neighborhood, but they could fix it up. And they wouldn't be there long. Why, in no time he was going to be running the doughnut store. Maybe soon he'd boss everyone around. That's how it was going to be, you see?

Katie shook her head with a wry smile. "Otis, you worry me."

"What about me, mama?" Dusty asked. He didn't want to be left out. "I want to be a space cowboy and a rocket engineer. Do I worry you?"

She stared hard at the road ahead. "Dusty, you just make me happy."

"Dusty, you just make me happy," he parroted. Then, looking at Otis, he said, "Come on, big fella, you gots to say it, too."

Not used to giving others much attention, Otis smiled and said, "Dusty, you make me happy."

45813567R00218

Made in the USA
Charleston, SC
28 August 2015